"Scarily good."

— BESTSELLING AUTHOR, LEE CHILD

"I'm used to cool, hard killers—in fiction that is—but I don't think I've ever come across a cool, hard killer as vulnerable as Edith Airey... Bisley-grade crack-shot, she could drop you at half a mile..."

— JOHN LAWTON, BESTSELLING AUTHOR OF THE INSPECTOR TROY AND THE JOE WILDERNESS THRILLERS

"DANCING ON THE GRAVE is a thriller that delivers on all levels. I found it impossible to walk away until I knew the end of the story."

— LINDA WILSON, CRIME REVIEW UK

"Male and female crime fiction readers alike will find Sharp's writing style addictively readable."

— PAUL GOAT ALLEN, CHICAGO TRIBUNE

"Zoë Sharp is one of the sharpest, coolest, and most intriguing writers I know. She delivers dramatic, action-packed novels with characters we really care about."

— BESTSELLING AUTHOR, HARLAN COBEN

"This is hard-edged fiction at its best."

— MICHELE LEBER, BOOKLIST STARRED REVIEW FOR FIFTH VICTIM

"I loved every word of this brilliant, mind-twisting thriller and even yelped out loud at one of the genius twists."

— BESTSELLING AUTHOR, ELIZABETH HAYNES, ON THE BLOOD WHISPERER

"This is a dark drama but a highly compelling one, unexpected, beautifully done and intelligently plotted."

— Liz Barnsley, *Liz Loves Books*

"Superb."

— Ken Bruen, bestselling author of the Jack Taylor series, **THE GUARDS, BLITZ**

"This is a straightforward, no holds barred, thriller. No one writes this kind of book better than Zoë Sharp."

— Ted Hertel Jr, *Deadly Pleasures Mystery Magazine*

"Dancing On The Grave is a dark, tense read that caught me off guard. The author takes us on an exhilarating ride full of twists and turns that had me clinging on to every word. Brilliant book and highly recommend it."

— Sarah Hardy, *By The Letter Book Reviews*

"I highly recommend this series!"

— Ian Rankin, bestselling author of the Rebus novels, on Charlie Fox

"If you don't like Zoë Sharp there's something wrong with you. Go and live in a cave and get the hell out of my gene pool! There are few writers who go right to the top of my TBR pile—Zoë Sharp is one of them."

— Stuart MacBride, bestselling author of the Logan McRae series

"I bloody LOVED it!"

— Noelle Holten, *Crime Book Junkie*

BONES IN THE RIVER

LAKES THRILLER ~ GRACE MCCOLL & NICK
WESTON: BOOK 2

ZOË SHARP

First published in Great Britain 2020
ZACE

Registered UK Office:
Kemp House, 160 City Road, London EC1V 2NX

Copyright © Zoë Sharp 2020

ISBN-13: 978-1-909344-70-9

For Sue Bold
horsewoman, sailor, friend
(1950-2019)

ALSO BY ZOË SHARP

For Behind the Scenes, Bonus Features, Freebies, Sneak Peeks and advance notice of new releases, sign up for Zoë's **VIP list** at **www.ZoeSharp.com/newsletters**.

GLOSSARY OF ROMANI TERMS

boro rye – a great man
bostaris – bastard
chal – Gypsy lad
chavo – child, son
chi – child, daughter, girl, nothing
chingaripen – war, strife
chore – thief, to steal
churi – knife, blade
coco – uncle
coorapen – a beating
cooroboshno – fighting cock
cooromengro – fighter, boxer
craic – gossip, chat
dado – father
desh – ten
dieya – mother, nurse
dinnelo – fool
dook the gry – bewitch the horse
dosta – enough
dukkering – fortune-telling
familiya – extended family
gavvers – coppers
gorgie – female gentile or Englishwoman
gorgio, gorgios (pl) – Gypsy name for a non-Gypsy
grasni shan tu – a mare, an outrageous woman

gry – horse
gudlo-pishen – honey bee
hindity-mengre – the filthy people (Irish vagrant)
lel a curapen – get a beating
kampania, kampaniyi (pl) – an alliance of households of the same geographic area
kistro-mengro – horse rider
kris Romani – highest Romany court
luvvo – money
mam – mother
marimé – banishment
matto-mengro – drunkard
miro rye – my lord or gentleman
o beng te poggar his men – may the devil break his neck
pal – brother
paracrow tute – I thank you
puro dad – grandfather
racaire – chatterer or chatterbox
ran – rod or cane
ratti – blood
rawniskie dicking gueri – lady-like looking woman
rom – husband
Romani – language spoken by the Gypsies
Romany – Gypsy
Shera Rom – Head man
spinyor – carrot
tawno gry – little horse
tawnie yecks – little ones, children
t'aves baxtalo – greetings
vitsa – clan
yeckoro chavo – only son
yoro – an egg

PART I

TUESDAY NIGHT/WEDNESDAY MORNING

AUTHOR'S NOTE

As an author, I *hugely* appreciate all the feedback, reviews, and ratings my books receive from my readers. It helps others make an informed decision before they buy. If you enjoy this book, please consider leaving a brief review or a rating on goodreads or on the retailer site where you made your purchase.
Links can be found at **www.ZoeSharp.com**.
THANK YOU!

1

HIS EYES DRIFTED from the road only for a second.

That was all it took.

One moment he was driving up the winding valley, the stark blaze of his headlights making the dewed grass seem frosted in the darkness. No streetlamps out here, no white lines—no taxis, either, or maybe he would have called one.

Not that he was over the limit, by any means but, during the course of a leisurely evening's dinner with friends, perhaps he'd had one more than he ought. One more than was sensible, for a man in his position.

Enough to cushion his reactions so that, when he caught the flash of movement at the side of the road, he was just a fraction slower than he might have been.

He jerked the wheel, the shock of it a jolt to the chest.

And then came another jolt, as the nearside tyres rode up and over, as some *thing* thudded against the underside of the car.

Later, he would be ashamed that his first instant thought was annoyance at the damage to his vehicle.

He stamped on the brakes and staggered from the driver's seat. His breath came harsh in the still night. Using the flashlight on his phone, he edged back along the tarmac strip. During the day, the dark surface absorbed heat. Come nightfall, he knew sheep liked to lie on it. As he scanned the verges, he tried to persuade himself that what he'd hit *was* merely a sheep, or perhaps a badger.

Right up until he saw it, lying crushed on the deserted road.
A child's bicycle.

2

HIGH OVER MALLERSTANG, out of the peat bogs on Black Fell Moss, the River Eden rises. Once she was in Westmorland. Now she has one foot in the Yorkshire Dales, another in Cumbria, holding the front line and shaping the border.

Born as Red Gill Beck, she toboggans the steep valley side, rips and stumbles, blossoms into Hell Gill Beck. With a bellow, she launches over Hell Gill Force to tumble into Ais Gill Beck. Their twinned spirits trip and twine, combine, to become the Eden.

And as the Eden, she broadens, settles. Slinking alongside the cut of road and railway as if hoping for cover, she roams restless across the valley floor. Stealing from the fields at every turn, snatching at trees that dare to dangle their fingers beneath the surface of her skin. She soothes stones smooth, juggles boulders just for giggles.

At Water Yat, she skirts the Gypsy encampment widely, as if not liking to intrude. They have brought their buckets and kettles down to her but she has plenty to share. Early summer rains have left her fat and full-blooded.

Without judgement, she accepts the offered body, wraps him tight and holds on. No Charon's hand upon the tiller to guide him. No coin under his tongue.

No matter.

Night water black, she bears him downward. Onward toward Kirkby Stephen, she is unaware of her might, delighted as she is by the company and careless in that delight. Like a kitten toying with a butterfly, she has no understanding of delicacy, the fragility of flesh and bone.

At Stenkrith Falls she whirls him through the gorge in a froth of excitement. A wild ride, snapping bites from the rock over which she roils.

Though his slack limbs flail to her rhythm, he fails to laugh. She gathers him closer, binding him, shrouding him, over and colder. Under a shot-down moon, reflected back from the rippled surface of his grave.

3

AFTERWARDS, he couldn't remember the rest of the drive home. On some level he registered that it passed without further incident. He steered and braked, changed gear, accelerated when the road ahead dictated. And he knew, had he been stopped, they would have taken one look and demanded he give a sample, just to find out what else was in his blood.

As his vision was hemmed in by the reach of the car's lights, so his mind felt cornered. Tucked in tight and hiding from the horror and the shame of what he'd done. It railed against reality, denied it, and wove a different tale.

He recognised, dimly, that what he should have done was step up for it. Call it in and wait, stalwart, for the lights and uniforms to arrive, for suspicion and interrogations. But somewhere at the back of his brain, the part that coiled and slithered with all the baser instincts, a primeval will to survive kicked in.

It flooded his system with adrenaline, pushed into his bloodstream so hard it made his temples pound. He couldn't stop his hands from shaking, no matter how hard he clenched his fingers around the steering wheel. Or how much he tried forcing himself to adopt a coolly logical approach.

He knew there were no *obvious* signs of collision on the car. He'd had his wits about him enough to check, back there on the road. Bit of a scuff on the bumper but nothing that would stand out—certainly not on the grainy footage of the traffic cameras

before he got back home. Not that there were many between here
and there.

He'd put on gloves before he touched anything—always kept
disposable ones in the glove box in case they ran out at the diesel
pump. The ground was too dry to take impressions of his shoes.
There might have been a bit of a skid mark when he anchored
on, but the gritty surface of the road, half crumbling, wouldn't
yield much by way of a tread pattern. Besides, his tyres were a
common brand in an equally common size.

The steel band around his skull began to ease a little.

By the time he hit the motorway and turned north, the worst
of his initial panic had subsided. As long as he didn't examine it
too closely, it would remain beneath the surface—for now, at any
rate. He rehearsed what he'd say when asked how his evening
had gone. *Very pleasant, as it goes. Nice to catch up. Shame I couldn't
have stayed over—perhaps had something to drink…*

And that set him spinning off again through weakness, disas-
ter, guilt, despair.

Or not.

Not if they didn't catch him. Not if they didn't even suspect
for a moment that he was involved.

And especially not if they couldn't *prove* anything.

Before he knew it, he'd passed the first countdown marker
for his junction. He flicked his indicator on, even though his was
the lone vehicle on this side of the carriageway. Realised, as he
did so, that such an action marked him out as trying just a little
too hard. He cancelled it.

From there it was but a few minutes to home, rolling through
empty streets without needing to pause. He was steadier now,
lent a certain perspective by distance, if nothing else.

He hit the remote for the electric garage door when he was
halfway along his cul-de-sac, knowing that he'd just be pulling
onto the driveway as it reached the height of its travel. Straight
in without the need to brake. Normally, such slick timing gave
him a sense of satisfaction. Tonight, that was strangely absent.

When he'd lowered the door again behind him, he sat for a
moment with the car ticking over as if he contemplated…giving
in. Leave the door to the house closed and the engine running.
But, he knew that a modern car with its catalytic converter—
especially on a well-warmed engine—meant the build-up of

carbon monoxide in the exhaust fumes would make for a slow and desperate way to go.

He twitched, and twisted the key decisively. The engine died away into silence, replaced by the occasional soft ping as components cooled and settled at their own pace.

Still, it took effort to push open the driver's door, swing his feet out of the car and stand. Maybe he was just putting off what came next.

On a hook by the door were his coveralls. He slipped them on over his clothes, lifted down an inspection lamp and plugged it in, donned fresh gloves. An old yoga mat provided a little cushioning against the bare concrete floor but still he grunted as he got to his knees. Playing the light underneath the front wheel arch revealed an area dark and sticky, peppered with insects, gravel, and dirt.

He hunted through the bucket of car cleaning products Susanne was always buying, found one that claimed to shift splattered bugs and spots of tar. He sprayed liberally under the bodywork, left it to soak in while he checked further back under the floor-pan, inch by inch.

At the jacking point just forward of the rear wheel, he found a tuft of what might have been bloodied hair. He'd never been a squeamish man but that made him jerk back with a muttered curse.

And, when he reached to disentangle and remove it, he noticed his hands were shaking again.

It was another hour before he cleared away and went inside. He washed in the downstairs loo, told himself it was to avoid waking Susanne rather than because there was no mirror over the sink. He recognised the self-deception for what it was—a form of self-protection.

Recognised it, accepted it, and tried to move on.

Upstairs, he undressed in the dark and slid into bed beside Susanne. She stirred briefly, made a snuffle of sound and went quiet again. He willed himself to relax but sleep was impossible.

Every time he closed his eyes, he saw the flash of movement, heard the thump and clatter. He even imagined a startled cry and couldn't recollect if it was real or simply his imagination.

Morning was a long time coming.

Normally, he slept through Susanne's first alarm but he was

already staring at the ceiling when her phone began its irritating bleat, buzzing across the bedside table like a wasp in a Coke tin. She reached out groggily and swiped the snooze option, as she always did.

He contemplated getting up then but stayed rigid alongside her, careful not to break his usual pattern. Only when her alarm sounded again and she slouched into the en suite shower did he get out of bed. He timed his movements so they didn't meet face-to-face until he walked into the kitchen, showered and dressed. She was perched on a stool at the breakfast bar.

"Morning, love."

Susanne spoke without looking up from the homework she was marking, pen in one hand, coffee mug in the other.

"Thought you were planning to get all that done last night, eh?"

"I was. Then I realised just how little effort Year Ten had put into this assignment, thought 'sod it,' opened a bottle of cheap red and fell asleep in front of the telly." Her smile was wry. "How was your evening?"

He helped himself to coffee, glad of the excuse to have his back to her. "Oh, you know, very pleasant, as it happens. Nice to catch up. It was a shame I couldn't have—"

"*Dammit!*"

Her sudden exclamation made him stiffen and whirl. She'd slopped the dregs of her coffee over the papers. He grabbed a tea towel, helped stem the tide and blot out the worst of the stains.

"Thanks, love." She let out an annoyed breath. "So much for me looking all professional as new Deputy Head."

"Ah, don't worry about it. Back when I was at school, the English teacher would send back my homework covered in fag ash and cat hair half the time."

"Well, those days are long gone." She dabbed a kiss on his cheek. "We don't write with chalk on slate anymore, either."

"Yeah, yeah. Very funny."

He finished his coffee standing with his back to the sink while she scurried round gathering books, bag, and keys. He followed her to the front door to wave her off. She was still distracted by her own clumsiness, for which he was grateful, but as she blipped the locks on her four-by-four she seemed to register the otherwise empty driveway and her gaze sharpened.

"Where's your car?"

He jerked his head to the garage. "Put it away."

She frowned. "I wouldn't have thought it was worth it by the time you got back. Must have been a late one."

"It was a bit, I s'pose. But…old habits."

He saw her shrug it off, her mind already on the day ahead. She gave him another distracted peck on the cheek and climbed into the driver's seat. He heard the voice of the local radio disc jockey boom out before the engine fired. She gave him a last brisk wave as she reversed off the driveway.

After she was gone, he stepped back, closed the door and sagged against the wall just inside.

How do people do it? How do they act normal and live with what they've done, day after day?

He made another careful check around the car before he set off for work himself. For once, the morning playlist on Classic FM on the way in failed to soothe him.

In the main car park, he left his vehicle nose to the wall, just in case there was something he'd missed, strode quickly into the office and hung his jacket on the back of the door. The day was already warm and looked like being warmer still before lunchtime.

The phone on his desk began to ring before his computer had a chance to fire up. The hesitation before he reached for the receiver was momentary but he was aware of it, even so.

As he picked up, he injected as much authority into his voice as he could manage.

"Good morning, Head CSI Chris Blenkinship. What can I do for you?"

PART II

WEDNESDAY

4

"ALL RIGHT, LADS, LISTEN UP."

In the relatively short time Nick Weston had been with Cumbria Constabulary he'd never heard Detective Inspector Pollock begin a morning briefing any other way, regardless of the gender mix of his audience. And if any of the female officers present felt undermined by his collective terminology they never called him on it, so who was Nick to make waves?

He had learned to keep his head down.

Fitting in with his colleagues was still an ongoing process. Although he'd earned a bit of grudging respect from those around him over the events of last summer, it was going to take more time than he'd first thought to become an accepted member of the team.

"I don't think I need to remind you that Thursday sees the start of this year's Appleby Horse Fair," Pollock went on.

A collective groan went up. For weeks now, Nick knew that those further up the food chain had been grappling with the plan for handling the largest gathering of Gypsies and Travellers in Europe. Pollock's boss, Superintendent Waingrove, had been put in charge of co-ordinating the police response. Nick hadn't had much contact with Waingrove—lowly detective constables did not mingle with the high-ups on a regular basis—but rumour had it she'd been breathing down everyone's neck to put the agreed plan into effect on the ground.

"So, I *also* don't have to remind you that nobody's getting a day off or pulling a sickie until it's all over, right?"

One of the other DCs, Yardley, shot a hand up. "Erm, sir—?"

"I know, lad, I know—your missus is about to pop. Well, if she does, she does, and it can't be helped. But tell her I'd take it as a personal favour if she'd keep her legs crossed for another week, if it's all the same to her."

There were a few guffaws. Somebody slapped Yardley on the shoulder hard enough to almost knock him off the corner of his desk. Pollock let them settle.

"Uniform are bearing the brunt on the run-up, as always, but intel we've received from other forces suggests drug gangs are going to be operating on the periphery of the Fair, as well as sellers of fake or stolen leather goods. And the latest whisper is of a serious falling-out between two rival groups of Travellers, who are aiming to settle their feud—if that's what it is—in a bare-knuckle fight to be held some time over the weekend."

"Well then, sir," Yardley put in, "can't we just let them sort it out for themselves?"

Pollock regarded him from beneath unkempt eyebrows. A big man, he had the look of a brawler himself, although Nick understood that any tendencies in that regard had been exhausted on the rugby pitch, and twenty years ago at least.

"If I thought it would stay one-on-one, I might be tempted, lad," Pollock admitted now. "But as we well know, these things have a habit of getting a bit out of hand. And this year we've got the added problem that they've lost their *Shera Rom*."

Pollock's eyes flicked towards him but before his DI could launch into any explanations, Nick said, "Their head man, sir, yes." He risked a small smile. "We came across our share of Gypsies down south."

Pollock nodded. "Last one was a good bloke, by and large— Hezekiah Smith. Had a reputation for not suffering fools at all, never mind gladly. He wasn't keen on us interfering but if we had a real problem with somebody and we dropped a word in his ear… Well, let's just say they tended to get put in their place, one way or another."

"What happened to him, sir?"

"Old age, lad. Same as happens to most of us, sooner or later —if we're lucky. I understand he was hoping to make this his last Fair but he died about a month back. As far as we know, nobody as yet has emerged as his real successor. So, it means that minor trouble he would have kept a lid on in previous years might just blow up in our faces this time. Rightly or wrongly, the Powers That Be have decided to take the 'iron fist in velvet glove' approach, so keep that in mind, eh?"

There were general nods and Pollock began assigning tasks. When he got to Nick, he said, "Right, lad, I want you down in Kirkby Stephen—a kid's bicycle has been found trashed in a skip put out for the Gypsies who were camped on the road toward Garsdale Head."

Nick's heart sank. He didn't miss the sly grins aimed in his direction.

"Yessir," he said, expressionless.

"Don't be like that. This is exactly the kind of thing that needs stamping on before the rumour mill gets going," Pollock said sharply. "Because that kid's bike, it appears to have blood on it."

5

HALFWAY along the Mallerstang valley road, Grace McColl processed the bicycle and tried very hard *not* to think about the child who had been riding it—or what might have become of them.

Instead, she concentrated on the procedure, her hands taking her through the familiar ritual, as calming as a meditation.

She had placed the dull gold-coloured bike on a piece of plastic sheeting on the grass near the skip in which it had been found. It lay isolated in the centre, the white space around it emphasising its size—or lack of it.

Throughout her training, they had warned her it would be the cases involving children that would affect her the most. But Grace had come late to the job of Crime Scene Investigator, after the demise of her childless marriage. Perhaps those extra years allowed her enough maturity to maintain a certain detachment.

"I thought it were paint or oil or something on it at first, like," said the man who'd been driving the skip lorry. He watched her work from ten or so feet away, nervously twisting a rag in his hands. Grace had already swabbed them and taken samples as well as his prints. She'd had to tell him more than once that this was purely for elimination—not because they seriously thought he might be involved.

"When did you realise it was blood?" she asked.

"Soon as I put it down. You could smell it and, this weather, there was the flies…"

"Where *was* the bicycle, when you got here?"

"It were shoved down that side of the skip," the man said, starting forward. "Just behind the—"

"If you wouldn't mind staying outside the tape, Mr Felton," Grace said gently. "There might be boot prints I haven't yet got to."

"Oh, aye, right you are. Sorry, lass. I've got grandkids, see—six and eight. Grow like weeds at that age, don't they? That's why I thought... It's fair upset me, this, I don't mind admitting it."

"It would upset anyone," Grace agreed.

Normally, she would have started at the perimeter and worked her way inward. But the priority here was to identify to whom the bicycle belonged, and where that person—that child—might be. The uniforms who were first on scene had already done a sweep of the immediate area. They had now gone to enquire at the nearest farm building just further up the valley.

"I've found all sorts in skips, over the years," Felton said suddenly, seizing on the familiar. "Never ceases to amaze me, what folk will chuck out—you wouldn't credit it. A full set of original window shutters once; half-a-dozen of those big old cast-iron radiators. Even a rocking horse—still had its horsehair tail."

Grace photographed a close-up of dark transfer on the bike's mangled front forks. *Paint? No...plastic. From a bumper, perhaps.*

She scraped a sample into an evidence bag, sealed it and scribbled a note before asking, over her shoulder, "Doesn't your boss mind you cherry-picking what gets put into the skips?"

Felton grinned, uneven teeth under a tobacco-stained moustache, and stabbed a thumb toward his own chest. "Aye, but I take no notice of me'self."

"Ah, no offence intended."

"None taken, lass. I tried sitting in the office all day but paperwork, it's not really my thing. Me daughter handles all that now." His pride was obvious. "She leaves me to do what I'm suited to—pick-ups and drop-offs. Anything that might be a bit problematic, like, I do them me'self."

Grace raised an eyebrow as she met his gaze. "Were you expecting this particular collection to be difficult?"

Felton returned her look without embarrassment. "With this

lot, you never know," he said stoutly. "There have been times, in the past. I mean, I sent one of the lads to pick up a ten-yarder from right here a couple of years back and—"

"A 'ten-yarder'?"

"Holds ten cubic yards, same as this one."

"Ah, right. I'm sorry, do go on."

"Well, it didn't look overladen, like, so he doesn't bother putting the legs down on the truck—thinks he'll get the job done quick and grab himself a bit of lunch and a pint at the Black Bull down the road. Only, when he hooks up the chains and starts lifting, the thing's so heavy it pulls the front end of the truck clear off the ground. Turns out it was full of engine blocks, hidden at the bottom, like. Ruddy great big diesel engine blocks —out here, I ask you?" He jerked his head to the surrounding hills and walled fields with barely a house in sight. "Where on earth did they get hold of those? That's what I'd like to know. And how on earth did a bunch of Gypsies *get* them here, with nowt but a load of horses and carts, in the first place?"

On her way to Mallerstang, Grace had driven past several garages which claimed to specialise in agricultural or commercial vehicle engines, but she thought it best not to speculate. Likely as not, Mr Felton did not expect answers to his questions.

She turned the bicycle upside-down, balanced on its handlebars and seat, and inspected the underside of the frame and the crank for an identification number. There was nothing on the rear chain stays or the headstock. At the base of the seat tube, she found a label that had been painted over. Whether this was because the painter couldn't be bothered to remove it, or a deliberate attempt to conceal the number, she wasn't sure. Although, judging by the quality of the paint job, she'd plump for the former rather than the latter.

She sighed and stepped back. As she did so, Grace noticed another label underneath the bicycle's seat. Someone had tried unsuccessfully to remove it, but there was part of a logo still visible. She raised the Canon to her eye and worked the zoom lens to get a better view.

Ah…

The sound of a car fast approaching from the direction of Kirkby Stephen brought her head up. The engine note was raspy and distinctive, and clearly not out for a leisurely drive.

A flash of bright blue appeared around a corner in the narrow road, the driver blipping the throttle as he changed gear for the short stretch of downhill before the cattle grid leading onto the open ground.

"Ruddy boy racer," Mr Felton surmised.

Recognising the car, Grace smiled, more pleased than perhaps she should have been. "Oh, without doubt," she agreed. "But fortunately, that's not *all* he is."

6

NICK PARKED his Subaru Impreza WRX behind Grace's dusty Nissan pick-up and the truck that must have come to collect the overflowing skip. It was on a wide flat area of grass, open on both sides of the narrow road. Far to the right he could see the curve of the River Eden. To the left was rugged rising ground, the grass yellowed and coarse.

The last time Nick had cause to travel this road, he remembered, it had not ended well. As he climbed out of the car, he could not suppress a shiver, despite the blustery sunshine. He eyed the far hills as if expecting to see the glint of reflection from the scope of a sniper's rifle.

Nick shook himself and walked across the road to where the crime-scene tape fluttered from slightly drunken rebar uprights surrounding the skip. He did not attempt to go closer. An older man wearing a shirt bearing the logo of the skip hire company watched him approach and gave him a cautious nod in greeting.

"Morning," Nick said.

"You a copper, then?"

"That's right." Nick unfolded his warrant card. "DC Weston, sir. And you are?"

"Name's Felton. That's my skip."

Nick glanced at the empty grassland, noting several blackened rings of stones that indicated recent campfires. "What time did you turn up to collect it?"

Felton shrugged. "About seven, I s'pose. First job on the sheet and I like to get a head start on the day before the traffic gets bad." His lips twisted below the moustache. "Hard to credit it, out here, but get behind one of them horse-drawn caravans on the A66 and the queues back up for miles."

"Was anybody else here when you arrived?"

"No, there wasn't, as a matter of fact."

"You sound surprised."

"Aye, I s'pose I was, a bit. They're not allowed onto the field at Appleby until a couple of days before the Fair. And you lot have clamped down on 'em clogging up the verges—quite rightly, of course," he added hastily. "They used to line both sides of the main road all the way from Kirkby Stephen up to Brough and that's a quick bit of road. Not safe when there's dogs and kiddies and ponies all over the shop. This is a good pitch—common land, see? What with fresh water, plenty of grazing and somewhere to dump their rubbish, I wouldn't have expected 'em to move on until they were ready to go straight to the Fair."

He went silent but Nick could almost hear the accusatory question lurking on Mr Felton's tongue.

"Why up sticks unless you've summat to hide?"

The man may well have spoken the words aloud but at that moment a warbling ringtone began, somewhere in the vicinity of his back pocket. Felton rolled his eyes at Nick and fumbled for his phone, turning toward his truck as he answered the call.

Nick left him to it.

"Morning, Grace. What've you got for me?"

She straightened. A tall, elegant figure, even in cargo trousers and a sleeveless T-shirt. She wore her long red hair in a loose plait at the nape of her neck but strands of it blew around her face. She pushed them back behind her ear with a gloved hand and shifted the bulky Canon camera onto its shoulder strap.

"Hello Nick, I'm glad you've turned up." Just when he might have made too much of that, she added, "I could do with a hand, if you wouldn't mind?"

"Sure. What do you need?"

"I don't suppose you have a blanket or a coat in your car—something heavy—thick, anyway—and dark?"

"I've got a waterproof in the boot, if that would do?"

"Please."

He fetched the waxed-cotton jacket and held it out to her but she lifted the crime-scene tape and beckoned him under it.

"I need you to hold it for me, too."

"Well, I don't see any puddles to drape it over—nor any maddened bulls to fend off. What's this in aid of, Grace?"

"The sun's too strong to see a UV light. I need you to create a bit of shade."

"I see," Nick said blankly.

But he allowed her to direct him to drape the jacket over the frame of the bicycle while she huddled underneath the cloth, light in one hand and camera in the other. Nick tried not to look at the mangled front end, the buckled wheel and sprung spokes.

His daughter, little Sophie, was almost five. She was desperate for a proper bicycle to replace her old trike, and alternated between pleading and tantrums as part of her ongoing campaign. The prospect of her being out on it anywhere near traffic had Nick frankly terrified.

After a minute or so, Grace emerged. Her face was flushed but whether with exertion, triumph, or simply the heat, he couldn't tell. He folded the jacket over his arm.

"*Now* are you going to tell me what that was all about?"

"Sorry. I found a sticker underneath the saddle—there. Someone's tried to remove it, as you can see, but they're designed to tear, so there's enough of it left to identify."

Nick looked but could discern no more than a few swirling lines of what was perhaps a stylised logo. "Which is?"

"One of the security companies who provide micro-dots people can glue to any property that's likely to be stolen," Grace said.

Finally, the penny dropped. "And you've just found the PIN number on one of the dots that will identify the registered owner."

Her smile was wry. "The *original* owner, yes. I wouldn't get your hopes up, though."

"Oh, why not?"

"Because the bicycle has been through at *least* two sets of hands—possibly more."

Nick sighed. "I think you better start at the beginning. Tell me what you know."

"What I know, or what I can infer from the evidence collected thus far?"

"OK, option two. At the moment I've nothing to go on. Anything's got to be better than that."

"According to Mr Felton over there, he dropped off the skip, empty, four days ago. Water Yat—that's the name of this unfenced area next to the river, before you ask—had maybe a dozen Gypsy caravans here then. Vardos and bow-tops, mainly, but a few modern ones, too. When—"

"Hang on, a 'bow-top' I think I can guess—those traditional looking Gypsy caravans with the green canvas top, yeah? But what's a 'vardo' when it's at home?"

"Ah. A vardo is a wooden caravan that widens at the top. The roof is usually curved slightly and they often have a row of roof lights in a raised section from front to back, and a porch where the driver sits."

"Got it, thanks. You were saying?"

Grace paused momentarily, as if checking she was not being mocked. Nick gave her a bland smile.

"*As* I was saying," she agreed, "when Mr Felton came back this morning, they were all gone and he found this bicycle in the skip with what he realised was blood on it."

"Human, or animal?"

"That we won't know without a lab test, I'm afraid. But it *is* definitely blood of some kind—I *have* checked."

"Of course you have." He smiled. "But I fell off my bike numerous times as a kid and often bashed myself up pretty badly with no foul play involved."

She pointed to the distorted front forks. "This damage was caused by crushing rather than a simple impact. The evidence points to the bike being first hit by a vehicle—leaving trace, as you can see—which then also ran over it."

Nick felt the tightness in his jaw, forced it to relax.

"There have been no local kids reported missing overnight," he said. "We checked the local hospitals, too—nothing."

"Maybe you're not looking at the behaviour of a *local* victim," Grace said. "What if they were part of the Traveller community?"

Nick frowned. "Well, that might add an interesting wrinkle," he said at last. "Can you tell me anything about the victim?"

She lifted a shoulder. "The bicycle was originally pink but it's been sprayed gold. And not done well, either. I'd guess with one of those rattle cans people buy for car repairs that never quite match the original colour."

"Which tells you...?"

"The original owner was most likely a girl but then the bicycle was acquired for—or given to—a boy. The family aren't wealthy or they would have bought him a newer replacement by now, and they either are not able to maintain discipline or don't bother trying."

"Oh, come on, Grace. I thought you weren't prepared to guess?"

Expressing his disbelief was a mistake, he saw. Her face took on that expressionless look, her voice so calm it was almost icy. "Who says I'm guessing?"

"OK, girl to boy I can go for. I mean, why cover up a good paint job with a worse one unless you were embarrassed by the colour?"

"If you could afford to be choosy, why accept a bicycle in the 'wrong' colour in the first place?" Grace said. "And look at the seat and handlebars. They've been raised as high as they can go. Higher than would be comfortable if there was an alternative solution."

Nick held up his hands in surrender. "OK, OK, I take your point. And the business about discipline?"

"Mr Felton arrived early this morning to collect his skip. It's possible, therefore, that the bicycle was put into it last night—in the dark." Her eyes strayed over the crumpled bike. "There are no lights fitted, and no marks on the frame to suggest any ever were. What kind of responsible parent allows their child to go roaming the countryside, on a bicycle with no lights, alone, in the dark?"

7

CHRIS BLENKINSHIP TAPPED his pen impatiently on the edge of his desk while the phone rang out long at the other end of the line. When it was finally picked up with a mumbled, "'Help you?" his temper sparked and took fire.

"What the hell way is *that* to answer a phone, Frost?" he demanded. And he heard a distinct clattering, as though Ty Frost had lurched instinctively to his feet.

"Erm, sorry, boss. I was just—"

"Oh, save it. Where's Grace McColl?"

"She's, erm…she's out."

"I *know* she's out, Ty, but her phone's going straight to voice-mail. Where is she?"

"I think she's down near Kirkby Stephen somewhere, boss. A kiddie's bicycle turned up in a skip along the valley road."

Blenkinship's heart bounced painfully behind his ribs. He forced the bite into his voice to still the quiver. "Since when do we send out CSIs to deal with lost and found?"

"Well, erm, we were told there was blood on it."

"Blood?" That shook him. What else had he missed, in the hurry, in the dark? "Who found blood on it?"

"Whoever called it in, I s'pose." Frost sounded puzzled now and Blenkinship knew he was making too much of this. Enough that it would stick in the younger man's mind.

"All right, all right," he said quickly. "But why didn't it get passed to Steve or Tony at Kendal. They're closer, aren't they?"

"I dunno, boss," Frost said. "I think Steve's away on a course today. Tony must have been out already."

Blenkinship grunted a response and tried not to slam the phone down. He spent a moment staring at nothing, rubbing a fist to the centre of his chest where the heartburn was trying to eat its way out through muscle and bone.

"Bloody Grace McColl," he muttered to the empty office. "It *would* have to be her, wouldn't it…?"

8

As they climbed the last long, slow pull out of Hard Hills to North Stainmore, Queenie was overwhelmed by a sense of poignant homecoming. It was always the same in this place, this time of year. A mix of emotions all jostling to be on top. Sadness and contentment. Anticipation and regret.

In front of her, between the shafts of the vardo, the old piebald gelding plodded on, nodding heavily into his collar, leaning into the grade. She could remember when he would trot all the way up, all flash and feather and needing a strong hand to steady him. Now she let the reins drape over the footboard, listening to him blow.

Bartley had walked the last mile or so by the horse's head, with Ocean alongside his father, striding out like a man. The boy had put on a spurt of growth in the last year. Reaching for his father's height, although in colouring he was dark like Queenie herself. Bartley's hair had a copper tint to it, shining now in the sun.

As they neared the final rise and the stone barn and farmhouse appeared, Ocean slapped the horse on the shoulder and said, "Nearly there now, look!"

Bartley turned to throw her a quick grin. "Told you," he said. "You always were a worrier, me darlin'. Told you he'd be fine, now didn't I?"

But she heard the relief in his voice and realised then how well he'd hidden his own doubts.

"Know that, don't I?" she said, and couldn't stop herself from adding, "But normally we'd have the mare to spell him. Had to work the whole trip by himself this time."

Behind the caravan, tied to the back runner, the mare let out a soft whicker as if she knew she was being talked about— Queenie swore she understood more than anyone gave her credit for. She leaned out and checked the led horse. The mare was twisting sideways, distracted, until the lead rope tugged her on again with a jerk.

"Where's the colt?"

Next to her on the front porch, Sky edged across to her side and swung outward to peer behind them, clinging by one hand to the decoration of the porch bracket for support. Queenie fought the urge to grab hold of the back of her little daughter's dress and haul her to safety.

"He's here!"

There was a scatter of hooves on the road and the foal came rushing to join his dam from the far verge, hustling in close alongside her as if something had startled him. Head up, nostrils flared wide, he stamped and snorted, showing every inch of the breeding that was in him.

Bartley laughed. "Got your dad's spirit, that one."

Queenie sat down again without speaking. His determined good humour was starting to grate. She'd argued against making the trip with the horses this year, what with the mare having foaled just weeks ago and only the old piebald to pull the van. She'd argued and lost, and now Bartley was close to crowing.

In truth, it was the colt she'd most wanted to leave at home.

Her father's last colt.

The old devil had lived just long enough to see his *tawno gry* —his little horse—safely delivered, as if that was all he'd hung on for. One life beginning as another ended.

Oh, she knew all the good reasons for bringing him to this year's Fair—hadn't Bartley been over them, time and again? The name Hezekiah Smith carried more weight now than ever. The bidding for his last-bred foal would be fierce—too good to miss. But by next year he'd be a scrawny yearling and another *Shera Rom* would have been long since chosen.

But still, she wished this time they'd brought no horses with them at all.

The old piebald turned in at the farm gate, hardly needing Bartley's hand to guide him. As they reached the yard, Wynter Trelawney emerged from one of the outbuildings, as though she'd been watching for them. A windswept woman with wild grey hair, she hurried across to a field gate and dragged it open, shooing ducks and chickens out of their way.

"Bartley! Queenie! Greetings—*t'aves baxtalo*, my lovelies. Welcome back to you all! My, Ocean, how you've *grown*. Go on straight through. You should know the way by now."

Sky put one foot onto the shafts and leapt, hitting the ground already in a run to be swept up and hugged by Wynter.

Ach, not yet six and that child will be the death of me. She has no fear.

Queenie let the old piebald take them the last few yards onto the grass, then gently took up the reins. It was only pure stubbornness made him pull against her for another half-a-dozen strides. He had a mouth like iron.

Queenie hopped down to give the piebald a pat on his sweating rump while Bartley set the brake. Wynter disentangled herself from Sky long enough to pull the gate closed behind them. Ocean was with her then, and she dropped an arm across his shoulders and hugged him close as they approached. A moment later she had enveloped Queenie in the familiar scents of washed wool and chicken feed and lavender.

"It is so good to see you again," she said. She eased back, met Queenie's eyes with concern in her own. "I was so sorry to hear about your father, God rest him."

"It was his time."

"But still…"

"And what of Agnes?"

"Oh, Mum's still with us," Wynter said with a wry twist of her lips. "Getting frailer now, though. And her eyes are not good."

"And, what of—?"

But Queenie's question cut off by Bartley's approach. He swept Wynter off her feet and twirled her around as if she were a slip of a girl, before setting her down again.

"Ah, Wynter Trelawney, aren't you a sight for sore eyes? I'd swear you get younger every year."

"And *I'd* swear you get more outrageous," Wynter said,

laughing. She squeezed his forearms, his hands still at her waist. "And brawny, too. I'm no lightweight these days."

"Ah, there's nothing to you, woman—a good wind would blow you away," Bartley denied, the Irish floating to the top. "Is Vano here yet?"

Wynter nodded toward the far end of the field where it dropped from view. "Already in his favourite spot," she said. "They came up from Mallerstang this morning. Got here so early I was still in my nightgown."

Bartley held up a warding hand. "Now, don't you be putting images like *that* in my head. If I weren't a married man…"

"Get away with you." Wynter slapped his arm. "I'm practically old enough to be your mother, only I'd wager you'd treat *her* with more respect." But she was still smiling. "Go on, see to those horses while I make your poor wife some tea."

He gave them both another grin and a wink as he moved away. The two women stood and watched him lead the piebald along the rutted track toward the bottom of the field. The mare ambled sedately behind the wagon and the colt darted about her. The children raced alongside him, excited to be reuniting with cousins and friends.

"Is that Hezekiah's last?"

"It is."

"He's going to be a beauty." Wynter paused. "I'm surprised you can bear to part with him."

Queenie swallowed and said nothing.

"Ah—I see," Wynter said quietly, her gaze following Bartley's figure as it disappeared. "You poor love. Will nothing persuade him?"

"No… No, it's for the best. It's getting harder to find the grazing close and he's going to be a little bugger to break to harness unless we have him cut."

"Oh, no, somebody will want to breed from him," Wynter agreed. "How could they not?"

"Besides, we're best to strike a deal on him now, while my father's name is still worth something…"

"Hezekiah was not a man who will be soon forgotten, lovely, don't you worry." Wynter laid a hand on her arm. "Is there any word yet on who will become the new *Shera Rom*?"

Queenie hesitated, then shook her head. Of course there had

been word. There had been talk of little else, on the road, except who would take over as head of their clan. But it was not something to be discussed with an outsider—a *gorgie*—even one as close as Wynter and her family had always been.

She glanced across to find Wynter studying her closely, as if she saw the conflict and knew the cause—the *real* cause.

"Stuck between your husband and your brother," Wynter murmured. "Can't be easy for you."

Queenie wrapped her arms around her body as if suddenly chilled, although the sun climbed still and the wind was but a breath in her hair.

Coming here was like coming home but it was never easy.

Wynter threaded her arm through Queenie's and pulled her close. "How about that cuppa, then? Come and say hello to Agnes. I'm sure she'll be glad to see you."

Queenie allowed herself to be ushered inside the farmhouse kitchen, with the beams so low even she had to mind her head. She watched Wynter wash her hands and fill the kettle. It still felt wrong to have only one sink for everything but, if Bartley was thinking of moving them into brick themselves, joining the settled community for part of the year, at least, she would have to get over herself on that score.

It was only once the tea was brewed and poured, and Wynter's local gossip had petered into silence that Queenie finally gathered her courage. The question had been on her mind if not her lips all through the journey northward.

"Has there been...any news," she asked, "of the boy?"

Wynter's face gentled. "No," she said. "I'm sorry, lovely. No-one's heard anything of him."

9

———

NICK OVERTOOK the horse-drawn caravans carefully, going as far into the outside lane as he could manage. Not that the traffic seemed to bother the animals, not even the heavy trucks, which thundered past only inches from the garish, flimsy vehicles. The horses trudged on, impervious, nodding into the load. Those holding the reins watched with expressionless faces as the tail-back streamed around them onto the dual carriageway, with no hint of embarrassment or apology for the delay.

In the front passenger seat, DI Pollock sighed.

"Hold-ups will be commonplace until the Fair's over—if we're lucky," he said. "Few years ago, a truck ploughed into the back of one of the caravans going along here. Splintered it to matchwood. Didn't do the young lad and his grandfather who were in it any good, neither—not to mention their horses." He shook his head. "Bad business, that."

"Can't we keep them off the main A66?" Nick asked. "Cut the risk?"

"Hardly. They reckon they've been travelling across the Pennines by this route, to and from the Fair, since the sixteen-hundreds. As far as they're concerned, it's up to the rest of us to make allowances."

It was hard to tell from the DI's voice, Nick considered, if he approved of their stubborn adherence to tradition or was annoyed by it. With Pollock, it could have gone either way. He had achieved his rank by persistence and was usually admiring of that trait in others.

Most of the time, at any rate.

Nick had not expected his boss's demand to be in on this interview and he was wary of asking outright. He drove on automatic pilot, flicking on his indicator as the turn-off for Brough Sowerby came up. And all the time he tried to work out what he might have done to cause a sudden collapse of confidence in his abilities.

He'd taken the PIN number Grace had revealed hidden in the micro-dots on the bicycle, run it with the company who held the data. They were used to such requests and, even though they said the bicycle wasn't reported stolen, they were happy to give him the details of the registered owner. That turned out to be a couple in Kirkby Stephen, local enough that Nick had been able to reach their address from the spot where the bicycle had been found in less than ten minutes.

There, things became more complicated.

The couple explained they'd given away the bike when their daughter outgrew it. Gave it to the small recycling site near the Co-op supermarket at the edge of town.

"The chap who used to look after the place, he ran a swap system," the wife explained. "Bring one child's bicycle in, take away another. Great idea, but the council put a stop to all that, wouldn't you know it?"

No, they'd no idea who might have the bicycle now and were shocked that their details were still registered with the micro-dot security company.

Nick had crawled along the main street, which was clogged with parked cars and lightweight horse-drawn buggies. He called at the recycling site and was surprised to find one of the current attendants knew the previous custodian.

"This time of day, you'll find him in the King's Arms," the man said.

Nick, who'd just battled past the pub on his way through the town, abandoned his car and walked back, without much hope of a result.

For once, he was surprised. It seemed the old guy who'd once run the recycling facility had a near-photographic memory for people and objects. Yes, he remembered the pink bicycle because it was taken away by a local woman who had a bevy of little girls. Name of Yvonne Elliot.

But no, he didn't have an address.

Nick had called it in, hoping for more information.

What he got instead was a terse instruction from DI Pollock to detour back to the Hunter Lane station in Penrith and pick him up before going to interview the Elliots.

He still didn't know why and the longer he left it, the harder it was to ask.

As they neared Kirkby Stephen, the grass verges had been roped off with warning signs for no horse-drawn vehicles posted at regular intervals. Most had been simply ignored, caravans and bow-tops and vardos crammed in wherever they would fit. The ropes and posts had mainly been turned into makeshift paddocks for grazing horses.

Pollock glowered at them.

"Told the Superintendent *that* would be a waste of time," he said at last. "Would've been a better idea to get a landscape gardening outfit to mow the grass flat. No grass for them to eat —no ponies. Simple as that."

Nick flicked his eyes sideways. "Sir—"

"I know, lad. You want to know what I'm doing riding shotgun on this one, eh?"

"Er, yessir."

Pollock swung his arm across the centre console and Nick almost ducked in instinctive reflex. "Take a right here, lad. No point in getting snarled up in the middle of town. We'll go round by the cattle market instead." He settled back in his seat as Nick took the side road. "Two words for you—Dylan Elliot. Name familiar?"

"No... I don't think so."

Pollock grunted. "It would be, if you'd been around here longer, you can bet on that. He's a right rascal and ne'er-do-well is our Dylan—like his dad before him. Has a ramshackle old farm further along the Mallerstang valley from where they found that bike."

"Sounds like you've got a bit of history with him."

"Aye, you could say that, lad. Felt his collar a time or two— receiving, theft, minor drugs offences—but never anything we could really get our teeth into. He's one of those cocky little sods who's just clever enough to get away with it, most of the time."

At Pollock's direction, Nick wound through a housing estate and turned again, back onto the main road. He was irritated to note they'd completely bypassed the main street with its glut of traffic.

"And Yvonne Elliot is…?"

"His missus. Nice enough to look at, but not the sharpest tool in the shed, as I recall. Married young and has been too busy popping out kiddies to do much else since. They've got half-a-dozen of 'em at last count. Five girls and one boy, Jordan. He's about ten or eleven and a right little tearaway."

"Grace—er, CSI McColl—seemed to think the bicycle most likely belonged to a boy, sir."

"Aye, now she *is* a sharp one, is Grace. That's why I've asked her to meet us up at the Elliots'. Best to go in mob-handed so they can't claim any kind of breach of procedure later."

"In that case…thank you, sir," Nick said. "If it's their boy's bicycle that's been found, well, I'd rather have someone with me who knows the family."

"Don't thank me yet," Pollock said sourly. "If it *is* Jordan Elliot who's disappeared, then his father is going to try every trick in the book to discredit us now, just so he can claim prejudice or harassment later."

Nick felt his eyebrows climb. "What about his son? If he plays awkward with us, he could hinder the entire investigation."

Pollock grunted again. "If there *is* anything to investigate. Still, I think you'll find, lad, things like that don't matter very much to a man like Dylan Elliot."

10

A WOMAN GRACE assumed was Yvonne Elliot took her time to answer DI Pollock's heavy knocking on the front door of the farmhouse.

She finally yanked the door open, a small child wedged on her hip and lips parted as if about to give her unexpected callers a mouthful of abuse. When she saw who was standing there, however, her mouth closed with a snap and she glared at them all equally.

She was a scrawny woman with a face that might have been pretty before discontentment carved the pinches into her skin. An old bagged shirt hung off one shoulder and there was a stain on the front that Grace didn't need a swab kit to know was probably baby vomit. She had long bare legs and dirty feet jammed into flip-flops.

"What the heck do *you* lot want?" she demanded. The child's face crumpled in response to the sharp tone. Yvonne began what might have been intended as a comforting jiggle. "If you're after my Dylan, he hasn't done nowt. He's here—and he's been here all day and all last night an' all!"

"It's not your husband we're looking for, Yvonne," Pollock said. "Not this time." His voice was gentle, somehow all the scarier because of it. "May we come inside?"

"You got a warrant?"

"Oh…do we need one—if your Dylan hasn't done nowt?"

She scowled at the three of them for a moment longer, then

seemed to fold, her bravado exhausted by this brief display. Underneath it, Grace saw trepidation leaching through.

"Come on then, if you must," Yvonne said, and turned on her heel, scuffing back along the darkened hallway. Pollock stepped inside, ducking under the lintel, and followed.

Grace gestured for Nick to go ahead of her. She was still clinging to the hope that her presence would be unnecessary. Regardless, she knew he needed to catch the expressions on these people's faces when they were first hatched and unguarded. Grace's task, if required, would come later.

Now, she merely observed. The house was generally dirty, that dark ground-in line at the edges of the carpet, the thick scab of dust on the skirting board and the grubby swathe running along the ancient wallpaper at the height of a child's hand. Dust highlighted the cobwebs that draped from every corner.

Yvonne led them through a door at the rear of the hall, into a sitting room crammed with mismatched furniture, including two three-seater sofas and an oversize TV. The space was made smaller still by the low ceiling, the beams bowing downward at the centre. Grace stood back by the doorway and watched the two policemen barely resisting the urge to crouch.

As they entered, a man lounging on one of the sofas lurched to his feet. He was small and wiry, his dark hair long enough to curl around the ripped collar of his T-shirt. His eyes darted between the now-blocked doorway and the open windows on the far side of the room. More out of habit, Grace judged, than any real attempt to plan an escape.

"Aw, 'Vonne!" he protested. "What you doin' lettin' this lot in?"

"Oh, give it a rest, Dyl'. What was I s'posed to do with 'em?" She flopped down onto the other sofa and pulled the little girl she carried onto her lap. The child had a cute face and dark curls like her father, flattened on one side where she'd slept on them. "'Sides," Yvonne added, her voice turning whiny, "*he* said"—she jerked her chin at Pollock—"it weren't about nothin' *you'd* done."

Dylan Elliot straightened, pulled back his shoulders. He was half a head smaller than the two detectives but more in scale to the room. That point seemed to bolster his confidence, Grace considered, despite the unannounced visit. "So, what *is* this about, then…Pollock?"

The DI heard the insult in the way Dylan over-pronounced his name and bared his teeth. No humour there but no animosity, either. He had too many years under his belt to be so easily offended, although Nick looked offended enough on his boss's behalf.

The little girl on her mother's lap reacted to the increased tension in the room by staring at the interlopers with wide eyes and jamming one finger up her nose.

Pollock glanced at Nick and said mildly, "If you'd like to inform the Elliots of the reason for our visit, Detective Constable Weston?"

Ah… Nicely done.

By deferring to an officer who was his junior—and making sure Dylan was aware of the fact—Pollock deftly put the man in his place.

"We are enquiring as to the whereabouts of your son, Jordan, if you wouldn't mind, sir?" Nick said.

"Why?" Grace caught a hint of alarm from Dylan. "What's the little bugger done now?"

"We have reason to be…concerned for his wellbeing."

Yvonne clutched at the toddler on her lap. "What does *that* mean? Dyl, what's—?"

"Shut up," Dylan snapped, without taking his eyes off Nick now. "But yeah, what *does* that mean? What's happened?"

"If *you* wouldn't mind answering the question first, sir."

"I should think he's at school," Dylan said. "Where else would he be?"

"But you don't know for sure?" Nick insisted. Grace didn't miss the way Yvonne's gaze latched onto her husband's face and stayed there. "When did you last see him?"

"Last night," Yvonne said, subdued now. "He had his tea, same as normal. He'd been…difficult, like, when I picked 'em all up from school, so I let him play out on his bike—after."

"Difficult? What was that about?"

She gave a shrug. "He saw the Gypsies was camped at Water Yat when we drove past and he wanted to go down there. He liked the horses."

"But you said no?"

She flushed, flicked her eyes toward her husband. "Dyl' don't like him hangin' around with 'em."

"Too right," Dylan said. "Bunch of tinkers and thieves, the lot of 'em."

"Did you see your son again *after* he went playing outside on his bicycle?"

"'Course. He came in and went to bed about nine-ish—usual time, same as the girls. Well, our Jess gets to stay up later but she's the eldest, so—"

"Did you actually *see* him go to bed?"

Dylan's snort was derisive. "The boy's old enough to put his'self to bed. Don't need tuckin' in and readin' a story."

Yvonne bit her lip. "I looked in on him just before I—*we*—turned in, 'bout half-ten."

"What about this morning? See him then, did you?"

Yvonne's face twisted. "N–no. I thought he'd got up early and gone to school on his bike. He does that sometimes, see…"

"So, you haven't seen your ten-year-old son since last night, and his school say he didn't turn up this morning," Pollock said, his voice flat. "And now a bicycle we believe belongs to Jordan has been found, a couple of miles away, having sustained what evidence suggests is impact damage from a collision with another vehicle."

He didn't mention the blood but he didn't need to. Yvonne let out a small shriek and clamped both hands over her mouth.

"What do you mean, you *believe* it belongs to him. Is it his or not?"

Pollock turned and nodded to Grace. Knowing this moment would probably come, she'd already downloaded one of the images of the mangled gold bicycle to her phone. Now, she stepped forward and showed the screen to Dylan, saw all she needed to from the way he flinched in response.

"Aye, that's his bike," he said. "Where was it found? And where's the boy?"

"Water Yat," Nick said, mispronouncing it as off-comers often did—"water" as it was spelt, rather than the local's harder "watter".

"Where the bloody gyppos was set up," Dylan said. "I *told* you not to let him keep goin' down there."

Yvonne, suddenly finding her voice again, cried, "Just shut

up, Dyl'. There's nowt wrong with the Travellers. It's *you* who—"
Dylan jerked to face her and she broke off abruptly.

"Who what, Mrs Elliot?" Nick asked.

Dylan glowered. She glanced across at him anxiously before muttering, "Jordan was always wantin' to be off down there, while the Gypsies were around. There's a kid comes every year with one of the families—boy about his age—and the two of 'em are sorta friends."

"I didn't want the lad mixin' with 'em," Dylan said. He shifted his glare to Nick, reproachful. "Everyone 'round here knows what they're like—the trouble they cause. I don't know why your lot didn't move 'em all on days ago."

"For pity's sake, Dyl', you're like an old woman repeatin' all that tittle-tattle," Yvonne shot back at him. "There's nowt wrong with the Travellers. Folk, just like the rest of us—they gotta be somewhere."

Grace caught the momentary surprise in the tilt of Nick's head. Not at Dylan's prejudice but at Yvonne's lack of it.

Interesting…

"And you've no idea where your son might be now?" Nick asked. "Other friends he might be with? Places he liked to go?"

The Elliots shook their heads silently.

"Was this usual behaviour for Jordan—taking himself off or cutting classes?"

"No, he always seemed to enjoy school, like," Dylan said, an element of bemusement in his voice. Yvonne gave a kind of hiccuping sob.

Grace cleared her throat. "I've been collecting forensic evidence from…where the bicycle was found," she said carefully. "I need something of Jordan's so I can isolate him from anyone else who might have handled it."

Dylan's eyes narrowed. "What kind of 'evidence'?"

Grace stared back without a flicker. "Well, fingerprints, for a start. Do you have anything only he's likely to have touched? Some personal item like a toothbrush, perhaps?"

Yvonne got to her feet, hefting the little girl onto her hip again. "Upstairs. I'll show you."

Grace climbed the creaky staircase behind her. The carpet runner up the centre of the treads was worn flat and was thread-bare at the half-landing. There were four bedrooms and a family bathroom. Yvonne nodded to a door covered with hand-drawn signs saying 'Keep Out' and 'No Girls Allowed'. Grace put down her crime-scene kit and pulled a pair of nitrile gloves out of her back pocket.

Inside, the room smelt of unwashed male, sweat and old socks. It was clearly the smallest room, with barely enough space for a single bed and a set of sagging shelves dotted with school books, artwork and painted action figures. A rail for hanging clothes went from wall to wall across the foot of the bed. It was not much used, with shirts and jeans and discarded underwear strewn across the floor.

The little girl wriggled to be put down and, once that aim had been achieved, made a beeline for the overflowing window ledge. Just in time, Grace spotted the jam jar crammed with pens, paintbrushes and pencils, and a green toothbrush with splayed bristles. She whisked the toothbrush out of the child's reach and bagged it.

"It's not much but he's the only one gets a room to his'self," Yvonne said from the doorway, watching as Grace looked about her. "The girls have to share, and Dyl' and me still got the baby in with us in her cot, like."

"How old is this little one?" Grace asked as the child latched onto her trouser leg at the knee.

"She's four. Startin' school in September, aren't you, Ollie?"

The little girl nodded vigorously. When Grace bent to deposit the sealed bag in her kit, she transferred her grip from Grace's leg to around her neck and clung on. Grace had little choice but to lift her into her arms as she straightened. The child, small but surprisingly weighty, grabbed a lock of Grace's hair, studied the red of it with absolute attention, and stuck it into her mouth.

Grace was not entirely comfortable around small children, never having any of her own. She and Max had skirted around the subject during the time they were married. Grace had never actively tried to *prevent* conception, but it hadn't happened and he hadn't pressed. She liked other people's well enough. She wasn't sure if it was the knowledge that she must soon hand them back that stopped her getting too broody.

"Aw, she likes you," Yvonne said.

"Mm," Grace replied, retrieving her slightly soggy hair and pushing it back behind her ear. "Would you have a current photo of Jordan we could borrow?" She saw the hesitation and added, "I can copy it and let you have it back."

"Oh, all right, then. I've got one the school took—that's probably the most recent, like. It's on me dresser."

She turned and went into another bedroom. As soon as she'd gone the little girl leaned close to Grace's ear and whispered, "We shouldn't be here."

Grace glanced at her in surprise. "Oh, why not?"

"'Cause this is *Jordan's* room and he don't like *nobody* to come in."

"That's OK, sweetie. Jordan's not here at the moment so I think we're safe."

"I come in sometimes, when he's at school," the child admitted with a shy smile. "But he'll be back very soon, though."

Grace tried to maintain her own smile. "Yes…I'm sure he will."

"He's got to," the child continued, nodding solemnly. "'Cause he hasn't got his puff-puff."

"His…'puff-puff'?"

She took her fingers out of her mouth for long enough to point them, stickily, at one of the shelves. And there, half-hidden behind an open can of fizzy pop and a plastic dinosaur, lay an asthma inhaler.

11

DYLAN ELLIOT STOOD JUST FAR ENOUGH BACK from the kitchen window not to be visible from outside. He watched the three coppers climb into their vehicles, circle through the yard and head off along the rutted drive.

All the while, he tuned out his wife's whiny voice, nagging on at him from the doorway.

The redhead took the pick-up truck. What was it with these posh birds and their big four-wheel drives? The two blokes got into the Subaru, the younger one behind the wheel. Dylan was into his cars—or he would have been, given either the money or the credit score to land a decent loan. He was aware of a burst of jealousy as the engine fired with a throaty roar. *Who knew the filth were so well paid?*

They'd given him a right jolt, appearing like that, mob-handed. He hadn't let them shake him, though, that was something at least. Dylan had a couple of nice little deals on the go at the moment. Deals that would not stand too much nosing about by the local cops.

They must have caught a whiff of something and had come round here, trying it on with some story about Jordan gone missing.

He wasn't over concerned about that. The kid came and went as he pleased most of the time. It was true he hardly ever tried to bunk off school, though—little swot.

Dylan shook off whatever unease he might have felt. The boy

had maybe just fallen in with the Gypsies, perhaps gone along for the ride to the Fair. Sooner or later, they'd get a phone call from him, cadging a lift home, or some other kiddie's parent would roll up and drop him off. Or he'd just arrive back under his own steam.

They'd never worried about him in the past, so why start now?

But behind him, Yvonne was droning on and on—something about the pollen count and Ventolin and never forgiving him. He turned.

"What the bloody 'ell are you on about, woman?"

She threw up her hands in exasperation. "Ugh! You listenin' to a word I say, Dyl'?"

"Only when you say somethin' worth listenin' to. So, half the time, no, I don't."

She jabbed him in the shoulder, hard enough to hurt. Almost without thinking, Dylan bunched his fist and hit her, high in the fleshy vee under her ribcage.

The air and the fight went out of her instantly. She fell back against the door frame, clutching at it to stay on her feet, shoulders heaving as she tried to drag in her next stuttering breath. The rasping sound of it reminded Dylan of the boy, when he was having one of his asthma attacks.

The guilt hit him at once. He'd done a bit of boxing, in his youth. A punch came natural to him, like those SAS blokes, just back from some war zone. He'd heard all the stories about how they turned on their own families if they were taken by surprise. Couldn't help themselves.

He put a hand out to help Yvonne but she swatted him away fiercely, still clinging to the woodwork. Milking it now, he was sure.

Dylan moved across to lean on the ancient range, put in when the farmhouse was new and still going, more or less. He hooked one foot onto the rail that ran round the hearth, got out his tin of tobacco and Rizla papers and concentrated on fixing himself a roll-up until the colour was back in her face.

He lit up, took a long drag, and gave her a narrowed stare through the exhaled smoke. "Now, you gonna run that by me again, 'Vonne? But without the lip, this time, eh?"

She eyed him with healthier respect. "J–Jordan. He didn't

take his inhaler with him. He *always* has it with him! You *know* he can't manage without—not this time of year, with all the pollen an' that."

Dylan shrugged. "Maybe he just didn't want to look like a wimp in front of them Gypsy lads. Hard as nails, some of 'em."

"If he had it in his pocket, how was they gonna know?" Yvonne saw him straighten and flinched. "Just sayin', that's all," she mumbled quickly. "It scared me, seein' it still by his bed. S'pose summat really *has* happened to him?"

"He'll be fine," Dylan said, picking a flake of loose tobacco off his lower lip. "Always is, little bugger. They're just trying to get to me and usin' any excuse to do it."

She looked down as Ollie, their next-to-youngest daughter pushed herself between her mother's legs. Yvonne bent down and swept her up, clutching the little girl to her chest like a shield.

For a moment, their eyes met across the hazy gloom of the kitchen. The TV still played in the sitting room at the back of the house. Flies buzzed against the kitchen window. The compressor in the ancient fridge fired up, trying to cope with the heat, rattling the shelves inside.

"I told 'em you was here last night, don't forget—*all night*," Yvonne said, her voice subdued now. "Are you gonna tell me where you *really* was, and what you was up to?"

12

GORGED with its fill of heat, the day stretches languid along the valley floor, warm and lazy like a sleeping cat.

Where it moves at all, it moves laboriously. Weighted down by its own mass, it makes half-hearted passes at Mallerstang Edge toward High Seat in the east, up the pitted track of the old Lady Anne's highway toward the Water Cut. But it lacks incentive for the climb. So it does little more than wash against the yellowed grass that lines the steep sides, and comes tumbling softly down again. So quietly, it does not even wake the trees.

On the far side, across the River Eden, vapour gasps from the boiler of an old steam train, brass bright and gleaming, working the grade from Carlisle to Settle. Behind the engine are four carriages of day-trippers. They press at the open windows for the movement's breeze as much as the view.

The train crawls on but its breath remains to hang flaccid over the tracks. Looming above, Wild Boar Fell shimmers in the western haze.

The ground has taken in the sun and can take no more. It sweats up dust, splits and pulls back. The sheep are listless as they crop the grass short as baize on a billiard table. Horses stand close, heads low, nose-to-tail against the flies.

The clamour of the insects is louder than the wind.

And then, in the turning of a moment, it is not.

It takes longer to notice the absence of the flies and the bees than their presence. The birds are first to know. The swallows, swooping in swathes through swarms of midges, now come up with beaks empty. The livestock are shaken from their lethargy to a skittish haste.

In the oldest farmhouse in the valley, the oldest farmer rubs his weather knee and eyes the cloudless sky, then tells his wife to take the washing in. She looks askance but brings her basket all the same.

The Travellers camped alongside the old Tommy Road that winds across the moors toward Ravenstonedale feel the dropping of the air and heed the warning. They live as much outdoors as in and can read the signs as well as any, and better than most. They send the largest of their number to hammer home the stakes that hold their horses tethered. Others tighten canvas tilts of the bow-tops, take in aired bedding and chairs, gather children and move kettles from fire to stove.

Breeze turns to blow. The warm air rolls upward, funnelled by the valley walls. It meets with cooler, then colder, as it rises and keeps rising. Convection turns to condensation. The air first weeps, then cries, white cotton tears that mound and bloom outward into ever expanding cumulus clouds. An avalanche in the heavens.

Ice forms in the freezing atmosphere, clashing drop to drop, splintering and sparkling as it collides, sparking with the charge.

The jostle turns to shoving. A hammer to the anvil, striking outright jagged blows. The crack of a whip's tail and the fearsome stamp of feet.

Breathing hard now, and uneven, the storm comes of age, spreads his arms and towers over the valley huddled down below. He roars his might, and smites anything that dares to raise its head. First with fire then with water.

The parched earth has been crying out for moisture. A few sips, carefully poured, would have quenched its thirst. Instead he pounds the ground with a deluge so heavy it hits and bounces into mist, runs over dry lips too fast to be swallowed.

Falling rain meets rising river. The Eden swells to the task, gathering all and pressing it onward, taking more and giving less.

Except the body of the boy. The river's been guarding him close, keeping him near. But now, attracted by this shiny new distraction, she pushes him aside. Tucks him into the crypt of a tree, exposed by the undercutting of the bank, pats his face and leaves him there.

Waiting to be found, or lost, and found again.

13

GRACE HAD FORGOTTEN the traffic detours that would be already in place through Appleby for the start of the Horse Fair. Just getting the participants to their designated camping grounds was an operation in itself, never mind the hordes of visitors who would soon descend on the town.

She drove down Bongate to the steady beat of her wipers. As she passed the Royal Oak and crested the next rise, she saw the Road Closed signs were already out and manned by a couple of uniforms.

She braked, buzzed down her window. The rain splashed in at her but the air still felt warm.

"Hello," she said to the nearest officer, a young lad who looked as if he might one day grow into his stab vest and helmet. "I'm trying to get up onto Scattergate, near the castle. Is there no way through?"

The young constable looked dubious. His eyes slid to his partner, an older woman who was clearly the more senior of the two. She came over, glanced at Grace and then took a second look.

"Oh...CSI McColl, isn't it?"

"Grace, yes."

"I doubt you'll remember me. We met at Kirkby Thore, a month or so ago—"

"Of course I remember," Grace said, thankful that nudge was

enough. "Someone had stripped a barn roof of its slate during the night."

"Don't suppose there's been any developments?" the woman asked without much hope.

Grace shook her head. "Not much to go on, I'm afraid. It was too dry for decent tyre impressions or boot prints. And whoever they were, they knew what they were about."

The woman cast her eye heavenward, blinking against the rain. "Aye, well, I reckon this is set in for the rest of the day. You may be thankful for it by the end of the weekend."

Grace frowned, then recalled someone once telling her that nothing quelled civil disorder quite as well as heavy rain.

"Are we expecting any particular trouble?"

"No more than usual, so probably plenty," the woman said wryly. "Still, I'm not complaining about the overtime, that's for sure."

Another vehicle pulled up behind Grace's pick-up. The young constable waved the driver round and off onto the designated detour road.

"Speaking of trouble, has it started already?" the female officer asked. "Is that why you're here?"

"Not as far as I know. I'm actually off the clock and trying to call in on my mother—she's only just moved back after years down south."

"Well, she picked her moment, didn't she?" The woman stepped back. "On you go, then. Just watch for any idiots already racing those ponies up and down Battlebarrow."

"I will," Grace promised. "And thank you."

She moved carefully around the barrier and continued down the hill onto an area by the river, called The Sands. Grace had always wondered about the name, as the only sand anywhere nearby was bagged and stacked in front of the local builders' merchant opposite the bridge over the Eden. Her mother would probably know the origin. She collected obscure facts the way a squirrel collected nuts for the winter.

As she drove across the bridge, Grace glanced at the river level. Sometimes it was barely a trickle through here. At others it flooded the road completely, not to mention the nearby houses and shop fronts. Today it was somewhere between the two.

At least Mum had the sense to buy something higher up the hill. Not that sense had much to do with it.

Grace had learned long ago that trying to dissuade her mother from anything she had set her mind to was a waste of effort. Eleanor had been a force of nature when she first married at twenty and was still one now, some forty-five years later.

During that time, she had buried two husbands. Grace's father—when Grace herself was in her early teens—and the second husband she'd taken after Grace's own marriage.

In the belief that her daughter was safely off her hands, Eleanor had moved down to the south coast and become the mainstay of various societies and committees.

And now she was back, and the two of them were still feeling their way toward balance in this new phase of their relationship.

Grace pulled up in the driveway of the well-proportioned old house, built of the red sandstone so prevalent in the local area. Any suggestions she made about the wisdom of looking for a modern bungalow had been quickly brushed aside.

As she climbed out of the Nissan and dashed for the shelter of the front porch, she noticed that her mother had already made a start on the somewhat neglected garden. She was still frowning over this when the door opened to the bell.

"I hope you didn't move those planters by yourself, Mum. They're far too heavy."

"And a good afternoon to you, too," Eleanor said, but there was a smile in her voice. Grace had inherited her mother's height and her colouring, and something of her inner composure. The older woman was still very upright and precise in her movements, putting her feet down like a dancer. She wore a long chenille sweater that was somewhere between mustard and gold. Her hair was set and her dress and make-up were lessons in flawless understatement. As always, Grace felt dowdy by comparison, ill-suited to her name.

Now, her shoulders dropped at the inferred rebuke. "I'm sorry, that wasn't much of a greeting, was it?"

"No, but I'll forgive you, darling. How's your day been? Was it very bloody? Would you like some tea? I've just made a pot of Earl Grey. Come through to the conservatory."

And with that Grace was swept to the back of the house

where a structure more like an orangery jutted out into the substantial rear garden.

"You've been busy here, too, I see," Grace said, noting the cut grass and pruned trees.

"Ah, well, I admit to having some help. I don't disregard *all* your advice, you know."

Grace was just about to ask who when it came to her. "Max," she said, rather flatly.

"Indeed." Her mother's smile was close to a grin. "For such an urbanite he's not afraid to roll up his sleeves and get his hands dirty, I will say that for him. The man's a gem."

"Mother—"

"Ooh, I know I've got under your skin when you call me that."

Grace paused, took a deep breath and steadied herself. "Mum, please don't give Max any cause to hope that things... Well, that we might get back together. We're divorced. It's over. And I've had quite enough trouble convincing him of that fact without *you* encouraging him."

Eleanor folded herself neatly into a chair without giving away anything further, and lifted the china teapot.

"Milk or lemon?"

Grace sighed as she took the chair opposite. Pursuing that line of questioning, she knew, would get her nowhere. "Milk, please. So, are you all prepared for your first Appleby Horse Fair?"

"Hardly my first, darling."

"Things have changed since you moved away."

"Not so much. Half the businesses in the town rub their hands with glee about all the extra income, and the other half shut up shop and treat it as an enforced holiday. Nothing new in that."

"It will be difficult driving in and out while the Fair's on. I only managed to get through now because one of the officers on traffic duty recognised me."

"In that case, I shall use your name shamelessly to cut a swathe—"

"*Mother.*"

She laughed. "Oh come on, Grace. Don't be so po-faced about

it. The Fair has been going on here for centuries. It's a fine tradition—one we should celebrate, don't you think?"

Grace sipped her tea. "You don't see the side of it that I see."

"What, you think there hasn't always been a bit of bother on the periphery?"

"There was more than a 'bit of bother' last year, I seem to recall—fighting, gambling, assault. Not to mention the amount of vandalism and theft that goes on."

"Ah, well, you must ask yourself how much of that is the fault of the incomers and how much of it is down to the locals," Eleanor said. "It's a well-known fact around the area that if you have a falling-out with your neighbours, then now is the ideal time of year for settling those scores."

"Because you can get your own back and blame it on the Gypsies," Grace murmured, almost to herself. She looked up, gave her mother an assessing stare. "I trust you haven't been here long enough to annoy any of your new neighbours quite that much?"

"No, but one or two of them have really annoyed me…" She flicked up a warding hand before Grace could speak. "I *am* joking, darling."

"Still, if you have any problems—this week or at any time— please, call me."

"I shall." Eleanor slipped her hand over Grace's, gave it a squeeze. "And don't worry too much about your ex-husband. I know going back would be a mistake—for both of you." She sat up and lifted her teacup delicately. The action did not quite hide her smile. "But if he's prepared to come and labour in my garden in the hopes I might put in a good word for him, well, who am I to turn him away?"

"Mother!" Grace said again but laughing now. "You *are* utterly shameless."

"Yes, I suppose I am, rather, aren't I?" Eleanor agreed placidly. She put down her cup. The smile had gone. "I heard today and I wanted to ask you… Is there any sign of the Elliot boy—the one who's missing down at Mallerstang?"

Grace put down her own cup, clattering it against the saucer in her surprise. "What have you heard? And where on earth did you hear it?"

Her mother waved a hand vaguely. "Oh, the local grapevine, you know. It works as well as ever, I see."

"Good grief… Well, no, there's no sign of him. Not yet, anyway. I've been told to wait for the house-to-house enquiries to come in before I…explore the evidence in any more detail."

Before she incurred any lab costs, in other words. But, if Jordan hadn't turned up by morning, one way or another, Grace knew the pressure would be on her to provide some kind of direction for the investigation team. She tried not to let the prospect of yet another run-in with the acting Head of CSI disturb her equanimity.

"I knew the family," Eleanor said, reflective. "Oh, not the boy but his father—and his grandfather, come to that. Now, he really *was* a rogue. Dylan's father died after a disagreement in a bar, from what I recall—stabbed, poor man. Still, everyone had half-expected that he would come to a Bad End."

Grace thought of the blood on the bicycle, the damage to the wheels and the frame. Whatever *had* become of Jordan Elliot, she feared that nothing good could come of it.

14

Nick stood by the lounge window, waiting and watching. Below the second-storey flat in what had been the old Organ Works in Kendal, two lanes of traffic passed along Aynam Road. The rain had eased back to little more than drizzle but the cars moved slow and sporadic. In contrast, the River Kent just beyond the road had started to pick up its pace, swollen from the earlier thunderstorm and sudden downpour.

Nick had sloughed off his suit and tie when he got in from work. Mindful of Sophie's usual bath-time antics, he'd changed into jogging pants, too, and rolled back the sleeves of his shirt, ready for the battle.

She was behind him now, asleep on the sofa—finally fed, bathed, and dressed in her favourite pyjamas. He glanced across at his daughter. All that was visible amid the soft throw and the plush bunny that was her most treasured toy, was a tousled mop of blonde hair. She let out a part-snuffle, part-snore, and tightened her grip on the bunny. Its wide embroidered eyes seemed to bulge as she did so.

Nick smiled, almost in spite of himself.

It was after nine in the evening. The storm clouds had turned the day gloomy. Not yet quite twilight, it was that indecisive time when only maybe half the cars trundling past below had their headlights on. The tarmac gleamed and glittered in the beams.

He leaned against the wall by the window, arms folded so the open bottle of beer in his hand rested against his shoulder. Condensation from the cold bottle had leached through his shirt and chilled a patch of skin until it was numb. Still, he hadn't taken a sip.

Not until she gets here...

Lisa had been a hairdresser when they first met, working at a big salon in Manchester. When they'd moved north, she'd reconnected with a girl she'd gone to college with. They were now partners in their own hair and beauty salon in Bowness-on-Windermere. Lisa wanted them to move closer, arguing it would lessen *his* daily commute up to the Hunter Lane police station at Penrith as much as it would her own. Kendal was as near as Nick felt they could comfortably afford. He'd been staggered to discover that property prices in the Lakes almost matched the south-east.

He knew he couldn't complain about Lisa working late, even if it *was* unexpected tonight. Nick had left a trail of so many abandoned dinners and broken dates behind him during his police career. Not to mention the days or even weeks when he'd disappear with no contact, saturation diving into some undercover job with the Met. He realised, on occasions like this, just how much Lisa had put up with over the years they'd been together—not graciously, sometimes, admittedly. And so he had no choice but to hold his tongue.

But tonight was not one of those when the salon usually stayed open late. Lisa should have been home long before now. It should have been her who picked up Sophie from her parents' house in Staveley on the way home. They were of a generation still suspicious of mobile phones. It wasn't until Nick arrived home to the unexpectedly empty flat he found their message on the landline answer-phone. He'd listened to them explaining Lisa hadn't turned up yet, swore under his breath and headed straight back out again. He never even got the chance to put down his car keys.

Nick recognised how lucky he and Lisa were that her parents were happy to baby-sit so frequently, what with the cost of child-care these days. In fact, they relished time with their grand-daughter and showed it by spoiling her rotten—something else

Nick would have liked to take issue with. He'd tried persuading Lisa to voice his reservations about them stuffing Sophie with her own weight in sugary snacks and fizzy drinks whenever they looked after her.

To that, Lisa had thrown, first a tantrum about his lack of gratitude, then whatever solid objects happened to be near to hand at the time.

At one point, an episode like that would have ended with them in bed, where they made love as passionately as they fought.

Not anymore.

Just after Nick transferred up to Cumbria Constabulary the previous year, he and Lisa had split up. Or rather, she announced she'd had enough of him and moved back to her parents', regardless of *his* feelings about it. He'd only put in for the transfer in the first place to appease her. It was either that, she commanded, or he choose a different career—one that wasn't likely to see him beaten half to death and hospitalised, *again,* as an occupational hazard.

Nick found himself an unwanted outsider not just at home but at work, too. It was only after he'd taken up the posting that he discovered it had been widely expected to go to a local officer. This did not prove the best way to ingratiate himself with his new colleagues. He'd been trying to make up the lost ground ever since.

Still, at least over the winter Lisa had undergone a change of heart about their relationship. Nick still wasn't quite sure why. At the time, he'd been too grateful to have Sophie back under the same roof.

But having Lisa back…well, that was something he was far more ambivalent about.

Especially on nights like this.

One car outside caught his attention. It was moving faster than the others, weaving from lane to lane as it cut through traffic. Finally, the driver braked hard and swerved left into the side street leading to their building car park, cutting up a delivery van behind. The van driver leaned on his horn and kept it there for a long, angry burst.

A few minutes later, he heard the rattle of Lisa's key in the front door. He listened to her kick off her heels in the hallway, dump her handbag on the side table and finally come padding through to the lounge, leafing through her mail. She seemed almost surprised to see him waiting for her.

"Oh, hello, gorgeous," she said over brightly.

Nick put a finger to his lips and nodded toward Sophie, still spark out on the sofa.

Lisa's face fell. "For heaven's sake, Nick, what's she doing still up at this time?"

Oh, so you do know *what time it is, then…*

"She particularly wanted *you* to tuck her in," he said, striving for a tone so bland she'd have nothing to dig her claws into. "If I'd known how late you were going to be, I wouldn't have agreed."

To his surprise, she gave him a chastened smile.

"I know. Sorry. It's all been a bit frantic today. Well, you of all people know how *that* one goes. I'll put her down now. Be a darling and pour me a glass of wine, would you?"

Nick levered away from the wall without comment. He retrieved a bottle of Lisa's favourite Chardonnay from the fridge in the kitchen area while she scooped a sleepily protesting Sophie out of her nest. By the time she returned, he'd poured out a glass, turned on the stove and was finishing a carbonara sauce over the heat.

"She hardly even stirred, poor little love." Lisa slid onto one of the stools at the breakfast bar that divided the kitchen from the living area. She took the clips out of her hair, massaging her scalp with a moan that, at one point, would have plugged straight into Nick's libido. Now, it left him strangely untouched.

"Long day," he commented, still so neutral that normally Lisa would take issue. She knew him better than anyone, after all.

All she said was, "Yeah, it has been a bit. Still, we'd be complaining more if things were too quiet, eh?"

Nick snapped a handful of spaghetti into a pan of boiling water and glanced back over his shoulder. He found her watching him with a slightly distracted air.

"Your wine's there."

"Oh, yeah…thanks."

"Supper will be about ten minutes—soon as the pasta's cooked."

"Thanks, darling," she said again, downing half the glassful in one long swallow. "You're an absolute star."

OK, now I definitely *know something's up.*

It wasn't until he had dished up the pasta and taken the stool alongside her that she seemed to pluck up her courage.

"Nick…how well do you know the other cops here? At Kendal, I mean."

"Why's that?" He finally reached for the bottle of beer and took a long pull. "Have you been caught speeding?"

"Of course not!" she protested. "I'm a very careful driver."

Nick thought of her madcap swerve off the main road and said nothing.

"It's, um…it's about Karl…"

He put down his beer with a sigh and simply looked at her. "What's he done now?"

"Nothing!" But as soon as the denial was out of her mouth, she flushed.

As well she might, Nick considered. Lisa's hulking brother, Karl, was a small-time loser who lacked any discernable talent—including the low cunning required to be a proper villain. He had no aptitude for crime other than a reluctance to work hard at an honest job. And he was a sucker for any enterprise that sounded like a path to a quick buck, regardless of how legal or illegal it might be. Quite how he'd avoided, if not arrest then certainly conviction and jail time, Nick was never sure.

Physically, he was the opposite of his sister, who was petite and delicate. Now, Nick held Lisa's gaze until she looked away, taking another mouthful of wine as an excuse to do so. He knew he should back down then, pick up his fork and let the awkward moment pass. Make small talk, say something innocuous, inconsequential.

But he was tired, he realised. Tired of pretending he cared about the soap opera that was Lisa's family, tired of indulging her pretentions, her mania for the latest fashions, her obsession with shoes, and her sheer bitchiness about the hairstyle, age, or weight of every woman he worked with.

Like any of that really matters.

It was down to Lisa's basic insecurity, he acknowledged, and he tried to make allowances. But the thought of her gradually instilling the same hang-ups and the same warped values into their daughter made him stubborn. So he stayed motionless, staring at her, until she began to fidget and eventually slammed the glass down hard enough to slop out some of the contents.

"All *right*, Nick!" she muttered, her voice compressed. "He bought this load of designer handbags, going cheap—"

Nick groaned.

"Aw, come on. Don't be like that! The bloke said they were buyer samples and overstocks—"

"What bloke?"

Her colour had begun to recede but now it bloomed again. "The bloke he bought them off—in a pub. And no, before you ask, I don't know *which* pub."

"So, in other words, they fell off the back of a lorry," he said flatly.

Lisa opened her mouth to form a denial, and then closed it again with a scowl. "They were decent mid-price brands—Danse Lente, Sensi Studio, Rey, Michael Kors." She threw out the names as if they should mean something to him. "Not obvious fakes of Hermes and Chanel, so you don't know *where* they came from."

"And neither do you. Why else would Kendal nick be involved?" He sat back, his appetite suddenly gone, and shook his head. "I'm sorry, but I think it's time your big brother finally stood on his own two feet and took responsibility for his actions."

"You mean you won't...do anything? Won't help him?"

"Not my area. Not my case."

Her face twisted and she, too, pushed her bowl aside. Nick rose, plucked their almost untouched dishes from the countertop and carried them to the sink. While his back was toward her, Lisa said quietly:

"What about doing it...to help me?"

Something in her tone made him turn and go very still.

"Lisa," he said then, in a soft voice she should have treated with caution, "what have you done?"

She was playing with the stem of her wineglass, twirling it round and watching the pale liquid climb the sides like a wall of death, inching ever closer to the rim.

"I... He asked if I'd help him—shift a few, you know? So, I let him put a display in the salon."

He bit back the instinctive rebuke and asked wearily, "How many have you sold?"

"Loads," she admitted. "They look really good and, at the price, they're a steal…" Her voice trailed away as she registered the poor choice of words. "It's just, if this goes…any further, it's bound to be in the papers, maybe local news. Our clients are bound to find out. They could demand refunds or—"

"Or report you," Nick finished for her. "Which could lead either to a conviction for handling stolen goods if these bags are the real thing—which I very much doubt—or one for fraud, if they're fakes. Not a good outcome for you, either way."

Temper flared in Lisa's eyes. To some extent, Nick was almost glad to see it there.

"What about it not being a good outcome for *you*, either?" she demanded. "After all, if I get done as well as Karl, what effect will *that* have on your precious career?"

He sighed in defeat. "Send it down the toilet, probably."

"Exactly. Besides, it's not the first time you've put in a good word for him, is it?"

In fact, Nick had done his best to see Karl got what was coming to him. But he knew that denying his supposed earlier intervention now would not be wise.

"I'll ask around," he said at last. "Can't promise more than that."

Lisa nodded. She did not hide her satisfaction well as she slipped off the stool and picked up her wineglass. "I'm going to grab a quick shower before bed. I'm exhausted."

Before she could turn away, Nick locked his gaze onto her face, the intensity of his stare at odds with his casual tone. "Is that where you were tonight, then—seeing Karl?"

Lisa hesitated. Only momentarily, but enough for a man who'd learned to read fractional intonation and micro-expressions as a matter of course. At one time, interpreting them correctly had meant the difference between life and death.

"Yeah," she said. "Yes, of course. Where else would I have been?"

When he didn't answer, she shrugged and went into their bedroom, shutting the door behind her with quiet care.

Nick let out a long breath, bracing his hands on the countertop. He'd long ago learned to distinguish truth from lies, too. And as soon as Lisa had spoken, all his cop instincts blared a warning like a klaxon going off inside his head.

Lie.

15

BLENKINSHIP STARED at the wildlife documentary on the TV screen without taking in a frame of footage or a word of the narration. He sat very still, almost outside himself. Occasionally, he lifted the whisky tumbler clasped in his right hand and took a sip. The twelve-year-old single malt was one of his favourites—taken with just a splash of water, thank you very much, and no adulteration of ice—but he could hardly taste that, either.

It was as though he was losing touch with all his senses as they became contaminated by the dirty floodwater of his guilt.

He hadn't stopped to draw breath all day, but by the end of it had achieved nothing. Perhaps because all the time he'd been waiting for Grace McColl's crime-scene report on the bicycle found at Mallerstang to come in. By close of play, however, it had still failed to arrive in his inbox.

He tried to tell himself there was nothing out of the ordinary about this. She might well still be tidying up her notes, going through her photographs. After all, as far as anybody knew, this could turn out to be nothing more than an overreaction. It was hardly a priority case.

Not yet, anyway…

Or she could have gone over your head because she's been able to reconstruct exactly what happened and can somehow link you to the crime. Even now, the boys from uniform could be gathering outside the front of the house, in the back garden, across the street. Waiting for the order to—

Something large sailed past his head, close enough to make him flinch back in the armchair with a convulsive upward jerk of his hands to protect his face. The whisky splashed out of the glass as he did so, trickling down his wrist.

Still, it took him another moment to focus on the cushion that had just flumped to the carpet beside his chair.

His eyes veered to Susanne, sitting on the sofa with her legs stretched out and surrounded by the inevitable stack of marking. She was watching him over her glasses, half amused but with a pinch of worry between her eyebrows.

"What the hell was that in aid of?"

"You tell me," she said, in the kind of voice he imagined she used on her least attentive students. "I've asked you twice if you're actually interested in the sex life of baboons and you totally ignore me."

He sighed and put down the tumbler, sucking the spilled whisky from the back of his hand rather than waste it.

"Yeah, sorry. Tough day."

She rummaged under her papers for the remote and muted the TV.

"Want to talk about it?"

I don't know… Do I?

Just for a second, the urge to blurt out the whole nightmare was almost overwhelming. Was a burden shared really a burden halved, as the old saying went? Or was it a burden doubled instead? For the first time, he began to understand how all but the most hardened perpetrators of crime might confess during police interview. Especially with apparently sympathetic listeners on the other side of the table, coaxing you to get it all off your chest.

He rubbed a hand around the back of his neck, took in a deep breath and opened his mouth. Just before he might have said anything he regretted, he glanced across again at Susanne.

Her attention had already moved on, back to her task.

He closed his mouth again, not sure if what he felt was disappointment or relief.

"Not much to tell," he said instead. "Staffing…concerns. You know the kind of thing."

"Hm?" Her eyes were still on the exercise book on her lap. "Oh, listen to this one, Chris. 'Queen Elizabeth the First could never get any rest because Mary Queen of Scots was always hoovering in the background.' Sometimes Year Eight's spelling is priceless."

He mumbled his agreement and went into the kitchen to rinse the sticky residue from his hands. As he stood at the sink he glimpsed his reflection in the window over it, shadowed in the blackened glass. Perhaps that was what made him look so... furtive. Restless, even—like a man about to bolt.

He turned away and refilled his glass with a more than generous measure.

Susanne looked up as he returned to the lounge.

"Sorry, love. I *was* listening. What kind of staffing concerns?"

He took his time about retrieving her thrown cushion and sitting down again, all the while hunting for some less inflammatory but still legitimate topic.

Eventually, he seized on: "You know when you first found out you'd got the Deputy Headship? It must have affected the way the other teachers behaved around you."

"Of course it did. The ones who've still managed to retain any shred of ambition were resentful that I'd beaten them to the punch, as it were. And the ones who've had it knocked out of them by years in the profession thought I was getting ideas thoroughly above my station." She gave a rueful smile. "And, on top of that, all of them were worried I might use their old staffroom whinges against them. I could practically see them desperately trying to remember what they'd ever said in front of me—about going through the motions in class or calling in sick when it was really a hangover. Why, is that what's happening with you?"

"It's a bit different, I suppose, in that we're spread all over the county, so we don't have a communal staffroom," he said. Not that he had the sort of relationship with the other Cumbria CSIs that invited those kind of confidences, in any case. "It's more that they don't always respect my authority. I mean, it was a damn shame, what happened to Sibson, but after him I was the one with the most seniority. There should never have been any argument over who was going to take his place."

That was not entirely true, he acknowledged privately. He had enough self-awareness to know he wasn't the most popular of people at work but, he reasoned, those who are good at what they do often invoked the jealousy of others.

They'd told him anti-discrimination rules meant they had to advertise the Head CSI position widely, although he had his doubts that was the real reason. And whether his promotion was confirmed, in the end, because he was the top man for the job, or the *only* man for the job, that was another thing altogether…

Susanne was nodding in agreement. "Oh yes, I had to put up with quite a bit of that kind of attitude. You've got to nip it in the bud, love. Show 'em who's the boss. Is it anyone in particular, or do I even need to ask?"

Now it was his turn to nod. "Yeah—that bloody McColl woman, mostly." Susanne had never met his work colleagues but it was not the first time he'd voiced his frustration on the subject of Grace McColl. The outright favouritism his predecessor had shown the woman described as his protégé—if that's *all* she was to him, and he had his doubts about *that* one, too—had always riled Blenkinship. Sibson had listened to her when she should have been doing all the listening and little of the talking. When she should have been making the tea and running the most mundane of tests, not being put in charge of important crime scenes.

"What's she got up to this time?"

"She's just not a team player. Take today, for instance. She goes haring off down to Kirkby Stephen for some minor offence —a simple theft, most likely—when she should have passed it on to the lads at Kendal instead. And that left only young Ty Frost to cover Penrith solo. I mean, he's come on leaps and bounds since I took over, but he's still a bit green for handling anything serious that crops up."

"And did it?" Susanne asked.

"Did it what?"

"*Did* anything serious crop up?"

"Well, no," he admitted, "but that's not the point. She should have passed the job on. Or kept me in the loop so *I*, as her superior, could have allocated the most appropriate personnel."

Susanne frowned. "To be honest with you, love, it sounds to me like she took the most logical option. Didn't you tell me Steve Scott was away on that Home Office course? You were complaining about the timing of it—clashing with Appleby Horse Fair. So, if you were down a man at Kendal—"

"Yes, yes, all right," he snapped, levering out of his chair as the frustration zipped along his nerves. He clutched the glass tight, almost hoping it would shatter between his fingers. He needed something sharp, sudden, shocking, to cut through the helpless rage. "Hell fire, it's bad enough that they're constantly second-guessing me at work, never mind the same damn thing when I get home!"

Susanne blinked at him for a moment, then said with careful precision, "I know you've had a difficult day, Chris, but so have I. All I'm doing is trying to look at the situation as a whole so I can help you reach the best solution." She shoved the marking aside and got to her feet with dignity. "Throwing a tantrum will not achieve anything except *you* spending a night in the spare room, so I'll thank you not to take that tone with me, hm?"

For a long moment their eyes cut, thrust, and parried across the coffee table. Eventually, Blenkinship let his gaze droop in surrender.

"I'm sorry," he muttered. "I'm just on edge at the moment, what with the Fair about to start and being a man short—"

"And I've got three members of staff off long-term sick with stress, another who's just announced he wants paternity leave, and an Ofsted inspection due any minute," she shot back. "Either accept my help in the spirit in which it's offered, or deal with it yourself!"

PART III

THURSDAY

16

WHEN QUEENIE WOKE the following morning, she lay watching the play of shape and shadow across the wood-lined ceiling of the vardo. She was both at peace and tickled by a nervous antici-pation. Same as every year at the Fair. Every year going back the last ten, anyway. Beside her, Bartley snored on gently with his arm anchored across her. The weight of it gave comfort.

Down in the lower bunk, the children slept top to tail, as they always did. Ocean closest to the rear wall and Sky to the inside. She was restless, that child, no demure little princess to be dressed up in ribbons. As often as not, she'd be up before any of them so much as cracked an eye. But the journey yesterday had tired her. For once, their curtain stayed drawn and all was quiet below.

Queenie gauged the time of day from the angle of light slanting through the windows that ran along each side of the central raised mollicroft roof. It was a little after six, she reckoned.

No rush yet.

Today they were due to go the last stretch to Fair Hill, to the field she'd been coming to since the year she was born. Never missed a single one. First in her grandfather's wagon, then her father's, now her husband's.

Bartley had built this vardo himself, not long after they married. He'd based it closely on the one she'd grown up in. Tradition didn't allow for inheritance, not of possessions. She and her brother had taken a keepsake from among their father's things, then everything was smashed and his wagon burned, as was the way.

If the heads of the clans used the Fair this year to select the next *Shera Rom*, then this adherence to tradition would sit well with them.

Vano was playing on that commitment to the old ways, too, like an election campaign. Didn't matter that he lived half the year in brick, or that he'd trailered his horses and his bow-top wagon up as far as Scotch Corner, just the other side of the Pennines, and come on from there.

Vano had tried to brush it off by saying his new daughter was less than six months in the world. Reading the spaces between the words, Queenie's opinion was that Vano's wife, Nell, had got more used to her luxuries than was good for her—an indoor bathroom, if you please!

Queenie had more sense than to voice that belief. Vano had been quick to temper as a boy. Now near thirty, age had not served to mellow him. Like as not, Nell had kept him wanting to force the issue. He'd been horny with youth and the years had not slowed him much in that respect, either.

Queenie lay on her back, eyes roaming the familiar design of the interior. Her parents' wagon had been almost exactly the same as this, and her mother had kept it gleaming. After she died, it had fallen to Queenie to step into her shoes. She'd taken pride in it—still did. There was a dash of her mother's taste here, some of Queenie's own. Others might think it gaudy, with the clash of pink and red, yellow roof, green tiles around the stove, dark polished wood. And gilt and brass everywhere, high-lighting carvings and decorating doors and the detail around the mantel, all polished to a high sheen.

And all of it dipped in memory and meaning. The plates and the figurines and even the coal scuttle, painted by hand, and the copper kettle she laboured over until she could see her face in it.

It was the texture of home. Of belonging.

Queenie watched the impromptu sundial ease around the walls. Its fingers seemed to touch the frames of every family photograph and linger with affection, until at last it sparkled in the mirror at the foot of the bed. She breathed out softly, tried to wriggle onto her side. She'd thought Bartley still asleep, but as she moved his grip tightened almost in reflex, using the curve of her hipbone as a hand-hold. Before she knew it, his stubbled chin was burrowed into the crease between neck and shoulder. That and his deliberate outward breath riffled the hairs, sending them rising all over her body. She quivered, tried to squirm out from under his touch.

"And where d'you think *you're* off to, me warm wee wife," he murmured.

She twisted, landing a not-quite-accidental elbow to his ribs, and hopped down out of the bed.

"A cuppa tea and on the road," she said firmly, felt his eyes roving her back as she pulled on a robe. "If we want to stay off the A66 over to Appleby, it puts another six miles on the journey. More than five hours, all up—and that's without a stop to rest the horse. Vano will be getting restless to be off—"

"Oh, he's gone already."

She stilled in the midst of pulling her hair into a plait, glanced over her shoulder.

"When?"

"Off at the crack of daft, he was. You know what he's like when the urge is upon him."

"No...when did he tell you he was starting out early?"

"Last night, it was—after you'd gone to your bed. Why? What difference does it make?"

He sat up, shoving a pillow between his back and the carved bed head, then sprawled against it and regarded her. He should have looked less than he was, with the white broderie anglaise sheet bunched at his narrow waist, but the feminine in the linen only emphasised the masculine in the man.

She averted her eyes.

"Without the colt to worry him, Vano will go the straight way. He'll be there by noon."

"Ah, don't you worry about that, me darlin'. If your brother wants to slink in ahead of us, let him. It's not a race now, is it?"

But it was, in a way. A race for the good opinion of the other clans. A race to secure their approval and support. And this for a man who was no blood relation to the Romany her father had been. Her brother already had a head start, and she worried that Bartley was too damn stubborn to see the dangers.

"No, but—"

"Ah, but nothing. I know how to time an entrance. He'll arrive with the nobodies and I'll be stridin' in with your father's last colt and his lovely daughter." He smiled. A grim smile that made her shiver despite the summer warmth. "Trust me, darlin'. There won't be a man's eye fixed on me who wouldn't sell his very soul to trade places."

17

"You're in early."

Grace was sufficiently engrossed in her work that she had not heard the door to the workshop swing open behind her. But she had no trouble picking up the disapproving note in the man's voice.

"Good morning, Christopher," she said, without looking up from her task.

The bicycle—now confirmed as belonging to Jordan Elliot—lay on its side on the large examination table in the centre of the workshop floor. Grace had rigged up spotlights from every angle to eliminate any possible shadows. She was going over every square centimetre of the frame with a magnifier. Her cameras, one with a macro lens attached for extreme close-ups, lay near to hand.

She straightened, noted down the number of the last shots, and finally glanced over at the man who was now her boss.

Chris Blenkinship was a big Geordie—tall, and wide across the shoulder—who still moved like the footballer he'd apparently been in his youth. Grace sometimes suspected he made the most of that aggressive physicality to ride roughshod over people who didn't quite see eye-to-eye with his way of doing things.

She didn't know if he'd been told to tone down his somewhat confrontational management style but, since taking over as Head CSI, he was growing out the military buzz-cut he'd always favoured to disguise his rapidly receding hairline. In Grace's opinion, the softer style did not suit his blocky features, but she would be the last to tell him so. But, as he would have been the last to listen to her, she considered that only fair.

"Was there something I can help you with?" she asked now, keeping her voice perfectly pleasant.

There was a twitchiness about him this morning. As though he was on the cusp of telling her something he knew she wasn't going to like. She mentally braced herself.

"No, no, just thought I'd check in, seeing as how I had to be in Penrith anyway," he said quickly. He nodded to the bicycle. "Going a bit overboard on this, aren't you? I thought it was down as a possible theft at most, and I've got the budget to think about, eh?"

His attempt at light-hearted banter was too forced to quite come off but Grace appreciated him making the effort to pass for human, at least.

"I assumed you'd been given the update. The ten-year-old child this belongs to"—she indicated the bike while carefully sticking to present tense—"hasn't been seen since last night. We're looking at a possible hit-and-run incident, or maybe an abduction."

Blenkinship fell silent. He moved up close alongside her. If he was trying not to loom, he failed in the attempt. As she watched his eyes skim over her notes and equipment, she swallowed down a minor bubble of resentment.

That he had never liked Grace—nor made any secret of the fact—was one thing. She was sanguine enough to recognise that not everyone she worked with would do so. But he'd never respected her abilities, either, and she found this far more difficult to stomach.

When Blenkinship had been one of her colleagues rather than her superior, he'd satisfied himself with the odd sly dig whenever the opportunity arose. But Grace had always known she could rely on his predecessor, Richard Sibson, to back her up when necessary.

Sibson had been her mentor as well as her boss. He was the one who had persuaded her to turn a good eye for photographic detail into a forensic one instead. Coming comparatively late to the job merely meant she'd time to experience life, he told her, to develop both a practical attitude and some common sense beforehand.

She still missed him fiercely.

To Blenkinship's mind, who'd come into scenes-of-crime the old-fashioned way, she was an upstart interloper and would no doubt remain so.

"I was expecting your report on this before close of play yesterday," he said with more than a hint of censure in his tone.

"I was called from the crime scene to the parents' home to collect elimination samples. Then, with the storm forecast, I felt it was more important to prioritise securing the evidence and having it transported."

He was silent for a moment. Looking for the holes, she thought. His huff of breath revealed he hadn't found any and was not pleased by it.

"All right, Grace. See to it that I've got a copy today, though. If something *has* happened to this lad, it's important to prioritise the paperwork, not just the glamorous stuff, eh?"

"Of course," she said blandly. "I'll see to it."

"So, what have you got so far?"

"Hair, prints, and saliva from the home. Plus blood and prints from the scene, as well as some transfer from—presumably—the vehicle that hit the bicycle."

"Now, now. You should know enough by now never to *presume* anything. That transfer could have got there because the bike was left lying about somewhere. You know how careless kids are."

No, I don't. But then, Christopher, neither do you…

"Of course," she said again.

"What kind of transfer are we looking at?"

He was crowding her again, not just physically but professionally as well. Grace took a calming breath to quell her annoyance and re-centre her equilibrium.

"Obviously, I have taken a sample for the lab, so I'd hate to guess as to its exact nature," she said with precision, "but if you asked me to offer an opinion, I'd say it may well turn out to be the kind of black plastic residue from the coating on a modern car bumper or protective side moulding."

If she expected him to remonstrate—either for the guesswork

or the trace of sarcasm—she was rewarded by a frown of concentration instead.

"Where were the prints?"

The question surprised her. "On the bicycle, you mean? There were quite a few, but the most recent seem to be on the seat stem and head tube." She leaned over the frame with gloved hands outstretched to demonstrate. "Where you would naturally grab to lift it, like so. The bicycle was found dumped in a skip, so perhaps whoever ran over it—with or without rider—probably heaved it into the skip afterwards."

"Right, of course," he murmured. "Good, well... As I'm here, I'll suit up and give you a hand, shall I?"

He posed it as a question but was already turning toward the shelves filled with disposable Tyvek suits, still in their wrappers.

Grace cleared her throat, making him pause.

"I'd rather you didn't, Chris, if you don't mind," she said firmly. "I have a system and I'm working through it."

"Come on, Grace. Many hands make light work, and all that."

"And too many cooks spoil the broth," she returned, adding a smile to soften what he clearly took as a personal blow.

He hesitated a moment longer, scowling, then turned away. "All right, but make sure you finish that report and have it in my inbox by lunchtime, if you don't mind."

"I will do my best," she promised.

"Aye, well, see that you do." He stomped toward the door, had almost reached it before Grace felt unable to hold her tongue any longer.

"I know you have your doubts, but I *do* know what I'm doing, Christopher," she said, halting him in his tracks. "I have been absolutely meticulous with the trace evidence in this case, as I am with *every* case. You bring me a suspect vehicle and I will be able to match the material I've collected from the bicycle to it with enough certainty to stand up in court, have no fear."

For several seconds he didn't respond, just stared at her with, she felt, a quantity of doubt in his face that was downright insulting.

Then he gave a jerky nod and turned on his heel.

As the door closed behind him, Grace allowed herself to sag a little against the table and took a couple of steadying breaths.

Damn the wretched man.

There was something he'd said that niggled at her but then, so much of what he'd said niggled at her in one way or another. It was hard to put her finger on any point in particular.

She shook her head. Then she straightened and reached once again for her camera.

18

BLENKINSHIP CLIMBED INTO HIS CAR, slamming the door behind him. He slumped in the driver's seat, let his head thump back against the rest and closed his eyes.

When that failed to generate a sense of calm, he swore under his breath instead. Every expletive he could think of, uttered with venom and feeling that was only intensified by the near-whisper of his voice inside the car.

Bloody Grace McColl. It would *have to be her, wouldn't it?*

Privately, he admitted that most of his dislike for the redheaded CSI was down to jealousy, pure and simple. He'd had to work hard to get where he was, put in the hours, slogged through the courses when sometimes it felt as though he was trying to take in an utterly foreign language.

It had been the same when he was still at school. He would be the first to admit he was not the most gifted academic. His father was an unforgiving man who'd kept him hard at it, more with stick than carrot as incentive. Blenkinship's overall performance had been doggedly persistent, achieving middling grades no matter how diligently he studied. It had grieved him that some of his classmates did nothing but loaf through the school year, yet were always in the top few percent when it came to the exams. It seemed they never even had to *try*.

Some people just had everything in life handed to them on a silver platter.

Grace McColl, he felt, was another of those people.

His annoyance with her was not because she was *bad* at her job, far from it. Instead, it was because she had an instinctive flair for reading the scene and listening to the story being described by the evidence that Blenkinship recognised he would never have. Not in a million years.

However much he wished for it.

Oh, he was good *enough*, he knew that. Reliable, sound. A solid member of the team.

He could follow the trail as well as anybody and probably better than most. But when it petered out he couldn't quite make those same leaps across the void. He could observe the scene, but that only meant he could see it as it *was now*, not as it *had been*.

Not like Grace.

He thumped a fist on the steering wheel. That made him feel no better, either.

As he started the engine, he replayed the conversation they'd just had in the workshop. However casually he'd tried to behave around her, he knew she'd sensed something was slightly off. Was that why she had refused his offer of assistance? Or was it down to territorial pride?

And as he went back and forth over it, he tried to work out—had it been any other case—if he would have stood his ground, insisted. As her superior, he had a right to monitor her work occasionally, after all. Some kind of ongoing performance review, he could call it.

Trouble was, the longer he spent around her, the more he got the feeling she'd suspect.

Damn it.

He rubbed his fist into the hollow ache at his sternum, fished in his pocket for a couple of antacid tablets.

"You need to stay out of her way," he murmured to himself. But he knew that wouldn't help him keep an eye on how the investigation was progressing.

Because soon it would turn from a missing persons case into one of manslaughter. Even then, he knew he was fooling himself. As soon as he'd taken the decision not to report the boy's death, the only way this was going to end was in a full-blown murder enquiry.

And it was imperative he stayed close to that.

His only hope was for a sudden crime wave in Penrith to

give him a legitimate excuse for reassigning Grace. Or that she might screw up in some way. OK, so the prospect of her making a mistake wasn't particularly likely, but a man could dream, couldn't he?

That last crack she'd made—about the black plastic trace. Oh, he knew exactly where it had come from and she couldn't have been any more accurate if she'd witnessed the collision first hand.

How does she do *that?*

He cranked the engine and reversed out of his parking space, aware all the time of those incriminating scuffs on the front corner of his bumper. What had seemed almost insignificant at the time now felt as if they were painted in Day-Glo and lit with neon arrows.

He needed to get the damage sorted as a priority. The trouble was, this was his work vehicle. Any repairs went through the official garage. And if he went to some private body shop, got it done on the sly… Well, that opened up a path to more potential complications than he wanted to explore.

He headed slowly for the exit, still lost in furious thought. Out of the corner of his eye, he saw another vehicle swing into the narrow approach to the car park. Instinctively, the muscles of his right leg tensed to shift his foot from throttle to brake. Then he realised the golden opportunity being presented to him.

The incoming car wasn't moving quickly.

But it might just be moving quickly enough…

Afterwards, he could hardly analyse the rapid progression of his thoughts. He stamped down on the accelerator and his car lurched forward, the front corner swinging out into the gap between the other parked vehicles.

The driver of the other car reacted immediately. It wasn't enough. The two came together with a graunching thud.

Blenkinship's footballing youth had taught him that the best form of defence was attack. He switched off the engine and was out of his car in a flash.

"Oi, why don't you watch where you're damn well going?" he demanded.

The other driver unfastened his seatbelt and took his time about getting out. A twinge of dismay set Blenkinship's heartburn off again when he saw who it was—that smart-arse detective who'd transferred up from the Met, Nick Weston.

The same Nick Weston who was, he recalled, particularly pally with Grace McColl.

In fact, at one point during the big sniper case the previous summer, the rumour mill suggested they might be more than simply colleagues. Well, with Sibson out of the way, a woman like that was always going to try getting her hooks into somebody else pretty sharpish, wasn't she?

Of all the bloody people...

He disguised his sudden uncertainty by fisting his hands on his hips, pushing his chin out and shoulders back.

Weston eyed him as if—like Grace—he, too, could read far more in another man's stance than Blenkinship was happy to reveal.

"I thought you'd seen me and stopped," Weston said after a moment, with only a hint of annoyance in his voice. The car was one of those suped-up Subaru Imprezas, Blenkinship saw, all bulging bodywork and big wheels, in a girly mid-blue. If it had been *his* car—and it could only have been Weston's personal vehicle—Blenkinship would have been livid. If anything, Weston seemed resigned.

"And *you* were going like an idiot in that thing."

Weston didn't reply to that. He merely raised an eyebrow before squatting to inspect the damage. Blenkinship moved round the front of his own car, relieved when he saw the existing marks had been obliterated by the second impact. The front corner of his bumper had broken loose from its mounting points, distorted and split. His headlight lens was cracked, too. Weston's vehicle hadn't come off much better. It had some kind of lower lip below the bumper—some fancy ground-effects that only worked on a rally stage or a race track. *Poseur.*

It wouldn't have much aerodynamic effect now, though, since it had ripped free and was hanging mostly on the ground under the car. His bumper had taken a pounding, too. Blenkinship felt the smile trying to stretch his cheeks and bit down on it hard, turning it into a grimace.

"Bit of a mess on both sides, eh?" he said, aiming for casual. "We'll just put it down to experience and go knock-for-knock on this one, shall we?"

"Perhaps we ought to take a look at the video before we make any decisions on that score," Weston said.

"Well, you can if you like"—Blenkinship jerked his head to the nearest camera, mounted on a corner of the building and pointed firmly away from them—"but I think you'll find the CCTV only covers the marked bays. They tend to assume that trained police drivers can manage to get in and out of here without the need for surveillance."

Weston smiled then, a tight smile with little humour in it. "That wasn't the video I was referring to." He straightened, leaned across and tapped a finger to his windscreen, up near the rear-view mirror. Blenkinship nearly let out a groan.

A dash-cam.

He hid his dismay behind pursed lips, twisting slowly to take in a good long look at the angles and lines of sight. The roads of Cumbria were often tortuous, and thronged with tourists, summer and winter. Road traffic incidents were commonplace and fatalities often a sad result. Blenkinship had been to his share. He was experienced enough to know that the view from Weston's car—or the mounting position of his camera—was not good enough to prove anything conclusive.

"I'm not exactly inexperienced at reading the evidence," he said, authoritative now, "and it's my opinion that by the time I saw you, it was too late to avoid a collision."

"If you'll forgive me for saying so, your opinion doesn't make much difference."

"Oh, you reckon?" Blenkinship bristled. "I'll have you know—"

But Weston didn't let him finish. Instead, he stabbed a finger toward the other car windscreen. Blenkinship wouldn't have been human if he hadn't turned to look.

His stomach dropped away like he was on a rollercoaster.

"You may not want to believe *my* dash-cam," Weston said then, a definite edge to his voice. "But I hardly think you can ignore your own."

19

NICK RAPPED SMARTLY on DI Pollock's office door, waited for the bark of "Come!" and reached for the handle. His inspector glanced up from the report he was reading as Nick entered, caught his glowering expression and froze, pen poised in mid air.

"Hell's teeth, lad. Who pissed on your chips?"

"Don't ask," Nick said sourly. He quickly thought better of it, took a breath and flashed a wry smile. "Sorry, sir. Mr Blenkinship just managed to get up to ramming speed in the car park."

Pollock sucked in a breath of his own, more loudly, as he waved Nick into a chair. "Oh dear. Not that nice snazzy motor of yours?"

"Yessir."

"Will she live?"

"Minor surgery, I think, rather than intensive care." Nick's smile was more heart-felt this time. "Mind you, she gave as good as she got."

"Ah well, I daresay the insurance companies will sort it all out—although I don't envy you having to argue with a CSI over who was to blame."

"Dash-cam," Nick said shortly. "Good job, too…"

"Oh?"

Brian Pollock had been a copper too long not to pick up on the trace of bitterness in his voice, Nick realised. He paused. The DI had never liked tales told out of school but even he didn't have any particular regard for Blenkinship. Nick shook his head, shrugged it off.

"I don't know. He seemed to see me coming, slow down, then accelerate again. Maybe his foot slipped and he's too embarrassed to own up."

"Aye, lad. There's two places where no bloke cares to admit he's anything other than world class. One is in the bedroom and the other is behind the wheel of a motor vehicle."

They shared a grin that reminded Nick why he was beginning to feel a considerable amount of loyalty as well as respect for his superior. At first meeting, Pollock had seemed an old-fashioned blunt instrument. But the longer Nick worked under him, the more he'd come to appreciate there was often a surprising subtlety there, too. Not to mention a sense of humour so dry it could be arid.

"You wanted to see me, sir?" Nick said now.

"Jordan Elliot," Pollock said, opening a folder and spinning it round to face Nick's side of the desk. Inside was a blow-up of the picture Yvonne Elliot had given them of her son. A head-and-shoulders shot of him, self-conscious in his school uniform, his dark hair plastered flat to his forehead. The boy's eyes were anxious and his smile just starting to deflate, leading Nick to suspect the photographer had made him hold it a second too long.

Grace would have got the best out of him, he thought suddenly. At his request, she'd taken a couple of snaps of Sophie at a mutual colleague's wedding a month or so ago. Candid shots that had turned out far better than any of the posed studio portraits they'd tried to have done. Even Lisa was reluctantly impressed.

"Our Grace has confirmed that the blood she found *is* from the kid. And the damage to the bicycle is consistent with it having been involved in a collision with a vehicle, which then also ran over it."

"And the boy?"

Pollock shook his head. "Not enough blood to say he was still on it at the time, apparently. Or bone fragments or other tissue. So, as far as we know, Jordan Elliot is injured—severity unknown—but still alive. And that's the basis we'll continue to work on until we know different."

"There's been no sign of him?"

"Not a sausage. We've got uniforms searching the area around Water Yat where the bicycle was dumped and doing house-to-house all the way along the valley." He sat back heavily in his chair, which groaned under him. Pollock's wife was always trying to modify his eating habits but his biscuit addiction was beyond cure. "It's a damn nuisance we weren't able to locate the site of the original collision before that thunderstorm washed away whatever residual evidence might have been available to us."

"If only the parents had reported him missing earlier…"

Pollock snorted. "If only they'd *noticed* he was missing earlier, you mean."

"Sounds as though we've not much to go on, sir."

"Well, I didn't say that, lad."

Nick's turn for a simple, "Oh?"

Pollock plucked another folder from his desktop and chucked it in Nick's direction.

When Nick opened it he saw another face staring out at him. This one was of a man perhaps in his late twenties, dark eyed, dark haired, with heavy brows and a face tanned either by genes or weather. The man's expression was one of weary resignation, perhaps tinged with defiance.

"Not his first arrest," Nick said, a gut reaction.

Pollock eyed him from under bushy eyebrows of his own for a moment. "You know him?"

He shook his head. "I don't think so, sir. Who is he?"

"His name is Vano Smith—one of our Travelling brethren."

"Smith? Really?"

"No joke. It's a fine old Gypsy name, apparently. In fact, Mr Smith's related to royalty, in a manner of speaking."

Nick raised his eyebrows for a moment, then said, "Ah, yes— the *Shera Rom* you mentioned yesterday."

"Aye, we're going to miss old Hezekiah. He wasn't a bad bloke. Kept his house in order, dealt with the troublemakers and if he didn't entirely put a stop to some of the dodgier deals that go on at Appleby every year, at least he made 'em keep it off the main street and out of the public eye."

Nick frowned. "Since when are we only interested in crime that happens where we can see it, sir?"

"Don't take that line, lad. I appreciate your zeal but when you've had as many years coping with this annual invasion as I have, *then* you can pass judgement. Until then, our biggest priority is keeping the peace. For the most part that means stopping any trouble from brewing up between the locals and the incomers, of whatever stripe, rather than sorting out internal strife. Got it?"

"Yes, sir," Nick said but knew there was still doubt in his tone. "How is Vano Smith connected to the missing kid?"

"We don't know, and the last thing we want to do right now is start accusations flying and a witch-hunt, understand?"

"Yes, sir."

Pollock eyed him a moment longer, as if checking his sincerity, before he continued. "Prints that came back to Smith were found on Jordan Elliot's bicycle."

"So, he might have been the one who ran him down?"

"No. And that's exactly the kind of leap we're trying to avoid. All we know is that, at some point between young Jordan going out on his bike, and it turning up in that skip the following morning, Vano Smith handled it."

"Do we know where Smith is?"

"We've had FLO going over the footage our lads have shot so far of people getting to Appleby. She was able to identify Smith's caravan arriving there earlier today. He's currently camped on Fair Hill for the duration."

Pollock's shorthand almost had Nick asking who on earth Flo was before he realised the DI was referring to the Fair Liaison Officer. Instead, he asked, "When you say 'caravan' do you mean horse-drawn? If so, it would have been difficult for him to have knocked Jordan off his bicycle."

"Aye, but not impossible. Besides, his home address comes back as Sheffield and he has several commercial vehicles registered in his name. He could easily have trailered everything up to one of the outlying areas and Dobbin'd in from there. In fact, what better way to hide the evidence? *If*, as I say, there's any evidence to be hidden."

"So we're picking him up are we?"

Pollock shook his head, almost regretfully. "A missing kid… Feelings are likely to run hot with this one. Word has come down from on high that we're to take a very softly-softly approach. So, that means someone has to go and beard the lion in his den, as it were. Have a quiet word and see if we can get his story as to how his prints got on the kid's bike, without kicking off a bloody riot in the process."

Nick sighed. "And you've called *me* in because…?"

"Aye, lad." Pollock's smile widened to a shark-like grin. "You're the lucky bugger who gets to volunteer for the job."

20

BLENKINSHIP PARKED UP AGAIN, as far away from prying eyes as he could manage, and switched off the engine. His hands trembled where they rested on the steering wheel.

How the hell did I forget about the dash-cam…?

He knew exactly how, of course. He'd never bothered with one for his personal car. Well, if you were a half-decent driver, on the ball, you didn't need one, did you? He'd tried to talk Susanne into a dash-cam for her car last Christmas, though. Her four-by-four was always picking up new knocks and dents in the school car park. She blamed the students. Blenkinship privately thought the teachers were more likely to be the guilty ones. Some of them were too dozy to survive out in the *real* world.

He glanced over, remembering bitterly of the care he'd taken to make sure the workshop positioned the camera so it wasn't in his line-of-sight when he was driving. It had a permanent display running on the back of the unit that he'd found irritating. This one was tucked away to the left of the rear-view mirror.

He knew they had run him through the basics of how it worked at the time, but the whole idea of them was, he recalled, that it was a fit-and-forget device. It came on and went off again with the ignition, unless something bumped the car when it was parked up. The unit could be unplugged and stowed in the glove box if you found yourself in a really rough area, but otherwise you left them alone and…forgot about them.

Unless you had an accident.

Blenkinship felt the prickle of sweat forming at his temples. He wiped his forehead, took a deep breath.

Stay calm, man and just think *for a moment…*

He knew the camera had a memory card that stored the video input. And that it worked on a continuous loop, over-writing the oldest footage with new. But he couldn't for the life of him bring to mind how long that loop might last.

And it was almost certain to go back weeks, rather than days.

In which case…

Blenkinship undid his seatbelt and flung it aside so abruptly the metal tongue clattered against his driver's window. He ignored it, leaned across and yanked the camera from the front screen. It was attached to a suction mount that peeled away from the glass, leaving a grubby ring behind like the stain from an old coffee cup.

He dropped the camera into his lap and fumbled with the casing until part of it flipped open to reveal the memory card inside. When he thumbed it out, he registered the capacity of it and did a rough calculation.

He'd been right—this thing could store *weeks* of video. Every journey was recorded. Every time he'd parked on double-yellow lines when he wasn't strictly on official business. Every time he'd overtaken where perhaps he shouldn't have done, or crept over the speed limit—OK, ignored them completely—or committed any other minor driving offence.

Or any major one, come to that.

He plucked the memory card out of its slot. He needed to replace it and get rid of the old one, and the sooner the better.

Blenkinship dug out his cellphone and stabbed his thumb on one of the speed-dial numbers, waited with barely suppressed impatience while the line connected and rang out. He had the card between his forefinger and thumb, end on, amazed how hard he had to squeeze the apparently flimsy plastic casing for it even to flex in the middle, never mind break. He was probably going to have to take a hammer to it.

"Good morning. This is CSI Frost. How can I—?"

"Yeah, never mind all that, Ty. Where are you, right now?"

"Er, who's that?"

"It's Blenkinship, you moron. Who d'you think it is?"

"Oh, er, sorry, boss. It didn't sound like you at all,"

"That's as maybe. Where are you?"

"Er, in the office, boss. I'm just working on—"

"Do you have any spare memory cards?"

"What for?"

"Never mind what for!" Blenkinship squawked. "It doesn't bloody matter what—"

"Hey, steady on, boss, I didn't mean it like that," Frost managed to break in. "I just meant, you know, what's it going into—so I can check I've got the right sort."

"Oh, why didn't you say so right off, eh?" Blenkinship grumbled. "It's, er, for a dash-cam. Mine's…stopped working."

"Ah, well, they changed from Mini SD to Micro SD halfway through the model year. Or it could be—"

Blenkinship let out an audible groan.

"Why don't you pop in next time you're passing and I'll swap it for you," Frost suggested quickly. "Easier all round."

Well, why didn't you damn well say that to start off with? But out loud he forced a smile into his voice and said, "Ah, thanks, Ty. Sit tight. I'm here right now, as it happens. I'll be with you in just a minute."

And it wasn't much more than a minute or two later that Blenkinship strode into the CSI office, making Ty Frost jerk guiltily in his chair. He was more of a computer geek than a crime-scene specialist, but Blenkinship was prepared to overlook his inexperience in the field in the face of his expertise when it came to tracing digital evidence.

Now, he took one brief look at the card still clasped between Blenkinship's finger and thumb and dived in a desk drawer, pulling out a tiny clear plastic case.

"There you go, boss. That's the one you need. If you give me the camera, I've got a charging lead here. I'll check it's all formatted for you."

Blenkinship handed over the camera but kept hold of the original card. With one eye on Frost, he moved casually nearer to Grace McColl's desk, gaze skimming over the paperwork stacked there.

"Where's Grace this morning?" he asked, all innocence.

"Oh, in the workshop, I think—processing the kid's bicycle. Did she tell you we got a positive match on one set of the prints she managed to lift?" Frost asked. Without taking his eyes from what he was doing, he waved a hand toward one of the in-trays. "They came back to one of the Gypsies, here for the Horse Fair. So, accident or not, it looks like there'll be trouble over this one."

Blenkinship took a breath to hide the adrenaline that crashed through his system at Frost's initial statement. He reached for the report Frost had indicated. His hands were shaking again, to the extent that he fumbled the papers. Some of them fanned onto the desktop. He gathered them together quickly, glad the other man was too wrapped up in his task to notice.

"Gypsies, eh? Well, no surprises there."

"Mm, a guy called Vano Smith. He's got a bit of previous form, although nothing like this."

"Ah well, they tend to escalate over time, most criminals."

Frost didn't look convinced. He studied the view-screen on the rear of the camera for a moment longer, then powered it down and unplugged it.

"There you go, boss. Good as new."

"Thanks, Ty." Blenkinship hesitated a moment, then joined the dots from Nick Weston to Grace McColl, and from Grace to Ty Frost and back again. "I, er, only realised it wasn't working because that bloody southern DC, Weston, came into the car park like it was the Monaco street circuit and thumped the front end of my car," he said. "If he thinks I'm going to take the blame for him driving like a lunatic, though, he's got another think coming, eh?"

"Oh, er, yeah, too right, boss."

It was only when Blenkinship was almost at the front entrance that he realised he no longer had the old memory card in his hand. He turned back, aware of the beat of his own pulse in his ears.

When he got back to the CSI office, Frost was on the phone. Blenkinship stood for a moment or so but it was clearly a call that was not going to be over quickly. He cleared his throat and mimed what he was looking for. Frost merely tapped the metal rubbish bin next to his desk with the toe of his shoe.

Blenkinship hesitated a second longer. He was aware that he was making too much of this. Had probably done so already.

Frost looked up, frowning.

Blenkinship showed his teeth, designed to reassure but not quite managing to do so, then waved and left again.

As long as the memory card had been thrown away, what did it matter?

———

TY FROST WAS STILL FROWNING about Blenkinship's odd behaviour when he finally put down the phone about ten minutes later. He'd found the old memory card just after the Head CSI had departed. It was on the corner of Grace's desk, the casing slightly displaced from the abuse it had suffered at Blenkinship's hand.

Automatically, Ty dropped it into the bin. Leaving corrupted devices around was asking for trouble.

Maybe that's why he wanted it back?

Ty had never been Chris Blenkinship's biggest fan when he was simply another CSI. Now the big man was…well, the big man, he liked him even less. Nick Weston, on the other hand, had put his neck on the line for Grace the previous summer, when no-one else had the balls to do so.

So, if there was anything on that memory card that might show Nick was *not* to blame for the accident Blenkinship mentioned, well, it might be worth a bit of his time to find out.

He bent and retrieved the memory card, spent a moment pressing the casing back into shape. Before he could slide it into the card reader on his desk, however, the phone rang again. Ty dropped the card into his desk drawer as he listened to the caller, pulling a notebook toward him to scribble down the details.

By the time *that* call was over, his mind had moved to other things. Absently, he pushed the desk drawer closed and turned his attention back to his work.

21

THERE WERE times Queenie hated the Fair as much as she loved it.

Oh, she loved seeing old friends—people who'd known her father, even those who still remembered her mother, and would speak of them fondly. She loved meeting again the giggling girls she'd grown up alongside, now matured into women with children of their own.

She loved the tradition of being among her own people and being together in force, drawn from all corners of Europe and across the Irish Sea, like Bartley's folk. And having *gorgios* by the thousand lured by the spectacle—come to admire them rather than to drive them out.

She loved to stroll among the many traders and see the glitter of the goods they brought to bargain over. But most of all she loved seeing the horses that came to be flashed and dealt.

Her brother Vano had always had a special way about him with the horses. There wasn't one foaled that he couldn't tame. And if he managed with sweat and struggle what Queenie herself could achieve with a quiet word and a calming touch, well, nobody thought any less of him for it—nor any more of her.

But what she hated about the Fair, she hated in measure enough to cancel out the rest of it. She hated what it did to her men.

Every year, she had seen it in her father, as the gathering

began. His manner hardened. She went from being daughter, friend and confidante, to his servant, a lesser being in his eyes.

All year, she had been the one who cooked his meals, cleaned the wagon, and washed and mended his clothes—her brother's, too, until he took a wife. And all year Hezekiah had seemed to recognise it was not simply her duty but her pleasure to do so. Her choice. But come Fair time, that changed.

It became all she was fit for.

And now she saw the same in Bartley, who was a good man overall, grown from the cocky lad who'd befriended and charmed her. Once, she'd seen him as a friend. The possibility of him becoming something else had seemed absurd. How could he, when her heart was already taken?

How things change.

Bartley had been there when Queenie had needed him most. He'd stood for her—stood up for her. And when he'd set himself to woo her, she'd been in no fit mind to refuse. She'd fallen to him as salvation.

But since her father had passed, it seemed he'd determined to take on more than just the old man's mantle, but his manner, too.

He hadn't discussed with her the idea of him throwing his hat into the ring to become the new *Shera Rom*. Hadn't asked what she thought, or even if she *minded* him challenging her brother. By the time she found out, the die was cast and it was more trouble than it was worth to speak out against her husband.

Bartley was many things. A wheeler dealer who could cut the line thinner than was good for him. A man who liked the drink more than the drink liked him. A man who fought and loved with equal fervour, so that sometimes there was little to choose between the two. A stubborn mule when he felt in the right. A sentimental fool when he knew he'd got it wrong.

A husband who knew her secrets, who held her when she cried, loved their children equally, more than life itself and who would do whatever it took to protect them.

She'd once thought she would feel nothing ever again. Bartley had made her feel many things since the day they wed, from the deepest sorrow to a joy she thought had gone forever.

But he'd never made her feel like property before. Not until he'd mentioned them all in one breath, as he had this morning at the farm.

"Queenie!"

The voice calling her name brought her head up suddenly. She realised she was amid rows of stalls selling extravagant furniture, mostly in diamanté-studded white leather, shrouded in clear plastic against the muddy ground from the recent rain. She had little memory how she'd got there. The sun was climbing fast, the sweat already sticking her blouse to her back. Yesterday's thunderstorm had done little to ease the heaviness. She flushed, aware of looking a little bedraggled when all around her were at such pains to be worthy of the show.

And show it was. Not just a time for catching up but a time for catching, too. When the boys strutted and the girls fluttered and many a match was made.

The old man who'd called her name called again, offering condolences on her father's passing. Queenie accepted with a quiet dignity, solemn as the occasion befit. She asked after relations, and relations of relations. It was a trick of memory she'd possessed since she was a *chi*, when it was brought out almost as a party trick. The old man nodded his appreciation and asked after Bartley, as if the approval transferred to Queenie's husband by default.

A customer to the man's stall gave Queenie the chance to slip away. She ducked out of the lane, between two vans with rear doors open and the stock piled up high. Trade at the Fair was always brisk.

As she weaved between the vehicles in the traders' parking area, a sudden clanging thud nearby made her start.

But not as much as the words that followed.

"Now there you are, *Bartley Smith*—as if taking *that* name's going to keep you from what's coming, eh?"

Queenie froze, flattened herself against the side of a horse trailer and slid an eye to the corner, peeping round. Across the grass, two men had Bartley hemmed in between car and van while a third loomed over him.

It was no secret that Bartley had become a Smith when they'd married. A sign of commitment to her father, she was told, proof that he was gaining a son, not losing a daughter. She'd never heard of it causing him trouble. Not like this.

It wasn't hard to recognise the big man. Name of Jackson, he was close to seven feet, a shovel-handed brawler, who made money from other Romany and unwary *gorgios* alike in bare-knuckle brawls. More by betting on the outcome than from the purse, from what Queenie knew.

But what does Bartley have to do with him?

Jackson leaned in, angling his jaw as if to take a bite out of Bartley's throat. She saw Bartley tense, then relax as the big man stilled a hairs-breadth away to whisper in his ear. Frustrated, Queenie darted closer, gripping the chains at her throat so even the tinkle of her jewellery didn't give her away.

Oh, watch him, Bartley. Watch his hands—

Moving faster than a man of his size ought to, Jackson whipped back a fist and drove it up and under Bartley's ribcage on the left-hand side. Her husband gave a great explosive whumph of sound as the air was blasted from his body. She would swear the force of the blow lifted him to his toes before he began to sag.

Queenie abandoned stealth and ran. The attention of the other pair was on the giant. The one closest never knew she was there until she boxed his ears for him and shoved him aside. He gave a roar, and Jackson's head jerked up, stepping back from the man he had pinned. Bartley wrapped his arms around his body and fell back.

The top of Queenie's head barely came up to the giant's chest but she'd no need of height for the target she had in mind. Without a pause, she reached for the crotch of the thin tracksuit pants Jackson wore—one of the few items off the shelf that fit his frame—grabbed tight and gave a vicious upward twist.

Queenie's youth had been spent training horses, carrying water buckets and three quarter-hundredweight bales of hay and straw. Of holding the reins of a bolting pony and not letting go no matter what. She had the iron grip of a farrier despite the size of her hands.

Jackson's eyes bulged in his cadaverous face. He tried to pull back and found out the hard way what a mistake that was. His colour drained, his mouth fell open and his Adam's apple bounced convulsively in the telegraph pole of his throat.

"For the love of God, Queenie—" Bartley managed but it was too late. The red mist was on her.

She got right into the giant's face and told him what she thought of him. At the top of her voice. People came running, her brother among them. But the crowd stopped a safe distance and didn't try to intervene.

Only when she'd run out of curses and was starting to repeat herself did Vano finally edge close enough to rest his hands upon her shoulders.

"Queenie, the man's sorry for your trouble," he said, speaking loud and slow. "Aren't you, Mr Jackson?"

Jackson made a small sound of assent, rigid and sweating now. Vano's hands slid down her arms to her elbows. His touch appeared gentle but, where the onlookers couldn't see, he dug his thumbs deep into nerves that sprang her fingers open as though he'd picked a lock.

Jackson gave a strangled groan as she released, stood bent over with hands braced on knees while he tried to catch his breath. Vano steered her away from him, caught her wrists and ducked to stare into her eyes as if checking she was still inside herself.

"*Very* sorry," Vano repeated. "Very sorry indeed. Isn't that right, Mr Jackson?"

"Oh yes," Jackson agreed, fervent.

Vano nodded. "Then that'll be the end of it, whatever it was."

There was laughter. Jackson's pals slunk in to help him away. Vano offered his hand to Bartley, heaved him to his feet. The crowd, recognising the show as over, began to drift with nods and a few bawdy remarks.

"You want to tell me what that was all about, my sister?" Vano asked, more quietly.

"It was nothing," Bartley said quickly. "A misunderstanding, that's all it was. Queenie…misheard and came in all guns blazing like the little firecracker she is. Isn't that right?"

Queenie did not miss the note of pleading that crept into Bartley's voice. After a moment's hesitation, she nodded without speaking.

Vano continued to stare for a moment longer, not fooled and not pretending that he might be. He was half a head taller than Bartley, more open of face, and a far better liar when he wanted to take that road.

"Well, if—"

"Excuse me, I'm looking for Vano Smith."

They all turned as if uniting, all differences aside. The voice was a mix of Manchester and London, but it was the tone that sent a warning through Queenie's head.

It was…official.

The man wore jeans and boots, a waterproof jacket slung over one shoulder and his shirt sleeves rolled up. His eyes went from one to another of them with focus like a hawk on a hare. Pale blue eyes, electric, piercing. She shivered.

"Oh, you've just missed him," Vano said without missing a beat. He glanced across the field, gave a vague wave of his arm. "I think he was heading over that way."

"Really? Well, perhaps you can help me then," the man said. His voice slipped from silk to steel as he added, "since you must be his *identical* twin."

"Ah, but you can't be too careful these days." Vano's grin was unabashed. "Was you wanting to buy a horse? I've a couple of real beauties I might be persuaded to part with, if the price was right."

"Would those be the horses you had with you down on the Mallerstang road the night before last—at Water Yat?"

Queenie reached for her brother, clinging to his sleeve as she murmured, "*Gavver.*"

The stranger flicked those unnerving eyes to hers. "Yes, I *am* a copper," he said. "And I'm here because a young boy was knocked off his bicycle, near where you were camped that night, and has been missing for two days."

"I wouldn't know anything about that, sir," Vano said calmly. "I certainly didn't go knocking any children off their bicycles and if you'd any proof that I had something to do with it, you'd have been down here mob-handed, so—"

"Your prints were on the bicycle," the copper said, cutting across Vano's smooth denial. "So was the boy's blood."

Queenie went cold, despite the increasing glare of the sun. She was suddenly aware of movement, looked about her quickly and found the crowd had re-formed around them and moved in close. Arms were crossed, heads were tilted and expressions stony.

"Anything goes wrong and you blame the Gypsies, is that it?" she demanded. "You should be ashamed, picking on us.

That's not just lazy, that's racist, that is. That's a hate crime. You should be investigating yourself."

There were mutterings of agreement. The man's gaze moved steadily over the people ranged against him. Not scared—not yet —but definitely wary and right to be so.

Queenie saw his eyes widen a fraction and lift. She turned and found Jackson and his mates had returned, were now standing behind Vano and Bartley.

There's nothing like a common enemy to bring the clans together…

The copper sighed. "All I want to do is eliminate you from our enquiries and move on," he said. "The bicycle was found in the skip put at Water Yat for *your* use."

"That proves nothing," Vano said. "Anyone could have put whatever they liked into that skip. Sitting there on open ground, wasn't it? Not locked."

The copper raised an eyebrow. "Could anyone have put your prints on the bike, too?"

Vano said nothing.

"Look. If you simply found it and dumped it, it would help us to know *where* you found it." He looked at the faces again, saw no help in any of them. His glance returned to Queenie. "I don't care if you're Gypsies or Martians. All I want to do is find the boy, or find out what happened to him. If you have children of your own and you care about them, then you'll help us to do that. It's the *human* thing to do. Anything else really *would* be a hate crime, don't you think?"

22

THE RAIN HAS STOPPED but the river rages on.

It runs fast and fat, greedy for its share of field to either hand. The water, churning silt turning it white-coffee brown, boils along the twisting course. It skips the apex of every bend, then whirls back on itself to take another bite.

At the outside of each turn, the river grabs and gouges, voracious in its appetite. It rebels against the confines of its banks, rides up and over, and spills across the open ground. Exploring field and home and road and garden without discrimination.

In less than five miles, from Outhgill down to Kirkby Stephen, the valley drops more than two hundred and seventy-five feet—almost eighty-five metres. No surprise, then, that the run-off from Edge and Fell thunders onward, downward, like a wagon train and bolting horses.

It takes most of the night for the swollen waters to ease back. Residents along the upper course of the Eden emerge into a new dawn to face deluge, damage and dirt, with determined forbearance. This isn't the first time and won't be the last.

Farmers make rounds of fields and hillsides on quad-bikes and in their four-by-fours. From elevation it is easier to note the places where the river has re-routed itself, side-stepping by as much as twenty feet and scouring a new track through the bank to do so.

One man spots a gleam of something he fears might be the carcass of fallen stock down in a crook of the river's displaced elbow. He *approaches slow, wary that further sections of the banking might give way beneath him.*

He doesn't get too close to the crumbling edge but doesn't need to. Even a brief glance tells him this is no dead sheep the rains have revealed. Shocked, he moves back a safe distance, as though to ward away some nameless contamination.

The farmer re-mounts his quad and pulls his mobile phone from his pocket, stabbing his thumb three times on the nine key.

"Emergency Services. Which service do you require?"

"Well now, tha's a good question," the farmer responds. "Tha'd best send a policeman and yon ambulance. No rush, though. 'E's not goin' anywhere…"

PART IV

FRIDAY

23

VANO MIGHT HAVE BEEN NEWLY dead.

Queenie, watching him from across the bow-top wagon, could barely even detect the sound of his breath. He lay utterly still in the bunk, sprawled on his back with one arm flung across his eyes. Didn't fidget or twitch, like their father had done— didn't snore and mutter half the night, either. Queenie knew some childhood chest infection had left her with a slight whistle when she slept. She'd never been able to shake it.

But Vano? Vano had always been the quiet one. In the years after their mother passed, Queenie remembered waking often in the night and reaching for him, just to check he hadn't slipped away and left her, too.

Now, though, she was aware of time passing. She leaned forward on the stool she'd taken and called his name softly.

For a moment she thought it hadn't reached him. Then he gave a start and a snort, like a dog roused from a dream of rabbit chasing, and was instantly wide awake.

He shifted the arm from across his eyes, saw her and let out a squawk, lurching up in the bunk and dragging the thin sheet tight around his waist.

Queenie laughed. Vano swore at her in return.

"Are you trying to give me heart failure, sister?"

"You still wake as quick as you sleep, then?"

"Did you think I'd be any different?" He rubbed his face with one hand to hide the smile, still keeping tight hold of the bed sheet with the other. "What a *grasni shan tu*."

"Oh, so I'm a mare, am I?" Queenie said tartly. "Well, my brother, what does that make *you*?"

The smile went as quickly as it had arrived. "And just what are you meaning by that?"

Queenie ignored the warning, such as it was. "The copper who was here looking for you yesterday—about the bicycle?" She paused. "With…the *ratti*?"

The blood.

"What is it you think I've done?"

Queenie clenched her fists in frustration. "If I knew that, I would have no need to ask, would I? Just tell me, brother. How can I protect you if—?"

"*I've* no need to hide behind a woman's skirts."

A dig. A dig at her husband. She realised, belatedly, that Vano might use her intervention with Jackson against Bartley. Might? He would, unless she gave him cause to think twice.

"I've been hearing that he disappeared—the boy with the bicycle. From Water Yat Bottom at Mallerstang, the night you were camped there."

Vano crossed his arms and stuffed his hands into his armpits as if to cover his chest. He was still clasping the sheet firmly.

"They don't know where he disappeared from," he said now. "They're guessing—trying to put the blame on us, just like you said."

"Did you knock him down, Vano?" Queenie asked, almost a whisper. "Is that why you left so early to come on to the farm? Wynter said you got her out of bed and she's up with the lark."

Vano gave a twitch like he was about to strike but thought better of it. He let out a long, annoyed breath through his nose.

"I never saw the lad," he said. "I found the bicycle, that's all. Found it by the side of the road. Saw the damage and the blood…" He broke off, gave a helpless shrug. "I knew, if I left it there, the first *gorgio* happening by would see it and see us and—"

"Think the same as the *gavvers*," she murmured, thinking of the man with the electric blue eyes who'd so unsettled her. Not least because clearly he knew the Romani word for copper. That didn't bode well.

"So I got rid of it. Never thought they'd go through what we left behind, not if it was all tidied away."

Queenie bit her lip. "It makes it look like you were trying to hide it, purposeful, like."

"What else could I do, sister? You know what they're like, some of the *gorgios* around about here. Always after an excuse to bad mouth us, do us down and move us on. You were right, it *is* hate crime."

She reached across, put a hand on his foot, sticking up under the sheet, gave it a reassuring squeeze. Vano smiled at her again but the light wasn't behind it this time. He glanced about him as if realising only now that they were alone.

"Where's my Nell?"

"She's taken Sky and the baby down to see the river," Queenie said. "If the water goes down enough, perhaps they'll stoop to letting us take the horses in to wash them this afternoon."

The evening before, the police and the animal welfare inspectors had gated off the sloping entrance to the Eden, by the bridge, saying the level was too high, the flow too fast and the risks too great. It had not gone over well with those who'd brought horses to sell and wanted them looking their best. Many tempers would be salved if they could get into the water today.

"Then I'd best be up and see what I can do to help convince them, hadn't I?" Vano said. He gave Queenie a stern look. "Off with you. Let me into my clothes in peace."

She rose. "You've nothing I haven't seen before, brother. And many times, over the years."

"Well, there's only two women see me naked these days. And one of them won't remember after she's grown her first tooth."

It was only as Queenie reached the bow-top's front porch that she paused to ask a final question. "Why did you camp at Mallerstang that night, rather than come on to the farm? Surely, when you were so close—"

"Will you stop your bloody questions!" Vano roared. "It was another ten miles, all right? The mare was tired, Nell was tired, and the baby wanted a feeding."

He threw back the sheets, regardless, slid from the bunk and grabbed his jeans and T-shirt. As he stalked past her in the narrow space, he veered close and stuck his face into hers.

"You ask too many questions, sister. I've a mind to tell that husband of yours he needs to take his belt to you more often! Remind you of your place."

Queenie flinched back, averted her gaze while he stormed into his clothes and clattered down the wooden steps onto the grass.

Only then did she realise that he'd come to Mallerstang from Scotch Corner, over on the east side of the Pennines. Unless he'd turned south at the old Tan Hill Inn, through Birkdale and past Nine Standards Rigg, the logical route would have taken him up closer to the A66, through Rookby, Winton, and Hartley.

And passed only a mile or so from North Stainmore.

By choosing to go down to Mallerstang, setting down there for a night, then coming back up to the Trelawneys' farm the next day, he'd added maybe thirty miles onto the journey.

As she climbed more sedately from the bow-top after her brother, Queenie worried over the reason for the detour.

And she prayed that a missing child had nothing to do with it.

24

BLENKINSHIP WAS LATE. He'd chosen to take the motorway south from Carlisle. It was the obvious route and, by rights, it should have been the quickest, too. Except for a broken-down caravan—straightforward grockle rather than Gypsy—in the roadworks going over Shap Fell. An already restricted piece of carriageway was further reduced from two lanes down to one.

He'd muscled his way through the tailback and the jam, losing time and temper in roughly equal amounts. It had always infuriated him that other drivers were so totally unaware of those around them, *some* of whom might have a genuinely urgent reason to get by.

When he finally reached the crime scene, just up the valley from Kirkby Stephen, he was sweating despite the car's air conditioning running full blast. He pulled onto the grass between a patrol car and the BMW convertible belonging to the Force Medical Examiner.

Cumbria still had its own pathologist when Blenkinship had first started working crime scenes. Now they were all free-lancers, contracted in when the need arose. Dr Ayoola Onatade lived in the Trough of Bowland, out in the middle of nowhere, on the other side of Lancaster. He'd hoped to beat *her* to the body, at least.

The uniforms had already cordoned off a section of field alongside the river. In the centre of the area, right at the edge of the bank, were the white easy-up tents, protecting the find not only from the elements but also from any passing gawpers. Not that there were likely to be too many of those around here. Not without four legs, horns and a fleece, at any rate.

He pulled on a fresh set of Tyvek coveralls and gathered his kit, aware of a tightness in his chest that was not his usual response to being called out on a job.

It wasn't hard to work out why this one was different.

He was surprised, though, what with all the run-off and the rain, that the body hadn't travelled further. Something must have snagged it, kept it back.

Still…

He traipsed across the grass, aware of a suddenly squidgy texture underfoot as the sodden sub-soil slithered under what appeared to be a dry layer of turf.

"Ah, good morning, Christopher. How nice of you to join us," Dr Onatade called cheerfully across the open ground. As if trained for the stage, she could project her voice without apparent effort. Any thoughts of keeping his late arrival quiet, of sneaking in and pretending he'd been here all along, were quickly discarded. "And you will need your Wellington boots!"

"Morning, doctor," he shouted back. "I'm OK, I think—it's not too bad on this side."

"Yes, but unless you intend to have very wet feet all day, there is the small matter of getting over to *this* side of the river."

It was only then that Blenkinship realised the tents had indeed been set up on the far bank. Without answering, he turned and trudged back to his car, digging out the Wellingtons that lived permanently in a bag in the back. The extra delay before he had to look at the body was half-torture and half-relief.

Animals had worn a track through the scrubby grass to the easiest crossing point, a little further upstream. The banks flattened out and he could see the stones and rocks on the bottom clearly. The river level might have dropped quite a bit overnight but it was still running strong. He almost went back to the car for the long trekking pole he kept in the boot, just to give him some extra stability in the water, but his guts were tied in enough knots as it was.

Instead, he crossed with care, moving one foot forward at a time and then bringing the other to join it, almost a hutching movement. As he did so, he made sure he kept his crime-scene kit carried high in his arms so it was clear of the water.

As he approached the cordoned area, it seemed to Blenkinship's critical eye that the main tent had been sited in a somewhat precarious position. All right, so you couldn't choose where a body was found—*well, not usually*—but this was perched right on the very lip of the bank.

Anywhere near to the edge would have been a bit risky, what with the flash flooding of the last few days. You could tell just from the river debris spread all over the grass that this whole area had been submerged. No telling when it might start to rise again.

Plus, what if more of the ground gave way? It was clear from the clods of mud and rocks at the foot of the bank, plus the fresh revealed earth, that it had recently done so.

He was still frowning when he reached the tape cordon. One of the uniforms met him there—a young Community Support Officer Blenkinship didn't recognise. The crime-scene log was being kept on a clipboard leaning against one of the tape poles. The youngster signed Blenkinship in and was already moving back to his search as the CSI ducked under the tape. Not quite procedure, but Blenkinship knew they didn't have the spare manpower to station someone there doing nothing else.

As he moved toward the tent, looking dubiously at its positioning, Dr Onatade thrust aside the flap and emerged.

She was the daughter of a Nigerian diplomat and a Jamaican astrophysicist. That she was accepted into Roedean School was a testament to her parents' wealth and influence. That she went from Roedean straight to a Double First at Oxford was entirely achieved on her own merits.

The first time he'd met her, Blenkinship had been so knocked flat by the force of her personality, so wrong-footed by her formidable intelligence, that he almost overlooked completely the fact she was a woman. Never mind that she was black…

Even *he* recognised that anyone who attempted to pigeonhole the good doctor by those factors alone would meet with very short shrift—from a woman who knew exactly how and where to hide the bodies.

"Hasn't anybody done a risk assessment for this?" he asked, jerking his head toward the first tent.

"Well, no-one has fallen into the river so far," she said briskly. "Except for part of our poor victim, of course."

"So, what can you tell me?"

She tilted her head to one side and regarded him for a moment. "Why are *you* taking the lead on this, Christopher? The nearest CSIs are in Kendal, surely—or possibly Penrith? *You* have sole charge of Carlisle. Shouldn't you be practising the forgotten art of delegation?"

"I have sole charge of all of it, if you want to look at it that way," he countered. "So, if something else comes up, I'll get the chance to put my delegating skills to good use, won't I?"

"Hm." She turned back toward the tent. "In that case, follow me and I'll bring you up to speed."

Blenkinship waited until the last moment to pull on a pair of nitrile gloves. Even in winter, they made the wearer's hands sweat like nobody's business. In summer you ended up with finger ends like prunes in minutes.

The last person he'd expected—or hoped—to see as he entered the tent was DC Nick Weston. The fair-haired copper was wearing a crime-scene suit but no gloves, although he was standing right up against the side of tent, as far away from the crumbling bank as he could manage. A notebook and pen were in his hands.

"Weston, what are you doing here?" The question was out before Blenkinship could prevent it and he added, almost defensively, "I didn't see your car."

Weston raised an eyebrow. "My car's at the garage while they estimate the cost of repairs," he said, somewhat pointedly. "And they're hardly going to assign anybody more senior, are they? Not yet—not for this."

Blenkinship frowned. His eyes slid to the edge of the bank. Dr Onatade was climbing down a short ladder into a second tent that had been butted up against the first, albeit at a lower level. Between the two, a chunk of bank had collapsed, leaving a gaping hole in the reddish-brown earth. He edged closer.

"You two are acquainted, I gather?" Dr Onatade said.

"Oh, yes," Weston said. "We've...bumped into each other, you might say."

Blenkinship ignored them both. He was near enough now to look down into the hole where it gaped toward the riverbed. At the bottom, partially uncovered, were nothing but bones, including a spinal column and skull. The long bones of the legs had spilled out onto the exposed stones that bordered the river, the metatarsals and phalanges scattered. To Blenkinship's suddenly uncomprehending eye, they obviously belonged to an adult, and had been there for some time.

Not a child, then. Not a young boy with a bloodied skull and slack body.

"But…what the devil's this?" he blurted.

"Human remains," Dr Onatade said, a little tartly. "And based upon my preliminary examination of the sciatic notch of the pelvis and the posterior ramus of the mandible, I can tell you with absolute confidence that we're looking at an adult male of the species." She paused. "Why, what were you expecting, Christopher?"

"I—" He broke off, scowled. "I was expecting something a bit more…"

"Exciting?" Weston put in, his tone dry.

"No—*urgent*," Blenkinship snapped. "I mean, how long has he been in the ground?"

"An unembalmed adult, buried without a coffin, in ordinary soil." She pursed her lips. "Say…eight to twelve years. But in order to narrow that down any further, you'll have to wait until I get him back to the lab," Dr Onatade said. She sounded almost gleeful at the prospect. Blenkinship had to remind himself that, when she wasn't acting as FME for Cumbria, her speciality was forensic anthropology. For her, the condition of this victim would be of particular interest.

He sighed. "OK, then, what about a *cause* of death?"

"I saw no visible injuries during my initial observation of the remains although, of course, I did not want to disturb the scene unduly." She straightened and smiled. "But, now that *you* are here to document the evidence, I may examine him more closely. Shall we get to work?"

She always sounded so damn cheerful for one in a profession that dealt with the dead. Blenkinship found it grated on his already raw nerves. Without responding, he set down his kit and started attaching the flashgun and battery pack to the body of his camera.

"Well, I'll leave you to it and let DI Pollock know what we

have so far," Weston said. He glanced down at the notebook. "Adult male—I think you said somewhere between eighteen and twenty-five?"

Dr Onatade nodded, sweeping a hand between the skull and pelvis. "Between the fully erupted wisdom teeth and the development of the pubic symphysis, that's as much as I can say at the moment."

"No problem. It gives us a starting point, anyway. I'll hit the Missing Persons database and see what pops."

She laughed. "Well, good luck. And you may need it. I seem to remember that people go missing in the UK at a rate of something like one every nine seconds."

"Not in Cumbria, they don't, fortunately—more like one every two or three hours," Weston said, grinning at her like a fool.

"Indeed. Including this young boy I've been hearing about— the one with the bicycle. Has there been any sign of him yet?"

"No. And the longer it goes on…" Weston shrugged.

"Well, let us hope for a positive outcome on that one, hm, Nicholas? That when he *is* finally found, you do not require my services."

"I'll second that. And it's just Nick, by the way. That's what it says on my birth certificate. Not Nicholas. I think my old man was in too much of a hurry to get back to the pub to write it out in full."

"How wonderful!" Dr Onatade said. "I would have preferred to be simply Ayo, but *my* father insisted on Ayoola and—"

"If you've *quite* finished swapping your family histories," Blenkinship said between his teeth. "Shall we get on with the job in hand?"

25

As he walked away from the crime-scene tents, Nick was already peeling off his Tyvek coveralls. The material was thin and supposed to be breathable but it was still an extra layer he could have done without in this weather.

One elasticated cuff caught on his watch and he struggled with it briefly before it pulled free, glad he was out of sight of the irritating crime-scene tech.

"Who's rattled *your* cage this morning, Mr Blenkinship?" he murmured.

As far as he could tell, the new Head of CSI had few redeeming features—no, make that none whatsoever. The bloody man couldn't even turn up on time...

Nick settled for stripping the coveralls half off and knotting the sleeves around his waist. There was no way he was going to take his boots off until he got back to the car his garage had loaned him. He found Blenkinship's reaction to his unexpected presence interesting and...revealing. Beyond a natural embarrassment, why should running into Nick's car at Hunter Lane make the man so obviously unsettled around him?

He still couldn't shake the feeling there was something odd about that 'accident'. Even the way he subconsciously emphasised the word when he *thought* about it, pointed to something hinky going on. And if there was one thing Nick's years of undercover work had taught him, it was to trust such metaphorical taps on his shoulder.

Back at the car, he sat with the door open on the passenger side to shed the coveralls and change back into his shoes. He sat for a moment, looking at the expanse of flat ground where the Gypsies returned to camp, year after year. His eyes shifted to the crime-scene tents, the peak of the lower one just visible from his position.

Was it coincidence, he wondered, for a long-buried body to turn up here? He'd encountered Gypsies, Romany and Travellers when he'd been with the Met. Yes, there was a criminal element among them, but you could say that about any group of people. And particularly when they tended to be marginalised by the rest of society.

If you treat someone as an outcast, you shouldn't be surprised if they start behaving like one.

Idly, he registered the sound of a vehicle approaching up the valley, heading toward Kirkby Stephen. Heard the rumble of it hitting the cattle grid on the approach to Water Yat. He half-expected, as it rounded the bend and came into view, that the driver would slow down. It was the usual, instinctive reaction to spotting a marked-up police car lurking by the side of the road.

Instead, the car—an old Volvo estate—gave a lurch and accelerated hard, engine screaming as it bore down on him like a battleship in full ramming mode. The car left the road and bounded onto the rough grass, pitching wildly as the elderly suspension tried to cope with the terrain.

What the hell—?

Nick leapt from his vehicle and crouched, ready to dive out of the way of the collision. He couldn't see the driver because of the sun's reflection on the windscreen.

At the last moment, the Volvo swerved away from him and headed directly toward the crime-scene. As it did so, Nick caught a glimpse of a kiddie-seat in the rear of the car, with a terrified looking child strapped into it.

"Hey!" Nick yelled, as much to attract the attention of the two uniforms on the far bank as the driver. He took off after the Volvo at a dead run, cursing having changed out of his boots.

Sheer momentum carried the car some way onto the grass, but the flooding from the night before and the heavy-footed use of the throttle meant it was never going to get far.

The front wheels began to judder, then to spin, sending liquid mud splattering along the side of the car. Nick saw the driver's door fly open. The slight figure of a woman scrambled out and ran, slipping and sliding in the mud. The car itself kept rolling forward.

Nick thought of the child's face in the rear and put on an extra burst of speed. He reached the open door and managed to throw himself across the driver's seat, yanking on the handbrake and shoving the transmission out of gear.

Only then did he glance into the back of the car. There were three children shrieking in the rear seat.

"It's OK. It's all OK. You're safe now," he told them. It had little effect. He grabbed the keys to kill the engine and backed out of the car again.

The woman was still going. She'd clearly fallen once and had lost a shoe, but wasn't going to let that stop her.

Nick set off in pursuit. In utter panic, she'd headed straight for the tents without working out she needed to cross the river first. He caught up with her on the bank directly opposite the scene, grasping her shoulders just as it looked like she was about to throw herself in to swim across.

"Mrs Elliot?" he said, finally recognising the woman. "Yvonne?"

It took him a while to get through to her, by which time the two uniforms had reacted, splashing across the river and running to join him. Dr Onatade and Blenkinship had both been drawn outside by the commotion. The Medical Examiner wore a look of concern. Blenkinship seemed to be enjoying the show.

Nick normally had no problem subduing awkward or violent suspects during an arrest but this was different again. Yvonne was a distraught mother, as much a victim as—possibly—her son. As soon as he realised who she was, he'd also known what she must have thought, seeing the crime-scene tape and the tents and police presence.

As a parent himself, his heart broke a little for her.

"It's *not* Jordan, Mrs Elliot," he told her, over and over, keeping his voice calm but loud enough to penetrate. "Yvonne, listen to me. It's not your son. It's *not* him."

Eventually, she stopped fighting and just slumped, sobbing. Nick tried to keep her on her feet but the sudden change threw him. All he could do was control her descent. She ended up on her knees on the ground anyway, arms wrapped around his legs and her face burrowed into his hip. He caught a glimpse of the leer on Blenkinship's face.

Oh, yeah, he's definitely enjoying the bloody show…

It was Dr Onatade who called across, "Is she all right, Nick?"

"I, er… She will be." He held out a fending hand to the young PCSO who'd signed him in to the crime scene. "Give us a minute, will you? And there are kids—in the car. Can you check on them? I think they're OK. They were terrified and screaming blue murder."

"Better that than too quiet," the copper said, turning away.

Nick managed to prise Yvonne Elliot's hands away from his legs. He bent so he could look her in the face, make sure his words were going in.

"Yvonne?"

She reacted to his voice this time. Her eyes were bloodshot and swimming but they managed to focus on him, at least.

"It's OK," Nick repeated gently. "It's definitely *not Jordan* that we've found—do you understand?"

"It's not?" Only the rising inflection in her wavering voice made it a question. "Who–who—?"

"We don't know who it is yet, but the bones are old, OK? They've been in the ground for some time—years. It can't possibly be your son." He kept his voice soothing, expecting her to start to relax. Instead, she tensed afresh.

"O–old?" she echoed. "*How* old?"

He hadn't been expecting that, either. Giving out information to anyone who wasn't part of the investigation team was a complete no-no, Nick knew that. But how could he tell her nothing at all. He hesitated, picked his words with care.

"Well… we don't know, as yet. But certainly an adult, OK? So it can't—"

But Yvonne wasn't listening anymore. She clamped her hands to her face, curling inward as though she'd been kicked in the stomach, and gave another howling wail of utter despair.

26

UNSETTLED, Blenkinship turned away from the sight of the woman on the far bank and the detective who comforted her.

To begin with, he thought he was witnessing an episode in DC Weston's private life, being enacted on a very public stage. And yes, he'd be the first to admit that, initially, he'd found amusement in watching him struggle to hold her. He would have assumed—what with Weston's supposed reputation as some hot-shot from the Met, up here to show the hayseeds how things *should* be done—that he'd know how to handle a woman.

And then one of the uniforms, a local man, had made a passing comment as he'd jogged past on his way to assist. Only then had Blenkinship found out who she really was.

The mother of the boy who was…

Missing.

The one who…

He tried to block out the woman's gut-wrenching sobs and the detective's voice as he reassured her. Weston was not, it seemed, one of those blokes who didn't know what to do with an over-emotional female. Blenkinship himself always felt at a bit of a loss. His first instinct was to tell them to calm down and pull themselves together. It had not, in his experience, proved an effective response.

He was not an emotional man at the best of times, was never reduced to tears either of joy or sorrow. When the people he worked alongside experienced some significant event—the death of a loved one, the birth of a new baby—he found that to a certain extent he had to take his cue from others on the appropriate behaviour. Apart from the obvious, like birthdays and Christmas, it never occurred to him to send a card bearing Get Well Soon wishes or a message of Sympathy. The only reason he had the date of his and Susanne's wedding anniversary marked firmly in his diary was because he'd made the mistake of forgetting it just that *one* time…

It was why, on the whole, Blenkinship preferred to stick to the nitty-gritty of the physical evidence. Then, his ability to remain clinical and detached, no matter what the circumstances he was asked to deal with, was an asset. Once, when he was trying to piece together severed limbs at a particularly gruesome pile-up on the M6 motorway, he overheard a traffic copper describe him as a cold-blooded bastard. He'd taken *that* as a compliment.

So, why were his hands trembling now?

He clenched his fists, took in a long breath and shut his eyes for a moment.

You've been careful. You've been clever. Keep your head and you'll be fine. Even when the body is *found—if* it's ever found—*there's nothing to link it to you.*

"Is everything all right, Christopher?"

He opened his eyes and found Dr Onatade regarding him with an anxious gaze.

"Yes, yes of course, doctor. I'm fine," he said. "Shall we get on?"

But her eyes slid past him, to the opposite bank, to where Weston was crouched close to the woman, holding her hands in his, pouring his attention into her. It really was quite sickening.

Blenkinship opened his mouth but Dr Onatade put her gloved hand on his arm. "It's all right. I understand," she said quietly. "I cannot *imagine* what that poor woman is going through right now."

"No," he said and found his voice was strangely gruff. He cleared his throat, said with more conviction, "No, neither can I…"

27

GRACE HAD ALWAYS FOUND that the closer she wanted to get to someone for a candid photo—the deeper inside their head—the further away she needed to stand. So, she had positioned herself well back from the rows of stalls selling the most lurid array of merchandise, and had attached a zoom lens to her Canon digital camera.

Purely from a photographic perspective, she found the Horse Fair fascinating. The character displayed in the faces both of the Gypsies and their animals made her want to capture everything she possibly could. She took snaps of the jewellery on display, a mix of artisan work, hand-made by traditional craftspeople within the community, and cheap imported tat of the type you found anywhere. By making best use of her telephoto lens, Grace was able to take her pictures of it without getting close enough to be given the hard sell.

Professionally, she was there to wander the camping and parking areas, looking for any vehicles showing damage that might have occurred during a collision with Jordan Elliot's bicycle. In the hour or more she'd been there so far, she'd found plenty to keep her busy. Sadly, quite a lot of the vans and cars had minor scuffs and dents, any one of which could have had such a cause.

The hostile reception Nick received the day before had been mentioned in DI Pollock's briefing that morning—to the amusement of his colleagues, she was sure. Word had been sent down that anyone intelligence-gathering at the Fair should take pains not to arouse the suspicions, or the wrath, of the Travelling community.

Grace was therefore being very circumspect, hence the long lens. The nice thing about the 55-250mm she was using was that its compact size meant few realised the range it had.

Take the gaggle of Gypsy girls walking toward her, for instance. They had no idea they were centred in the split-prism of her shot as they sauntered past a group of boys.

Grace pressed the shutter and kept it pressed. In the digital equivalent of motor-wind, the camera committed a continuous stream of images to its memory card. Of the girls swinging their hips and tossing their long hair back like the manes of horses. They pranced on impossibly high heels, tanned legs showcased by mini-skirts or tiny shorts, with painted faces, painted nails, and draped in gold jewellery.

The girls were half-a-dozen strides past the boys. *Any moment now,* Grace thought. Her forefinger hovered.

Then one of the girls looked back, caught the boys craning after them. All of them burst into giggles, nudging each other in their excitement and pleasure at being the centre of attention. Two of the boys were grinning, pink in the cheek. One punched another's arm in celebration.

Grace captured a final burst and knew without needing to check the view-screen on the back of the camera body that she'd got the shot she was after.

Not quite the intended purpose of today's outing but one for her portfolio, all the same. Besides, if anyone—and for *anyone,* make that *Blenkinship*—complained about the excessive number of images she'd taken, she could write them off as no more than a sensible precaution. Camouflage.

Most of the horses and ponies brought to the Fair were there to be sold. They were taken down to The Sands, the stretch of road running parallel to the River Eden. There they were left, tied to the temporary barriers, for interested buyers to wander past and inspect. Periodically, they'd be ridden or driven up the steep hill at Battlebarrow to Long Marton Road, known as the flashing lane. There, they'd be shown off at the fastest trot Grace had ever seen a horse perform without getting its legs in a tangle.

The Gypsy boys who rode them—and it seemed mainly to be the boys—did so with only a bridle. They rarely used a saddle but rode bareback instead, adopting a leaning-back seat with legs well forward. Grace suspected this was as much to prevent any vital bits of their anatomy bouncing around on the horses' narrow withers as it was for style.

Although she was interested to see them, Grace stayed away from the more crowded areas. Where the crowds gathered were the most heavily policed and she had no wish to have her cover blown, as it were, by a friendly wave from officers she'd encountered previously at crime scenes.

She paused to take a couple of shots of a pretty vardo van— either an old one or perhaps just a traditional design, although in such good condition it was hard to tell. Next to it, on a staked tether, was a heavy-set piebald mare of the type known as a Gypsy vanner. And beside her, free to roam but sticking close, was a foal that looked impossibly young to have made the journey to the Fair.

"Now, you *are* gorgeous, aren't you?" Grace murmured. The foal turned on dainty feet and butted against its dam, leaning to suckle. As it fed, the foal's fuzzy mop of a tail wriggled with pleasure, like a puppy.

The little horse was very interestingly marked, Grace saw. Its body was mostly black but it had a large white patch covering its neck and shoulder on one side that looked almost exactly like the outline of another horse's head. Captivated, she raised the camera to her eye.

"It's a fiver a picture," said a voice behind her.

Grace turned. A little girl of maybe six stood on the front steps of the vardo, hands on hips, watching her with wary eyes. She had curly dark hair in high pigtails, tied with green ribbon that matched her dress. Only the grubby knees of her bare legs spoiled the picture of a young lady in-the-making.

"You must be making some money today, then," Grace said cheerfully. "He's magnificent."

"He is *and* he's for sale," the child said, adding hopefully. "*You* don't want to buy him, do you? I'm sure we could do you a good price."

Grace suppressed a smile at the serious tone and shook her

head. "He's too good for me," she said. "I can't afford quality like that."

A young woman—not much more than a girl, although it was hard to judge—appeared in the open doorway of the vardo, drawn by the child's conversation. She had long dark hair pulled back from her face, dark eyes and tanned skin. By the standards of the Fair, she was dressed down, in a floral skirt that came almost halfway down her thighs and a strappy top under a denim jacket.

By comparison, in her usual cargo trousers and a shirt, Grace felt as concealed as a nun.

"The young lady was just inviting me to make an offer for the horse," Grace said, nodding to the foal. "I told her he's out of my league, I'm afraid. He's magnificent."

Her face softened a little. She came down the steps and moved to stand beside Grace, her eyes on the foal. "Oh, he is that," she agreed.

"You *have* come to sell him, I assume?"

She shrugged. "Maybe."

Grace regarded her. All the Gypsies she'd ever met would not need a better invitation to start their spiel. It was interesting that this girl did not immediately launch into a sales patter, even though the little girl was almost hopping up and down for the chance to try.

"Have you travelled far to the Fair?"

"Over from the north-east," the young woman said. "Took us a while to get here—had to stay off the main roads, what with the colt."

The north-east, Grace thought. Even avoiding the A66, that still did not put Mallerstang on the logical route...

"You're local, are you?"

Surprised by the question, Grace glanced at her. "Yes. I live about ten miles south of here. Why do you ask?"

The young woman bit her lip, as if trying to make a decision, and glanced at the child, who'd gone to stroke the mare's ears as she grazed. Then said suddenly, "Only... I heard some kid's gone missing—local, like. Awful shame, it is. We were shocked to hear it, all those of us who have kids of our own."

"It is." Grace listened to the threads in the woman's voice, all being pulled in different directions. Anxiety and defiance and a measure of justification.

She reached out a hand and stroked the mare's velvet nose, careful not to get between her and the foal. The mare, her eyes hidden behind a mass of forelock, snuffled at the proffered fingers with a remarkably strong and agile upper lip, but lost interest quickly when no titbits were forthcoming.

"Only…" the young woman said again. "I heard… I heard something had been found—this morning. A body. Do you know…?"

"Well, I haven't heard much," Grace said with care. "But from what I can gather, it isn't the missing boy. They're saying it's a much older set of bones. They could have been there ten years or more."

The young woman paled at the news, took a step back.

"He's owing!" she muttered.

"Owing? What's owing?" Grace took a step after her but the young woman began to hurry then, scuttling away from her, almost running back to the vardo. "Wait, please! What do you mean? Is it like a debt, or an argument?"

But the young woman had scrambled up the steps into the van and disappeared. All Grace heard was the slam of the wooden doors and the sound of a bolt being firmly drawn across.

28

NICK SAT BACK in his swivel chair and hunched his shoulders, trying to ease the ache in his neck. It was not altogether successful. Still, it could have been worse.

Nick had learned to touch-type when he was still a teenager —taken evening classes at the local technical college, mainly as an excuse to meet girls. He'd mastered their old electric and electronic machines, and managed to improve his manual dexterity in other ways, too, although strictly speaking that was not part of the syllabus. At the end of it, he came away with a fancy diploma and keyboarding skills that had stood him in good stead ever since.

He rubbed absently at the knuckles of his right hand where they'd begun to stiffen. One of the many reminders of his undercover role with the Met. Or, more to the point, why he'd given up all that and moved north in search of a police career that might prove less injurious to his health.

Yeah, and some mixed blessing that *turned out to be…*

Behind him, the CID office was perhaps a third occupied. He tuned out the murmur of voices, the occasional phone ringing or the ping of an incoming message.

Nick had been combing through the Missing Persons database, starting with records logged eight years ago and gradually working back from there. Dr Onatade had given that timescale as being the minimum amount of time the body had been in the ground, although she'd stressed it was only a preliminary estimate, with a whole heap of provisos attached. Still, it gave him somewhere to start and he'd every confidence in the FME's opinion. So far, in Nick's experience of the cases where her services were required, she'd been just about spot on every time.

Unless, of course, once they worked the crime scene more thoroughly, they came to the conclusion that the body had been buried elsewhere—or perhaps not buried at all, until after the bones had been picked clean.

And from what he'd seen of the location where the body was found, it looked like his clothes and effects were with him at the scene, in close proximity to the bones. Everything that hadn't rotted away or been eaten, anyway. Surely, those would have been lost, had he been moved long after he was dead?

Nick wasn't keen to think about that. It was one thing to die —suddenly, violently. But somehow, having your corpse shifted from pillar to post afterwards, like an inconvenient package, well, that was another thing.

He'd allowed a few years' leeway on the age range of the body, too. Better to be able to further narrow it down later, rather than have to run the searches again.

Dr Onatade had been able to tell him that the bones showed a few signs of old injuries, so that was another filter he could apply. He'd have more details when the full PM report came through but, at this stage, all he knew was that they'd required no surgical pins or plates, which was unfortunate for identification purposes. He had good teeth with little dentistry and no implants or complicated bridgework. Apart from the fact he was dead, the unknown victim seemed to have been in remarkably good health at the point of his demise.

Chris Blenkinship was currently working on the items found surrounding the body, including, so Nick had heard, an old mobile phone. The battery was as dead as its owner, of course, but Ty Frost had been delegated to find out if it could be resurrected or if any data could be gleaned, even so. The phone had once been an expensive model. That didn't mean the dead man —Nick dubbed him Eden Man, like some anthropological missing link—had owned it from new, of course. Technology moved on so fast, became outdated and was sold on or given away. Nothing to say it wasn't a later hand-me-down, donated to someone who was grateful for anything he could get.

If it had been Grace assigned to this one, Nick admitted privately that he would have been down in the workshop right now, leaning over her shoulder and absorbing each new detail as it was uncovered. With Blenkinship in charge of the evidence, he preferred to keep his distance and wait for the official report. Not that he would have been welcome as an observer, in any case.

Nick blinked his eyes back into focus and returned to the database. Fortunately, the instances of missing persons in Cumbria were indeed considerably lower than most of the neighbouring areas. The vast majority of people who went missing were found within the first day. Almost three-quarters of those who were found, turned up within five miles of home.

Didn't go far. Didn't go for long.

Only a small percentage remained missing after a week. And, of those cases, a tiny fraction—usually less than half of one percent—resulted in a fatal outcome. Including, of course, those who fell off mountains, drowned in lakes, died of exposure on some Lakeland fell when the weather turned unexpectedly. Or those who committed suicide.

Or were murdered.

Eden Man must have disappeared from somewhere, so why hadn't more of a hue and cry been raised for him? Instead, he'd apparently been lying in his makeshift grave for ten years or more. His death *could* have been accidental or self-inflicted, Nick reasoned, but then someone had deliberately hidden his body rather than call it in. Had gone to great pains to bury him deep enough not to be found, in the normal run of things.

Until the river had other ideas.

He made a note to find out how much the Eden had changed its course over the last ten years or so. Had anyone done that kind of research? Some local university, perhaps?

He sighed and went to the gents just for the chance to stretch his legs, rotate his back until his spine popped. When he returned to his desk, he found DC Yardley had brewed up. A gently steaming mug of tea was perched on a pile of paperwork next to Nick's computer monitor.

He took a sip—just a small one to begin with. It wasn't so long ago he was the butt of every practical joker in the station. The tea was thick and strong and—as far as he could tell—

unadulterated. He took a longer swig, hoping that the caffeine hit might sharpen his brain.

"Thanks," he said, raising the mug in salute to Yardley.

"No problem," Yardley said and for once there was no sneer or snub in his voice.

"How's your Other Half doing?"

"Ach, being driven crazy by back ache and kept awake half the night by the little 'un playing football with her bladder, so she reckons," Yardley said but Nick caught the wonder in his face, the slightly dazed air of someone who has no idea of just how much his life is about to change. "Apart from that, she's...blooming."

"My girlfriend, Lisa, was the same when she was carrying our little girl," Nick said, reaching for common ground. "It sounds corny to say it, what with the swollen ankles, and itchy patches all over her body, and the fact she could belch for Britain, but to me she never looked more beautiful than in her last six weeks."

"I know!" Yardley grinned. "But will they believe you when you tell 'em that, eh? No chance."

"How close is she?"

"Any day now."

"Ah, you'll have her hospital bag permanently by the front door then?"

"Nah, she's hoping for a home birth," Yardley said. "I've got the midwife on speed-dial, though."

Which, Nick reckoned, taking another mouthful of tea, was probably the longest conversation he'd had with any of his CID colleagues that wasn't entirely related to work. But it seemed Yardley was feeling chatty.

"Heard you had a bit of excitement at your crime scene this morning, eh?"

For a second, Nick thought he meant the discovery of Eden Man, then realised Yardley was talking about the dramatic arrival of Jordan Elliot's mother.

"Yeah, she was lucky," he said. "If that car had gone anywhere near the river, she could have been fighting social services over the rest of her kids."

Yardley took a slurp of his own tea. "Mind you, poor lass, she must be getting frantic by now. Two days and still no sign of the little lad, eh?"

He sounded genuinely sympathetic. The imminent onset of parenthood was clearly having a humanising effect.

"What's the story with the husband—Dylan?" Nick asked, making the most of this unexpected armistice. "He's certainly a cocky little sod."

"Oh aye, he is that," Yardley said. "Handy with his fists, too, from what I've heard. Not above knocking the wife about a bit if she steps out of line, if the rumours are true."

Nick frowned. "Has he ever hit his kids?"

"Heck, I hope not! That would…open up a whole new line of enquiry, eh?"

Yardley's phone rang. Nick swung back to his computer, opened up another screen and typed in Dylan Elliot's name and address. Moments later, he was skimming through the details of the man's tawdry criminal past. It was, as DI Pollock had suggested, mostly petty stuff involving property theft.

There were two instances where Dylan had got physical, however. Once when he was arrested fleeing from the scene of a burglary as a teenager and scuffled with the uniforms trying to cuff him.

The second was only eighteen months previously. During a night out with his mates on a pub crawl in Carlisle, an apparent stranger had accused Dylan of having an affair with his wife. The man ended up losing several front teeth for his trouble.

The cuckolded husband pressed charges. In court, Dylan Elliot gave every appearance of contrition to get off with a hefty fine and a suspended sentence. One of the witnesses to his good character as both a husband and father was his wife, Yvonne.

That, in itself, set Nick's antennae quivering. Something about the way Yvonne had behaved around her husband, when Nick and DI Pollock had called on them at the farm, meant her portrayal of Dylan as a loving family man did not quite stack up.

But what clinched it was brief testimony from one of the mates Dylan had been out with that night. Not the statement itself—which was of the 'didn't see him do anything wrong, yer honour' variety—but the identity of the man who made it.

Lisa's brother, Karl.

29

QUEENIE HEARD the commotion before she saw it, and then saw it before she realised what it meant.

It didn't take her long, though.

She broke into a run across the camping field, dodging between the horse trailers and vans. The closer she got, the louder the cheers and shouts and jeers. She caught a glimpse of a big man on a big bay horse with a white face and white feathers stretching way up past knee and hock. It was being ridden in tight circles beyond the next row of vehicles. The ground shook to the thunder of hooves the size of dinner plates.

A Clydesdale. Usually a dray or plough horse, it was not a common breed among the Gypsies and Travellers. Took too much feeding and too much finding space for.

In fact, there was only one man she was aware of who'd brought one to the Fair.

Jackson.

She knew for a fact the horse was more than eighteen hands high but, with the giant on his back, he looked no more than a pony.

Jackson was up on the horse now, bareback with just a head-collar and a knotted lead rope to guide it by. Making the animal twist and turn so tight, it was a feat of horsemanship. At first, she thought that was plenty to warrant the excitement of the gathered crowd.

Until she got closer.

Close enough, that is, for someone to spot her approach and let out a warning, "Uh-oh…"

Alarmed now, Queenie elbowed her way through to the front. It took her precious moments. People stood their ground, seemed set to block her in a way they wouldn't have dared while her father was still alive.

By the time she pushed through the final rank, she was near to both temper and tears.

What she saw horrified her.

Bartley had the brood mare by her tether. He'd said he was going to take her down to The Sands, just a little walk to show off both mare and foal—no flash, no dash. Would do no harm to let those who might be interested lay their eyes on Hezekiah's last colt, with his unique markings and regal bearing. Ocean had a halter on the colt, had led him away proudly, like a rite of passage.

But they'd run into Jackson on the way. Not just the giant alone but his animal besides. Descended from an ancient warhorse breed with the fire still in his belly and spoiling for a fight.

Jackson was kicking the Clydesdale on, tugging it round in ever-smaller circles about the frightened mare and her terrified offspring. Bartley was trying to calm the mare and that was bad enough. But it was all Ocean could do to cling on to the rope with the panicking colt at the other end.

As Queenie gave a cry and launched herself forward, ripping free from the hands that tried to hold her back, Jackson overshot his mark. He let the big horse run on two or three strides, then wheeled and sent it leaping back toward his prey.

There was nothing Bartley could do to avoid the clash. He had his hands full and more besides. The colt was trying to hide beneath his mother's belly. She yanked against the man who held her head and strained to swing free. Her hindquarters thumped against the foal, sending both animal and boy sprawling into the path of the thundering Clydesdale.

Ocean refused to let go while the colt thrashed on the ground, ungainly, letting out a shriek that brought every hair bolt upright on Queenie's body.

She threw herself forward, into the path of the oncoming pair. A great shout went up from the crowd of watchers. There are some who believe a horse will do everything to avoid trampling a person. Anyone who knows better will tell you they're as likely to step onto you as step over you. And there are some who will do so with a song in their heart and come back for a second try.

The Clydesdale's head was up and its eyes were wild. Queenie knew she came barely halfway up the horse's shoulder. It could have barrelled over and through her without noticing the check.

Still, she stood her ground. Horse and rider were barely a stride away now. She felt the earth tremble beneath her and saw Jackson heave uselessly at the rope tied to the headcollar, in a desperate attempt to turn aside. The colt was still not on its feet, too young yet to have full mastery of his limbs. Ocean hauled on the lead rope in vain.

And then, for no reason anyone could afterwards name, the Clydesdale bunched itself and sprang sideways, stiff-legged, as if spooked by some unseen predator. The pair passed so close by Queenie that Jackson's knee just scuffed her shoulder.

It was a glancing blow—compared to what might have been. All the same, it was hard enough to spin her round and bowl her off her feet.

And if Jackson hadn't been born to horses, riding almost before he could walk, he would have hit the ground, too. As it was, he was thrown sideways and held on only by the skin of his teeth. Fifty yards shot past before he got himself back on top and brought the heavy horse skidding to a stamping, snorting halt.

By that time people had flooded around Queenie, all talking at once. She struggled to rise, fighting off their insistence that she should lay quiet and still.

"Ocean! Where is he—?"

"Me darlin', he's fine," came Bartley's voice, a near croon.

"And the colt?"

"They're both fine. It's *you* that concerns me."

He must have handed the mare off to Ocean because all at once he was there. He gathered Queenie up, helped her stand but kept a bruising grip on her arms. "And what the devil were you tryin' to do, wife—throwing yourself under the very heels of such a beast?"

"But the colt—"

"Never mind about that. He's had a bit of a scare but there's no harm done, eh?"

In some corner of her mind, Queenie registered the warning in his tone but she was too far gone to heed it.

"*No harm done*?" Her voice rose to a howl. "That *matto-mengro*… That *dinnelo*, he almost flattens the pair of us and all you can say is 'no harm done'?"

Jackson did not like being called a drunkard or a fool—and certainly not in the presence of the other clans. He nudged the Clydesdale forward with a determined gleam in his eye.

Bartley thrust Queenie roughly behind him and stepped forward to stand braced in front of them.

"That wife of yours should watch her tongue," Jackson said darkly.

"It's not my tongue you should be afraid of!" Queenie shot back.

Bartley spun, grabbed her arms again and pushed her back a pace, almost a shove, then raised his hand as if to strike.

"Will you be *quiet* for once, woman, and just be lettin' *me* handle this?" he demanded through his teeth.

Shocked, Queenie complied. She realised then how still the crowd had become, how close they pushed in. All wanting to see. All wanting to hear. She shrank in on herself, aghast.

"You're right," Bartley said, more loudly now, lifting his chin to meet Jackson's gaze. "She is *my* wife. And because of that, what she does with her tongue is *my* business. I'll thank you to keep yourself out of it."

Jackson's shoulders came back. The Clydesdale shifted, made restless by the tension. Jackson stilled it, glaring down. "You may have married true Romany but that doesn't make *you* more than you are, or ever will be. All here will bear witness that you'll never be anything other than *hindity-mengre*!"

Queenie heard the gasps that escaped those around her at his words. As well they might. To call Bartley one of the 'filthy people'—a name given to vagrant Irish by the Gypsies for their dirty ways—was the gravest insult.

One Bartley would not be able to let pass unchallenged.

He spat in the grass at the Clydesdale's feet.

"Name your time and place."

———

AFTERWARDS, Bartley would *not* discuss it with her. Would not listen to her pleas, her arguments or threats. Just like her brother, he'd been taught from a boy never to back down from a fight and he was not about to start now.

Not least because the choice of new *Shera Rom* was as yet undecided.

It was all down to stupid pride, of that she was sure. It was not so much that her husband didn't like to lose—it was that he hated to lose to Vano. Oh, the two men got along well enough but there had always been a rivalry running close beneath the surface, even so.

As for Jackson, she held no sway there. She acknowledged privately that her fierce defence of Bartley the day before had made certain the giant would never listen to anything she might have to say.

Jackson had no wife to whom she could appeal. And the family matriarch was growing physically more frail as she grew more set in her ways. Both meant she had refused to travel to this year's Fair.

So, Queenie was on her own…

She'd spent some time with the mare and the colt, settling and calming them after their scare. Then she wandered alone down to The Sands and walked the rows of horses and ponies on display there. Nothing matched the colt for quality, in her opinion, which was both reassuring and disheartening.

Reassuring because it meant the colt was more likely to sell— and for a good price.

And disheartening for exactly the same reason.

Further along the row, she saw the big bay Clydesdale tied to a tree amid the smaller animals, like a truck parked among cars. It was directly across from one of the pubs. Not hard to guess where Jackson would be right now.

She was still smarting from the whole encounter, not least for the humiliation of being seen to be put in her place. Nevertheless, she remembered the way the heavy horse had shied at the last moment to avoid her—her and the fallen colt.

It would have been ungrateful not to thank him.

With care as to who might be watching, she sidled over to the horse. It turned toward her as she neared, swinging that huge head round to meet her, lowered so he offered her the sweet spot behind the ears. She rubbed the sweaty patch beneath the strap of his headcollar obligingly. He leaned in toward her, eyes shut.

Despite herself, Queenie smiled. She murmured praise to the huge animal for his gentleness and bravery.

"And don't you let him hurt me and mine, hm?" she added. "You hear?"

The Clydesdale rubbed his brow against her hand another couple of times, up and down. She knew, honestly she did, that he was simply scratching an itch.

But, still, she could have sworn that he was nodding.

30

GRACE WAS ALMOST HOME. Tallie, off her lead and feathering back and forth across the grass verge ahead, reached the gateway and came to an abrupt halt. By the way the dog lowered her head and stood with the hair up in a mini-Mohican at the back of her neck, Grace knew she had a visitor.

And that the visitor was male.

Since she acquired the young Weimaraner only *after* her divorce, Grace had been accused—not least by her ex-husband—of training the dog specially to react that way. Grace denied it. After all, there were times when such behaviour was not an asset.

She clicked her fingers but for once Tallie was too fixated on the new arrival to obey the command to come. At least she didn't advance any further. Grace hurried the last few yards and bent to clip the lead onto the dog's collar.

"Nice to see she hasn't forgotten me," Nick said, his voice dry.

Grace straightened. A vehicle she didn't recognise was parked in her driveway. Nick leaned against it with his arms folded.

"That's not your car, is it?"

He nodded to the dog, who still hadn't moved but was now growling softly. "What—you think she simply doesn't approve of my choice of transport?"

"That's always a possibility," Grace agreed. "It's not a patch on the Subaru. What's happened to it?"

"Your boss happened," Nick said darkly. He gave her the bones of the story while she unlocked the door to the cottage and shed her boots in the tiny hall. She had to shoo the dog ahead of them into the living room. Tallie kept wanting to stop and herd the interloper back out of the door. Eventually, she retreated to her bed near the sofa and watched the goings on with anxious, gold-coloured eyes.

"I know the breed is supposed to be smart but you can't blame poor Tallie if she's forgotten you," Grace said, moving round the breakfast bar into the kitchen area. She ducked into the fridge and came out with a bottle of Sauvignon Blanc. "It has been a while, hasn't it?"

She made sure to keep the reproach out of her tone. When she was off work through injury the previous summer, Nick had been a regular visitor. Tallie had learned, if not to welcome him, then at least to tolerate his presence.

The dog stayed indoors with more than a hint of a sulk about her, while Grace dug out two glasses and led the way onto the small flagged area outside the French windows. It was late afternoon. The fierce grip of the day had begun to loosen and, with a gentle breeze rustling through the garden, it was a pleasant spot to sit.

"I confess I've never noticed Chris Blenkinship was any worse a driver than anyone else," she said now, pouring a modest glass for them both. "Although, if I voiced such a possibility I've no doubt his masculine pride would be mortally wounded."

Nick took a seat at the wrought-iron garden table. "It almost felt like he did it deliberately." He lifted a shoulder. "I don't know. There was just something slightly *off* about the whole thing."

"Well, there's nothing to say he wasn't having a thoroughly bad day *before* he hit you and that just put the icing on it. Who knows what *else* might have gone wrong for him?"

Nick frowned. "Hm. I suppose so. I did wonder... I remember years ago, not long after I joined the force, having to deal with a road accident where some woman claimed this guy flashed her out of a junction, then drove straight into the side of her."

Grace raised her eyebrows along with her glass. "Did you get to the bottom of it?"

Nick took a sip of wine, paused a moment to savour and swallow. "We caught him on CCTV hitting a traffic bollard earlier the same day." And at Grace's frown, he added, "Turned out he only had third-party cover, so he needed to engineer a claim on someone else's insurance for the damage, or pay for it himself. Happens more often than you think."

"Ah. But surely Chris doesn't have that kind of problem? You said he was driving his work vehicle. They're covered every which way."

"I know. Maybe you're right. Maybe it's just his ego at play here—Brian Pollock seemed to think so." He held his glass up to the light, looked at the translucent colour of the wine. "Speaking of inflated egos…how's your ex?"

"Max is fine—as far as I know. I haven't seen him recently," Grace said sedately. She smiled. "In fact, it would rather seem that he's been directing his charm at another woman."

Nick leaned back in his chair and regarded her with a quizzical eye.

"Why do I get the feeling there's more to that than—?"

"My mother. He's been thoroughly ingratiating himself."

"Uh-oh. Is that going to make life awkward for you?"

"Oh, I doubt it. She's wise to him but not above making use of his labouring skills to help get her new garden beaten into submission, the minx."

"How's she settling in? Didn't you say she lived in Appleby before?"

"Yes, years ago now. Still, it hasn't taken her long to re-establish herself. I think she's already plugged-in to the gossip hotline. When I was up there the other day, she reminded me the week of the Fair is known locally as a good time to settle old scores. You can get your own back on the people who've annoyed you all year, but you can blame it on the Gypsies."

Nick was silent for a while after that, his face serious. Watching him, Grace remembered the first time they met, when he was both in a foul temper *and* hung-over, but she'd itched to photograph him. She still did, if she was honest. Had contented herself with taking some portrait shots of him with his daughter, Sophie, a few months before.

At last, he said, "I wonder if that was what happened to the guy whose bones were uncovered at Mallerstang—a settled score? And then his body buried at a place where the Gypsies often camp, just in case it ever *did* come to light."

"Or a deliberate attempt to make them look guilty."

"True. But until Dr Onatade carries out her post-mortem exam, we don't even know if he was murdered, or died accidentally."

"Well, considering where and how he was buried, someone will have questions to answer, certainly."

Nick shrugged. "For what—failing to register a death? Failing to gain consent of the landowner before carrying out a private burial? Hardly big league stuff, is it?"

"And you haven't identified him yet, your John Doe?"

"I spent most of today trawling through the Missing Persons database but there are no obvious matches."

"I suppose, if he was part of the Traveller community, it's likely he was never officially reported missing. They don't exactly trust the police."

"Tell me about it! We'll just have to wait and see what we get from the PM—or from the effects found with the body. I understand there's even an old mobile phone, although what use it will be is another matter."

"Well, if anyone can do something with it, I'd put my money on Ty Frost."

"So would I." Nick stood, stretching out his back with a groan. "Ah well, time I was making tracks. Lisa's working late tonight, again, so I need to pick up the little one from her grandparents' place."

Something in his voice tapped at her. "How *are* things with Lisa, since the two of you got back together?" Grace asked.

Another shrug. "OK—some of the time."

"Oh, I was hoping for second honeymoon territory." Her voice was gently teasing but when he didn't smile she sobered. "What is it?"

"Again, I'm not sure I know." He rubbed a hand around the back of his neck. "She's been acting…strangely. Secretive, defensive. Just…half a beat out of step with me. Or maybe it's me that's out of step with her." He flashed a quick smile. "Oh, just ignore me. I'm tired. It's been a long day."

"Perhaps," Grace agreed. "But you have good instincts and I'd be tempted to trust them."

"And do what, though?"

"Whatever you know is right."

He picked up his glass and went back inside the house without answering. Grace followed, bringing the remains of the wine and her own glass. Tallie lifted her head, saw Nick and gave a brief token growl, then flopped down again, as if it wasn't worth the effort.

Nick placed his empty glass on the breakfast bar and turned to her, car keys already in his hand. "Thanks, Grace—for letting me talk. I always feel a little better for it."

"Then my work here is done," she said. "Look after yourself, Nick."

It was only as the exhaust note of his car died away up the lane that she remembered her encounter with the unknown Gypsy woman at Appleby. Grace wondered if she should have mentioned the woman's response to the discovery of the old bones, or her outburst about something that was owing…

How did the settling of old scores fit into that?

31

———————

AT THE END of the lane leading away from the cottage, Nick braked slowly to a halt. The road ahead was clear but still he sat for a moment, arms braced against the steering wheel.

"Why do you do it to yourself?" he murmured.

He didn't expect an answer—but then, he didn't need one.

He knew why.

Ever since he'd first encountered Grace, at the start of a long and difficult case the previous summer, he'd fought against the attraction he felt toward her. Why else would he be so minutely aware of the moment she entered a room? Or, on the occasions when she had cause to call him, to report findings or update him on something they were working on together, he often *knew* without needing to see the incoming number, that she was on the other end of the line.

He didn't like it, this...*awareness* he had of her, but there didn't seem to be much he could do about it. Avoiding her was not an option. Despite Chris Blenkinship's occasional snide comments, Grace was probably the best crime-scene technician they had. He'd be a fool to settle for anyone less.

Was that what he'd done with Lisa—settled for somebody less?

Nick occasionally wondered, if Lisa *hadn't* broken up with him just after he transferred up to the Cumbria force, if he would have been able to keep Grace firmly in the Friend Zone. But, almost as soon as they'd moved north, Lisa announced she was leaving and moved out, taking little Sophie with her. At the time, Nick suspected it was what she'd been planning all along.

It was only after Lisa had gone that he'd met Grace for the first time. He wasn't on the rebound exactly, although he wouldn't deny his male ego was still smarting from the rejection. But, the usual restrictions—that absolute loyalty to the woman who was his partner, the mother of his child—seemed no longer to have any meaning.

Perhaps that was why he'd felt the pull of the lanky redhead and had allowed himself to become…enthralled.

He shook his head as if to clear his ears, like a dog coming out of water. He was still sitting at the junction and the road was still empty. He put the car into gear and turned south, heading sedately out of Orton village toward the motorway.

A few months after Lisa left, she'd started to backtrack. It was subtle at first. Rather than making him fight for every minute he wanted to spend with Sophie, Lisa began inviting him to join the two of them on picnics, days out, family gatherings.

Once the relief of being able to see his daughter without all the hassle had sunk in, Nick soon realised what she was doing. Rather than admitting that she might have made a mistake, Lisa was setting out to…re-seduce him, all over again. Only, this time, she had the added lure of Sophie on her side.

What Lisa could *not* have known was that, during the weeks they were apart, Nick had come to recognise that their little girl was more or less the only thing they had in common. In some ways, she'd done him a favour by forcing him to assess the situation with the clarity of distance, however slight.

Bluntly put, Nick simply didn't want her anymore.

He discovered, to his surprise, that he was developing a taste for lanky redheads over petite blondes.

Not that he made any moves in Grace's direction. Her ex—Max—had not taken their divorce well and was still trying to reassert his claim. Nick realised that offering anything other than friendship, at that point, would have sent her running in the opposite direction.

If Lisa had remained determined to do without him, who knows what might have developed with Grace. But Lisa *had* changed her mind. And, thinking of his daughter's happiness and sense of security, Nick had agreed to a reconciliation.

Even though, he acknowledged privately, it was with resignation rather than joy.

Of course, Lisa knew things weren't quite right between them. Initially, she'd tried a little too hard to pretend everything was exactly as it was. But her smile was too bright and she couldn't quite carry the forced note of cheerfulness in her voice. Not for long.

Eventually, she exploded, yelling and throwing breakables along with insults and accusations. Nick had responded with a weary calm where once there would have been desperation. And maybe Lisa had realised, at last, how badly she'd misjudged both him and the situation.

The fact they were still together was due to inertia rather than anything else. She didn't have the nerve to move in with her parents again. And Nick found that sharing his life with Lisa, however uncomfortable that might be, was a small price to pay for being able to see his daughter every day and tuck her into bed nearly every night.

But, just sometimes, he needed a small reminder of how things *might* have been.

"Yeah," he said aloud and heard the rueful edge. "*That's* why you do it…"

PART V

SATURDAY

32

When Blenkinship walked into DI Pollock's office the following morning, he was irritated to see that, once again, Dr Onatade had beaten him to it. The FME was already ensconced in one of the visitor chairs facing the DI's desk. She sipped from a glass of water rather than accepting Pollock's truly awful coffee, and had what could only be the post-mortem report balanced across her knees.

"Ah, there you are, lad," Pollock said darkly. "I was just thinking of sending out search parties."

"Sorry sir. My wife's car wouldn't start." He gave an apologetic shrug to accompany the lie. It was probably more believable than admitting he hadn't been able to sleep until the early hours—*again*—and avoided any discussion of a possible reason for that state of affairs.

Blenkinship declined a cup of coffee from Pollock's personal filter machine over on the filing cabinet. The DI bought only the good stuff but then spooned in so much for every jugful, it practically qualified as an offensive weapon. The thought of something so acidic made Blenkinship's stomach surge. He took a deep breath to quell it, slid into his chair.

"Dr Onatade has already gone over the PM results," Pollock said, with only a hint of censure. "The full report will be in your inbox, of course, but if you'd just like to give Mr Blenkinship the gist, Ayo?"

"Of course," Dr Onatade said. "Blunt-force trauma to the back of the head. His skull was smashed like a ripe melon."

Blenkinship took another calming breath. "Are we sure that couldn't have happened after he was put in the ground? After all, half the bank collapsed around the body, by the looks of it."

Dr Onatade straightened in her chair. "As surprising as it may seem to you, Christopher, I *am* able to tell the difference between ante-mortem, peri-mortem, and post-mortem injuries," she said with great precision. "Yes, the fractures to his right femur, pelvis and jaw all happened some time after death. The bone around the breaks is brittle, almost crumbly. *That* damage, without doubt, took place some time after he was buried." She tapped the report with her forefinger but didn't need to consult it. "The greenstick fractures to the radius and ulna of his right arm happened several years *before* he died. Both exhibited considerable formation of callus. The break to his right clavicle was even older—possibly even in childhood. Again, it was well-healed—*clearly* ante-mortem—"

Blenkinship lifted his hands in surrender. "OK, pet, you've made your point. I—"

"*But,*" Dr Onatade over-rode him, her voice round and rich and forceful, determined to finish now she'd started, "the fracture to the base of the skull showed all the hallmarks of occurring to *living* bone with a blood supply. Therefore, the considerable expertise for which Cumbria Constabulary pays me so handsomely, leads me to conclude that this was the defining peri-mortem injury, occurring immediately before death. Obviously, the brain is no longer available for me to examine but I can *assure* you that, in my professional opinion, sufficient damage would have been caused to the underlying brain tissue to make your victim's demise almost inevitable."

She sat back in her chair and beamed at both men. Pollock cleared his throat.

"Yes, thank you, Ayo. That all seems…very clear cut."

"I don't suppose it was possible to establish what kind of weapon *caused* the fatal injury?" Blenkinship asked, determined to find *something* the blasted woman didn't have an answer for.

"He was killed by an upward blow to the underside of the skull with a thin bar or rod," she said promptly. "Bring me an object matching that description and I will be able to tell you, one way or the other, if it caused the wound. However, bearing in mind the possibility that he was not killed where he was buried, this would rely on *your* people being able to discover the primary crime scene, when it could easily be a decade after the event." She paused. "So, what do *you* have so far?"

Blenkinship felt like a snooker player whose opponent has just utterly barricaded-in the cue ball and then cheerfully handed back the table with no shots available to play.

"Not much, I can tell you that," he admitted. "There were some clothing fragments found in the immediate vicinity of the body but they're generic and don't tell us much. Some plastic buttons, probably from a cotton shirt that's rotted away. Rivets from denim jeans, which again have rotted to nothing. If he was wearing shoes or boots, the river took them, along with his feet. No watch, no wallet. No ID, either. He was wearing some kind of medallion round his neck on a chain but that's corroded badly. We're doing what we can with it."

"What about the phone?" Pollock asked.

"Well, *that* could prove interesting but at the moment it's so covered in crud that we're having to go fairly slowly cleaning it up."

"Does young Ty Frost think he can do anything with it?"

"Well, he doesn't expect to be making calls from it anytime soon, eh?" Blenkinship said, trying to lighten the mood. Neither Dr Onatade nor DI Pollock smiled in response. "Ah, yes, the electronics are scrap but Frost reckons that the serial number is likely to be on a label inside the case. Rush it, and we risk destroying our only means of identifying who the phone was sold and registered to. And that's *if* it's not a Pay-As-You-Go phone, and *if* the service provider still has records going back that far."

"I have taken the liberty of sending off a DNA sample with a rush on it," Dr Onatade said. Pollock shot upright in his own chair and she raised a finger to silence his imminent protest. "It was something DC Weston said this morning that made me think of it."

Pollock raised his eyebrows. "This morning? How early did the lad get in?"

"He called me just before I examined the body, to ask if there were any indicators that the victim might come from the Gypsy or Traveller community."

Pollock allowed himself to slump back again, frowning as if the steam had gone right out of him. "Did he now?"

"Waste of time and resources," Blenkinship said. "There was nothing to suggest—"

But again Dr Onatade did not let him finish. "On the contrary," she said, "the more I thought about it, the more logical a suggestion it seemed. There were no matching reports in the Missing Persons database. The body was found on a piece of land regularly used by Travellers. And the old injuries I found might be consistent with riding—or falling off—horses."

"Aye, and they *might* be consistent with riding or falling off a mountain bike, an' all," Pollock muttered.

"Very true. And if there was, currently, happening nearby, a huge gathering of mountain bike riders from all over Europe, I would have rushed the test then, too."

Blenkinship had read all about the new integrated microfluidic system for rapid DNA analysis. It cut the turnaround time from around seventy-two hours, down to just four. But he'd never had a case that warranted the extortionate cost, and he wasn't sure he had one now.

Dr Onatade watched the realisation hit Pollock with, Blenkinship thought grumpily, a satisfaction bordering on smug. Then she nodded and got to her feet. "The Gypsies are here until Monday and then they'll begin to disperse. You know as well as I do, Brian, that once they leave, you may never see them again—particularly anyone who might know something about the dead man. You won't get a better opportunity than this."

"Aye," Pollock said, his voice still gloomy. "And I'll pay through me nose for the privilege."

33

WYNTER TRELAWNEY PUSHED her old Land Rover as fast as she dared, keeping one eye out for speed traps. They always put in lower limits along the road between Brough Sowerby and Kirkby Stephen during the run-up to the Fair, but there were hardly any vans camped on the verges now. Most of them were already up at Appleby.

She found the turn-off to Warcop just before she reached the edge of the town itself, swinging sharp right and accelerating again, hearing the ringing rattle of the gearbox and the diffs whining. She leaned forward and scanned the road ahead anxiously.

The voice on the phone had been vague—deliberately so, but she was used to that.

"Come quick, *dieya*," it had said. "Appleby Road out of Kirkby. Come quick!"

And knowing better than to ignore such a summons, she'd run across to one of the neighbouring cottages to get someone to sit with her mother, grabbed a bag and jumped straight into the Landie.

Now, she was looking for a cluster of vans, so she nearly missed one boy standing next to a piebald pony in a gateway by the weir. She braked and slid back her window.

"Was it you—who called me?"

The boy regarded her for a moment as if he didn't understand, then shook his head and said briefly, "Me *puro dad*."

My grandfather, Wynter translated as she climbed out and slammed the door behind her. Just as they'd called her *mother* when they phoned. But then she saw the blanketed form lying in the grass by the edge of the river.

And she remembered that *dieya* also meant *nurse*.

"What—?" she began before she heard the fast clip of hooves on the road surface. The boy had swung himself up onto the pony's back and was now disappearing in the direction of Appleby, leaving Wynter alone in a tiny paddock with...*something* wrapped in a blanket.

She approached the shape carefully, edging closer, noticing how trampled the grass was around it and how wet. Whatever it was, it had come from the river.

Leaning down, she took hold of a corner of the woollen cloth between forefinger and thumb, lifted it slowly and with great care. She was not aware of holding her breath until she saw what was inside the bundle. Then the air gushed out of her like a pricked balloon. She dropped the blanket into place and scuttled backwards half-a-dozen paces, until she felt the wooden fence at her back.

She fumbled in a pocket for her phone.

Then it was her turn to tell those who answered: "Come quick!"

34

ALONE IN THE workshop at Carlisle HQ, Blenkinship was absorbed in his task and thankful for it. It stopped him having to think—or worry—about anything else.

He'd been over every item recovered with the bones of Eden Man and prioritised two—the mobile phone and the medallion. The phone, he'd dropped off with Ty Frost in Penrith. He'd chased him a couple of times but knew doing so was likely to make Frost work slower rather than faster, paranoid about making a mistake.

So, reluctantly, he'd forbidden himself to check up again until he'd finished with the medallion.

It was round and flat with a small hole at one side, almost like the kind of tag you'd put on the collar of a dog or a cat, engraved with the owner's telephone number. The thin chain on which it had been threaded was so delicate with age and corrosion that it practically fell apart on the bench, but the disc itself was made of a thicker material—perhaps stainless steel.

That didn't mean it *wouldn't* rust, of course—there were many different grades of stainless. But at least this had stood up to being buried next to a watercourse better than most metals. Maybe, he speculated, it had been hidden inside clothing, which offered a small amount of protection until that, too, had rotted away.

Blenkinship had already soaked the disc in a mix of acids, ferric chlorides, and water to clean away much of the looser surface material. Now, he clamped it in place on the bench and began very gently rubbing one side with waterproof abrasive paper, lubricating it as he went. He moved through progressively finer grades of paper until the surface began to smooth out and gleam, meticulously documenting his process in both note form and photographs as he went.

When he had the disc polished to an almost-chrome finish, he set up his camera on a small tripod, with a flash mounted off to one side, and photographed the surface in detail.

There was nothing to see.

Blenkinship swore and stood up, stretching out his aching back and flexing his fingers. He peeled off the disposable gloves, revealing sweat-swamped hands with prune-like fingers. He washed and dried them, made himself a coffee, and thought about putting through another call to Ty Frost. He managed to talk himself out of doing so.

Instead, he stripped another pair of gloves out of the dispenser, turned the disc over, and began work on the reverse.

With no obvious back and front to the thing, he knew it was pure luck which side he'd worked on first. But, by the time he was halfway through the polishing process, he knew that his earlier efforts had never been going to reveal anything.

"Hah, Sod's Law," he muttered.

But the gradually emerging outline was enough to keep resentment at bay. Particularly as it looked as if the medallion might have been engraved with a pair of initials, the right-hand one of which appeared to be a slightly flowery capital G.

He redoubled his efforts. The left-hand side of what he now realised was the front of the disc was more corroded, but he slowly managed to coax an image out of it. To begin with, he thought it might be a back-to-front capital C, but then it appeared to have an extra, smaller curl at the top, so that it could even have been a reversed capital E, or the number 3.

Whatever the two letters were, they had been placed back-to-back, overlapping to form a single spine up the centre. And sprouting inside the curve of each letter was what looked like the wings of a butterfly. The one inside the C—or 3, or whatever it was—was the Eye of Horus. The one inside the G was a Lotus flower. Or as far as he could tell, anyway.

Blenkinship photographed the revealed image, then took to the internet in search of meanings.

The individual elements produced a mixed bag. The Eye of Horus was a symbol of protection. The Lotus flower meant ultimate perfection, a thing of beauty rising above the mud in which its roots were embedded.

The letters were more difficult to define. A reversed and a forward-facing C, back-to-back with spines touching, was the anti-sigma character, part of extra letters invented and introduced by the Roman Emperor Claudius and meaning, as far as Blenkinship could discern, absolutely bugger all, except that the man was vain and powerful enough to do whatever he liked and get away with it.

Blenkinship even searched on designer labels, such as Gucci and Coco Chanel, but none of them were even a remote match to the odd lettering on the medallion.

And the butterfly wings, in various belief systems, meant change, joy, colour, the soul, or an advertisement of the availability of an unmarried girl.

He sat back and rubbed his hands—they still felt vaguely pulpy from the gloves—over his face. His eyes were gritty from concentration and lack of sleep, despite the frequent caffeine boosts he'd been giving himself all day.

He typed up a brief report with all the facts, such as they were, and digital images attached of the image on the medallion, with the recommendation that an appeal was put out to the media for the public's help in identifying the man. They had no description other than an approximate height and age, but this insignia, whatever it was, might prove a useful additional factor. Might just jog someone's memory.

And then, finally—*finally*—he allowed himself to reach for the phone and call Ty Frost.

"I think I've gone as far as I can with the serial number of the mobile, boss," Frost reported. He sounded as weary as Blenkinship felt. "It was printed on a label inside the casing, so the bits that are missing are gone for good and there's no way to retrieve them. The manufacturer was able to tell me which retail chain bought that batch, but that's as much as I could do, I'm afraid."

"Well, I'm sure you've done your best. *I've* managed to reveal an image on the medallion and maybe initials, so it gives DC Weston *something* to work on, eh?"

Frost muttered a response that Blenkinship took to be hurt pride that his boss had outdone him. *Well, only to be expected…*

Then his brain caught up with his ears as he registered part of what Frost had just said.

"Run that by me again, would you?"

"I said what a shame it is, that's all—about the boy."

"What boy? What about him?"

"The Elliot kid," Frost said. "I thought you'd have heard by now. Grace left about an hour ago. We got a call from some woman just north of Kirkby Stephen—he's been found…"

35

"WELL, LASS—IS IT HIM?"

Standing just inside the crime-scene tape, Grace hesitated. "We think it might be, yes."

"You *think*?" DI Pollock repeated. "*Might*?" There was annoyed disbelief in his voice, until the ramifications sank in. Then he paled. "My God... How bad...?"

"Bad," Grace said flatly. "Dr Onatade is talking about another fast-track DNA test, just to be sure. I know, I know—it's expensive," she went on when Pollock would have spoken, "but, Brian...you don't want to let the parents see him. Even if they *could* make an identification. Not like this..."

Pollock was silent for a moment, then he nodded. "All right, lass," he said, gruff. "Do what you have to."

He signed the log and struggled into a set of coveralls, gloves and bootees. As he and Grace tramped across the grass to the tents, he indicated one of the police vehicles where a shaken woman sat, wiping her eyes.

"Is that who found him, then?"

"Well, she's the one who called us..."

"Oh?"

Grace sighed. "I'm afraid, as contaminated crime-scenes go, this one's a mess. I've been over the bank but there are almost a dozen different boot prints there alone," she admitted. "The woman is Wynter Trelawney. She lives up on North Stainmore, looking after her parents' farm up there. It's been a stopping-off place for the Gypsies for years, apparently, on their way to and from Appleby. They trust her. So, when a group of them pulled a body out of the weir this morning, she was the one they called."

"And by the time our lads arrived…?"

"They were long gone," Grace agreed. "To be fair, she reckons they had all upped sticks by the time *she* got here. Just one boy left behind to mark the spot. And as soon as he'd done so—"

"Don't tell me—he scarpered, an' all."

"That's about the size of it." She pulled aside the flap of the tent and stood back for Pollock to enter first. He took a deep breath and stepped inside. Almost immediately, he put a gloved hand up to his nose and mouth. Grace couldn't blame him for that.

Dr Onatade looked up, her eyes sombre above her mask.

"Sorry about the smell," she said briskly. "Clearly, the poor little chap has been dead for several days. In fact, from the level of decomposition, I'd estimate he probably died the same night he went missing."

Pollock stared down. Grace saw his throat move in a convulsive swallow and she heard his quiet, "Poor little bastard looks like he's been savaged." He lifted his hand away just long enough to ask, "Any ideas yet on cause of death?"

"Plenty," Dr Onatade answered, "but, as you can see, the body has been severely…traumatised. Until I can get him onto my table and examine him more closely, it's hard to say with any certainty where one injury finishes and another begins."

Pollock scowled, although whether at the pathologist's caution or the fact she was making him stay inside the tent for longer than he wanted to, it was hard to tell. He wafted his other hand against the irritation of insects that buzzed and crowded around living and dead alike.

"The bicycle Grace found had been run over," he said shortly. "All I need from you is to know if *he* was run over along with it."

"And *I* need the time and the facilities in which to examine the body in greater detail," she returned. "I'll do the post-mortem exam as soon as I get him back, and Grace can collect what's left of his clothes the moment they are removed. They may tell us as much as the body."

"Hm, if he's been in the water all this time, there probably won't be much left to tell," Pollock muttered, turning toward the tent flap again.

"You should have a little more faith in your own people, Brian," Dr Onatade said. "If there is evidence here to be found, then naturally Grace and I will find it."

She handed Grace the folded blanket the body had been wrapped in. Grace bagged and tagged it. Both of them knew the blanket had probably been in contact with the body for a short period—only since he was rescued from the river. The woollen material was wet but not sodden. But still it needed to be examined minutely, and samples taken and fibres analysed.

As she left the tent herself, Grace was warmed by the pathologist's matter-of-fact tone to Pollock as much as the words. It was a vote of confidence that straightened her spine and rationalised her scattered thoughts.

Grace did not shock easily, but this one *had* shocked her, she admitted privately. The brutality that had been visited upon the body spoke of…hatred. More than that, it spoke of something deeply personal. She had always veered away from using the word "frenzied" in connection with an attack, but something about this one suited the description. Even outside the tent, out in the sunshine, she could still see the detailed injuries of the corpse burned into her mind's eye.

It was not the first death of a child she'd attended but it was the first one with such an edge to it. She swallowed and reminded herself that part of the reason she became a crime-scene technician in the first place was as a form of penance, not because it was the easy path.

But the only way she could stay on that path now, she realised, was by concentrating solely on the task at hand. And by not allowing her imagination to run riot.

Pollock was waiting for her by the crime-scene tape, talking to one of the uniformed officers who'd taken Wynter Trelawney's statement. The detective inspector turned at her approach.

"I suppose you're going to want to search the whole bloody river between here and Water Yat," he said gloomily.

"About that—I'd like to bring in Ty Frost."

"I thought he was working on that mobile phone for the skeleton case? What is it they've dubbed him—'Eden Man'?"

Pollock queried. "Well, I won't deny this has priority, but is it best use of the lad's geek skills?"

"When I left Penrith, Tyson had almost finished recovering the phone's serial number," Grace said. "I believe he was going to hand it over to DC Weston to follow up with the manufacturer."

"Right. So, does he have some secret obsession with sub-aqua that we're not aware of?"

"No," Grace said. "But he *does* have a not-so-secret obsession with flying drones…"

36

QUEENIE SAT on a blanket she'd laid out on the grass near the river, Sky alongside her, and watched the drama unfold. The Eden had been high—too high for the police, the animal inspectors, the officials, and the all and sundry who stuck their noses in, to allow anyone into the water. It was dangerous, they said.

Outrageous, is what Queenie thought it was.

The Gypsies had been coming to this spot, washing their horses in the Eden, for more than three hundred years. It was in the manner of a ritual, a cleansing—maybe even close to a religion. But still *others* thought they knew what was best.

There were always these *concerns*, they called them. Not *restrictions*, not *limitations*, but always voiced just so, in such a way as to paint the Travellers in the wrong if they disagreed. Yes, there were risks, but sheer living was a risk. Getting up in the morning and putting on your boots was a risk, but nobody suggested you should stay all day in your bed.

Well, maybe not yet…

Further along the riverbank, near the slipway, she could see her brother arguing with the *gavvers*—the coppers—in charge. Well, perhaps 'arguing' was too strong a word. But she could tell by the angle of his head, the set of his shoulders, that he was doing his best to drive a bargain. He could be the devil of persuasion when there was something he wanted, she knew.

And, sure enough, a few minutes later the barriers that had been blocking the slipway, closing it off, were dragged aside.

The first man down to the water was perhaps the best one to check its depth and flow. There was no denying that Jackson was the tallest man there, and riding the tallest horse by a hand or three.

The Clydesdale walked placidly down the angled concrete, head low for balance. At the bottom, he paused to sniff the water sliding past and blew out a noisy breath through his nostrils. Queenie, seeing the horse's ear flick back and forth, seeking reassurance, got to her feet and moved forward, suddenly uneasy.

Jackson didn't like the hesitation, not when every eye was upon the pair. He gave the big horse a couple of kicks and a slap with the loose end of the lead rope.

The Clydesdale dithered a moment longer, then half-stepped, half-jumped into the river in slow-motion, sending up a tremendous splash.

The crowd cheered and Jackson grinned at them, lifting his hat. The horse kept going, still snorting loudly, lots of knee action. Through the shallows at the entry side of the river and heading for the deeper channel. Jackson tried to turn him but the horse just bent head and neck to the side while his shoulders carried on moving him forward.

Recognising the evasion for what it was, Queenie sucked in a breath. She murmured, "Pull him up, *chal*. Pull him up…"

Jackson sat back and heaved. The horse's head was round almost to his rider's knee but he was still not for turning aside. The river level was past his belly now, and climbing fast up his flanks.

A moment later, the Clydesdale stumbled on the uneven and rapidly deepening river bed. He floundered forward, loosing a huge bow wave, but with his neck pulled round so tight he had no chance to regain his balance. Horse and rider went crashing sideways into the water and completely disappeared beneath the surface.

There came a great shout, initially of laughter, that the giant had taken a ducking. But a second later, the sound veered into alarm. Queenie stared at the churning water where horse and rider had fallen. From this angle, she could see nothing beyond the reflection and the chop. The only sign of Jackson was his hat, floating upside down like a makeshift craft, rotating slowly in the current.

Then the horse reared upward, breaking surface like a breaching whale, coughing and gasping, with red-rimmed nostrils flared, and the white showing all around his eyes.

Men were already running down the slipway, wading through the shallows toward him. They spread their arms, tried to snag the lead rope dangling below his headcollar without getting in the path of those huge feet. One man—she thought it might have been Vano—dived into the deep water after Jackson.

The Clydesdale, thoroughly spooked now, dodged his would-be captors and, with another stumble and lurch, made it onto a high patch of shingle near the side of the river. Ears laid back, he put on a burst of speed, from trot to a near gallop, heading for the bank with a determined look in his eye. People on the grass scrambled out of the way, leaving shoes and bags and spilled drinks behind.

The horse reached the bank in two long strides and launched himself up and out, his huge feet carving great divots of earth and grass as he powered up the steep incline, on a straight path for Queenie and her daughter.

Queenie knew she, too, should dive out of his way but she had suddenly taken root. She curled her arms around Sky's body as if she could protect them both by doing so. At that moment, she could no more have moved her feet than she could have flapped her arms and flown.

Just when she began instinctively to flinch, to close her eyes and tuck in her head, she was aware of the big horse juddering to a stiff-legged halt, very like the colt did, when he was at play in the fields with his dam.

She risked opening her eyes. The horse was standing right in front of her—towering over her, in fact. He was still blowing hard, his sides pumping like the bellows for a furnace. Sheltering Sky's body with her own, she reached out a shaky hand for the sodden lead rope hanging loose under the horse's whiskery chin. All the while, she murmured calming words of nonsense to him, relying on tone to get across her meaning.

She glanced past the horse, saw Vano cradling Jackson. He had him on the surface if not yet out of the water. The big man was not moving. His limbs floated slack and there was blood on his face.

Queenie put a hand to her mouth to cover her gasp of shock.

And, as if he'd heard her, Vano glanced up sharply. He saw her standing there, with the rope to Jackson's horse in her hands, and his expression darkened. Like he knew exactly what she'd done, by asking the horse to look after *her* family before his own.

And, all at once, Queenie felt the chill of fear quiver across her limbs, as if she, too, had taken a plunge into the cold waters of the Eden.

"Here, let me take him," said a voice at her elbow. And Bartley reached across to take the horse from her.

"No." She twitched away from his hand. "I have him. Leave us be."

"But Queenie, darlin'. You're pale as a ghost," he said gently, swinging Sky up into his arms. She clung around his neck and buried her face in his shirt.

Queenie didn't reply, just turned and started walking slowly, clicked to the horse to walk with her. He took a moment to start moving, as if he couldn't quite remember which order to shift his feet.

Bartley fell into step alongside. Even looking down, she could tell he never took his eyes off her face, like he was watching her for signs of guilt. They walked the length of The Sands in silence, the four of them, until the horse had stopped shivering and going up on his toes at every sound. Until his head started to lower, nodding to each stride.

Until the ambulance had nosed through the crowd and Jackson had been loaded inside.

Someone came and took the Clydesdale from her then. Vaguely, she recognised him as one of the pair who'd been with Jackson when he'd threatened Bartley, up on the field—members of his clan. There were no threats now, just sober thanks.

Queenie stood and watched them lead the big horse away without apparent recrimination. That was something, at least.

She turned toward Bartley. Sky, she saw, was fast asleep, still cradled against him. Without needing to be told, he put his free arm around Queenie, pulled her close and held her. Without needing him to say anything, she let him.

After a moment or so, though, she felt the tension in him that didn't let up. She lifted her head from his shoulder, stared into his worried eyes.

"What is it?" she asked. "What else has happened?"

She felt his chest rise and fall on a deep breath. When he spoke it was with a hesitancy that wasn't like him.

"Queenie...I don't know how to... They've found a body..."

37

IT WAS MORE in hope than expectation that Nick rang the twenty-four-hour support line for the retailer of the mobile phone found with Eden Man's body. Sure enough, his call was passed from one extension to another, with him having to repeat his explanation of who he was and what he was after to each person he spoke to.

After the fourth—or it might have been the fifth—time of going through all the details, the frustration was making his brain throb. The guy at the other end of the line said, "No, I can't help you with that, mate," and just when Nick was about to hang up, he added, "*but* I do know someone who might be able to. Let me just check if Alex is in today."

Nick tucked the phone against his shoulder to muffle the awful distortion of the on-hold muzak and rubbed his eyes. They no longer felt quite lined up with the holes in his face.

"Hello? Hello? You still there, mate?"

"Yeah, sorry. Still here."

"As I thought, Alex is off this weekend."

"Oh, well, when—?"

"But, under the circumstances, I think I can let you have a mobile number, eh?"

He thanked the guy and quickly dialled. The phone rang out so long Nick was on the point of giving up when a groggy female voice answered with a bark of, "*What*?"

"I'm sorry to bother you, but I'm trying to contact Alex. Is he there, by any chance?"

There was a long pause, then the voice finally said with awful precision, "'*He*'?" It sounded a lot more awake, but no less annoyed.

Uh-oh.

"Or she," Nick amended quickly. "No reason at all why Alex couldn't be female. None at all. Absolutely not."

There came a short laugh. "Oh, well rescued. Well, not *quite* but nice try, anyway."

"Sorry. *You're* Alex, I assume?"

"Yeah, you got me. Running on too much caffeine, not enough sleep, and a dollop of pissed off that work have given out my number on the only day off I've had in the last month but yeah, you go right ahead. How can I help?"

Nick's turn, if not to laugh, then certainly to smile before he introduced himself and ran through his spiel one more time.

There was another long pause. But just when Nick was expecting another blow-out, Alex said, "Sorry, I was just grabbing my laptop. So, you have only a partial serial number for the phone. What about the serial number for the SIM card itself? Should be between twelve and twenty digits long."

She sounded completely awake now, revving. Nick checked his notes. "Ah, there wasn't one on it, and CSI have tried switching the SIM over into a working phone but it doesn't want to play ball, apparently."

"No number," Alex murmured, almost to herself. "Must be an old one, then…"

"We reckon it could have been in use anywhere from eight to twelve years ago."

"Ooh, a challenge. If you email me whatever you've got of the serial number from the equipment, I could run a search."

"Well, I'm not really supposed—"

"Lighten up, DC. I'd bet you're handling your searches manually, right? You give me as many parameters as you like and I can filter out a lot of the chaff, leave you with the wheatie goodness." She paused. "*Or,* I can just send you a great wodge of data and let you pick through it by hand. Your choice, but it could take you *weeks*."

Nick did laugh then, not just at her tone but at the fact she used his rank as a nick-name. "OK, OK, I'm sold."

"Good. If I'm going to have my first-day-off-in-a-month ruined, at least it will be for something interesting." She reeled off an email address and Nick sent the digits Ty Frost had managed to recover. "You mentioned eight to twelve years ago. Is that when the phone was *first* used, or *last* used?"

"We think that would be when it was last used."

"So, you want someone who had one of our mobiles, with a serial number that matches your partial, but who's shown no activity for at least eight years, and who hasn't upgraded, asked for a PAC code to move their existing number to another network, or cancelled their contract," she said. "Anything else?"

"Males only, aged between nineteen and twenty-four."

"OK, that it?"

"I think so."

"How do you want them sorted?"

Nick thought for a moment. "Geographically, if that's feasible," he said. "Cumbria residents first."

"No problem. You got an email address I can send the results to?"

Nick rattled off his work email. "Alex, thank you *so* much. And I appreciate it's your day off, but when do you think you might be able to get those over to me?"

"Check your inbox, DC," she said cheerfully. Almost on cue, Nick's computer let out a ping to signal incoming mail.

"Wow, that was fast."

"Yeah, well, that's why they pay me the big bucks." Her tone was dry. "Now, your turn to do *me* a favour."

"What's that?"

"Let me know if this leads anywhere—I don't need the details, just the result, OK?"

"Deal."

"Great. Now, sod off would you, and let me go back to sleep."

38

Ty Frost was at his desk when Grace got back to the CSI office at Hunter Lane.

He glanced up when she came in, his expression wary.

"Are you OK?" he asked. "How…was it?"

"Not good." Grace put down her camera bag and dug in the end pocket of it for the memory cards she'd used at the crime scene. As she sank into the chair at her own desk, she felt the energy drain out of her body. "Oh, Ty," she said, not troubling to hide the anguish in her voice. "Never mind run over… He looked like he'd been mauled by a bear."

"Ah…"

Frost got up, looked about to speak, then gestured uncomfortably to the door and went out. Grace hardly noticed him go. She took a deep breath and flicked the memory cards out of their protective cases, fired up her laptop and plugged in the card reader. She'd just set the first one downloading when Frost returned, carrying a cup of weak milky tea that was the same shade of beige as the magnolia paint on the walls. He set it down carefully on the corner of her desk.

"There you go—I put sugar in it," he said. "For the shock."

Grace started to say, "There was no need—" but he looked so crestfallen she simply finished with, "Thank you, Ty. That was very thoughtful."

He sat down again, frowning. "Never easy, when the victims

are young, is it?" he offered at last. "I mean, my first one, I got called out to a bad smash on the M6. Pitch black, freezing fog, a truck jack-knifes, wipes out a family saloon. Parents, grandma and two kids—gone, just like that. It wasn't until the next day, when it got light, we found out grandma had been holding the baby on her lap. Thrown clear in the crash with not a mark on him, but landed down the embankment in a water-filled ditch." He shrugged. "I've always wondered, what might have happened if we'd found him sooner…"

Grace was silent for a moment. For all his air of being an overgrown puppy, Ty was a fully qualified CSI. He had been to more than his share of crime scenes and coped with gathering whatever evidence he found there in a thorough and competent manner. Sometimes, it was easy to forget.

"I know,' she said gently. "The only thing we can do is find the answers—the *what* and the *how*, even if the *why* is sometimes a mystery." She picked up the tea, took a tiny sip and tried not to wince. It was tooth-achingly sweet. As a distraction she nodded to his computer screen and asked, "What are you working on?"

"Oh, Chris Blenkinship's got me running image searches on the design on the medallion he found with Eden Man," he said, tilting his swivel chair backwards onto two of its castors and balancing there. "It's some kind of weird symbol. Not sure what it means—if it means anything at all. I s'pose, sometimes people just decide to wear stuff because they think it looks cool, not because it signifies anything special, right?"

The first card finished downloading. Grace checked all the images were in the correct folder without looking at them too closely. That was something she was going to have to work up to.

"What's the symbol?" she asked, clearing the first card.

He leaned forward and tilted his screen in her direction. "Here, see for yourself."

Grace was just inserting the second memory card. She set that downloading before she looked up, without expectation. And froze.

Frost let the chair rock forward again and land with a thud of wheels on the thin carpet. His eyes were on her face. "You've seen it before," he said. It was almost an accusation rather than a question.

"Yes, I rather think I have…"

"So, what is it?"

"That I *don't* know."

39

"So, what is it then?"

Blenkinship asked the question as soon as he was halfway through the door into the Penrith CSI office. Both Ty Frost and Grace McColl looked up in surprise as he strode in.

"Good morning, Christopher," Grace said, in that infuriating tone of placid condescension she seemed to manage as easily as breathing.

He scowled by way of reply. "I've got a dead body and a ticking clock until half my suspects scatter to the four winds," he snapped. "But, oh, let's not forget the niceties of small talk, by *all* means!"

There was a moment's silence that Blenkinship realised was shock. And—belatedly—that they might just have good reason to view his outburst in that light. He swallowed, took a deliberate grip on the frayed strands of his temper.

"Sorry," he said shortly, "but I've got all the top brass above me breathing fire down my neck to get answers faster than anyone below me seems able to provide them."

Frost looked suitably chastened, but Grace favoured him with a cool stare. "In that case, I would suggest better results *might* be achieved by you keeping that heat *away* from the people who work 'below' you, as you term it, rather than holding a proverbial blow-lamp to the soles of our feet."

"And *I* would suggest that you keep your insubordination to yourself, McColl!"

She raised an eyebrow. "If you feel I'm being insubordinate for objecting to you charging in here without any concession to the norms of decent human behaviour, then let's take this upstairs, by all means."

He stood, hands on hips, and let his breath out between his teeth. "I apologise," he gritted. "I'm under a lot of pressure—"

"As are we all."

"As are we all," he echoed. "But that was no excuse for taking it out on my staff." He closed his eyes for a second, trying to ignore the mental image of putting his hands around her throat and squeezing until she finally lost that icy poise. "Now, would *one* of you, *please*, like to bring me up to speed about the symbol on the medallion, eh? What does it mean?"

She sat back in her chair. "I have no idea."

He threw a disgusted look at the pair of them and whirled away. "Oh, for—"

"*But*," Grace said, her tone cutting through whatever expletive he'd been about to utter. "I *do* know I've seen it before—and recently. *And* I can tell you where to go"—she smiled and put in a measured pause—"in order to find out."

"Where?"

Grace gestured to her computer screen. Blenkinship waited, narrow-eyed, until she tilted it slightly in his direction before he moved to look, wary of being treated as more of a fool by her than he had already.

But as soon as he saw the screen, his interest quickened. There, in close-up, was a whole stack of medallions of varying sizes. The symbol he'd so painstakingly revealed was portrayed in stark clarity among half-a-dozen other hieroglyphs and pictograms.

"Where did you take this?"

"At the Fair," Grace said. "When I was up there yesterday, looking for any vehicles with damage that might correspond to that on the boy's bicycle. I was trying not to make it obvious that I was photographing only vehicles, so I took some other snaps as well—of the stalls and the goods they were selling." She clicked the mouse and zoomed out so the full shot was in view. He saw one stall in a row of others, selling the usual Gypsy tat.

"Where was this stall?"

"Well, I didn't draw a map at the time but I can tell you roughly what area of the field it was in so you—"

He was already shaking his head. "Not me, Grace—you," he said. "You're the one that spotted this and remembered it. Only right that *you* should be the one to follow it up."

She seemed momentarily taken aback, he thought with a certain satisfaction. *About time, too.*

"But…I can't."

"Why not? It could be an important lead."

"It *could* be, or it could be a complete dead end," she said with the first hint of losing her composure. She pointedly checked her wristwatch. "Besides, I don't have time to traipse across to Appleby right now."

"And what's so important you can't be bothered to collect evidence, eh?"

She ignored the jibe. "I have to leave here shortly to get to the boy's post-mortem examination." She rose. In heeled boots she was almost on a level with Blenkinship's own height. On the whole, he preferred it when she was sitting down. "This man— whoever he is—deserves justice. I won't argue with that," she said, her voice entirely reasonable and all the more irritating for that. "But he's been dead a long time and you know as well as I do that the chances of catching his killer, perhaps a decade after the event, are slim. The boy, on the other hand, is a new and active case that surely *must* take precedence?"

"You're right," Blenkinship said. His sudden acquiescence seemed to take the wind out of her. She stared at him blankly. He squared his shoulders. "Which is why *I*, as Head CSI, will attend the PM personally."

Her mouth actually opened and closed without any words emerging. Blenkinship could not help a private victory cheer that he'd finally struck Grace McColl speechless.

"I… You can't," she said, which was no argument at all. "It's *my* case."

"And I'm *your* boss," he said. "So, suck it up, McColl, get your arse to Appleby, and find that medallion, or I *will* be writing you up for insubordination, all right?"

40

Queenie managed to hold herself together until she reached the vardo and climbed stiffly inside. Bartley was with her, his arm apparently loose around her shoulders.

But she could feel him trembling, all the same.

And once they were inside and the doors were closed behind them, she felt her legs go from under her. Bartley scooped her up and laid her onto the bunk, boots and all, despite her half-hearted protests.

"Now then, darlin', calm yourself," he said, as though gentling a horse. "You've had quite the shock."

"Where's Sky?"

"It's OK, Nell's taken her."

Queenie pushed his hands away but when he let go she gripped his sleeve. "How do you know it's…him?"

He stilled his fussing and met her gaze, holding it for a long time. As if he was reckoning how she'd take a piece of news he *knew* she wouldn't want to hear. At last, he took in a deep draught of air, let it out again. And something of the man himself seemed to go with it.

"Because of where they found him," he said simply.

"Because of where they…?" Queenie started to echo. But then her brain caught up with her mouth and the full weight of what he'd said—of what he'd admitted to—settled onto her, pressing down on her chest until she could hardly fill her lungs. She sat up, heard something break inside her head that might have been her very soul. She whispered, "Oh, *Bartley*…"

"No." He took a step back, raised both palms to ward off her grief, her pain. Her accusation. "*I* didn't kill him, Queenie. I swear to you by all that's holy, we only meant to—"

"'*We*'?"

He closed his lips on too much said. She snatched at his hand, held tight when he would have pulled free of her.

"'We'?" she queried again, quieter this time. She saw shame in his eyes, something small and base, and she knew. "You and Vano."

He started on a denial, she saw it plain in his face. But he recognised a lost cause when it was right in front of him. His shoulders slumped a little and he nodded. "Aye."

"So, scaring him wasn't enough for the pair of you?" she said, her voice bitter. "A beating wasn't enough?"

He said nothing, folding in on himself with the guilt of it. A heavy burden, she thought, carried all these years…

"When?" she asked roughly. "How long…?"

He swallowed. She saw the convulsive bob of the Adam's apple in his throat before he mumbled, "Eight years past."

"Eight years," she repeated flatly. "*Eight. Years*? Eight years you've known what became of him. And you never told me. You never told me…"

Her hand dropped away. She pulled her knees up to her chest, wrapped her arms around them.

Bartley stepped back, almost stumbled. "How could I?" he asked, the pain twisting his voice into something close to anger. "*When* could I? When would the time have been right to say to you, 'oh, by the way, you want to know what we did—me and your brother…?' You answer me that, hey—when? On our wedding day?"

"No—"

"Well then, that's—"

"Before then, Bartley. You should have told me *well* before then."

And if you had, *there might have* been *no wedding.*

He nodded, as if she'd said the words out loud, and blew out a quick, derisive breath, sounding like the colt when he was up on his toes and ready for flight.

"Vano, I can understand," she said at last. "But you? What did *you* get from it?"

He looked at her with disbelief. "Are yer blind, Queenie?" he demanded. "Only, he had the last laugh, didn't he? Because I may have got you, but I never really got the whole of you, all this time, did I?"

She stared at him, feeling the tears pool behind her eyes. A fierce pride had her willing them not to fall.

"That we'll never know," she said. "Because you and my brother never gave me the chance to put him behind me."

She turned her head away, rested her cheek on her knees and closed her eyes.

His hand touched her shoulder and she flinched.

"Queenie, I—"

"Go," she said. "Leave me be."

She thought he'd argue. Maybe she even hoped he would. But his hand fell away. She heard his boots on the wooden floor, the latch of the doors opening, closing, and the shudder as he jumped down on the grass. Then nothing.

Queenie wept.

41

───────────

THE ADDRESS NICK was looking for was on the outskirts of one of the little villages just south-west of Penrith. It was an area of pretty stone cottages and converted barns, with not a house number in sight. Property names, where they appeared at all, were on signage that was designed specifically, it seemed to him, to be virtually invisible from the road.

He was getting used to that since he moved up to Cumbria.

Eventually, after waylaying a couple walking two stout Labradors—who turned out to be tourists with less idea of local geography than he did—Nick asked the woman delivering the post. She pointed him to a house he'd driven past three times already because it bore a different name from the one he was looking for.

"Oh yes," the postie said cheerfully. "They changed it a few years back, I think."

Nick smiled wearily at her, left his car where it was and walked down the driveway indicated. There were two cars parked outside, which he took as a good sign of occupancy, and bed linen flapping gently on a line strung between two apple trees.

He'd already worked his way through half the list of dormant phone owners emailed to him by the efficient Alex—the ones who lived in Cumbria, at any rate. He'd divided the others into the different force areas and sent them off to colleagues around the country with a plea for a speedy response. How effective that might prove was anybody's guess.

Some of the names in his own area he'd been able to cross-reference against the local authority property register. If they were still listed, he knew he could discount them. He very much doubted that the long-deceased Eden Man had kept paying his Council Tax all these years.

Nick wasn't entirely sure why he'd decided this particular name deserved a personal visit, though. Only that something about it set his Spidey sense tingling. It seemed to tick all the wrong kind of boxes but in the right kind of ways. Even down to the fact that the young man in question—Owen Liddell—had never been officially reported missing.

And that in itself was suggestive.

There didn't appear to be a doorbell of any kind, but the rusted iron knocker made enough racket when he rapped it against the door to set off frenzied barking somewhere inside the house.

"Oh joy—dogs," he muttered. "I should have brought Grace…"

The door opened at that moment to a woman who was perhaps in her early thirties. She was Asian—possibly of Indian or Pakistani descent, if Nick had to guess—and not quite what he was expecting at all. But, having learned his lesson from the phone call with Alex, he produced his warrant card and said in an entirely neutral tone, "Hello, I'm DC Nick Weston with Cumbria police, ma'am. I'm sorry to trouble you but I'm making enquiries about Owen Liddell. I understand he was living at this address?"

The woman was clearly startled by his presence, both by sight of his official ID and mention of the man's name. Nick felt his pulse rate step up, just a little, as adrenaline pushed into his system.

The woman turned her head slightly, still keeping her eyes on Nick, and called, "Catherine! I think you better come."

She had a classless English accent and long bare legs below frayed cut-off denim jeans and a loose shirt.

"Can't you deal with it, Shanaya? I can't really leave this right now." The voice, also female, drifted from the far reaches of the property.

"Not really," Shanaya said, rolling her eyes at Nick. "It's—"

At that moment there was a terrific scream from the direction of the second woman. Nick charged past Shanaya into the house, shouldering through the doorway off the square hall.

He found himself in a long kitchen-diner with a huge island unit in the centre. A woman wearing an apron and brandishing a very large chef's knife was chasing a pair of Irish Wolfhounds around the island, yelling. One of the Wolfhounds appeared to have an entire joint of meat clenched in its jaws.

When Nick burst in, the dogs saw an escape route and sprinted for the doorway. The woman pointed the knife at Nick and roared, "Stop them!"

More out of instinct than anything else, he succeeded in snagging a hand through the collar of the main culprit as it bounded for the gap. The jolt of it almost took his arm out at the shoulder but he managed to keep his grip and bring the dog up short. Just in time for Shanaya to arrive and cup both hands beneath its jaws with a firm command of, "Give!"

The dog, realising it was outmanoeuvred, dropped its slightly chewed and spat-on prize, with great reluctance, into her hands.

"Oh, well *done*, that man," said the woman with the knife, rushing toward him. Nick let go of the dog's collar and took a precautionary step back with both hands raised.

"*Catherine*," Shanaya protested. "For heaven's sake put that thing down. You're going to get the pair of us arrested. I'll throw these two out into the garden. You…make a cup of tea or something."

"To hell with that," Catherine said, dumping the knife in the Belfast sink. "I think I'm going to open a bottle." She ran the tap, washed her hands and picked up a towel, giving Nick a shrewd gaze. Her voice held the faintest trace of a local accent, long since smoothed over. "So, apart from being slightly pushy but very good at dog-catching, who are you?"

"DC Nick Weston, Cumbria police," Nick said again. "I'm here about Owen Liddell."

The woman froze, just for a second or two, her eyes losing focus. Then she threw the towel onto the worktop and said, "That settles it—I'm *definitely* opening a bottle."

"So, what's all this about Owen?"

It was Shanaya who put the question. Nick frowned, was about to pick his way into the conversation with as much delicacy as he could manage, when Catherine reached over to squeeze the other woman's hand.

"Whatever you would say to me, you can say to Shanaya as well," Catherine said. "We've been married for two years, and were civved for another seven before that."

Now he saw them together, he saw the tell-tale lines beginning at the corners of her eyes and mouth, and realised Catherine was the older of the two by half-a-dozen years. Her hair was a glossy brown with a few hints of grey in her parting, which he knew Lisa would have tutted over. Both were dressed with casual trendiness.

The two women were sitting side-by-side on the high-backed sofa in the sitting room. The fireplace was filled with dried flowers and the French windows were open onto a part of the garden that was *not* accessible to the thieving Wolfhounds—or so Nick hoped. He sat across from them in a wingback chair, his notebook open on his knee. The paint scheme in the room was bright—sunshine yellow walls and sage green woodwork. The contrast between the décor and the very old-fashioned furniture was marked.

"First of all, if I may, what's your relationship to Owen Liddell?" He glanced from one to the other.

"He's my brother," Catherine said. "Although I haven't seen him since before our parents died." She gave a ghosted smile. "We were not exactly what you'd call a close-knit family."

"I understand he hasn't been seen for around ten years, would that be correct?"

"I... Yes," she said, more cautiously now.

"But nobody ever reported him missing?"

"As I said, we were not a close-knit family." Any trace of humour about her had vanished. "Look, what's this about?"

"Oh." Shanaya turned abruptly, straightening, her eyes flicking between Catherine and Nick. "It's to do with those bones found in the Eden valley, isn't it?" she said. "It was on the news this morning."

"My God, is that true?" Catherine said softly. "Have you found Owen?"

And there was something in her voice that Nick had heard many times before in his years as a copper, a combination of both hope and sorrow.

"Things are at a very early stage, ma'am. We have a list of possible identities and we're just trying to eliminate as many as we can from our investigation. Your brother's name—and this address—came up during our enquiries."

He reached into his inside pocket, brought out his phone and opened up the image of the medallion that Blenkinship had issued.

"Can you tell me if this looks familiar? Is it something you might have seen your brother wearing?"

Catherine took the phone with trepidation that turned to puzzlement as she looked at the design. Shanaya leaned in, too. Neither of them showed any hint of recognition.

"I'm sorry," Catherine said at last, disappointment in her voice as she handed back the phone. "It doesn't look like his kind of thing at all. But I left home when he was still at school."

"Any other siblings?"

She shook her head. "No, just the two of us—both disappointments to them in our own way."

"How so?"

Catherine gave Shanaya's hand another squeeze. "Well, they didn't approve of my...life choices, for a start."

"And your brother? What did he do?"

"Fell in love with the 'wrong sort of girl', if you please."

"In what way was she 'wrong'?"

"I don't know that much about her. I'd left by then, don't forget. She was Romany, that I *do* know, which made her beyond the pale as far as my parents were concerned—and far too young for him."

Nick raised an eyebrow, frantically running the numbers in his head. If the date of birth he had for Liddell was correct, he'd only be twenty-nine or thirty now. So, if he'd been missing ten years or so...

"How old was this girl, do you know?"

"Not old enough to be legal, when they first met, that's for sure. They met at the Horse Fair, of course. And I don't know if you've seen those Gypsy girls, detective, but some of them are very...*adult* for their age."

"She led him on, you mean?" Nick tried to keep the scepticism out of his voice.

"*I* don't know," Catherine said. "But her tribe, or clan or whatever it is, didn't approve any more than ours did. They set about him—put him in hospital."

Nick made a note on his pad. "There would be some kind of record of that, presumably?"

"Maybe not." She shrugged. "He wouldn't press charges, so..."

"How badly was he injured?"

"They broke his arm, apparently. Apart from that and concussion, he was just battered and bruised."

Nick hesitated. "Did your brother have any other injuries—broken bones when he was a kid, perhaps?"

"I don't think so... Oh, wait, no, he broke his collarbone years ago. We were both pony mad. I grew out of it before he did. I think that's what drew him to the Horse Fair to begin with."

Nick made a note of that, too, circled it and the arm.

"Would you still have anything of Owen's here?"

"Something that might contain his DNA, you mean?" It was Shanaya who asked.

Catherine threw her a glance that held amusement, despite her alarm.

"She watches too many cop shows on TV," she said. "And I'm not sure there's anything like that around."

"If we have a place to start, we can request his official medical and dental records," Nick said. "I was thinking of diaries, letters, photos?"

"Oh." She let go of Shanaya's hand and rose. "There might be something still in his room. I'll...go and have a look."

When she'd gone, Shanaya asked bluntly, "Is it him?"

"It's really too early to—"

"If you hadn't thought there was a good chance, this would have been a phone call, not a home visit."

Nick returned her level gaze. "Yes. It might be him."

"Oh, thank God for that." She slumped, gave a half-hearted smile at his slightly shocked expression. "You have no idea of how this has been hanging over her—over us. Her parents never made Wills. So when they died, this place passed equally to Catherine and Owen. We've been putting rent money aside for his half, every month since. Just in case he came back." She gestured to the sofa and the wingback chair. "She wouldn't even get rid of the furniture, just in case he might want it."

"You shouldn't get your hopes up," Nick said, unconsciously echoing, "just in case."

"I know but, still… It would be such a *relief*, finally just…to *know*."

Catherine returned, empty handed. She faltered in the doorway at their expectant air.

"I know I boxed up some of his stuff but…I'm not sure where we put it," she said. She sounded almost forlorn.

Shanaya jumped up, went to her and rubbed her arm. "Don't worry, love, we'll look for it later." Her eyes went to Nick. "Can we drop it in to you—when we find it?"

"Of course," Nick said. He dug in his phone case for a business card, held it out. As Catherine moved to take it, he asked, "Tell me, why did nobody report your brother missing, all that time ago?"

Catherine frowned, staring at the card as if it might provide answers. "When he wouldn't give up his Gypsy girlfriend, my parents gave Owen an ultimatum—something along the lines of shape up or ship out. Then, when he went, I think they assumed he'd simply…made his choice."

42

IF THERE WAS one thing Bartley Smith was good at, it was the putting on of the brave face. Well, to be right, it was but one of many things at which he considered himself a pretty handy sort of feller. A man with a little of all trades at his fingertips, you might say. And, if he was pushed to boast, mastery over one or two of them as well.

So, he'd spent a few hours abroad on The Sands, taking in the *craic* with any of his large circle of friends and acquaintances. Smiling and laughing and joking for all he was worth. Being seen about with Ocean by his side, showing him for the good family man.

He was only too aware of the fact that the Fair was three days in and as yet there had been no word at all on the choosing of the next *Shera Rom*.

If truth be told, he didn't want the responsibility of the position and all it entailed. He could feel the weight of it already, dragging at his shoulders, making him stagger. And all he'd done so far was throw his hat into the ring—with little thought and less effort.

Beneath the swagger and the bravado, the thought of taking on the charge of Queenie's clan was scaring him half to pieces. He'd rather face a dozen flaming giants across the blood and straw of any makeshift boxing ring than try to fill old Hezekiah's boots.

The man was a legend. A true *boro rye*—a great man.

Living up to him would take another who was cut from the same cloth.

And in the cold depths of a dark night Bartley feared that he was not the man to do it.

Even for a woman like Queenie.

The way she'd drawn away from him, after he'd told her about the… After he'd told her. It sliced him deep, to see the pain in her eyes, the disappointment, and the fear. But news spread fast at the Fair, it always had. Part of its reason for being was to keep the wheels of the gossip cart turning. He couldn't run the risk that someone else might take it upon themselves to put the word in for him, knowing what they knew.

Especially not if that kindly soul happened to be her brother.

He and Vano had started close, like brothers themselves. But of late they'd drifted—more so since the old man's passing, he'd be the first to admit the fact. Didn't like the direction Vano's thoughts were leading him, if he was speaking plain.

Like most folk born of Travelling blood, Bartley had been taught from the cradle never to back away from a fight. And he'd gained a reputation in the ring, for sure—as a *cooroboshno*, a fighting cock. He'd take on all comers with a wide smile and enough of the gab to make them lose their cool. And, if he was lucky, to forget all about the quickness of his feet, and his fists that were quicker still.

But he never went about *looking* for a fight.

Vano, on the other hand, had something he needed to prove that Bartley suspected his brother by marriage might never be man enough to do. It pushed Vano a step past brave and into downright reckless, if truth be told. The thought of being honour-bound to such a man did not fill him with anything other than foreboding of the bleakest hue.

Now, though, as he and Ocean hopped down from the trap belonging to a *pal,* outside one of the many pubs that Appleby had to offer, he was all smiles, no worries.

Doing a fine job of making like a man without a care in the world.

More of his *pals* arrived, most by trap or on the backs of their ponies. They tethered the animals to the railings and went inside the main bar of the Lady Anne's Arms.

And as soon as the door was closed behind them, the temperature inside the place dropped to winter frost. Bartley looked about him, taking note of suddenly grim faces where only the day before had been, if not smiles of welcome, then at least the straight faces of acceptance.

It was the barmaid who came forward, bunching her glass cloth and tossing it onto the counter as she stepped around it.

"I'm sorry, but I can't serve you," she said, a fierce determination in her voice he hadn't heard before.

"Oh, Maisie, darlin', is *that* how it is between us now?" he said, still smiling. "Does our coin not spend as well as any other?"

"Not today." She moved in a little closer, a pleading for no trouble in her eyes, even as she kept her voice loud and cold. "I'm sorry. Publican's discretion. I'm afraid I'll have to ask you all to leave."

"And yet, there we were, in here only yesterday and there was you, who welcomed us like returning knights from a quest, and with a thirst to match. What's gone to change your mind, hey?"

It was one of the other customers, already seated and drinking, who spoke up.

"A dead child, pulled from the river, that's what."

Bartley looked about him but couldn't place the one who'd said the words. All the faces around the bar looked unfriendly in equal measure.

"That's awful sad. I feel for the family. We all do, to be sure." He glanced left and right, saw nods at his words. He placed a hand on Ocean's bony shoulder and went on carefully, "But whatever happened to the child had *nothing* to do with any of us."

The crowd shifted, disbelieving. Bartley tried not to tense. He had half-a-dozen others with him but one was an old man, leaning on a cane, and Ocean only a *chal* not yet in double figures. Not good odds against maybe *two* dozen with a righteous anger lighting them.

Not good odds at all.

"You would say that, wouldn't you?" someone jeered.

He would have reacted to that. How could he let it lie? But Maisie beat him to it. She turned on them, face flushed.

"Shut up!" she snapped. "Shut up, the lot of you!" She

whirled to face him again, lowered her voice. "If you take on anyone, Bartley Smith, you take on *me*, you hear? *I'm* the one in charge. *I'm* the one that says who drinks in this place and who doesn't. And *I* say not *you*. Not *today*. You say it's nothing to do with you. Well, when that's proven, you'll all be welcome. But until then… I'm sorry."

43

As soon as he had a signal on his mobile, Nick rang DI Pollock. It was only as the phone connected and started to ring out that he realised his inspector was likely to be at lunch.

"Weston," Pollock barked. "This had better be important, lad!"

"Well, sir, I—"

"Wait!"

Nick's voice dried. He realised he was out of the speed limits for the village where Catherine Liddell and her partner lived and was still dawdling along at thirty, much to the disgust of the driver following on behind him. He was so close that Nick could barely see the front of the car's bonnet, never mind the registration plate. He put his foot down. That seemed to infuriate the other driver even more.

"Right, lad," Pollock said then, his voice normal. "What've you got for me?"

"Well, erm, I'm sorry to disturb you at lunch, sir," Nick began. "But—"

"Oh, don't worry about that, lad. To be honest, pie and chips at my desk would have been my choice, and a damn sight faster, an' all. But Superintendent Waingrove demanded I help wine and dine some local big-wig she's intent on schmoozing, and a duller man may I never have the misfortune to meet. So, you could be calling to tell me you've just heard the first bloody cuckoo of spring for all I care, but I try to keep my superiors happy. Now then, talk to me—and if you could drag it out for twenty minutes or so, I'd be much obliged."

"Ah, right you are, sir. Well, I think I may have a line on the identity of Eden Man."

He briefly ran through his contact with the phone importers over the serial number recovered, and his subsequent visit to Owen Liddell's sister.

"Sounds promising, lad," Pollock said. "Good work."

"Thank you, sir. I've already got calls in to chase down Liddell's medical and dental records. I'll get them to Dr Onatade as soon as they come through."

"Damn shame we couldn't have found this out before we fast-tracked the DNA test," Pollock grumbled. "Ah well, all spilt milk under the bridge now, eh?"

"Erm…yes, sir. DC Yardley's looking into the assault the sister mentioned. It happened around eleven years ago. Two Gypsies broke Liddell's arm and put him in hospital, apparently. There were arrests but no charges were brought, so there isn't much to go on."

"Sounds like once he got over the initial shock he had sudden amnesia brought on by an acute attack of realism," Pollock said. "Still, I'll ask around with some of the old lads. I was still in uniform back then and I've a fair idea of who might have been sent to pick 'em up. Most of those Romany lads were hard buggers and if we needed to nick anyone we tended to use the biggest meanest coppers we'd got."

"Right, thank you, sir."

"Presumably the sister didn't know the name of this young lass Liddell was seeing?"

"She said not. She says she was living away from home around then so she only had a vague description of the girl."

"Which was?"

"Jailbait, basically."

Pollock gave a snort of laughter, quickly stifled. "Speaking of Gypsies, have we had any luck getting our hands on Vano Smith —he of the fingerprints on the Elliot kid's bicycle?"

Nick felt his stomach drop. "Er, not yet, sir, no."

"Ah. Ran you off, did they?"

"To be fair, sir, I was pretty heavily outnumbered. And I *was* trying to be diplomatic."

"Well, I'll have a word with Waingrove, see if she can apply a bit of pressure from her side, although it's not going to go down well if it seems like we're only looking in one direction when it comes to suspects for *both* these bodies," he said, almost more to himself than to Nick. "Right, I'm out on the terrace and my superintendent is giving me daggers through the dining room windows. As soon as you've got confirmation of an ID, I want you to dig deep into Liddell's background, lad. See if you can find anyone *else* who might have wanted him dead."

44

ELEANOR McCOLL LINKED her arm through Grace's and leaned her head close.

"Just remind me, darling, what is it we're looking for again?"

Grace suppressed a sigh. Not so much at her mother's question, as at the entire situation. It was ridiculous, sending a qualified CSI on an errand that could be just as easily accomplished by anybody with half a brain who could match an object to a photograph. A child could do it.

Oh God…

"Are you all right, Grace?" Eleanor asked.

Grace gave herself a mental shake. She threw a quick smile in Eleanor's direction.

"Of course," she said. "We're looking for the symbol I showed you. I came across it on one of the stalls along the next row, I think, but I can't recall exactly which one. We need to know what it means."

"Ah, yes, and I'm here as your wing-man, to provide back-up, in case they make you for a rozzer." Her mother's voice was filled with glee.

"A what? Honestly, what kind of TV programmes have you been watching lately?" Grace murmured, not *quite* managing to hide a grin. "That doesn't sound like it came from an adaptation of the Brontë sisters."

"It all depends," her mother returned dryly, "on who's done the adapting."

"Anyway, no—no back-up required." *I hope*, Grace added silently. "I asked you along to help make me look *less* suspicious, not more."

"Ah, like covering fire?"

"No, like local colour."

Eleanor patted her arm, then let go with a light laugh.

"I know. Your face was a picture, though."

Grace gave her a look of mild reproof as they walked the next row of stalls. It took a while, as her mother was interested in everything. She stopped frequently to ask questions of the merchandise, as if she was seriously considering a set of display shelves shaped like a two-metre-high stiletto heel and covered in rhinestones.

"So, Max was round again yesterday," Eleanor said, her eyes on a huge white leather armchair, covered in clear plastic against the dirt and the dust.

"Oh yes," Grace said, entirely noncommittal. "How nice for you both."

Eleanor laughed at her tone. "He firmly believes that you're punishing him for not paying you enough attention while you were married. And that, eventually, you'll get tired of playing at real life, and come back to him."

"Really?" she drawled. "How *fascinating*."

"Yes, it is rather, isn't it? I didn't have the heart to tell him, poor boy."

"Hardly a boy any longer, mother. He's plenty old enough to know better."

"Well, you know what they say, darling—there's no fool like an old fool."

"We *are* still talking about Max?"

"Hm, I fear he won't stop dreaming until he knows for certain there's no hope—that is, until he sees you settle down with somebody else."

"Why on earth should I need the company of anyone else in order to be happy? I *am* settled—with myself. And I have Tallie. Why would I want another man when I have a dog? Far better company *and* she never complains about my cooking."

Eleanor smiled with a certain indulgence that Grace didn't know whether to take with anger or relief.

They drifted apart to walk the next row. When Grace reached

the end and turned, it was to find Eleanor had stopped halfway along the opposite side and was beckoning her over.

"Here, darling, don't you think *these* look rather interesting?" she said as Grace joined her.

The layout of the goods on the stall was not the same as she remembered, but maybe the woman manning it set her wares out differently every day, just to attract a new crowd of potential buyers. But there, tucked away behind window stickers showing the official green and blue Romany flag with the red sixteen-spoke wheel in the centre, was a box of unstrung pendants, all bearing the same design as the one found with Eden Man's remains.

"I'm not sure," Grace said, trying to play it cool.

Eleanor held one up as if picturing it around Grace's neck, then turned to the stallholder. "What does it mean?"

"Mean?" the woman asked, heavy-set enough to be unhappy in the heat. It came through in her voice. She had clearly assessed the pair of them with a quick flick of her eyes and knew they were not fellow Travellers. She did not seem pleased to be mixing with the public and made no pretence of charm.

"Yes, this design, it's rather curious. Does it have any significance?"

The woman shrugged and Eleanor pursed her lips as if in disappointment and leaned across to put the pendant back in its box.

Realising that being unhelpful was going to actively cost her money, the stallholder had a sudden change of heart. She even tried a smile that Grace decided was the stuff children's nightmares were made of.

"Is for luck," the woman said.

"Luck?" Eleanor pressed. She frowned. "I thought that was horseshoes, or four-leaf clovers?"

"This, too," the woman insisted. "And protection. Will protect you *against* bad luck."

"How wonderful. I should get one for you, Grace," Eleanor said. She glanced at the Gypsy. "Or does it only work if you're Romany?"

"No, no. For *gorgios* too."

"Excellent. In that case, I'll take it," Eleanor said. "I haven't seen these anywhere else. Do you make them yourself?"

Out of the corner of her eye, Grace saw a little girl skip up alongside Eleanor. The child was wearing a yellow dress today, and matching ribbons tying her pigtails. Still, Grace had no difficulty recognising her as the girl who so boldly tried to charge her a fiver a time to photograph their colt.

"My *mam* makes those," the little girl said.

Eleanor turned. "Does she? Well, your mother must be *very* clever," she said gravely, her eyes wide. "But mothers often *are*, I find. Don't you?"

The little girl nodded mutely. Not wanting to spook her—or be remembered—Grace moved away, eyes on other items for sale, while her hands went to the camera slung across her shoulder. She moved a suitable distance while her mother was paying for the pendant and discreetly took a couple of wide shots of the stall, making sure to include the registration plate of the open van parked directly behind it. She caught the little girl in a couple of the pictures, looking up at Eleanor. It was hard to tell who was more enamoured of the other.

Then, from between the stalls, slipped a skinny boy of perhaps ten or eleven, who came to stand protectively at the girl's shoulder. He was dressed in jeans and jodhpur boots, a shirt with the cuffs rolled back and an unbuttoned yellow waistcoat in a style twenty years too old for him. His chin was out, aggressive, very much the man.

She saw him say something to Eleanor by way of a challenge. Her mother responded with a serene disregard that clearly threw him, although Grace was too far away to hear their exchange. She knew from experience how hard it was to put Eleanor off her stride. A mere boy, no matter how much cocky swagger he possessed, would be eaten up and spat out in seconds.

And, sure enough, when her transaction was complete, Eleanor walked away, leaving the boy scowling in her wake. Grace snapped a quick shot of the pair before he tugged at the girl's arm to lead her away. *Big brother*, she surmised. Not only watching, but watching over as well.

Eleanor crossed to join her and pressed a brown paper bag into her hand.

"There you go. Mission accomplished."

"What was the boy after?"

Eleanor glanced up from rooting in her handbag. "Hm? Oh,

wanting to sell me something else, I expect. I purposely didn't let him get his foot in the door." She took a quick look at her wrist-watch. "Now then, do you think your boss would stand us a glass of wine on expenses?"

Grace thought of Blenkinship's manner in the office. He had never been exactly good humoured and seemed to be getting worse. Perhaps the added stress of being made up to Head CSI—even in an Acting capacity, as yet unconfirmed—was proving too much for him?

Whatever the reason, being forced to miss the post-mortem exam on the boy from the river was infuriating. Oh, she had no doubts he'd do a competent job but she couldn't help wondering about the little things he might miss. Things which, she knew, *she* might divine.

"I don't know about a glass of wine," she said, her voice dry. "But, knowing Christopher, you'd be lucky to get a glass of water out of him, even if it came out of the river."

"Speaking of the river, one of the other stallholders was telling me they had an accident in there today, with one of the horses…"

45

BLENKINSHIP HAD NEVER *ENJOYED* ATTENDING post-mortem examinations. He wasn't squeamish, far from it, but it all took up valuable time, which, he considered, would be far better spent otherwise engaged.

To his mind, if you had a decent pathologist on staff, you let them get on with the job and didn't interfere—not something he had managed to get across to *all* the people on his team. So, it had not occurred to him, when he pulled rank on Grace McColl, that the prospect of watching Dr Onatade about her work on this *particular* case would cause him undue anxiety.

But it had.

In fact, he got as far as the outer doors before his nerve failed him. As he reached for the handle, he noticed that his hand had a slight tremor. The next thing he knew, he was doubled over the nearest waste bin, bringing back his last meal in racking painful heaves.

"Christopher? Are you all right?"

It *would* have to be Dr Onatade herself who found him, of course. Even if her voice held nothing but concern for his welfare —however much he suspected she might laugh about this with her colleagues later.

She brought him inside, sat him down with a hot damp cloth to wipe his clammy skin, a paper cup of water to wash away the vile taste in his mouth, some gum. Considering she was more used to ministering to the dead than the living, she took care of him with enough thought and skill that he found himself unaccountably emotional.

At last, she perched on the edge of the desk in her office, where he half-sat, half-lay, sprawled on the visitors' sofa. She eyed him critically, as he imagined she did with most of her work. The only difference being that he wasn't about to leave here with a large Y incision decorating the front of his chest—or so he hoped.

"Sorry, doctor. I'm holding up proceedings," he managed at last.

She dismissed his apology with an airy wave. "My patient will be just as dead an hour from now as he was an hour ago," she said. "It's *you* I'm concerned about, Christopher. Are you sick?"

"Might have been something I ate, maybe, eh?" he suggested. "Anyway, we best get on." He tried to rise. The room tilted wildly, seeming to whip the sofa out from under him. If Dr Onatade hadn't grabbed his arm to steady him, he doubted he would have found it again on the way down.

"*You* are staying put," she said firmly. "Have a nap or something—you won't be disturbed here."

"Away with you. I'm fine—"

She gave him a hard stare and there was no mistaking the grit in her voice. "Don't make me go over your head, Christopher, and have you declared unfit for duty." She patted his shoulder. "I know how important this case is to you—to all of us. I'll put his clothes to one side for you to bag up and I'll come to find you as *soon* as I have the results."

———

"THE BODY IS that of a young boy, aged approximately eight to ten years old," Dr Onatade began in a measured tone. "His injuries are…extensive. There is major trauma to the head, chest, and torso, and considerable damage to the limbs. Also, bruising and abrasions on most areas of the body. At this stage it is not immediately apparent which of his numerous injuries might have been fatal."

She stopped, rested her gloved hands on the steel table in front of her and fixed Blenkinship with an implacable eye across the boy's corpse.

"My goodness, Christopher, when you do something, you certainly go all out, don't you? What did you do—back the car up and run over him again?"

Blenkinship gaped at her, the buzz of shock zipping over his scalp. Before he could form a response, the boy sat up and turned toward him, his one remaining eye wide open, milky. He tried to speak, his ruined jaw unable to form the words. All that emerged was a wrenching gargle. He tried to lift his arm, to point an accusing finger, but the bone of his upper arm was fractured clean through. It first began to tremble, then gradually to droop from the fracture site. As it did so, the sheared end of the bone became visible through the torn skin.

Horrified, Blenkinship lurched back away from the table, hands up to ward him off. He saw Dr Onatade watching the scene calmly, as if this was entirely normal. As if this happened all the time during her post-mortem examinations.

She put a hand on the boy's shoulder—in the same way she had with Blenkinship, only a short while before—and hushed his inarticulate moans.

"Don't try to speak," she told him. "I promise that *I* will speak for you. Grace and I will speak for you."

The boy snarled again and she nodded, somehow understanding what he was struggling to say. Like a dentist communicating with a patient in the chair when she had both hands and a drill in his mouth.

"I know," Dr Onatade said, her voice almost a croon. "You can tell me and we will tell the world. Grace and I will make sure that *everyone* knows what *he* has done to you."

"But…" Blenkinship's voice trailed away. What could he say? That only *parts* of the boy's injuries were down to him? That *none* of it was intentional? That if he'd known the damage the river would do, he would have…what?

Not done it? Not consigned the body to the Eden and watched as the darkness swallowed him like the water?

And he knew, to his shame, that the answer would still have been yes.

The boy continued to wail but now his limbs flopped and flailed, also. Dr Onatade ignored the erratic movements. She carried on preparing for her task, laying out her instruments—scalpel, saw, and rib-spreader.

Blenkinship moved forward again, realised as he did so that he was up to his ankles in water. He glanced down, thankful he was wearing rubber boots and wondering when he'd changed into surgical garb. The water level was rising rapidly, floating detritus from around the room. A box of latex gloves bobbed past, a half bottle of whisky. The same brand he'd been drinking that night.

I had only the one! Or was it two…?

The water was up to his knees now, flooding over the tops of his boots and drenching his feet with biting cold. Dr Onatade appeared not to notice that her autopsy table was starting to lift gently with the rising tide.

The double doors leading out of the suite began to rattle fiercely. He eyed them with apprehension, trying to climb onto a cabinet to escape the encroaching water level. He slipped and fell back with a splash.

"Doctor!"

As he shouted, he looked for her, found both her and the boy now perched on top of the steel table which was hovering somewhere up near the ceiling, bumping against the extractor unit, well clear of the water. Three eyes stared down at him.

Treading water, fighting the forces pulling him under, Blenkinship coughed, managed, "I'm sorry!"

"So am I, Christopher," Dr Onatade said. "But you must realise that you have only yourself to blame."

Then the doors finally gave way and a tidal wave crashed in, crushing him with the weight of his own guilt.

Blenkinship jerked upright, deafened by the rasp of his own breath. His lungs felt sodden and his clothes soaked through. They clung to his body as he shivered.

"Are you all right?" Dr Onatade asked from the doorway.

He glanced about him, slightly dazed. He was in her office, sprawled on the visitor sofa. Everywhere was dry and still. She moved into the room, still in her scrubs, although minus gloves and disposable apron. He wasn't sure if that meant she had finished or was yet to begin. All sense of time had left him.

"Erm, what…?"

"Here, I've made you some ginger and honey tea. No, don't pull faces. It will help to settle your stomach."

He took the proffered cup with bleary thanks, checked his watch and was momentarily dumbfounded by the time that had passed.

A dream. It was just a dream.

Or a nightmare.

He scraped a hand across his scalp, tried to force his brain back into gear. At least he no longer felt in imminent danger of throwing up.

Or he didn't, until he asked, "So, how did the PM go? What did…you find?" He so nearly phrased it, *"What did he tell you?"* but managed to switch course at the last moment.

Dr Onatade frowned and leaned back against the edge of her desk again. "It was…hard to say."

"What do you *mean*?"

Of all the times for her to sound uncertain, this was not one where he wanted to invite speculation. Clear-cut, brief, final— that's what he'd been hoping for.

Now, she sipped her own drink, some kind of fruit tea by the smell of it, before responding. "A huge amount of…damage was done to the body, much of it either at or immediately after the time of death," she said then. "It has served to obfuscate matters —which may have been our killer's intention."

"Aw, come on, pet. He was hit by a vehicle, plain and simple —knocked off his bike, dead, into the river. End of story."

Her eyebrows, visible over the rim of her cup, shot up. She put down her tea, very precisely, onto a coaster on the desktop, before she spoke.

"Since when, Christopher, do *we* dictate the evidence rather than letting *it* dictate to us?"

He rubbed a frustrated hand around the back of his neck. It was still clammy to the touch. "That wasn't what… Well, it's obvious, isn't it—what happened, I mean?"

"Oh?" Rarely had one word been so imbued with scepticism.

Aware of the sheer size of the hole he might be digging for himself, nevertheless Blenkinship plunged in.

"Well, take the bicycle. Grace McColl examined that and came to the conclusion—all right and proper, I've no doubt—that he was hit by a…vehicle of some kind, that ran over the frame of the bike. There was transfer from both the vehicle and the vi— the boy"—he amended quickly—"onto the bicycle."

"Agreed. I've seen Grace's report. It was very thorough."

He nodded. The room was beginning to rotate again and was suddenly very hot. He was aware of the sweat blooming at his armpits and around the waistband of his trousers where his shirt tucked in.

"So, it's logical to assume that…that whoever hit him, realised he was dead and…and…"

"Dumped him in the river like a piece of trash?" Dr Onatade had a way of enunciating her words very clearly when she was annoyed, or upset. She was doing it now. "We all know what happens when we *assume*, Christopher. And why would he—or she—bother to check? After all, the perpetrator had just run over a child. They must have known what they had done, or why did they stop—not to call for help, as you or *I* would have done—but for the sole purpose of disposing of the incriminating evidence?"

Blenkinship silenced the mental alarms going off inside his head and ploughed on, dogged.

"You surely cannot think that, having stopped, as you say, they put the kid into the river without wanting to make absolutely certain that the poor little bugger was actually dead? I mean, maybe they *did* stop to help, like, but when they realised they'd…what they'd done, they panicked, weren't thinking straight?"

"Perhaps they had been drinking, you mean?" She looked thoughtful. "It's a possibility, I suppose, but choosing to get behind the wheel of a motor car when you're inebriated makes you fully responsible for all that happens next, in my opinion. Anyway, speculating on the mind-set of the criminal is rather outside my purview. And yours, too, I would have said."

"But, at least you can confirm that he *was* dead before—"

"Not at all," she interrupted. "That's just it, Christopher. The entire body underwent severe trauma, as I said. In fact, it would be easier to list the bones that are *un*broken rather than the ones that are. The chest cavity has been ruptured and the lungs compromised. Any foam that might have been present in the bronchial passages would have washed away. This makes it impossible to say with any degree of certainty if he died as a result of injuries sustained in the initial collision, or if what *actually* killed him was being put into that river while he was still alive…"

46

Queenie had just checked on the mare and her colt. The little feller was still unsettled from his run-in with Jackson's Clydesdale, looking tucked up and nervous whenever anybody came near. She couldn't help but regret that they'd brought him to this year's Fair, despite all Bartley's persuasions.

It took the colt a while to emerge from sheltering behind his dam to investigate her pockets. She felt sad for him. That he'd learned so soon the world outside the paddock where he'd been born could be a scary and dangerous place.

Walking away, she turned to stare back at him for a few strides, still frowning over this knock to the horse's confidence.

Maybe that was why she didn't see him.

As she turned, head down, an arm dropped around her shoulders, dragging her to the side. Instinctively, she drew in a sharp breath to scream but a hand clamped over her mouth.

She thrashed, lashing out, until a voice growled in her ear, "Queenie! For pity's sake, woman!"

It took her a moment to recognise her brother's voice. It didn't stop her from stamping hard on his instep, just to reinforce her anger at this downright stupid move. There were simpler ways to get her attention, if that's what he was about.

And, if she were honest, she'd admit that it was a relief to be able to take out her frustration on someone, however brief an opportunity that might be.

She stilled and his hands dropped away, but hesitantly, as if he expected her to start on him again. For maybe half a second, she was tempted to do just that.

"Vano! What the devil d'you think you're playing at, brother?" she demanded, shaking herself free of him. He looked about, grabbed her wrist and towed her between two wagons where they were mostly out of easy view.

Then he said meaningfully, "Ah, and I could be asking you the very same question, sister."

"And what is *that* supposed to mean?"

"That horse of Jackson's—what did you do to him?"

She jerked her arm round and out to break his grip. "Nothing. Of course not. Did you not see him come right to me? I caught him, that's all, and walked him about until he'd got over the shock that big oaf put him through—"

"Not then—not *after*," Vano said. "I mean before they went anywhere *near* the river. Did you…intervene with him, like?"

"Did I what?"

She knew what he was getting at, of course she did, but, made truculent by his behaviour of late, she determined to make him spit it out, all the way.

"Oh, come on, Queenie. You know very well what I'm asking. There are those who say they saw you yesterday with the horse —that you were *talking* to him."

She laughed to hide the increased beating of her heart. "Since when is that something to be ashamed of? I've just been talking to the colt, too. Are you going to take me to task for that?" She waited but he didn't answer. "No, I thought not."

"Queenie, you know I'm not a big believer in the old ways but you've always been good with the horses. They do things for you…somehow without you ever having to ask. And there are those who think there's more to it than just an ordinary skill. Look at how the big horse jumped aside when it looked for all the world as if you'd be trampled. And now there's talk—that you had something to do with the accident."

"Put him up to it, you mean?" But even as she scoffed, she remembered asking the horse to take care of 'me and mine'. *Is that what he did?* She felt the fight go out of her like water from a leaking bucket. "Well, I never asked him to hurt anyone."

"Oh, *Queenie*. You *know* how that's going to sound to some of them."

"I know. I'm sorry. Will he be all right—Jackson, I mean? After his ducking?"

"Well, he sank like a rock, so I guess we can say for sure *he's* not a witch," Vano said. Still, the levity of his words did not quite reach his voice. "The doctors reckon he's got the concussion, seeing two of everything, and the headache from hell. They're keeping him at the hospital for a few days. Then he'll be doing nothing more strenuous than laying down for a week or two." He started to turn away but Queenie put a hand on his arm.

"There's more going on with you than this. What is it?"

"Nothing." Vano's smile came too quick and was gone too fast. "It's just…ah, the timing stinks."

"Why? At least Bartley won't have to take him on over some stupid…" Her voice trailed off as she watched the flit of emotions across her brother's face. "Oh, no, what have you done, the two of you?"

"It's nothing that need concern you."

"Oh yes it *is*, brother. When it's *my* man you're using in your latest scheme. Tell me, or…"

"Or what? You've nothing to hold over me on this one."

Not now our father's passed on…

"Tell me," she repeated, icy, "or I'll start running my mouth that you and Bartley had this fight between him and Jackson fixed." She saw his start of surprise and her eyes widened. "You *didn't*! Oh, you pair of fools. You'd start *chingaripen* between the clans—now?"

He bristled, checked again for eavesdroppers anywhere close by, stepped in. "You watch that mouth of yours, my sister. It wasn't like that. As if I'd do anything to cause strife between the clans. I met with some local *gorgio* who wanted a little private entertainment for the purposes of placing bets, that's all. We were to provide the fighters in return for a cut of the take. We thought if it seemed like a genuine feud being settled, they wouldn't…you know."

"Suspect the fight was rigged, is *that* it?" she finished for him. "And no doubt *you* were planning to make a pretty penny on the outcome, seeing as how you'd know it in advance." Queenie tried not to groan out loud. "So, how are you intending to get the pair of you *out* of this fine mess?"

"I don't know." He shrugged a restless shoulder. "Jackson's

in no condition to fight. And even if he *was* prepared to risk it, who'd bet on a man who can't tell which of the two opponents he can see he ought to aim for?"

Her eyes sharpened. "Who else knows of this…*arrangement* of yours?"

"Just me, and Bartley, and Jackson. And I don't think *he* said a word to anyone—not even those two lads who go about with him, although one or other would've been his bottle man in the fight, no doubt."

"What if another steps up for Jackson—wants to take his place and take on Bartley? Some *cooromengro* you've had no dealings with before. What then?"

"Well then, I'm sure we can have a quiet word between us, form an alliance of some kind."

He was trying to placate—she could hear it in his voice, but still the anger welled in her. "I can't *believe* you'd encourage Bartley to go up against that giant. He swore to me he'd put all that behind him."

"It was a chance for some good *luvvo*," Vano protested. "Too good to turn away."

"*Dinnelo*! What use is *money* if he's crippled or killed?"

He stared her down. "Now then, if that's the way things are, you'd know as well as I do that the *only* thing of any use is money."

Queenie closed her eyes a moment. When their father was ill —dying—and it was either continue in one stay for him to get the care he needed, or travel and work… Well, yes, *then* they had known what it was like to go without.

"And just who *was* this local *gorgio* you were meeting?"

But he shook his head, a stubborn jut to his chin. "Nobody you've met."

"*Yet*," Queenie put in, ignoring his scowl. As a thought came to her, she asked abruptly, "Was *that* why you camped down at Water Yat, the night the young *chavo* went missing—to meet with the *gorgio*?"

Reluctantly, he nodded. "This was nothing to do with us. They've nothing on us."

"Oh, you think they need *proof* to condemn us now?" She fisted her hands into his shirt and shook him. "Don't you *know* what you've *done*? The word has spread. *Two* of the pubs in the town turned us away today because of the *chavo* who came dead out of the river. We were there when he was lost and we were there when he was found again. And now even those who've been friends to us in the past are turning against us. And if you can't see—"

But Vano just slapped her hands away and pushed her—a hard shove to the chest that stole her breath and made her stumble.

"As I said before, you best watch your mouth, my sister. If that *rom* of yours is not willing to put you in your place, *I* am." His face, his voice, was tight with anger. "I'm man of this family and I won't be held to account by a *chi* such as you!"

Trembling, Queenie watched him stride away. And a part of her mind numbly registered that the Romani word *chi* not only meant *child*, *daughter*, or *girl*.

It also meant *nothing*.

47

As NICK WALKED into the CID office at Hunter Lane, DC Yardley spun in his chair to face him.

"Ah, the very man."

Some residual wariness put a momentary hitch in Nick's stride. It took him a second to remember that things had moved up to a slightly friendlier level in recent months.

"What's up?"

"Well, mate, I've been digging up the dirt on the pair of gyppos who—"

Nick paused again, halfway through sliding his jacket onto the back of his seat, to give Yardley a hard stare. "You what?"

Unabashed, the other man merely grinned at him. "Sorry—I meant to say the 'two esteemed members of the Travelling community', of course."

Nick sighed. "I know you think it's only a word, Dave, but you can't deny it's an attitude as well. Can you imagine if anybody here used that kind of derogatory slang to describe someone who was black? Or a woman? Pollock would kick their arse for them. And quite right, too."

"OK, reverend, I take your point." Yardley held up both hands in surrender that was not quite as mock, or mocking, as it might have been. "Now we've got *that* out of the way, you interested in what I've found out or not, eh?"

"Of course."

They moved across to the murder boards. Half the time, they

had no need for a board at all. Now they had two going at the same time—one for the bones labelled 'Eden Man' and one 'Jordan Elliot'.

While he was out, Nick noticed that Yardley had written 'Owen Liddell?' under 'Eden Man'. Next to it was a hastily printed-out DVLA picture from Liddell's driving licence. The image did Owen no favours but, until his sister dug out something better, it was all they had.

"Have we had confirmation on Liddell yet?" Yardley asked, picking up a marker pen.

Nick shook his head. "I'm waiting for Dr Onatade to compare his medical and dental records."

Yardley pulled a face. "Shame, because if it *is* him, I had some big news for you. Well, it might *still* be big news but—"

"Just get *on* with it, Dave, will you?"

Yardley came over all businesslike. "Care to take a guess who was nicked for beating up Liddell eleven years ago?" Nick glared at him and he grinned again, pinning up a picture Nick recognised onto the Liddell board.

"Vano Smith," Nick murmured.

"The very same," Yardley agreed, drawing a connecting line between the two boards. "Back then he was of No Fixed Abode, although he now has an address in Sheffield. Bit of form but nothing violent. Couple of 'handling stolen goods' but mostly traffic and trespass offences going back donkey's years, from just about every force in the country."

"What about offences on our patch?" Nick asked.

Yardley glanced at the print-out in his hand. "Last one was… eight years ago, by the looks of it. He was pulled over in Kirkby Stephen for leaving the scene of an accident, no number plate lights, and neither he nor his passenger were wearing their seatbelts."

"Sounds like a real Al Capone," Nick said dryly. "Nothing since then?"

"Not round *here*, anyway." He wagged a finger. "And hey, they caught Capone for tax fraud in the end, don't forget, mate. He didn't exactly go out in a blaze of glory."

"All right, all right. What about the second guy?"

"One Patrick Doherty. Also of No Fixed Abode at the time. And there we hit a problem."

Nick glanced at him. "No photo?"

Yardley shook his head. "Apparently we had a big purge of old custody photos after some ruling by the High Court a few years ago. One of the associations who deal with the legal rights of gy—er, the Travelling community—made a mass application to have the arrest photos of all 'unconvicted persons' deleted."

"No driving licence pic or *anything*?"

"Nope. The original arrest record said he was an Irish feller, though, so maybe he went back over there?"

"Hm." Nick studied the picture they *did* have, of Vano Smith. He remembered the man's cocky self-confidence when he'd tried to speak with him.

"So," Yardley said with another grin when Nick didn't immediately comment further, "it looks like you're going to have to take another run at those dragons, eh, St George?"

"Who's doing what with dragons?" demanded Pollock as he came striding in. "Because I'm pretty sure they're currently out of season."

Superintendent Waingrove was hot on Pollock's heels. A tall rangy woman with the wide shoulders of a swimmer, her ability to play the political game earned her both admiration and distrust among the lower ranks. Both DCs shot to their feet at the sight of her, murmuring, "Ma'am," as they did so.

"Sit," she said, as you would a pair of dogs. Her gimlet eye landed on Nick. "I understand you may have identified our mystery man, DC Weston. Let's hear it."

Nick wasn't sure why he should have been surprised that she knew his name but he was a little unsettled by it, even so. He pinned on a neutral expression and gave her the bare facts of it, then sent the ball firmly onto Yardley's side of the court to explain about the men who'd been arrested—if not charged— with Owen Liddell's assault.

"Hm, not bad—both of you," she said when they were done, sounding strangely disappointed to be dishing out such praise. She turned to Pollock. "Brian—plan of attack?"

"Looks like dragons *might* be in season after all," Pollock said with just a flicker of humour in his tone. "We could try asking the Gardai in Dublin what they have on this Patrick Doherty. But my money's on this Vano Smith—if anyone knows where Doherty is, it's probably him." He paused, looking thoughtful.

"So, Vano Smith is connected to *both* our victims. If we want to scoop him up, though, we may have to go in mob-handed."

"Absolutely *not*," Waingrove thundered. "As head of the multi-agency committee, I will submit a request that this man voluntarily consents to interview—that's always supposing he *is* present at this year's event, obviously. But there will be *no* heavy-handed tactics, is that understood?"

"With all due respect, ma'am, FLO has already confirmed his presence, and this *is* a *murder* enquiry." Pollock's voice was deceptively mild. "If this lad *did* have anything to do with either Jordan Elliot *or* Owen Liddell's deaths, he's hardly likely to agree to just hand himself over, is he?"

"These are people who have dealt with prejudice and racial slurs their *entire* lives," Waingrove said. "Besides anything else, the *only* way we can police the annual Fair is with the co-opera-tion and support of the Travelling community." Behind Wain-grove's back, Yardley rolled his eyes. "Otherwise, it would be chaos. And with the leadership situation in a state of flux," she went on, "we don't want to do *anything* that might provoke them into electing a *Shera Rom* who is more…*militant*, shall we say."

"Ma'am," Pollock acknowledged shortly. Waingrove shot him a narrow-eyed glare but he'd kept it just a sliver the right side of insolence.

"I'm glad we understand each other, detective inspector," she said tightly. Her gaze skimmed over Nick and Yardley. "So, find a way to talk to these people that *doesn't* involve starting a riot, yes?"

48

"WHAT WAS THAT?"

Grace paused, frowning. "What was what?"

They were partway along the evocatively named Doomgate, a narrow street that ran parallel to the main thoroughfare, with rows of houses cheek by jowl on either side, their front steps leading straight out onto the footpath.

Grace had been checking the images on the rear view-screen of the Canon as they walked back up the hill toward her mother's house. She would be the first to admit that she was not paying her fullest attention to what might be going on about them.

"You always were in a world of your own," Eleanor said, smiling. She checked up and down the street, stepped off the kerb and started to cross over. As far as Grace could see, they were the only ones in sight. She slung the camera onto her shoulder by its strap and followed.

Up ahead, on the left, was a narrow gap between the terraces —no doubt an access ginnel to the tiny yards at the rear of each property. As they neared, Grace heard the sounds of a scuffle, muffled blows and grunts. She put a hand on Eleanor's arm.

"Mum, just wait a moment, will you?"

"Wait?" Eleanor repeated in an affronted whisper. "It sounds like someone's taking a beating and you want me to *wait*?"

"Yes, I want *you* to wait here while *I* take a look. I am the professional here, after all."

"I hate to break this to you, darling, but strictly speaking you're not *actually* a police officer." Eleanor looked about her, as if hoping one might magically appear at any moment. With the number of them present in the town, Grace considered, it wasn't an unreasonable prospect.

Still there was no-one else in view. She sighed.

"No, I'm not," she agreed, "but *they* won't know that, will they?"

She slipped the camera bag off her shoulder, dropped it behind the nearest parked car, and handed the camera over to her mother. Then she took a deep breath and stepped into the open end of the ginnel.

The fight was five against one. Hardly fair, even if two of the attackers seemed to be playing little part in the proceedings other than egging-on the rest. If any of them were yet in double figures, Grace would have been very surprised.

And that, somehow, made it all the more shocking.

Their victim was on the ground. She caught no more than a glimpse, his back hard up against the stonework, arms curled protectively around his head. They had given up with their fists and were now using their feet, kicking him in desultory bursts. The grunts she and Eleanor heard were from that effort. The boy on the ground made no noise at all.

"And just WHAT do you think YOU'RE doing?" Grace thundered in her best taking-charge-of-a-crime-scene voice.

The kids leapt back in conditioned response. For a moment she saw them hesitate, as if unsure whether to bluff it out or run. She sensed movement behind her, snapped her head sideways to see Eleanor had completely ignored her instruction and was now standing at the mouth of the ginnel. She had the Canon raised to her eye as if about to record their wrongdoing.

That was enough to make the kids scatter. They bolted for the far end of the alleyway in a clatter of boots on cobbles, and disappeared from view.

Grace had no intention of trying to catch up with them. Instead, she threw her mother a brief look of reproach and hurried to the boy on the ground.

Tucked in tight like a hedgehog, he still hadn't moved. But when Grace gently touched his shoulder he flinched. It was the only outward sign of consciousness.

"It's all right. They've gone. You're OK."

For a few moments longer, he remained motionless, then he brought his hands down very slowly and raised his head.

And at once she recognised him as the Gypsy boy she'd last seen through the lens of her camera—he and the little girl she took to be his sister. Apart from a nasty cut to his forehead, his arms had saved his face from damage, although his eyes were bloodshot and swollen. He knuckled away the tears that streaked his cheeks, scowling furiously. Grace understood his distress—as much at being caught in a position of weakness as at the physical harm.

So she didn't touch him, as instinct urged her to do. And she held Eleanor back when she would have done the same.

Treat him as the man he's desperate to be.

She stepped back, curbed the words of sympathy and comfort, and instead asked, "Can you stand?"

He glanced up at her then, a wary surprise in his face. After a moment, he thinned his mouth and gave a small nod. Grace hardened her grip on Eleanor's arm as he struggled to rise, leaning heavily on the stonework behind him for support. As he straightened, some inner pain snagged him. He sucked in a breath that, in turn, made him cough, and that doubled him over again.

Eleanor wrenched free and crouched beside him, her arm around his bony shoulders. Over his head, her gaze met Grace's with concern.

"We need to get him to a hospital or, at the very least, a doctor," she said. "Even the St John's Ambulance, if they're here."

"No!" the boy said instantly. His voice was high and cracked. It set him coughing again and he bent into it, banding his arms around his ribs while he did so.

"Well, we certainly need to get him off the street," Grace said. She frowned, thinking through the logistics of it. "If I—"

Before she could get much further, a warbling tune she recognised began to play. Eleanor ignored it. Grace rolled her eyes. *She can hear a street fight in an alley but can't recognise her own mobile.*

"Mum, that's *your* phone ringing."

"Oh yes, so it is." Eleanor pulled the phone out of her bag and checked the incoming caller. "Oh, this might be rather handy," she said, and pressed a button. "Max! How lovely. Where are you?"

She must have had the volume up high because even without the phone on speaker, Grace heard Max say, "Sitting outside your house, darling. More to the point, where are *you*?"

"So you're in your car. Excellent, I'll guide you to us." And she walked back toward Doomgate with the phone still to her ear, leaving Grace and the boy eyeing each other with caution.

"That lady is my mother," Grace said. "She lives at the top of the hill here. We'll take you back there and get you patched up, is that OK?"

The boy said nothing. She could almost see the warring emotions flitting across his features, so she added, "You don't want them to *know* they hurt you, do you?"

"What, those *gorgios* who set about me?" he asked with a sneer. "What do I care about *them*?"

Grace didn't rise to that. "I didn't *know* any of those kids," she said. "But I recognised the look of them. And they weren't locals, were they?"

The boy's eyes narrowed. "That's racial stereotyping, that is."

"No, it's using my observational skills. Local kids wear trainers, or sandals. The boys were in boots—proper boots with steel segs at the toes and heels, as you must know to your cost. And they were dressed too smartly—all in their best. Local kids wouldn't bother, just for the Fair. But for the Travelling folk this is an important occasion. You dress for it, make a show."

She paused, watching his glower increase as he searched for a comeback, a denial, and couldn't find his way into one. Finally, he slumped, lifted one shoulder in defeat.

"What did they have against you?"

"'S'nothing," he muttered.

At the end of the ginnel, Grace saw Max's car pull to a halt. Eleanor waved her forward. She glanced at the boy. "Hm, well, before they decide to come back and finish the 'nothing' they started, shall we get you out of here?"

49

"WELL," Chris Blenkinship said, "that's a bit shit, isn't it?"

"I'm glad *you* think it's funny," the bar manageress shot back. "You're not the one who spent three hours this morning scrubbing that barbecue."

They stood in the beer garden of the Lady Anne's Arms, looking at a substantial brick barbecue with a gleaming stainless steel grille suspended over a tray already filled with charcoal and chips of hickory, ready for the lunchtime rush.

Right in the middle of the grille was the largest pile of recently-deposited excrement Blenkinship had ever had the misfortune to encounter. The flies were spinning themselves into raptures over it.

"And you saw nothing suspicious?" he asked, pulling on a second pair of nitrile gloves. There were times when you really couldn't be *too* careful.

The manageress, Maisie, glowered at him. "Do you honestly think, if I'd seen somebody taking a dump on *our* barbecue, that a) I wouldn't have screamed blue murder at 'em, and b) it might have slipped my mind?"

"All right, pet, I have to ask," he muttered. Maisie gave a muffled expletive and took a rapid step back as he opened an evidence bag and, for want of an alternative, picked up one end of the stool between finger and thumb.

It lifted almost as one long sausage link of ordure. He dropped it into the bag and peeled off the outer gloves, sealing them inside, too. If things went as far as forensic examination, he was more than happy to let the lab techs deal with separating them.

"Gawd, I wouldn't have your job, mate," called one of the pub regulars. A group of them had ventured outside to watch the entertainment, most of which was coming at his expense. Blenkinship noted that they stayed well out of olfactory range, though.

"So, d'you have any thoughts on who might be responsible for this?" he asked as he initialled the label.

Maisie folded her arms. "I hope you're not inferring that I might be able to recognise *anybody* by the shape of their shit."

"No, pet, *I'm* not implying anything. *You're* the one who's inferring it," he corrected. "What I meant was, have you had any trouble lately? Anybody you think might be holding a grudge against you or the pub?"

"It's them gyppos," another of the regulars said. "Stands to reason, don't it?"

Blenkinship turned toward them. "What does?"

"A group of 'em came in earlier, bold as brass, like nothing had 'appened," the man said. "But our Maisie, she wasn't 'aving none of it."

Blenkinship sealed the 'evidence' inside a second bag, just to be doubly sure none of it escaped, and glanced at the manageress again. "Were they causing a problem?"

"She didn't give 'em no chance to!" The man was in his stride now, aware of his appreciative audience and determined to make the most of the tale in the retelling. "Told the thievin' bunch straight out as how they wasn't welcome 'ere no more and as how they should take their business elsewhere." He gave a rueful laugh. "And they wasn't 'appy about that, was they, lads?"

"No, and it looks like one of 'em brought some of *his* 'business' back here, eh?"

He glanced around for support, received several nods in agreement. They jostled each other and grinned. Blenkinship wished suddenly for a Taser and free licence to use it with impunity.

Meanwhile, he tried to keep his attention on Maisie.

"Why the change of heart about letting them into the pub?"

She reddened. "We heard about that little boy they drowned," she said, lowering her voice. "Threw him in the weir at Kirkby Stephen, so *I* heard. Well, I could hardly let them keep coming into the Lady Anne after that, could I? The locals wouldn't stand for it, and I've got our reputation to consider for the other fifty-odd weeks of the year."

"Too right," agreed the spokesman. "About time we banned 'em altogether. Coming 'ere every year, bringin' nothing but trouble. If it's not red hot or nailed down, they'll be off with it, quick as a flash."

Blenkinship knew he should correct the wilder assumptions but... If the general feeling was that the Gypsies were responsible for the boy's death, well, that took suspicion further away from him, didn't it? He turned back to Maisie. "Had stuff stolen previously, have you?" And he was unable to keep the cynical note out of his voice entirely.

She set her jaw. "When the Fair was on, the year before last, they unscrewed every door in the gents' loos and carried them off for firewood," she said tartly. "After they'd gone, we found the handles and hinges among the ashes on the camping field. Good solid doors they were, too—and not cheap to replace."

"How on earth did they manage to get out of the place carrying a load of doors?"

She jerked her head toward the rear of the building. "Back way—the fire regs insist we keep it unlocked during opening hours."

Blenkinship sighed. He could feel the tightening at the base of his skull that did not bode well.

"So, who knew you were planning to use the barbecue today?" he asked.

"Anybody who could read," she said, jerking her head toward the traffic on the main road running past the pub. "Had it on a board out front, didn't we? 'Lunchtime barbecue—all you can eat'. We've done a few of them. Very popular. Or, it was. Not sure anybody's going to want to eat *anything* that comes off that grille now."

Blenkinship sighed again. The chance of getting a viable suspect in the frame for this was marginal at best, but he knew he had to go through the motions. His lips twisted bitterly at his own unspoken pun.

Yeah, in more ways than one.

Much as he regretted not letting his phone go to voicemail when the call came in for this one, you couldn't pick and choose.

He checked back through the photographs he'd taken of the offending item in situ, and then studied the barbecue's construction. Brick and block outer supports with ledges for the charcoal tray and the grille above. The grille was at worktop height, convenient for cooking over. And the bricks extended upward on three sides to stop the smoke blowing in all directions. There was no way, he reckoned, anybody could suspend themselves over the grille without leaning heavily on two of those walls to maintain the position—particularly if they had their trousers around their ankles at the time.

He mimed placing his gloved hands above the bricks, looking at the angles. This was greeted by howls of laughter from the regulars. Blenkinship gritted his teeth and did his best to ignore the catcalls as he reached for his fingerprint powder and dusted the area.

Sure enough, he managed to lift a couple of decent prints as well as numerous smudges and partials.

He could have run the prints from his laptop while he was still out in the beer garden, but chose to retreat to his vehicle parked in front of the pub. At least he wouldn't have a crowd of boisterous gawpers to cope with there.

He was just squeezing through the bin area along the side of the pub itself when his mobile rang. Blenkinship fumbled for it, juggling his crime-scene kit and evidence samples, and just managed to get to the Receive icon before it went to voicemail.

"Yes!" he barked.

"Oh, er, is that CSI Blenkinsop?" asked a girl at the other end of the line, sounding hesitant.

"*Head* CSI Blenkin*ship*, yes." He lifted the phone away from his face just long enough to see an unrecognised number on the display. "Who the hell's this?"

"Oh, er, I'm with the forensics lab. I'm just calling to let you know we have the results of the urgent DNA test on your unknown adult male and—"

"Wait a minute," Blenkinship cut across her. "I thought that had been cancelled. We're ID'ing him via medical and dental instead!"

"Ah, I see… Well, I don't have anything to say that on my system. When did you say the cancellation was made?"

"I don't know! I…"

But as he spoke, Blenkinship realised that he *did* know. It had been top of his To Do list before he'd been called out to this farce at the pub. He'd tried, mind you, but the line was busy and rather than sit all the way through the telephone system's menu choices and finally leave a voicemail, he'd decided to do it later instead.

Only, now, *later* had become *too late*.

He swore under his breath, although judging by the girl's sharp intake of breath, not far *enough* under his breath for her not to hear, and to assume it was aimed in her direction rather than at himself.

"I'm sorry, Mr Blenkinsop," she snapped. "But if there's nothing on the system here, then the communication breakdown must be at *your* end."

"All right, pet, don't get your knickers in a twist. Put me through to your manager, would you?"

"No," she said. "She's not here today. In fact, *I'm* the most senior person in. You'll have to try again on Monday morning. Goodbye!" And with a loud click, she ended the call.

Blenkinship was still muttering, much less under his breath this time, when he reached his vehicle.

The Lady Anne had a large car park at the rear, as well as a handful of slots for nose-in parking on the forecourt. These were usually the first to fill, so Blenkinship had left his car, with two wheels on the kerb, in front of one of the neighbouring cottages.

The car was enough in the sun to be baking inside. He stripped half out of his Tyvek suit, knotting the arms around his waist, and climbed into the driver's seat, balancing the laptop on the centre armrest. Cranking the engine, he twisted the air-con onto full cold and adjusted the vents. It took a few moments of feeling like a joint of meat in a fan-assisted oven before it began to take the edge off the stifling heat. At last, some semblance of calm prevailed.

He had just finished uploading the prints and was running them through the database, when someone rapped on his driver's window. He jumped, so sharply that the point of his elbow cracked against the hard plastic grab handle on the door.

Rubbing it, he glared out at the man who appeared to be glaring in at him.

Having attracted his attention—and possibly his wrath—the man took this as invitation to open the door and stick his head in through the gap.

"Oi, what do you think *you're* doing, parking there?" the man demanded, his moustache bristling with affront. "Don't you think I have enough to put up with? My garden's already become a complete no-go zone, what with the noise and the smoke and the fumes, and now you want to take over the *front* of my house as *well*!"

Another strand of Blenkinship's temper stretched, frayed, and snapped.

"What does it *look* like I'm doing?"

"How should *I* know that? You could be surfing porn sites for all I…"

The man's brain finally caught up with his mouth and his voice died away. He had belatedly registered the crime-scene paraphernalia spread over the front passenger seat, and the prominent Cumbria Constabulary logo at the head of the site visible on the computer screen. He stepped back, surveyed Blenkinship's unmarked car with a frown.

"Shouldn't you be in a proper police van or something?" He still sounded aggrieved, as though the lack of decals and reflective tape was a deliberate attempt to trick him.

"Why?"

"So that ordinary members of the public—tax-payers like myself, who, after all, *pay your wages*—can identify you as police personnel from the outset."

Sparks lit flames inside Blenkinship's skull. He clenched his fingers inside the remaining pair of nitrile gloves, attempting to resist the urge to squeeze them around the man's scraggy throat as hard as he could manage.

"Well, now you *have* identified me as police personnel, *sir*," he said, with acidic emphasis, "perhaps you'd better identify *yourself*, if you wouldn't mind?"

"Stubbins," the man mumbled. "Dennis Stubbins."

Blenkinship reached for a notebook and pen and wrote it down, just to make him sweat. "And the address?"

With all the eagerness of a man giving up teeth, Stubbins jerked his head toward the house closest to the pub.

"Thank you, *sir*. You may be aware that there's been an offence committed at the Lady Anne's Arms some time this morning. I don't suppose *you'd* know anything about it?"

The man squirmed and shook his head.

"Well, I'll have one of our uniformed officers pop round shortly to take a statement from you, all the same," Blenkinship said. "Weren't planning on *going* anywhere, were you?"

"What! Why?"

"This afternoon, sir," he repeated innocently. "Are you going to be at home for the next hour or so?"

"Oh! Oh, er, yes, I expect so."

"Good. Now, if you'll excuse me, sir. I have a crime scene to process."

Stubbins just managed to shift his fingers away from the top of the car door before Blenkinship slammed it shut again. In his door mirror, he watched the man scurry back into his cottage, glancing over his shoulder several times.

"Shifty little bugger, aren't you?" Blenkinship murmured.

His eyes flicked to the door, where the man's clammy fingers had left prints clearly visible on the glass.

"Ah well, in for a penny…"

And he reached for his crime-scene kit.

50

VANO SMITH CONSIDERED himself a careful sort of man. Never more so than when there was something he needed to be careful about. In this case, he was balancing on a fine edge between being seen about the Fair by the right people, and *not* being seen by those he was doing his best to avoid.

Without, of course, being *seen* trying to avoid them.

He'd just spent an hour or so strolling the horse lines on either side of The Sands, looking at animals with Nell and the baby, playing his part as the family man. He'd left Nell to gossip while he talked serious business with the men, weighed up breeding and condition and bone with a narrowed eye. And from the way they'd listened to his opinion, nodded in agreement when he spoke, he was quietly confident of himself.

There was just one moment that troubled him. One of the fellers who had his eye on a pony for his daughter to cut her teeth on, asked if *Queenie* might give it the once-over. Vano had laughed, until he'd realised the man was serious. Then he'd quickly pursed his lips and said he'd see what he could do, as if considering the loan of a fiddle or some other fine instrument.

As if she was his to control.

Vano had long since realised that his sister followed her own star.

Maybe it was something to do with losing their *dieya* so young. A girl learned from her mother, how to grow like her—in deed if not in thought.

And yes, after a bit of a wild start, she'd taken to the traces of her life, as it were. She'd married the Romany *chal* her father had chosen for her, borne him children, kept their vardo looking polished as fresh paint.

But still…there was something behind her compliance that didn't always lay as *quietly* as it should. Times when Bartley gave her too much free rein. And if Vano pushed her occasionally, maybe it was by way of seeing how far she'd let him go before she pushed back. Like worrying at an aching tooth, hoping there would be one last explosion of pain and then it might, finally, subside.

Only, he wasn't too sure he wanted to be close by, if Queenie ever *truly* erupted.

Now, he cut alongside the river on the footpath that ran between the woods and the playing fields of the grammar school near the top of the hill. He was heading for the flashing lane, and while he *could* have walked up Battlebarrow with the rest, somehow he'd rather just turn up from place to place, without being seen to hurry from one to another. It was one thing to have a definite plan of where he was going. It was another to telegraph it to the world.

So he walked quickly between the trees, avoiding the muddy patches from the recent rain as he climbed the track. One hand was in his pocket, feeling the fat roll of cash there, which was always a happy happenstance.

When a man appeared at the top of the path and halted, with every sign of both intention and intent, Vano felt his step falter. He glanced around out of instinct, saw another coming up behind him. Nothing casual about it—the man following was there with a purpose.

No choice but to brazen it out.

Even if, as he drew closer and recognised the feller waiting for him, he felt a tightening in his gut. He tipped the brim of his hat a little further up so he had a better view of the man's face, and pasted on a cool smile.

"Now then, *miro rye*, what brings you here?" It hurt his teeth to call him "my lord" but Vano knew there was as much to be gained by the *spinyor* as the *ran*—the carrot as the rod. At least until there was no other option to be taken…

"Heard about the big man, eh," he grunted, straight to the

point and no bothering with the niceties. It was something that the *gorgio* referred to Jackson as "the big man" when he was well over six foot himself, with bulging arms dangling from those wide sloping shoulders. Vano had once seen a great ape in some safari park years before, up so close they could almost have reached out and touched one another. The beast had moved with the same kind of deliberate, slow menace, as if it knew it could crush him without thinking twice about it, so what was the hurry?

"Jackson? T'was indeed an awful shame, that accident," Vano said, keeping his tone absolutely neutral. "A miracle he wasn't drowned."

"Oh aye?" the *gorgio* said, not sounding convinced, regardless. His eyebrows met above the bridge of his nose. "Never mind can he swim—what *I* want to know is, mate, can he fight?"

"Can he *fight*?" Vano repeated blankly. He glanced from the *gorgio's* face to the man behind him. Now there were two of them —where had the third appeared from? A cold feeling pooled at the nape of his neck. "Man, he can barely see nor stand. A lesser man's skull would have been cracked like a *yoro*—that is to say, an egg."

"So, he *can't* fight?" the *gorgio* persisted, worrying at it like an old dog that barks and keeps on barking.

"No, he can't fight."

"Well, that's *unfortunate*, eh? Seeing as we had an...*understanding*, like."

"We're as disappointed as yourselves. And Bartley? Well, he was hoping to get a few decent blows in, to make up for the way Jackson's had about him, these past few days. But what can you do?" He shrugged, palms up and out. "Maybe next year."

He made to step past then, but the big man lumbered sideways, blocking his path. The men behind edged nearer. Vano turned between them and they closed again, the threat all too evident now.

Vano cast about but saw no-one. A part of him was dismayed by the lack of potential allies, and a part relieved there were no witnesses to his humiliation.

The big *gorgio* said, "That don't follow."

"What?"

"Just 'cause the big man can't fight, it don't follow that

there's no fight at all, eh? Must be someone else from his...tribe, or whatever, who's up for it? Always up for a bit of a scrap, you people, eh?"

"Oh, now, it's not as easy as all that. Those two had a bit of a blood feud going, if you catch my meaning? It was sure to turn the fight we talked about into something special. A settling of scores. There's not many wants to get in the middle of something like that."

The man said nothing for a moment, merely dipped into his pocket, deliberately enough to send Vano's pulse rate soaring, and brought out a pack of cigarettes he didn't offer round. When one was stuck between his lips and lit, he blew out his first breath and glared through the smoke.

"Fair seems busy," he said then.

Alarmed by the sudden swerve the conversation had taken, Vano eyed him cautiously, trying to spot the traps he just *knew* lurked behind the words, before responding. "Aye. It is a good year."

The big man took another drag and snorted the smoke out through his nostrils like steam. "So, what with *all* these folk here, you really tellin' me you can't find nobody else prepared to take your lad on? That good, is he? Funny how you never mentioned *that* before, eh?"

Vano caught a gleam of low cunning slither behind the man's eyes. He gave an inward curse that he'd made the old mistake of seeing a slow body and thinking a slow mind.

"'Course he's *that* good," he said, robust. "But against a man like Jackson, well, it's hard to measure up. I mean, the man is, after all, literally a giant. I tell you what, let me see what I can do, hey? Don't hold out too much hope, what with the time we have, but I'll ask around, see if—"

"Oh, you don't need to worry about that none, eh. Sorted it, haven't I?"

"Sorted it?"

"Aye, a mate of mine knows somebody who's a bit handy, like. And he's *more* than willing to go up against your lad. *Gagging* for the chance, he is."

Vano's tongue was so dry it had glued itself to the roof of his mouth. He was forced to swallow before he could ask, "And who might *that* be?"

"Lad called McMahon. Reckons he knows *your* boy from *way* back—before he was all respectable, like. Bit of history *there*, too, I'd say."

"McMahon?" Vano whispered. He cleared his throat. "Now, not so hasty, *pal*—"

"What's your problem, eh?" the *gorgio* demanded. "We wanted a fight and you promised us a good 'un. If there *were* as much bad feeling between them two lads as you reckoned, what's the difference now, eh?"

When Vano didn't speak, he loomed closer still. Close enough to smell the cigarettes on his breath, the garlic of his last night's meal. Vano felt rather than saw the other two surround him. He forced himself to calm, not to start anything that would end badly for him.

"One fighter or another—what's the difference?" The *gorgio* shrugged and then went on, more meaningfully, "that's supposing it *was* all fair and square, like? Because, *if* you *was* trying to pull a fast one on us, well, there are some as would really take *exception* to that, eh?"

"Of course not!" Vano smiled broadly. "Why would we even think of doing something like that to the Gentile folk here, who welcome us back year after year?"

The *gorgio* grunted. "Better not." He stepped back, turning slightly as he did so. Afterwards, Vano realised it was so he wouldn't see the coiling of one long arm, nor the bunching of a hand not much smaller than Jackson's.

As it was, he knew nothing until that fist was buried knuckle-deep in his belly. The air burst from his lungs. He dropped and folded like wet cloth slipping from a line. And he stayed there, hands in the dirt while he fought for his next breath. The three *gorgios* stood around him, looking down.

"Take that as a taster of what will be coming your way if you try anything *stupid*, like," the big *gorgio* said, bending toward him. "Not just you, but your 'pal' Bartley, an' all, if *he* thinks of changing his mind."

"All–all right," Vano managed, still struggling to pull in enough air. "He'll fight your man... I guarantee it."

"See that you do," the big *gorgio* said. He straightened, waited until Vano was recovered enough to get one foot under him, at least. Then he added, "Because, that's a pretty wife you've got—and a prettier sister, eh?"

Vano glanced at him sharply. "Now just wait a minute! You leave my family *out* of this."

The *gorgio* nodded, as if they finally understood one another. "Oh, I will, mate. Unless you force me to do otherwise…"

———

THE THREE MEN watched the Gypsy stumble away along the edge of the playing field, arms still wrapped around his stomach. By the time he reached the far end, where the school had opened up its hard standing for visitors to park their cars, he'd recovered enough to put on a show of nonchalance that was *almost* convincing.

"Nice punch, Karl," one of them said. "You didn't half put the wind up him."

"Had it coming, though, didn't he?" Karl muttered. He finished his cigarette with one last pull and ground the butt underfoot.

"D'you reckon he'll keep his word?"

"Better had do, or there'll be *real* trouble if he don't. They think they can walk in here mob-handed and do what they like. Well, if they try that with me, they're in for a big surprise, eh?"

51

THE FIRST THING NICK NOTICED, when he pulled up outside the address Grace had given to him, was the horse tied to the front porch.

A sturdy looking piebald, it wore no saddle on its back, and the reins of its bridle were buckled around one of the main timber posts of the porch roof. Nick hoped the animal didn't decide to take off, or there was an outside chance of it pulling part of the house down.

So that *was what she meant when she said "You can't miss it."*

He edged cautiously between the flowerbed and the horse's rounded rear end, but it didn't stir beyond a swish of its tail against the flies. One hind hoof rested jauntily on its toe. Nick, who had no experience of horses, wasn't sure if that meant it was completely relaxed or poised to kick out.

He removed his sunglasses and rang the doorbell, keeping a wary eye on the horse while he waited. He couldn't see the animal's eyes at all to gauge its intent. Between the mass of forelock covering more than half its long face, and the blinkers that formed part of the bridle, they were completely hidden.

The door was opened by a very well-preserved and upright older lady.

Nick smiled at her. "Ah, I'd know you for Grace's mother anywhere. She has your bones, ma'am."

The woman blinked in surprise and then laughed.

"Well, I can't make the same claim for you, young man,

because you're not quite what *I* was expecting, but you *have* to be the upstart detective she tries so hard *not* to talk about all the time."

His smile eased into a grin without effort. "Guilty as charged, ma'am."

"Oh, please, call me Eleanor." She opened the door wide. "We're in the kitchen. Do go on through." He stepped past her, carefully shuffling any dust off his shoes on the mat, and noted the little sideways appraisal as she added in a murmur, "And as *we've* been handling things with kid—or perhaps even *velvet*—gloves, I do hope that *doesn't* mean you've come to play the iron fist?"

Nick paused. He'd left his suit jacket in the car, parked in the driveway behind Grace's truck, had loosened his tie and folded back the cuffs of his shirt. He guessed it did serve to make him look as if he meant business.

"Believe it or not, I can be amazingly domesticated when the mood takes me."

"Oh, I do believe you," Eleanor said lightly. "After all, you even wiped your feet…"

She motioned him on toward the back of the house. Nick was reminded of the contrast between this gracious home and the Elliots' dark and dingy farmhouse. The hallway was decorated in shades of pale green and grey, lined with what looked like old family photographs. Nick took in a brief glimpse of a small girl with pigtails in one picture and wondered if it was Grace as a child.

Then he stepped through into the large kitchen that faced out into the rear garden. He got a snapshot of granite countertops and shaker-style cabinetry. In a bay window to one side was a circular oak table, where sat two women.

One was Grace. If he didn't know her better, by her pose he might have thought she was relaxed. But because he *did* know her well, he saw the watchful air.

The other woman at the table was also not entirely a stranger. And if her startled reaction when he entered was anything to go by, she recognised Nick as easily as he recognised her.

It was the mouthy Gypsy woman from Fair Hill. The one who'd made him for a copper and accused him of hate-crime, when he'd made his abortive first attempt to speak with Vano Smith.

"What's *he* doing here?"

Grace regarded her calmly. "You said you'd talk to a friend of mine, Queenie. This is Nick Weston. He's—"

"Oh, I knows what *he* is, all right," she muttered. "Ocean!"

There was a rustling behind the open pantry door and a boy appeared, chewing, with a lump of sticky cake in his hand. He was dressed in jeans and a yellow waistcoat. The waistcoat was unbuttoned and his lack of shirt underneath it showed the livid bruises forming all over his skinny torso.

Nick glanced at him sharply. The boy glared back, his chin up, as defiant as it's possible to be with a mouth stuffed full of lemon drizzle. The action showed the Steri-Strip dressings holding together a cut on his forehead.

Mindful of Eleanor's warning, Nick kept his voice neutral as he asked, "So, would anyone like to tell me what's going on?"

The uneasy silence that followed was broken by Eleanor, breezing in with a small shirt in her hands. "There you go, Ocean," she said, holding it up for his inspection. "A quick sponge and a press and it's good as new. Ah, I see you found the cake. Excellent. I made it fresh this morning."

The boy, Ocean, slipped off the waistcoat without a word and turned to slide his arms into the sleeves of the shirt she offered out to him. Nick's eyes narrowed as he saw the discolouration of the boy's skin continued onto his back.

When Nick turned his attention back to the woman, Queenie, he found her scowling at him.

"He was set upon, so don't go thinking the worst of me and mine," she said. Her eyes went to Ocean, buttoning up his shirt. "What do you say to the lady?"

The boy swallowed his cake and gave Eleanor a shy smile. "*Paracrow tute, baba.*"

Eleanor looked to her for a translation but it was Nick who said, "I believe '*paracrow tute*' means 'I thank you' and '*baba*' means"—he glanced at Queenie, saw her blush—"'grandmother', among other things." It also meant 'old woman' and 'hag' but he wasn't about to tell Eleanor that.

"Where did you learn your Romani?" Queenie asked him and for the first time her voice had lost its edge.

"Oh, I picked it up here and there." Dealing with rogues who made the occasional foray onto the Met's patch, mainly. Nick had always found it an advantage being able to understand what was said around him.

He pulled out a chair and sat alongside Grace, careful not to face the other woman directly and turn this into an interrogation. But still, he couldn't prevent himself from asking, "What happened to Ocean?"

Queenie's scowl was back at once. "Like I said, he was set upon. So don't—"

"Mum and I were on our way back from town when we came across the altercation and were able to…intervene," Grace said. "We brought Ocean back here to patch him up a bit and persuaded him to let us call his mother, Queenie. Queenie *Smith*," she added.

"Ah, any relation to Hezekiah Smith?"

Queenie nodded. "My father. And yes, before you ask, *Vano* Smith, for whom you were searching when we last met, he's my brother. You wished to speak with him about the boy from the river?"

Nick nodded. "I do. The boy was last seen out on his bicycle —a bicycle which was later found in a skip at Water Yat, with his blood on it, and your brother's fingerprints. We need to talk to him about how that came to happen, so we can try to piece together a timeline—a sequence of events."

"Things are…difficult at the moment. I know he would not agree to speak with you. *But*," she added when Nick couldn't suppress a sigh in exasperation, "Vano has already spoken with *me* of what happened. I can tell you what I know. Good enough?"

Nick paused. "Yes, good enough." *For the moment.*

"He had already picked up the bicycle before he saw the blood. He knew it for what it was, so he threw it away, knowing that if it was found in his possession then accusations would be laid against him. We are an easy target—the root of all evil."

"I understand that your brother lives in Sheffield when he's not travelling. Did he come by horse and caravan all the way from Sheffield, just for the Fair?"

If Queenie was surprised by the sudden change of subject,

she didn't show it. "Not this year. His wife just had the baby. They motored to Scotch Corner and came on from there."

"And what about you?"

"We walked all the way, with the horses and the wagon."

"You make charms, don't you?" Grace asked suddenly. "I believe we bought one of yours, earlier today, from one of the stalls at the Fair."

She laid a medallion on the table. Nick had last seen the design engraved into it as a corroded image on Owen Liddell's murder board.

Queenie leaned forward to study it, then nodded. "Aye, that's one of mine."

"What does it signify."

She almost snorted. "You bought it without *knowing*?"

"Well, the woman running the stall told us it was for protection."

"Ah, and so it is."

Nick nodded. "Thank you. That's been very helpful."

"That's it? We can go?"

She started to rise until Nick said, "Oh, there was just one more thing…"

She subsided back into her chair, her back stiffened. "Which is?"

"I know your brother got himself into a bit of trouble about ten years back, with a local guy called Owen Liddell. Can you tell me anything about that?"

"N–no." She frowned. "The name is not familiar to me. Is that all?"

"Almost." He tried a smile. It bounced off. "Do you know anyone called Patrick Doherty?"

"No." Queenie pulled Ocean close toward her, wrapped her arms around the boy as if for comfort.

Something about the action scratched at Nick's senses. "Are you sure?" he persisted. "This Doherty used to hang around with your brother."

"At one time, perhaps," she said, surer now. "But it is not a name I have heard in years. The man you speak of is no longer with us."

52

QUEENIE HUSTLED Ocean out of the house as fast as she could manage, hoping she didn't look as flustered as she felt. They unsettled her, all of them—even the old lady, who acted friendly enough but was a sharp one, for all that.

As they were leaving, she'd touched Ocean's arm, smiled down at him and held out her hand, palm upward. For a second, Queenie had thought she was asking for some kind of hand-slap greeting, the kind the youngsters used. Then Ocean, with hanging head, dragged a small china horse out of his pocket and gave it back to her.

Mortified that they'd caught him nicking, Queenie gave him a sharp poke in the shoulder. "Ah, you *tawno chore*!" She scolded him for the little thief he was. "I taught you better than that."

He twisted out between them, and busied himself unfastening the piebald's reins from the porch, his back purposely turned.

"Ah, he's young," the old lady said with an indulgent smile. "What age is he?"

"*Desh*," Ocean said over his shoulder, glowering. "I'm ten."

In fact, he was barely nine, but Queenie wasn't going to correct him. His pride had taken enough of a hiding this day.

"If you hear anything that might help us, please, call me," the *gavver* said, offering her a business card. Queenie nodded and took it because it was hard to simply refuse. She had no intention of calling. From the look on the man's face, he realised *that* well enough.

They stood watching as she gave Ocean a leg-up onto the piebald's broad back and vaulted up behind. Standing in the sun, the black part of the animal's coat was noticeably hotter under her thighs.

"Thank you, again," she said to the red-haired woman. "We'll not forget this."

She turned the old horse's head toward the gateway and nudged him into action with her calves. He must have realised he was going back to join the others in his temporary herd because he almost broke into an ambling jog.

Once they were out of sight of the house, Queenie wrapped her arms around her son, put her mouth close to his ear. "How *could* you?" she asked. And a beat later she added, "Let them *catch* you stealing?"

"The old lady was sneaky," he complained. "She acted like she wasn't paying no mind to me. But eyes like the hawk." He pouted. "That's not *fair*."

Queenie slapped a big kiss on his ear. He squirmed in protest, giggling. She wanted to ask if he was sure he was all right but knew he wouldn't thank her for fussing. Instead, she held him tight for a moment longer, then asked, more sober, "Who was it set upon you—*gorgios*?"

Because she wouldn't put it past them to engineer such a meeting, one where *she* was in their debt. Not after the way the *gavver*, Weston, had been run off the last time he'd tried to question her brother.

But Ocean shook his head. "They was Romany," he said sourly. "Jackson's clan."

"Did they tell you for why?"

"They said, if you *dook the gry*, then I shall *lel a coorapen*."

"If you bewitch the horse, then I shall get a beating."

"The horse slipped and fell," she said. "That doesn't take bewitching, just a bad *kistro-mengro*."

She felt only a twinge of guilt at calling Jackson a bad horseman. It was better than the alternative.

Ocean was silent while they jogged further down the hill. She saw his shoulders hunch a little before he asked, *"Mam…* That boy they mentioned—the one in the river. Was it…Jordan? Only, I thought I'd see him here, or on the way back, you know?"

Queenie gaped for a moment, then realised the dead boy was one her son had met in previous years. Whenever they camped along Mallerstang, he'd appear, shy, awkward, looking for Ocean, and they'd play together. She'd heard the news and not thought…

"They haven't said so, but I think it might be, yes," she said. "I'm sorry."

"'S'OK." He gave a shrug that tried so hard to be unconcerned it broke her heart.

She wrapped him close again until he began to wriggle. Then she said, "I don't think it would be a good idea to tell your father about…what happened today—or your uncle."

"Tell *Dado* or *Coco* Vano?" Ocean sounded affronted. "When they bested me? No way!"

Queenie almost sighed with relief. It was short-lived as Ocean put one hand on the horse's neck and twisted round so he could see her face. "There is one *other* thing, *Mam*. When they asked of Patrick Doherty, why didn't you tell them that—?"

"Because they didn't need to know," Queenie cut in quickly. "*None* of them *gorgios* need to know. So you keep *that* to yourself, all right?"

53

"Well, did you find out what you needed to know?" Eleanor asked.

The three of them had moved back into the doorway of the house to watch the Romany woman and her son disappear along Scattergate on the piebald gelding. As she spoke, Eleanor's gaze moved between her daughter and the young detective. Having only just met him, she couldn't be sure of his expression. And even as a child, Grace had been hard to read.

Eleanor knew she wasn't going to get an answer out of her when her mobile phone started to ring. Grace turned away to answer it, as if glad of the excuse, leaving Eleanor and Nick standing together.

"Some of it," Nick said. "It's what she *didn't* say that interests me."

"About this Doherty chap?" Eleanor saw his eyebrows rise and smiled. "Even *I* could tell she wasn't being entirely truthful about that."

"And you spotted him taking the ornament." There was added respect in his voice.

Eleanor looked down at the china horse in her hands. "No, I didn't," she admitted. "But I saw his eyes linger on it and, when we came out just now, I saw it was gone. Not exactly a Sherlock Holmes level of deductive reasoning."

"You do yourself a disservice, Eleanor. Not much gets past you, I'll bet."

Like the way you look at my daughter, you mean, when you don't think she's paying attention?

She sighed. "If he'd *asked*, I would have given it to him with pleasure, but I will not allow myself simply to be robbed."

"Well, if they decide to make a return visit, or you should ever need my help, I hope you'll call me," Nick said, handing her a card.

"Thank you." Eleanor thought of the contrast with Grace's ex-husband, who had happily come to their aid until he found out who they were dealing with, and then made his excuses along with a quick exit.

Not that Max was lacking in courage, when it was required.

Grace returned, tucking away her phone. The camera bag was slung onto her shoulder.

"I need to go," she said. "I'm meeting Ty Frost over at Kirkby Stephen. He's already left Penrith, and it would be embarrassing to be so close and then arrive *after* him."

"More trouble?"

If Nick hadn't asked the question, Eleanor probably would have done so herself.

"We're going to carry out a drone survey of the river, upstream from the weir—see if we can find out where Jordan Elliot was put into the water." She paused. "If it *is* Jordan who was found, of course."

"Still no official confirmation?"

"Not yet. I'm expecting the results of the DNA comparison any time now. The moment I hear anything, you'll be the first to know."

Nick grinned at her. "What, even before your boss?"

Grace arched an eyebrow. "He pulled rank on me at the post-mortem exam," she said. "He's not going to do it twice."

54

WHEN CHRIS BLENKINSHIP knocked on the front door of Dennis Stubbins' cottage next to the Lady Anne, he had not only one of the uniformed constables with him, but also the bar manager, Maisie.

"Yes, what's the meaning of this?" Stubbins demanded, drawing himself up to his full height. His nose was almost level with the top button on Blenkinship's shirt. "What's *she* here for?"

"An apology, Mr Stubbins," the constable said.

He sniffed. "Well, better late than never, I suppose. After all the months of inconvenience I've had to put up with—"

"No, sir. *You* are going to be the one to apologise to *her*."

The man floundered, mouth opening and closing several times before he said, voice low with outrage, "I *beg* your *pardon*! I will do *no* such thing."

"Well, that might prove awkward," the constable said, and Blenkinship could see he was struggling to keep a straight face. "I have to inform you, sir, that defecation in a public place is an offence under current legislation, punishable by a hefty fine. As well, of course, as the resultant adverse publicity…"

"*Publicity*?" Stubbins echoed, colour leaching from his face. "I deny it. You can't prove a thing."

"I wouldn't be sure about that, sir, when Mr Blenkinship here has just matched your fingerprints to those on the surround of the barbecue where the, ah…offending deposit was made."

"Downright *offensive* deposit, if you ask me," Maisie put in.

"That's ridiculous! I–I could have been into the pub recently and...come into contact with that barbecue under *entirely* innocent circumstances," Stubbins blustered.

Blenkinship favoured him with a tight smile. *Finally*, his day was taking a turn for the better. "I'm sure you're aware, sir, that we can identify owners who don't pick up after their dogs by analysing the DNA...left behind." He leaned in, conspiratorially. "That doesn't *only* work with dogs."

He thought for a moment the little man was going to faint. "You can't... I can't..." He swallowed. "I'm on the Parish council. And the committee for the bowls club!"

"You should have thought of that before you shit in my barbecue and hoped everyone would blame it on the Gypsies, then," Maisie said.

"Is there no way to avoid...any of this?"

"That's another reason she's here," Blenkinship said. "So that the two of you can work out some kind of suitable restitution."

"A nice healthy donation to The Donkey Sanctuary ought to do it," Maisie said. Just as the relief started to creep across Stubbins' face, she added, "And you can bring your marigolds with you right now, matey. You've got some serious scrubbing to do..."

55

It was around ten miles from Appleby to the weir just north of Kirkby Stephen. Twenty minutes by road, depending on the traffic. Grace took the back lanes through Burrells and Soulby to avoid any possible tail-backs on the A66 from the Fair. She met her share of locals *en route*, who no doubt had the same idea.

She left her Nissan pick-up parked at the roadside near to the gate. There was a chain and padlock wrapped around it that looked secure, but on closer inspection had been forced. Grace remembered the woman who'd reported the body—Wynter Trelawney—saying the Gypsies had called her. She wondered if it was they who'd broken the lock, for the sake of a bit of overnight grazing. Or perhaps the officers who'd first responded?

The metal gate actually had hinge pins rather than needing to be dragged. Grace opened it and went through onto the trampled grass. It was calm and quiet there, with only the murmur of the river tumbling over the weir, and the occasional buzz of cars on the nearby road up to Brough.

Someone, she saw, had laid a bunch of cellophane-wrapped flowers close by the water's edge, a small plush toy in the shape of a horse. Sad little reminders of a life that had not yet outgrown its childhood. And now never would.

She was reminded of the china horse which the boy, Ocean, had tried to steal from her mother's house. Had Ocean's mother lied to them for a reason, or just out of some ingrained distrust and dislike of anything representing rules, constrictions, and law?

Ty Frost arrived a few minutes later, beeping his horn in greeting as he swung his old banger of a Peugeot through the gateway and pulled up alongside the river. She saw the car lurch a little as he jerked the handbrake on with a graunch of the ratchet mechanism. He was a contradiction when it came to equipment. If he valued it, then he treated it with obsessive reverence. If he didn't, with disdainful neglect.

Now, Ty bounced out like a puppy taken to the beach, opened the rear hatch and flung out an arm.

"There you go, Grace. What d'you think of that?"

She peered in to see a spindly looking machine with a central body and two narrow struts leading to a T-piece, with a twin-bladed rotor at the end of each arm. Underneath was the camera, protected by articulated legs like those of a crab. She did not insult Ty's pride and joy by voicing the comparison.

"Very impressive," she said. "What does something like that cost these days?"

He named a figure that made her blink, and he flushed a little at her reaction. "Why do you think I still drive this old heap? I spend my money on tech instead."

"Well, I hope you're billing the force for flight time?"

His answering grin told her that, even if he wasn't making *money* out of the exercise, he was probably enjoying himself too much to care.

"Speaking of flying time, how long have we got in the air with this?"

"Twenty-seven minutes, max. I've got a couple of spare battery packs with me, and a charger, but I'd rather not have to fish it out of the river if I can help it."

As he talked, Ty was assembling his kit, hands working with the speed of familiarity. Grace watched over his shoulder

"What does it record onto?"

"Standard Micro SD card. I put a load in a box on the front seat, if you wouldn't mind grabbing them for me? Then we can get this party started!"

Grace reached in through the passenger door and picked up a plastic box filled with assorted cards. "Any one in particular?"

"Hm? Oh, the largest capacity you can find, if you wouldn't mind."

She sorted through with an exploratory finger. Picked one out and frowned at it. "This one has a note taped to it that says 'CB'. Is that for something special?"

"Ah, no, I brought that to give to you, actually." He flushed again, all but shuffled his feet. "You know that day when the boss ran into Nick Weston's car?" She nodded and he went on, "Well, he told me his dash-cam wasn't working and had me put a new memory card in for him. Said the old one was corrupted or something."

Grace caught the slightly haughty note in his voice. "But you didn't believe him," she said.

"Nah, I think he knew he was in the wrong and was trying to hide it, like. Anyway, he wanted me to chuck the old card but I thought, well, you might want to see if there *is* anything on there that can help Nick." He shrugged, embarrassed. "You never know."

"Thanks, Ty. That's really nice of you. I'll take a look later, when we're all done here." Grace tucked the card into the leg pocket of her cargo trousers. "Now, are we almost ready for take-off?"

56

As soon as they got down to the bottom of Boroughgate, Ocean was twitching to be let down off the piebald, like he'd sat on a nest of ants. Queenie let him off by the memorial on Low Wiend with the vertical sundial on the top of it.

She watched him dart away into the crowd and urged the old horse into a shambling jog-trot across the bridge. He reluctantly obliged, announcing his return with a deafening neigh as they reached the other side of the river.

Queenie leaned forward and stroked one of his long ears. "No point in trying to be stealthy with you about, feller, is there?" she murmured.

But she had a good vantage point from his back, able to scan above the heads of the people, looking for two in particular.

She caught sight of Vano first, in the shallows of the Eden with their father's last colt, washing him down. Then, further in, Bartley doing the same with the mare.

Her first reaction was of hurt—that they hadn't waited for *her* before taking the colt into the Eden for the first time. It was almost like a baptism, and it stung that they'd chosen to do it when she was absent. And without Ocean, who'd be more upset still.

That's when the anger took over. She shook the piebald up and rode him straight down the ramp into the water without a second thought. Vano looked up and saw her and, although he kept a smile pinned firmly on his face, it no longer went all the way up to his eyes.

Oh, you don't want to spoil your campaign image, now do you, brother of mine? Got to show everyone you know how to follow all the old traditions.

She nudged the piebald closer, leaned down to him and hissed, "What the devil d'you think you're about?"

"What do you *think* I'm doing? Trying to get the best price, to honour our father. *That's* what I'm about. Something *you* should have had in mind, my sister."

The piebald began to paw at the water, splashing the pair of them. Vano stepped back and said, more loudly than he needed to, "You'd best take him out before he rolls, with you still on his back."

Queenie, who could read the signs the horse was giving her without the need for such instruction, scowled at him but did as she was bid, growling at the animal when his knees began to droop.

Bartley had seen her arrive and, reading her mood, was already walking the mare toward the slipway, knowing Vano would have little choice but to follow. She moved to intercept her husband, leaned close to his ear and gave him a kiss.

The audience on the riverside laughed and applauded. Bartley grinned at them and caught her wrist, tugging her closer apparently to snatch another.

"What is it?" he demanded quietly.

"The *gavvers*," she said. "They're asking about Patrick Doherty." And she straightened in time to see the worry in his face before he covered it with smiling ease.

"Now then, me darlin'. Don't you be worrying about that."

"But—"

"Trust me, Queenie," he said, all trace of humour gone. "Patrick Doherty is a long time buried and he *won't* be coming back."

57

"Found something?" It was all Grace could do to keep her attention on the road and not on the view-screen held by Ty Frost, alongside her in the passenger seat of the Nissan. The photographer in her was captivated by the superb-quality images being relayed by the drone in flight.

"Not as yet. Ah, hold on…" Frost manipulated the controls with a deft touch that was almost delicate. The picture on the view-screen zoomed in, steadied and refocused. "Nope, just a piece of litter."

"You're coming up to Frank's Bridge," Grace said, glancing in her mirrors and flicking on her indicator. "Watch your altitude."

Frost flashed a quick grin at her, suddenly looking even younger than usual. "Don't worry, this thing's got built-in proximity sensors. Folk in the film industry regularly fly them inside buildings without any problem. Ah, there's a stone bridge just coming up. That the one you were meaning?"

He tilted the screen toward her and Grace risked a quick scan. "That's the one."

"Who was this 'Frank', anyway?"

"A local brewer, apparently. He had the bridge built some time in the sixteen-hundreds to allow the dead to be brought over the river, from Winton and Hartley to St Stephen's for burial. There are even stones at either end of the bridge where they used to rest the coffins."

"How do you *know* all this stuff?"

"I have an enquiring mind, Tyson," she said. "Plus, I was brought up in the Lakes, and I used to spend my spare time going out photographing local landmarks."

He shook his head. At the traffic lights in Kirkby Stephen, Grace turned left, past the Temperance Hall and started to head slowly along Nateby Road. Somewhere further over to their left, the Eden's course wandered in the same direction, weaving back and forth through the fields.

Frost took it slow, pivoting the camera from side to side and zooming in on anything that caught his eye. They knew they could review the footage in more detail later, on a larger screen, but anything that was missed might easily be swept away and lost completely by the time they went back for it.

"How far away can the drone get from us and still be controllable?"

"Four and a half miles, more or less, so don't worry on that score. We're not going to lose it anytime soon."

"Oh, I *do* wish you hadn't said that…"

"Ah, we'll be coming up on Stenkrith in a moment. That might be worth a closer look."

"OK. There's a little car park just the other side of the bridge over the falls," Grace said. "I'll pull in there, shall I?"

Frost nodded.

As soon as they stopped and she turned off the engine, they could hear the rush of water crashing over the waterfall. Frost started walking down the sloping path toward the river. Grace began to follow but an incoming call on her mobile made her pause.

"Go on ahead," she called to Frost, pulling out the phone. "I'll just get this—it's the lab."

She turned back for the Nissan, unlocking it and rifling in the door pocket for a notebook and pen as she answered the call.

"Ah, hello Ms McColl, it's the forensics lab," said a girl's voice, sounding tentative. "You *were* expecting the results of a priority DNA test through today, yes?"

"Certainly," Grace said. "What do you have for me?"

"Oh, right. Just to let you know that the profile you asked for has been sent."

"That's wonderful, although I can't get to my email right at the moment," Grace said, doing a quick mental calculation of time and distance. "Would you mind giving me a quick run-through now?"

"No problem. We actually recovered two distinct DNA samples from the asthma inhaler. One was male, the other female."

"Ah, I *thought* that might be the case," She recalled the little girl, Ollie, who seemed to have a magpie-like approach toward anything that belonged to her brother. Grace could imagine that extended to his asthma inhaler as well. "The male sample—was it a match to our victim?"

"Yes, no doubt about it."

"Thank you." Grace let her eyes close briefly. "Not the news his parents were hoping for, but at least they'll have some closure."

"You're welcome. Please contact me if I can be of any further assistance."

"Of course. Oh, the female sample—that was his sister, yes?"

"No…" The girl sounded hesitant. She said something else but Grace was distracted by a shout from Frost, down near the river. She tucked the phone against her chest while she called, "Just a moment!" And then lifted the phone again. "I'm sorry, I missed that?"

"I said, different parents."

"Really? That's odd. In theory, they should be full siblings."

"Well, I ran the tests myself." The girl's voice frosted. "There's no chance of error at *this* end, I can assure you."

"No, no, I didn't think that for a moment," Grace said quickly. "I know how professional you are there."

"Ah, well," the girl said, somewhat mollified, "I *did* make a pass through the database with both of them, actually, just out of interest."

"Oh, that could be rather useful. Did anything show up?"

"Yes, although I'm not sure if it helps you or makes life more complicated," the girl said. "We got a familial match on the female sample—one Dylan Elliot, Cumbria address. We tested and logged his DNA after an assault charge about eighteen months ago."

"When you say 'a familial match' are we talking *immediate* family?"

"That's right—father and daughter."

"Well, that makes sense, although, as you say, it *does* compli-
cate things somewhat—particularly if Dylan Elliot is no relation
to the *male* sample."

"No...*he* isn't."

"Ah, I wonder if—?"

But Grace's words, and her train of thought, were derailed by
another shout from Frost, slightly more urgent this time.

"Grace! There's something down here. Looks like a bit of the
boy's clothing maybe, but if we don't grab it pronto, we're going
to lose it."

"Look, I'm sorry, I'm needed and I have to go," she said to
the girl at the lab. "Thank you very much. I really appreciate
your speed on this one."

"Oh," the girl said again. "Oh, well, thank *you*. It's my pleasure, although your *boss*, if you don't mind me saying so, could
do with an attitude adjustment."

"Yes, he certainly could," Grace agreed. "And I'll be sure to
mention that to him…"

She ended the call, already hurrying toward the river where
she could see Ty Frost leaning precariously over the rocks at the
edge of the waterfall.

Something about the conversation rubbed at her like a new
boot on a raw heel. Perhaps it was simply that here was someone
else Chris Blenkinship had annoyed.

Whatever it was, she decided, she would deal with it later.

58

THE ELLIOT FARMYARD was deserted when Nick pulled up. He sat in the car for a moment, surveying the scene. He was getting used to the style of buildings on the eastern side of the Lake District, hunkered down into the landscape. The rugged stone farmhouse, built solidly to withstand the harsh Cumbrian winters, and the stone barn looming nearby.

The Elliots' small-holding was made up of old corrugated iron sheds, the sheets dark with rust and their roofs sagging. One had collapsed altogether and been left to die where it foundered. There were a couple of old railway goods wagons, too, which might have been worth something if their timbers weren't slowly rotting into the ground on which they stood. Plastic tanks lay discarded here and there, their purpose undefined, their sides stained green with lichen and mould. And where repairs had been attempted with tarpaulins, wind and weather had ripped them to fluttering tatters.

There was so much to be done to get on top of the place that Nick felt the energy being sucked out of him, just sitting there looking at it.

He climbed out of the car and approached the house. He could hear the sounds of children in the garden, raised in some kind of dispute. A woman's voice shouted at them to no obvious effect. Nick detoured through a rickety wooden gate that led down the side of the house. He emerged on an area of lawn, balding in places and divided by a washing line draped with bed sheets, which a pair of girls, perhaps in their early teens, were squabbling over the best way to peg out. Another, smaller child —Nick recognised Ollie from his previous visit—was making their life more complicated by trying to scale the sheet like a makeshift assault course, and shrieking with glee while she did so, to the overall annoyance of their mother.

Nick's appearance, however, brought an abrupt halt to the proceedings. He was aware of the silence as all eyes turned in his direction. He could see the family resemblance, echoes of Yvonne's face, shades of Dylan's, too, in their cheekbones, their mouth and chin.

He took a step forward and, spell broken, the children dropped the sheet where it lay and scattered as if trained for it. They left their mother standing by her re-dirtied laundry, looking close to the edge of temper.

"Not *you* again. What d'you want *now*?" she demanded.

"A quiet word, Mrs Elliot, if you wouldn't mind." His tone did not make it a question.

More high-pitched squealing broke out, this time from inside the house through the open French windows.

Yvonne gave him a look that was too tired to be as defiant as she no doubt intended. "Well, this is as quiet as it gets round here."

"Is your husband at home?"

"Dyl? He's in his workshop, most likely. Said as how he had some weldin' to do on a trailer. Why? Have you found him—our Jordan? What's the little bugger got to say for his'self?"

And Nick realised then the significance of his mistake in coming straight here. He'd got Grace's phone call about the lab results and, as he was still in Appleby and only a few miles away, had come straight here. He suddenly realised that news of the DNA confirmation of Jordan Elliot's identity had clearly not yet made it along all the necessary official channels, and that his parents had not actually been informed.

He swallowed.

"I have to tell you, Mrs Elliot, that we've had positive identi-fication of a young boy whose body was pulled from the River Eden this morning, near Kirkby Stephen. It *is* Jordan. I'm so very sorry."

It was not the first time Nick had been obliged to deliver such bad news. He'd seen most reactions from heartbroken sobbing, to rage, even hysterical laughter.

Yvonne just stood, frozen, gaze turned inward as if replaying a life not yet lived and finding few highlights to treasure. She gave a single, listless nod. An 'it figures' kind of gesture, as if things had always turned out badly for her, and this was just another in a long line of tragedies and failures that she'd long since learned to accept.

"Mrs Elliot? Can I…get you anything? Call somebody to come and sit with you, perhaps—a relative, or a friend?"

"No, no, there isn't anyone… I'm all right."

The harsh note had gone from her voice. What was left behind was thin, almost without substance, as though only her anger had been sustaining her.

Nick spotted a stack of four grubby plastic chairs near the back wall of the house. He wrestled one loose and planted it behind her.

"Sit down," he coaxed. *Before you fall down.* "Please."

She complied, her legs folding so suddenly that she flumped into the seat.

He moved round in front of her and her gaze tracked him now, silently pleading for the words he knew she wanted but he was unable to say.

That it was all a mistake. That it hadn't happened. And he knew she would be trying to cling to the fragment of time before he appeared, before she knew. When there had still been room for hope.

He crouched in front of her, took her limp hands in his. "We will do *everything* we can to catch whoever did this to Jordan, Yvonne. I *promise* you that."

She frowned, as if he'd offered to paint the grass purple. "What's the use of that? Still be *gone*, won't he?"

Nick found he had no answer to give her, so he just squeezed her hands and said nothing.

Whole minutes ticked past. She didn't cry, just stared sightlessly over his shoulder at the patchy grass and rocked gently in the chair.

The breeze picked up, rippling the sheets like sails on the line. He heard the cries of distant sheep and the buzzing of insects. Even the shrieks of the other children seemed muted.

"Mrs Elliot?" he said at last. "I'm sorry, but I *do* need to ask you some questions. You realise that, don't you?"

He got to his feet. Her eyes tracked him, which was something, even if they held no more comprehension than before.

"What questions?"

"Well, can you think of anyone who might want to...take Jordan—or to harm him?"

"'Course not," she mumbled but it was a knee-jerk response with no thought behind it.

"Someone your husband's had a...disagreement with, perhaps?" he persisted.

She gave a snort.

"I know Dyl's no saint, but he ain't the bloody mafia, is he?"

Nick hesitated, then asked, "And what about Dylan—how well did he and Jordan get on?"

That earned him a sharp glance but any words of reproof remained unspoken.

"Did Dylan know, for instance," Nick went on carefully, "that Jordan was *not* his son...?"

She shoved free of him and scrambled to her feet so fast the chair flew backwards. It bounced off the bone-hard lawn with a crack. He half expected her to run but she rounded on him, poised as if to attack, her voice crackling with fury.

"You sayin' I was unfaithful to my husband, are you? *Never!*" she spat. "We wed in church. I said my vows before *God* and I meant 'em. *I'm* not the one who strayed—"

She straightened and closed her mouth with a guilty snap, eyes suddenly feral.

"So Dylan has a wandering eye," Nick said. "When was this?"

She backed a step and he saw the leap of fear.

"*When*, Mrs Elliot?" His eyes narrowed as his mind made the jump after her. "The night Jordan went missing, perhaps? You told us he was here but that wasn't so, was it?"

He moved a step closer. She tensed to run, lips pulled back almost in a snarl as, finally, the tears came. "You can't prove it! You can't prove *nothin'*."

"Oh, you'd be surprised what we can prove. Modern forensics are amazing." He shoved his hands into his pockets, regarded her coldly. "Lying to the police is a serious offence, Yvonne. Could get you into a lot of trouble. And if we find—"

"What the bloody hell is going on here, then?"

Nick turned, aware of the sudden flare of his own guilt. Behind him, at the corner of the house, was DI Pollock, with Dylan Elliot at his shoulder. It was Pollock who'd spoken but when it came to which of the two men looked the more furious, there was very little to choose between them.

59

DYLAN WAITED until *after* DI Pollock had finished giving that jumped-up DC of his a right arse-kicking before he went after Yvonne. She'd fled indoors the first chance she got—wouldn't say boo to a chicken, that girl, never mind a goose.

Most times, his wife's timid nature was a source of mild irritation to him, but on this occasion it had actually turned out to be an asset. After all, old Pollock wasn't to know that 'Vonne was likely to dissolve into tears if he so much as raised his voice to her. And Dylan would be the first to admit that occasionally she pushed him further than that.

Sometimes, the girl was just begging for a good slap.

But right now he was more interested in what she might have said to that bugger Weston. She wasn't good at keeping secrets, either, which was why he never told her much about his business. Not that it was any of *her* business, what he did or didn't do. She stayed at home and looked after the kids, like she was supposed to, and he never took that much interest, outside the bedroom and the kitchen, *what* she got up to.

Or, so he'd thought.

He was aware that his mind was shifting between random subjects and put it down to shock. He might not have *liked* Jordan much, son or no son, but he never thought he'd have to bury the kid. He still couldn't quite believe it.

But right now he had more important things to worry about

—like if the dumb brood mare he was married to had said anything to the copper that might drop him in it…

He flicked his eyes over the pair of them. Pollock had gone in close, got right in the younger man's face while he tore a strip off him, so Weston had to blink against the flying spittle.

Yeah, well, serve him right.

But Weston wasn't just standing there and taking it. His shoulders were bunched and his hands were tight and there was a muscle jumping at the side of his jaw. If he clenched his teeth any harder he'd crack the enamel on all of 'em.

And when he began muttering back at his DI—and, more to the point, when Pollock stopped bollocking him long enough to listen—Dylan began to worry.

He eased sideways and slipped in through the French windows.

"'Vonne! Where the devil are you?" He paused in the hall-way, listening, but heard nothing. "Don't make me have to come lookin'!"

He heard it then, the creak of the floor joists upstairs. She appeared on the landing, looking down at him with her thin shoulders stooped and her face a ruin from crying.

"What have you been sayin'?" he asked, his voice a low growl, threaded with menace.

Her face crumpled again. "*I* didn't say nothin'!"

He grasped the newel post and put his foot on the first tread of the stairs, watching the way she tensed.

"An' what's *that* supposed to mean?"

"I didn't say *nothin'*, honest I didn't," she repeated, almost gabbling now.

He kept climbing. She backed up another step until she hit the bedroom door frame with a start.

"If you've told the filth anythin', 'Vonne—and I mean *anythin'*—you know what I'll do to you, don't you?"

She didn't speak until he was nose-to-nose with her on the landing, listening to her shallow gasps, the catch in her throat. Breathing in her fear.

"*Don't. You?*" he repeated softly.

"Y–yes." It came out as a whisper. Her whole body was trembling, so hard that if she hadn't been pressed up against the door, he doubted she'd still be standing.

"*Yes*, that's right. And whose fault will it be, eh?"

"M–mine."

"*Yours*, that's right again. So, what you gonna do *next* time them coppers come callin'?"

"Say n–n–nothing. Dyl', I—"

He reached for her, gratified by her instant silence, her flinch. He felt the goose-bumps form when his hand met the bare skin of her throat. He slid his fingers upward and around the base of her neck, tightening just enough to send her up on her toes, her eyes widening.

"Mr Elliot? A word, if you please." Pollock's voice bellowed up the stairs. "*Now*, lad. Shift yer arse."

Dylan held onto his wife for a moment longer, just to prove a point, then let her go and turned away, sauntering down the stairs with all the bravado he could manage. Pollock stood in the hallway, framed by the light spilling in from the open doorway at the far end so he loomed, filling the space. Weston stood just behind his boss and slightly to the right of him, as if blocking off Dylan's escape route. And he watched with narrowed eyes that Dylan didn't quite want to meet.

"You goin' to say a few words of comfort to a bereaved father in his moment of grief, then, Mr Pollock?"

"We'll get to that in due course, lad," Pollock said grimly. "But first, why don't *you* tell *me* where you were the night your boy went missing?"

"I already told you—"

"I *know* what you already told us. But in light of some *new information*, I was wondering if you wanted to…reconsider your story, like?"

"If you're meaning my 'Vonne, well, she don't know whether she's comin' or goin', half the time." He smiled, a quick baring of teeth. "Wouldn't know her arse from her elbow, eh? Not the sharpest tool in the shed, that girl."

He heard a gasp from behind him, turned and saw that Yvonne had slunk halfway down the staircase behind him, pressed against the faded wallpaper as if hoping to blend in to the pattern and slip past him unseen. When she'd caught his last words, though, she'd let out that involuntary noise and was now glaring at him. He threw her a brief, meaningful glance, trying to inject silent warning into it.

If you're too dumb to keep your mouth shut, you'll take what's coming to you, stupid tart…

"So are you telling us you *weren't* out on the night Jordan went missing, then?"

"Of course not. I was here, all night. *Isn't that right*, 'Vonne?"

She tensed, a hunted look about her. "I, er—"

"Only, we've been looking at CCTV footage and you'd be surprised what's turned up," Pollock said, rolling his shoulders as if he was about to start a fight.

Dylan smirked at him. "CCTV? How much of *that* d'you think there is round here?"

"Oh you'd be surprised." Pollock's voice was mild. "Just about every petrol station and convenience store has something covering the front of the building—amazing how much passing traffic they record while they're at it. Not to mention the ANPR cameras." He turned, said almost conversationally to Weston over his shoulder. "You may not be aware of this, lad, but trucks are not supposed to cut through the middle of Kirkby Stephen on their way from Tebay over to Scotch Corner. Supposed to go up to Penrith and across the A66, eh? But there's always a few who bend the rules, and then they wonder how we catch 'em…"

Dylan ran a hand across his suddenly dry mouth, tried not to fidget. He'd never given the Automatic Number Plate Recognition cameras a second thought. Well, you didn't, did you? He'd always thought they were just to catch the folk who had let their car tax run out, or maybe weren't insured…

"All right, all right, so I went out? What's the big fuss about that? I wasn't nowhere near Kirkby Stephen, was I? Just passed through, that's all."

"On your way *where*, exactly?"

"To see a man about a dog. In a pub—in Windermere, as it happens." That last bit, at least, was *almost* true.

"Which pub?"

"*I* don't remember. A few of 'em."

Pollock shook his head. "Oh, no, you're going to have to do better than *that*, lad. In—"

"I know *exactly* where you was *and* what you was up to!" Yvonne's voice had taken on the screechy note that always set his teeth on edge.

He swivelled. "For God's sake, woman! Will you just shut the—"

But she didn't listen. Why wouldn't the damn woman just *listen* for once?

"You was seein' *her*, wasn't you?"

He lunged upward and slapped her, opened handed, across that flapping mouth. Wasn't supposed to be much of a blow but he hadn't reckoned on her flinching downward, almost walking into it. Nor that her head would bounce off his hand and straight into the wall alongside her. Her legs went from under her and she dropped like a sack of potatoes.

Pollock darted forward with surprising speed for a man of his bulk. He grabbed Yvonne under the armpits before she went head first down the remaining stairs.

Dylan wasn't sure what happened next. He didn't see Weston move. But, the next moment, he found himself dragged backwards off the staircase, feet scrabbling unsuccessfully to stay underneath him. He was spun, landing hard, face down with his nose mashed into the hall carpet. There was a heavy knee in the middle of his back as his hands were wrenched up behind him and the cuffs went on.

"Dylan Elliot, I am arresting you for assault. You do not have to say anything. But, it may harm your defence if you do not mention…"

Dylan tuned it out, seething. Perhaps because he couldn't *see* Weston's face, the grim satisfaction in the man's voice came through loud and clear.

60

THE EMAIL WAITING in Blenkinship's inbox from Dr Onatade had for its subject line the name 'Elliot, Jordan' followed by the case number. As soon as he saw it, Blenkinship had the same churning feeling in his gut that he'd experienced at the post-mortem exam, right before he threw up.

He sat for a moment, staring at the screen without moving. Then he leaned forward and clicked the email open, doing it quickly as though otherwise he might lose his nerve.

The message itself was brief and businesslike. He would not have expected anything else from the ever-efficient doctor. But it did not tell him what he needed to know.

He downloaded the report and sent it straight to the printer, forcing himself not to seize each page from the tray as it spat out. He made himself wait until the whole thing was done before he picked it up, but then couldn't prevent his eyes from darting along the lines of text, snatching meaning from the key words and phrases.

And the more he read, the tighter the feeling in his chest, his ribs, became. His fingers were so tense that the paper quivered in his hand.

In truth, it was not as damning as he'd feared, from the conversation he'd had with Dr Onatade in her office in the immediate aftermath. He began, cautiously, to hope.

And then, when he was almost at the bottom of the conclusion section on the final page, one sentence hit him like a truck.

'I cannot state with certainty that the victim was dead at the time he entered the river.'

Blenkinship almost felt the blood drain from his face, his vision darkening at the edges.

"You *bitch*," he muttered out loud in the empty office, his voice choked.

He slumped back in his chair, seeing nothing. Seeing everything, too.

The whitened scene in the glare of his headlights.

The flash of movement from the side of the road.

The jolt.

The clatter.

The crunch.

And he saw, too, the exact moment when life had become death. He'd known it, at some instinctive, primeval level. Had *felt* it.

"Of course he was *dead* when he went into the water. Of *course* he was," he whispered. "He was dead the *second* he went under my wheels. Do you think I didn't *check*? Do you think I wouldn't *know*?"

He threw the pages onto his desk. They splayed across the surface, the last couple skidding over the side and fluttering to the worn carpet tiles. Rubbing his hands over his face, Blenkinship got jerkily to his feet. The office was too small to pace but he did so anyway, trapped like an animal in a third-rate zoo.

Some small logical part of his brain knew this made no difference to the way things stood. There was still no connection between him and the dead boy. The damage to his car had been fixed within a day of him 'accidentally' running into Nick Weston. He'd thoroughly cleaned the underside, got rid of the memory card from the dash-cam. What else was there?

He glanced back at the report spread across his desktop. And he knew that single damning sentence would haunt him. Almost as much as the continuous loop-tape of the accident itself, which he couldn't seem to purge from his head.

Especially at night, when he closed his eyes. Darkness made it worse. He'd tried leaving a light on when he got into bed, on the excuse that he wanted to read before dropping off, but Susanne complained that it was stopping *her* getting to sleep.

He'd tried booze but that just seemed to make the nightmares more vivid rather than less.

He'd even sneaked a few of the tablets Susanne's GP had prescribed, when she had that bout of insomnia during the last run-up to exams. Half her staff were off with some kind of mystery virus, and her stress levels were through the roof.

They had made him sleep, sure, but he woke feeling leaden, groggy and disconnected, as if looking out at the world through frosted glass that dulled his brain as well as his senses. After he'd come very close to pulling out into the path of a truck on his way to work, he daren't take any more. The last thing he could afford would be to have his ability to drive put under scrutiny.

With a heavy sigh, he dropped into his chair, bending to pick up the fallen pages. But as he reached out for them, his hand stilled.

They'd landed with one slightly overlapping the other. The corner of one page was just covering the end of the last word on one line.

It turned *'cannot'* into *'can'*.

Blenkinship froze.

'I can state with certainty that the victim was dead at the time he entered the river.'

Just three letters obscured but they made all the difference.

If only…

Just three letters…

Blenkinship picked up the pages and pulled open his desk drawer, rummaging through the stationery oddments stored there—boxes of paperclips and staples, a hole punch, a calculator. And there, right at the back, a bottle of correction fluid.

He had no idea why it was there—or even how long it had been so. Nobody used typewriters anymore, and erasing a typo on a computer document had long since become a matter of hitting backspace and trying again.

He shook the bottle, pleased to feel the contents were, at least, still liquid. Using the little brush attached to the cap, he very carefully covered the offending letters, blew on the paper to dry them. Then he scanned the sheet and reprinted it. By repeating the process on the copy of the copy, he judged the final version to be almost flawless.

He fed the original page, and the first copy, through the shredder alongside his desk and put the revised report back together, flipping through it one last time. He could detect no deterioration in the print quality of the altered page.

He sat back in his chair and that tiny bright flame of hope began to burn again in his chest. He clenched his fist against his breastbone, knowing it was only heartburn. But still…

All he had to do now was delete the original file from the server. But as he clicked open the email, he saw that Dr Onatade had not only sent the post-mortem report to him.

She'd also sent it to Grace McColl.

He reached for his phone, dialled her number and listened impatiently as it rang out. He had no idea what he was about to say. How could he ask her if she'd looked at the report yet, or persuade her *not* to do so without making her curious?

But when she answered, it was clear she was in a vehicle. He could hear road noise in the background, the rhythmic click of an indicator. The reprieve had him sagging in his chair.

"Christopher," she greeted coolly. "What can I do for you?"

"Ah, hello, Grace." Relief made his voice warmer than was usual. "Where are you?"

"Kirkby Stephen," she said. "Tyson and I have just been running a drone survey of the Eden."

"Oh aye? I don't suppose you've actually found anything of use?"

"Yes, we have, as a matter of fact. Trace evidence on the rocks of the waterfall at Stenkrith Park, showing the victim definitely went into the water upstream of here."

Blenkinship checked his watch, already on his feet and shrugging one arm into his jacket, the phone wedged in the crook of his neck. "Well, how much longer do you think you'll be?"

"As long as it takes to do the job properly," Grace replied with an icy note. "Why? Was there something you needed?"

"Oh, er, no, it'll keep," he said, too flustered to pull her up on that. "I've got to, er, call in to Penrith—thought you could update me on the case, eh?"

"Well, I'm not sure *when* we'll be finished, so please don't make a special trip."

He gritted his teeth. "Just keep me informed, McColl." And

he cut the connection before she could respond to that request. He left the office moments later, hustling for the car park with the doctored post-mortem report in his hand.

Maybe, just maybe, this might work…

61

GRACE ALLOWED herself a brief scowl as she ended the call. The man who was now her boss drove her to distraction on all but the good days—and those were becoming few and far between.

"Problem?" Ty Frost asked, eyes still glued to the view-screen of the drone controller.

She let out her breath noiselessly, tried to let go of her irritation at the same time.

"Oh, it's just our lord and master launching a new charm offensive."

That *did* make him glance up for a moment. "Really?"

"No, not really."

"Ah."

Grace shoved her phone back into her pocket and finished scribbling the details onto the sealed evidence bag, before dropping it into the open plastic box with the two others. She eyed them. A torn piece of fabric that was a visual match to the T-shirt Jordan Elliot had been found wearing, a bloodied piece of denim that might be a ripped-off repair patch from his jeans, and a scrap of what looked like human tissue that included skin and maybe half-a-dozen hairs.

In some respects, it wasn't much. In others, it was a miracle they'd found anything at all that had even the *possibility* of a link. Grace found herself ever more in awe of Ty Frost and his skill as a drone pilot.

Perhaps what was most remarkable, though, was the change

that came over him when he was flying it. She checked him now. He stood leaning against the front end of the pick-up, at ease, relaxed, thumbs making constant minor corrections to heading, speed, and height, swivelling the camera from one side of the river to the other. Normally shy and socially awkward, Ty suddenly blossomed in confidence when he stepped out into his own particular arena of expertise. It was a pleasure to watch.

She folded her arms, realising as she did so that she hadn't recapped her pen. The nib left a streak of permanent marker on her forearm. Digging in her pocket for the cap, her fingers brushed against something small and flat. When she pulled it out, she found the SD card Ty had given her when they arrived. The one that he said had come from the camera in Blenkinship's car.

Grace had a similar dash-cam in her own vehicle. If she slotted this card in place, it should play back what was on it—if indeed it *was* perfectly OK, as Ty suspected. She started to move toward the driver's door.

"I'm coming up on the far end of Water Yat now, Grace," Ty said over his shoulder. "There's sheep netting across the river, so I'm thinking he couldn't have gone in any higher than this."

Grace paused. "I agree. I think we're done here. Well done, Tyson. Is there enough juice left in the batteries to bring the drone back up here, or shall we go down there and collect it?"

He squinted at the corner of the display. "Best to go down there, I think. Just to be on the safe side."

She nodded, bending to collect the evidence box and her cameras. She dropped the memory card back into her pocket and dismissed it from her mind. For the moment, at least.

62

QUEENIE NEVER MEANT to eavesdrop but when the opportunity presented itself, well, she would have been a fool to turn a deaf ear to it.

The heat of the day had weight to it all of its own. By the time she'd been up the hill and back with Ocean on the piebald, plus a splash in the river, she needed a little quiet time and a change of clothes.

So, she'd led the old horse back up to the camp field, replaced his bridle with the headcollar clipped to the staked tether, and let him rub the sweated band behind his ears against her shoulder. He bent his head to it, leaning in. She had been about to climb the wooden steps up to the vardo when she heard their voices.

Bartley and Vano.

Not arguing, not quite. But talking fast and low, with a charge behind the words that sparked and stung.

She stilled like the hare when it first sees the dogs, hoping that stillness alone will keep it hidden. The voices carried on without a pause, oblivious to her presence. She eased her feet back and slipped to the side, leaning her head against the wooden boards. Their words seemed to come louder then, amplified by vibration through the framework of the van itself.

"Have you lost your mind?" Bartley was saying. "The man's a demon, right enough. Did you not see him go up against O'Reilly last summer? Had to be dragged away from the poor feller when he was lying there unconscious."

"Ach, he was faking. That was just O'Reilly's way of saving face."

"Says *you*. He limps now in the winter and doesn't hear well to the left-hand side…"

They were talking about a fight, Queenie realised. She remembered the one—by repute, anyway. It had been brutal, she was told. What was the feller's name, now…? Ah, *McMahon*, that was it. Surely there was no way Bartley would have agreed to go up against a man like that?

Not after all the promises he'd made her…

"Come on, my brother." Vano's voice had taken on a note of pleading. "You don't have to last the distance—just put on a good enough show."

"And what of the *luvvo* you've already wagered on me to win?"

"Well…surely they won't expect those wagers to stand?"

Bartley gave a short hard laugh. "Oh, you reckon not? You reckon they'll allow you to change your mind from the thought of me pitted against a giant of a man, with a reputation to match, to that wee scoundrel? You reckon they won't see right through what you're about and clean out the other side?"

"I…" For a moment, she thought Vano would throw another argument out there, full of his usual bluster. But then he cursed, long and loud, and it sounded suspiciously like he kicked the side of the cast iron stove in pure temper. "If *you* won't fight him…then *I* must."

"Don't be a fool, man," Bartley said calmly. "McMahon's a killer and you—"

"Be very careful of the next words that come out of your mouth, my brother!"

A pause. "You are not," Bartley finished simply. "Besides all else, you have Nell and the baby to consider."

"And you do not, I suppose? What about Queenie? Ocean and Sky?"

For a long time, Bartley made no response. Queenie found herself holding her breath. Then he said, "Queenie may *want* me, sometimes, but she doesn't *need* me. Not like your Nell needs you." And something contracted in her chest, sudden as a clenched fist, so that she almost gasped aloud. "So, if it comes to it, *I'll* be the one to tell them there'll be no fight."

"That's just it," Vano went on, sullen now. "If we don't stand on for the fight, he's sworn to come after Nell, Queenie, the little ones…"

She didn't wait to hear more. In two quick strides she was up the steps and bursting in through the vardo doors. Both men whirled to face the intrusion. She saw a swirl of emotions laid plain across their unguarded faces—anger and fear, frustration and regret.

Vano recovered first. "Leave us be! This is not *women's* talk."

"Oh, it isn't, is it not?" she demanded, shoulders stiffening at the scorn in his tone. "Well, considering what a fine upstanding job the pair of you are making of this business, I'll take myself off then, shall I, and not be offering you *my* help?"

63

WHEN NICK WALKED BACK into the Hunter Lane station, he was told there was a visitor waiting to see him. He was frowning as he hurried through to the Reception area. Partly because he wasn't expecting anyone—except maybe Lisa, which could only mean something had happened to Sophie. And partly because his mind was occupied with the questions he and Pollock would need to put together before they interviewed Dylan Elliot.

Which was perhaps the reason why, as he buzzed through the door, he didn't immediately recognise the woman standing near the front desk.

She seemed to know him, right enough. She greeted him with a familiar smile and turned to pick up a lidded cardboard box— the kind used to store archive material in, or old evidence. It was only the lack of the proper labelling that made him realise this was something else altogether.

"This is what Shanaya and I have managed to dig out," the woman said. "It's not much but I'm guessing Mum and Dad might have got rid of a load of Owen's old stuff after... Well, when he disappeared."

It was only as she spoke that it clicked. She was Owen Liddell's sister, Catherine. He buzzed keyed her through into the main building and found an empty interview suite where he could put the box down and open it with some degree of privacy.

"Have you looked through it all yourself?" he asked.

She nodded. "There are some photos. Including some I wasn't really expecting."

Catherine pushed aside the lid, rifling through the contents until she came to an old-fashioned paper wallet for standard-size photographs. The kind Nick remembered his dad picking up from the chemist's after family events, with the little extra pocket for the negatives at the front.

Catherine pushed a strand of hair behind her ear and leafed through the prints. Eventually, she picked out two or three and handed them across.

The top one showed a man that bore enough resemblance to his driving licence picture for Nick to recognise Owen. He was standing near the front of a yellow classic Ford Escort, with a dry-stone wall and fuzzy fields in the background.

And, in his arms, Owen was holding a baby swathed in a pale-coloured blanket.

He was grinning self-consciously, tilting the baby's face toward the camera, clearly nervous to be in sole charge of the child, but proud of it, too.

"Who *is* this with your brother?" Nick asked. "You didn't mention he had kids of his own."

"That's because, as far as I know, he *hadn't* any. But, like I said, we'd lost touch." She shrugged and jerked her chin at the picture. "I'm rather hoping, if you find out what happened to my brother, you might find out what happened to the child, too…"

64

CHRIS BLENKINSHIP almost had a heart attack when the door to the CSI office opened and Ty Frost walked in. Blenkinship was still sitting behind Grace McColl's desk, having just used his authority to go into her work email and delete the original post-mortem report from Dr Onatade.

And although Blenkinship was the one who'd been doing something he shouldn't, it was Frost who halted abruptly, with a slightly hunted look on his face, when he caught sight of his boss apparently sitting there waiting for him, not the other way around.

Watching him, Blenkinship thought sourly that if Frost ever committed any kind of crime—intentional or not—he wouldn't get away with it for half a day. Not with that open face. He could read just about every thought and emotion that flitted across it.

"How did it go with the drone flight?" he asked, just to break the awkward silence. "Find anything useful, did you?"

"Erm, yeah, we did, actually. I've already logged it all in," he added hastily, as if expecting a reprimand.

"No problem, Ty. I'm sure you did a bang-up job. And I've evidence to log in myself, so I'll leave you to it." Blenkinship rose, sauntered around the desk, nodding to the papers he'd left on the corner. "Tell McColl I've brought her a copy of Dr Onatade's PM report on the Elliot kid, would you? Where is she, by the way?"

"Oh, er, I'm not sure, boss. She was called to another scene, I think."

Frost dumped his kit bag by the side of his chair as he spoke, sliding open the top drawer and dropping his keys inside. Blenkinship tensed a moment while he did so, hoping that the young CSI wouldn't spot the fact he'd thoroughly rifled through the contents of all the drawers, just to double-check that Frost really *had* thrown away that SD card from his dash-cam.

"Oh, speaking of the Elliot kid," Frost said when Blenkinship was halfway through the door.

He froze, turned back slowly. "What about him?"

"Did you know we've got the lad's *father* locked up downstairs—can you believe it? And his car's been brought into the workshop for examination."

Time stopped. Between one tick of the clock and the next, a stream of thought rushed through Blenkinship's mind. Of the 'suspect' vehicle, waiting to be pored over, of Grace being unexpectedly—fortuitously—absent. And of the physical evidence from the boy's post-mortem exam—including all the clothing that had been on his body when it was recovered—sitting bagged up and ready to be deposited, but presently still under lock and key in the boot of Blenkinship's car.

The opportunity to...embellish, was too good to miss.

Too tempting to resist.

Blenkinship curbed his excitement. Instead, he heaved a put-upon sigh and made a show of looking at his watch. "*Where* did you say McColl had swanned off to? Oh, never mind," he said, before Frost could answer. "*I'll* have to make a start on processing the vehicle now, I suppose. If they're waiting to interview the suspect, time is of the essence, eh?"

"Oh, er, yeah, I guess so. Sorry, boss. I don't think she'll be long, but—"

He scowled. "Don't worry about it, Ty. Not *your* problem, is it?"

But as he left the office and strode away down the corridor, Blenkinship couldn't prevent the relieved smile that spread across his face.

65

GRACE PUSHED open her front door, still wrestling to remove the key from the lock, and gave Tallie a perfunctory rub across the top of her head on the way through.

She had already toed off her boots and was about to strip out of her T-shirt when she heard the sound of an engine outside and tyres on the gravel. Tallie scrabbled out from under her hand and rushed the front door, letting out a couple of warning barks as she did so.

Grace sighed. DI Pollock's call had been brief, explaining that she was needed at the Elliots'. When she'd tried to explain that she'd just been gathering evidence of Jordan's presence in the river, so she could be accused of cross-contamination by going straight from there to his home, Pollock was blunt in response.

"This one needs a woman's touch, Grace—and you're it."

It was high time, she decided, they recruited another female CSI into the team.

So she'd hustled from Kirkby Stephen back to the cottage in Orton to shower and change. This unexpected caller, whoever they were, was an unwelcome interruption.

She pulled open the front door with excuses on her lips that died as her visitor turned to face her.

"Ayo! What brings you here?" she said, surprised. "Oh, I'm sorry, please—come on in. You don't mind dogs, do you?"

"Not at all," Dr Onatade said. "Oh, you're *beautiful*, aren't you?" She dropped her bag off her shoulder and held her hands out to Tallie, who took a regal sniff and deigned to allow moderate petting from her latest admirer.

The pathologist glanced around, taking in the discarded boots. "Have I come at a bad time?"

"Well, I hate to say it but you have, rather. I have to go to one scene straight from another that's related, so I need to clean up."

"Ah, of course. I'm sorry—I should have called first. Please, don't let me hold you up."

Grace paused. "If you don't mind me multi-tasking, perhaps I could shower while we chat?" She smiled. "I'm not particularly shy and I'm sure I don't have anything you've not only *seen* before, but probably also dissected."

Dr Onatade laughed outright. "Lead on, sweetie."

In the end, she sat at the top of the staircase, making a fuss of Tallie. The dog sprawled alongside her, taking up an inordinate amount of the landing, and waving her legs in the air.

"I had a call from the forensics services lab earlier," Grace called from the bathroom as she set the shower running. "They've confirmed that the boy *is* Jordan Elliot. But the results also indicate that Dylan Elliot is *not* his father. I haven't been back to the office yet, so I haven't had a chance to update the system."

"Well, that certainly complicates matters nicely, doesn't it?" Dr Onatade remarked. "Although, I can't say I'm totally surprised. One of the unfortunate side-effects of more and more people buying each other these trace-your-ancestry home DNA kits has been the number discovering, when they get the results back, that husbands and fathers are not always the same person. There is even an acronym for it—NPE. It stands for Not Parent Expected."

"Really? Well, I had a quick call from Nick on the way over here—DC Weston. He's just been to the Elliots' place and said he raised the subject, briefly, with Yvonne Elliot, Jordan's mother. She flat-out denied having an affair, apparently, even though she did admit her husband wasn't always quite so scrupulous."

"I do hope she's bright enough to realise that's not quite how biological inheritance works."

Grace could hear the grin in her voice.

"Well, having met her, I'm not sure I'd put money on that," Grace said. She pulled a face, immediately contrite. "I'm sorry, that was probably most unfair of me but Yvonne is one of those dreary women who just seems to *accept* everything that's dealt to her, however rotten it is. It's as if she's been conditioned to believe that she doesn't deserve anything better."

"Ah, one of those. Well, perhaps she has. We are not all of us lucky enough to grow up loved and encouraged and supported, as we both see only too frequently in the victims who pass through our hands."

Grace stepped into the shower and shut the door behind her, raising her voice a little to be heard over the running water. "It doesn't make it any easier to accept, though, does it?"

"No. No, it doesn't." There was a pause, then Dr Onatade said, "So, if you haven't been back to base, you won't have seen the PM report on the boy? I sent it through earlier today."

"Ah, no, I haven't," Grace said. She rubbed shampoo into her hair and asked, almost diffidently, "How did he die?"

"Not well, or easily. That I can say with certainty. If you're asking what killed him, on the other hand—as I said to Christopher, that's a *far* harder question to answer."

"Oh?"

"I would say that *some* of the boy's injuries are consistent with cyclist versus motor car. Never a good outcome for the cyclist. He ticked all the wrong boxes there." Grace could visualise the doctor listing the points on her splayed fingers. "He was male—more than eighty percent of bicycle accidents involve males. Riders between ten and fifteen are *the* most at-risk age group—far more than either younger children or adults. And while almost *all* child cycling accidents happen during the day, when an accident *does* occur at night, it is far more likely to be fatal."

"You've been doing your homework," Grace observed.

"Of course. You see as many car-crash victims as I do and it becomes something of a hobby-horse. I mean, half of cycling fatalities take place on rural roads, where vehicle speeds are faster and there are no street lights. Three-quarters of cyclists killed have major head injuries, as was the case here. And, incidentally, cyclists are much more likely to be seriously injured or killed if the driver of the vehicle is over the limit—in terms of either speed or drink."

"You think that was a factor here?"

She heard the shrug in Dr Onatade's voice. "I deal in facts and that *is* supposition, but a reasonable one, even so. If he—or she—wasn't speeding or drunk, why didn't they stop? This person not only hit a child but ran over their bicycle as well, I believe? They must have been *aware* of what they'd done."

Grace frowned and ducked under the spray to rinse her hair. "Ty Frost and I surveyed the Eden today by drone, from the point where the body was found back toward Mallerstang. From the trace evidence we recovered, the boy was put into the water somewhere above Stenkrith Park, but we couldn't find anything to pinpoint exactly where. Perhaps the driver stopped, picked up the child and started to drive him to a hospital. But, at some point very soon into the journey, they realised he was dead and they simply panicked and...dumped him."

"In the nearest *river*?" Dr Onatade gave an unladylike snort. "Well, it's a theory that relies on both the best and worst aspects of human nature, I'll give you that."

Grace shut off the spray and squeezed the excess water out of her hair, deciding that her usual wipe down of the glass cubicle would have to go by the board for once. She stepped out into the bathroom, wrapped herself in a towel and ventured onto the landing.

"Come on, Ayo. You could have told me all this over the phone. What's bothering you enough that you've made a special trip?"

Ayo took a breath, met her eyes. "I'm...concerned about Christopher," she said flatly. "He was acting very strangely during the post-mortem exam on the boy. I know he claimed simply that he was ill but—"

"Ill? As far as I'm aware, there was nothing wrong with him when he left Penrith."

"Well, there you go. It wasn't just that, he seemed...not just *ill*, but ill at ease, too. Twitchy. Is he struggling with taking over as Lead CSI, do you think?"

Grace felt her eyebrows climb as she pulled on a set of clean clothes. "I *would* have said that he was positively *revelling* in his position of superiority. But now you've said that, I begin to wonder..."

"Well, I just thought perhaps you ought to be aware of it." She hesitated a moment, looking uncharacteristically uncertain.

"I don't interfere in office politics if I can help it, but if it impacts on his cases…"

"I understand. And thank you. I'll…keep an eye on him."

"Good. Speaking of Christopher's cases, you might like to tell him that I've had the dental records through for the bones from the river. I can confirm it *is* Owen Liddell."

"Hm, if you don't mind, Ayo, I'll let *you* deliver that news. It's probably better than letting him think we've been conspiring against him…"

66

When Dylan Elliot refused his right either to have a solicitor appointed for him, or to have his own legal representative present, Nick's cop instincts gave an uneasy twitch. Something was up, which he initially put down to Dylan's general air of smug over-confidence.

Pollock began the interview in a relaxed enough way. Without discussing it beforehand, the detective inspector fell naturally into playing an almost fatherly good cop role. As Nick had been the one to physically tackle Dylan during his arrest, continuing to play bad cop went without saying.

It's an old strategy, but it works.

"Now then, lad. As you *know*, as soon as you clobbered your missus right there in front of us, you left us no choice but to arrest you," Pollock said. "We have some questions for you about that but, before we start, is there anything *you'd* like to get off your chest?"

They'd arranged themselves on two sides of the interview table from Dylan. It was less combative than both sitting opposite. The man was sprawled in the hard plastic chair in the corner, putting on a good show of being unconcerned but picking at the plastic lid on his vending machine coffee, nevertheless.

"My 'Vonne will never press charges, so you're wasting your time there."

"You may not be aware of this, but the decision on whether to press charges or not actually rests with the Crown Prosecution Service, *not* Mrs Elliot," Nick said mildly. Not quite the whole story but he wasn't about to spell it out for him.

As it was, Dylan's grin stiffened a little, and his eyes flicked between them, looking for signs of deception neither of them were green enough to show.

Pollock glanced down at his notes. "Just before you thumped her, Mrs Elliot intimated that you might have a bit on the side. Was she right?"

"Like I told you, she's not the sharpest tool in the shed, isn't my 'Vonne. You can't believe most of what she says."

"Would that be 'most' of it? Or *any* of it?"

"Any of it, then. Same difference."

"So, we shouldn't have believed her when she said you were at home, *all evening*, the night young Jordan went missing, then?"

For a second or two, Nick thought Dylan might rise to that, but then he grinned at the pair of them.

"Nope, she were right about *that*. I was home all night, just like she said."

"I see," Pollock said. He paused. "Got any siblings, have you?"

"What? I got an older sister, over in Cockermouth. What's that got to do with anything?"

"No brothers, then? Especially no *twin* brothers?"

Dylan wriggled in his chair. "What *are* you on about?"

Pollock sat back and let Nick take over. Nick reached into the folder in front of him and pulled out half-a-dozen print-outs, turning each one to face Dylan. For stills taken from video images, they were remarkably sharp and detailed.

Dylan leaned forward, used his fingernail to draw the nearest one toward him as if wary of leaving fingerprints. He took in the time and date stamp in the corner, the location on that one, and the next. And the one after.

"For the benefit of the recording, I am now showing Mr Elliot a series of photographs taken from various traffic cameras between Kirkby Stephen and Ambleside, on the evening in question. They clearly show a vehicle registered in Mr Elliot's name, and being driven by him."

Nick saw the moment when Dylan's gaze changed, from

looking *at* the pictures, to looking through them, as his mind whirled.

"Where *were* you off to, Mr Elliot—*driving in your vehicle*—on the evening that Jordan was *run down and killed*?"

The emphasis was not lost on him, and Nick watched the panic bloom in his face, quickly stifled.

"You can't be serious. You think I'd do something like that?"

Nick shrugged. "Maybe it was an accident—to begin with, at least. Maybe you ran into Jordan in the dark? Unlit road, a beer or two in your system, perhaps? Who could blame you for not wanting to own up to something like that?"

"No! Is that really the best you lot can do? The countryside's swarming with Gypsies and you think *I*—?"

"You lied to the police, Dylan," Nick cut across him, his voice cool. "Why would you do that if you had nothing to hide?"

Dylan opened his mouth to respond, then closed it again. He swallowed. "Look, yes, OK, so I went out that night. Not admittin' it when you first asked was…unwise, probably. But I don't always want 'Vonne to know my business. And, havin' you lot turn up out of the blue, tellin' us something like that, well, I wasn't thinking straight. Shock, you know?"

"Of course you were in shock, lad," Pollock said. "Only natural. But you must see, in light of this new evidence, we have to check where you were and who you were with?"

Dylan's face twitched. It had begun to shine under the lights.

"We'll find out eventually, so why not save all of us some time and trouble, and just come clean?" Pollock coaxed. "I'd hazard a guess that, whatever you were up to, it wasn't exactly above board, but what's worse? Having your wrists slapped for some minor misdemeanour, or being accused of killing a child?"

"It weren't like that! I… I wasn't doing nothin' *illegal*, like."

But.

Nick heard it loud and clear, and knew Pollock would have done, too.

"Well then, where's the harm in telling us?" Pollock, the picture of warmth and friendliness.

Dylan's eyes skimmed from one to the other and he scowled.

Nick let his breath out, as if annoyed, gathered the print-outs and slapped them back into the folder. "We're wasting our time here, sir," he said to Pollock. "He's lied to us, he won't give us an alibi. I think we've enough to go to the CPS and charge him. The only decision left now is, do we go for manslaughter or murder?"

"For God's sake…" The anguish twisted Dylan's voice into a squawk. "*If* it *had* been me—and I'm not admittin' *nothing*, here —then I would have stopped, called an ambulance. I mean, come on! Why would I not try to save my own son?"

"That's just it, though, isn't it, Dylan?" Nick said. "Jordan *wasn't* your son, was he?"

He watched the micro-expression of surprise on Dylan's face. Not because of the information itself, Nick realised, but because they—the police—knew about it.

"I brought him up," he said at last, more quietly. "That makes him mine."

"Really? Are you sure you didn't come across him, out on the road, and decide it was a good opportunity to rid yourself of a kid that wasn't yours to start with?"

"If I'd wanted rid of him, there have been plenty of better chances than that," Dylan flashed at him, finally pushed into temper.

"You might only recently have found out about his…parentage," Nick suggested.

Dylan slumped in his chair and gave a short harsh laugh. "Do me a favour! I've known for *years* he wasn't mine."

"How did you find out?"

"With that colouring? It was obvious he was a cuckoo in the nest from *very* early on, I can tell you."

"But you never said anything to your wife, or to Jordan himself?"

"What would be the point in that?"

"You wanted a son," Pollock said quietly. "Three girls before him, another two after. You were desperate for a son, weren't you?"

Dylan said nothing, but his body language spoke for him.

"Mr Elliot, if you are *not* prepared to provide an alibi for the night in question, you will leave us no choice but to charge you in connection with the death of your…of Jordan Elliot," Nick said, keeping his tone expressionless. "And of dumping his body into the River Eden like a bag of unwanted trash—"

"That's *enough*!" Dylan jerked to his feet, sending the chair skittering back into the wall. He loomed over the table, jaw set, fists clenched so hard they quivered. "That's enough," he repeated, almost a whisper.

Nick did not react to the outburst, just eyed him impassively. "Sit down, Mr Elliot."

"Come on, lad. Why don't you just sit down and tell us where you were, eh?"

"All right," Dylan muttered. He rubbed his hands over his face slowly, finally letting them drop away as he sank into his chair again, shoulders rounded. "All right, I'll tell you." He met Nick's gaze, steadier now but hollowed out. "But you're not gonna like it…"

67

QUEENIE WOULD HAVE PREFERRED to wait for darkness but there wasn't time enough for that.

She would have preferred seclusion, also, but the opportunity did not present itself.

So she had to make do with what she had, which was a small element of surprise and, hidden in the folds of her skirt, a dagger with a long slender blade that tapered to a needle-sharp point.

Vano stayed long enough only to finger his man. A big feller, not quite fat, bulky in the shoulder and long in the arm. He was loitering in the crowds that lined the flashing lane, watching the horses with a brooding eye.

"And the pair with him," Vano muttered, then slunk away to the shelter of the other men he recognised as kith and kin.

Bartley was still by her shoulder. She threw him a final haughty glance. "Leave me be."

He looked as if he might argue. She was torn which way she wanted him to fall. He fell on the side of his own skin, as she'd prayed he might. He, too, blended into the crowd.

The pair Vano had indicated stood by the barrier—to the man's right, but you couldn't have everything. Queenie spent a moment longer watching the air between the three of them. They were together but apart, with no *craic* between them, no banter. Bound by some form of duty, rather than friendship.

Hard to know, from that, how they would react to a threat that might be more subtle than they were accustomed to facing.

Queenie closed her eyes for a moment, drew a breath deep into her lungs and let it out slowly. Then she moved forward, putting sway and swagger into the walk, a swing of the hips that still had the power to make men stare and trip over their tongues.

Not that the man by the barrier was watching her, of course, but it gave her a jolt of courage when it was most needed.

She squeezed in alongside, to his left, turning into him rather than away. His gaze jerked from the lane and was instantly lured down the front of her blouse. She'd left a button or two undone and knew without vanity that he'd find the view too enticing to resist.

"Hello, Karl," she murmured, her voice a throaty purr.

He moved his arm before she could press in close and she thought for a moment she'd been rumbled. But all he did was grab for the back pocket of his jeans, where no doubt he had his wallet, mistaking her moves for fakery.

Queenie pressed close, trapping the arm against his body with one hand wrapped in his sleeve. The other, still hidden from view, pressed the tip of the dagger low against his inner thigh. She smiled at him. A brilliant smile that furrowed his brow as she leaned up toward his ear.

"I don't believe I need to tell you to keep very still, friend, if you value living."

His response was to try to wrench free. Queenie tightened her grip and shifted the dagger a fraction. The tip slipped through the weave of the cloth with hardly a pause, and through the outer layer of his skin with even less hesitation.

"That little prick you feel in your pants?" she asked. "Well, *that* little prick is a whisper from doing you some serious harm, friend. At present, it's no more than a warning. Up to you if that's how it remains." She left a pause, felt him make a conscious effort to relax and drew back by maybe a millimetre. "There now. All I want to do is talk."

"Get that thing *out* of me," he snarled through frozen lips. "*Then* we can talk all you want."

"Oh no, I think I like your attention just the way it is, for the moment," she said. "But bear in mind you're surrounded by *my* people here. One wrong twitch and you'll be bleeding out on the ground before your *pals* know what's happened, and nobody around you will have seen or heard a thing, I promise you that."

"All right! Have it your way. Say what you have to, girl."

He daren't even twist his head to look at her, she realised. All the better for that.

"You'd a bare-knuckle fight arranged for tonight, had you not?"

"'S'right."

"As you well know by now, Jackson went for an unexpected dip in the river, cracked open his skull and is still in his bed in the hospital."

"So what? Not my problem, eh? We found an alternative who's prepared to step up."

"McMahon," she said flatly.

The man forgot his situation enough to start nodding, stopped again abruptly.

"Bartley Smith will not be fighting your man McMahon," Queenie said. "He retired from the ring."

"Since when?"

"Since a couple of hours ago. Family pressure, you might say."

"*You*, you mean?"

Queenie chose not to answer. After a moment, the man let his breath out, slow and careful. "I'm out of pocket. Can't just let that go, however...*persuasive* you might be, eh?"

She could almost admire the balls of the man, considering how close he was to losing them.

"I don't expect you to suffer financially for this...late cancellation," she said. "But let me tell you now, ask for more than we've a hope of paying and you'd best be prepared to sleep with one eye open from now on."

He let out a grunt that seemed to signify as much respect as it did disgust. Another horse came by in the lane, pulling a light-weight racing sulky. It was pacing rather than trotting, both legs on each side moving forward and back at the same time, rather than in diagonal pairs. The driver struggled for control as they tore along, the horse fighting for its head all the way. Full of spit and spirit.

They came within a hair's breadth of the barrier, so that Queenie almost flinched away. She felt him relax slightly under her hands, as if the sign of her weakness gave him courage of his own. She tensed, as though he were about to start something.

"I want that colt."

"That one?" she said blankly, thinking of the horse that had just flashed past. *Speed but no stamina.* "I think you'll find *that* was a mare."

"*Your* colt," the man said. "The one your father bred."

"No." An automatic response while her mind scattered into turmoil.

"Why not? Came here to sell it, didn't you?"

"Sell, yes. Give away, no."

"Think of it as barter," the man said. "Your man's life for the horse. A fair exchange, eh?"

She forgot herself enough to ask, "What would *you* want with a horse like that?"

"That's my business. Got contacts, haven't I? Know what he's worth."

So did she.

Everything.

But not *anything.*

Not that.

Swallowing back the acid taste in her mouth, she gave a single, jerky nod. "All right. He's yours. *If,*" she added quickly, "there's been no trouble, no comebacks, by the end of the Fair, and nothing after. Come for him then."

He did look at her then, pushed his face in close to hers. "You best not try to wriggle out of this. A deal's a deal, after all." He let his eyes wander over her features, slow and insulting, but making sure he'd know her again anywhere. "You break your word, girl, and I'll break *you.* You get me?"

"If *you* break yours, I'll do more than that," she threw back at him, bitter. "I'll curse you from the very grave."

Her only satisfaction was that she just had time to see the instinctive alarm flare in his eyes before he could mask it. She released him, disappearing the dagger up her sleeve as she slipped away into the crowd.

68

"WILL YOU GET *IN* THERE, you awkward, little—"

The sound of the workshop door swinging open chopped off Blenkinship's muttered invective. Levering with a pry bar and one last shove, he managed to trap the torn piece of T-shirt between the coil spring and its housing. He risked a last quick check. The cloth was barely visible—just enough to be spotted. Not so far it would look planted.

Even though it was.

He took a couple of hasty steps forward, inspection lamp in hand, and hooked it back over part of the front suspension. Then he reached up and continued what would appear to an onlooker to be a fingertip search of the steering rack and engine mounts. All the while, he listened intently to the footsteps approaching across the concrete floor. A throat cleared.

"Er, hi boss." Ty Frost's voice, hesitant, as usual.

"Oh, hello, Ty. Didn't hear you come in."

Blenkinship ducked out from under the side of the hydraulic lift, where he had Dylan Elliot's old Ford hatchback up in the air.

"Just thought I'd come and see if I could give you a hand, like."

Blenkinship blinked in surprise, aware of the sudden increase in his heart rate. A primal response to flee and keep fleeing from any source of danger. But something made him hold back on his instinctive sharp "No!" And not because he thought Frost might wet himself if he were shouted at.

Although that's a distinct possibility, even so.

"Well…" He frowned as if in consideration and didn't have to fake the brightening of his expression. "You know what? That would actually be a big help. Thanks, Ty."

"Really? Oh, er, right. I'll get suited up."

"Aye. Canny."

The young CSI trotted across to the office and disappeared inside. When he'd gone, Blenkinship wilted onto the toolbox in front of him, arms braced, and let his head drop.

That was too close for comfort.

By the time Frost returned, a minute or so later, he had regained something of his poise, making a show of documenting his examination so far and taking a couple more pictures.

"Right, boss. Where would you like me to start?"

Frost was almost pathetically eager to please. Blenkinship pursed his lips, looking at the car as if the choice wasn't screaming at him.

"Well, I suppose as I've made a start on the front end, if you wouldn't mind doing the rear and working your way forward, we'll meet somewhere in the middle, eh?"

"Right you are."

Blenkinship let him work in silence for a minute or two before he couldn't control the urge to add, "Make sure you have a good poke around in all the nooks and crannies, won't you? You can never tell what you might find stuck in the crevices in a case like this."

"Er, funny you should say that, boss," Frost said a moment later. There was excitement in his voice with no hint of suspicion. "I think I may have got something…"

69

GRACE STOOD by the doorway leading to the main bedroom of the Elliots' farmhouse, watching Yvonne weep into a soggy tissue on the unmade double bed. In one corner was the baby's cot, squeezed-in between a cheap flat-pack wardrobe and an overstuffed chest of drawers.

She had come galloping back from Orton after her hasty shower, hair still damp. Now, she realised that there'd been no need to hurry. Yvonne Elliot was unlikely to confide in her, however patiently she waited. Grace had never been one for crying, not even when her father died with all the longed-for praise left unspoken. It put her at something of a loss to know how best to deal with women who wept long and easily at every situation.

"I won't p–press charges," Yvonne managed now, on a hiccup. "If Mr Pollock had waited until I was more me'self, like, I could'a *told* him that."

"They still had the right to arrest Dylan, as he'd just assaulted you, regardless of whether or not charges are brought," Grace pointed out. "Domestic abuse is taken very seriously these days, I'm glad to say."

Yvonne cast her a doubtful look through red-rimmed eyes. The lower part of her face on the right-hand side was swollen and had started to yellow. It pulled the corner of her mouth down into a lopsided frown. So far, she had refused to allow anyone to photograph the result of her husband's handiwork.

There wasn't much Grace could do about that other than try gentle persuasion.

"This has happened before, hasn't it?"

"It's not *his* fault—I'm stupid, see? And he gets fed up with me goin' on at him, sometimes. Can't blame him for that, can I? Not really."

"That's not a good enough reason to hit you. Or an excuse for having done so."

Yvonne lifted one bony shoulder in a half-hearted shrug.

Grace let her eyes drift around the room, the small windows in the thick stone walls making it gloomy, even in daylight. A towering pile of ironing was stacked on the lone chair, a refugee from the kitchen by the look of it. On the far side of the bed, the side table held a messy stack of car magazines, their pages well thumbed and curling. On Yvonne's side was a frame with cut-outs in the mount for half-a-dozen photographs. It had been filled with baby pictures of each of the Elliot children, mostly fuzzy snapshots, glaring with too much flash. She tried to work out which was which, couldn't quite do it. There were no obvious clues to gender, so she couldn't even pick out Jordan from his sisters, apart from one baby with a wisp of dark hair.

She turned back to Yvonne to find her staring vacantly at the far skirting board.

"Has Dylan ever…hurt the children?"

That got a reaction, at least. Yvonne's head jerked up and for the first time there was some fire behind her eyes.

"No! He loves them kids."

"I'm sure, when we ask him, he'll swear he loves *you*, too," Grace said. "Didn't stop him knocking you down the stairs, though, did it?"

"That were accidental, like. He didn't *mean* it…"

Her voice trailed off, perhaps as the feebleness of the argument sounded hollow in her own ears.

"So he's never given the girls a bit of a cuff round the head when they were playing up?"

"Well, that's different, isn't it? Not the same at all, if they was bein' little buggers."

"And what about Jordan? If girls can be naughty, boys can be worse, can't they?"

Yvonne wagged a finger. "Oh, I know what you're tryin' to

do. You're tryin' to put words in me mouth an' it won't work! Yeah, if any of the kids is really messin' about, they get a bit of a slap, but no more'n that. Not like *my* dad used to—"

She stopped abruptly, looked away.

"Did your father hit your mother as well?"

She nodded, sniffing as she crumpled the disintegrating tissue between her fingers.

"And how did it make *you* feel, when he did?"

That earned her another lacklustre shrug.

"Did it ever make you wish she'd just found the courage to pack up and leave him? Got out of there and taken you with her?"

"I knew she'd never do it," Yvonne said sadly. "What's the point of wishin' for summat you *know* is never goin' to happen?"

Because that's why it's called a wish…

"Besides," she added, "leavin' with half-a-dozen kids in tow, well, that's easier said than done, eh?"

And Grace knew Yvonne was no longer talking about her parents. *Even if she now has only five children left…*

She raised an eyebrow. "Who says *you* would have to be the one who moved out?"

Just for a moment, she saw the spark of hope like an ember in the ashes. Then it dulled and faded out to grey.

"Like I said, I *know* I ain't the sharpest tool in the shed," she muttered, "but you must think I'm *really* dumb, if you expect me to fall for *that* one again."

Grace was genuinely puzzled and didn't try to hide it. "Fall for *what* one again?"

"For *that* load of guff. Oh, I know what *you* lot are like. You come in here, makin' like you're all sympathetic—makin' all these *big* promises about how you're gonna help me and the kids. Then, soon as you nick my Dyl' for summat, *boom*, you're off, an' I don't see you for dust."

"I'm not looking to arrest anybody for anything. It's not my job. I just gather the evidence," Grace said. "Professionally, it makes no difference to me if I leave here with photographs of what he's done to your face or not. *That's* not the reason I'm trying to help you."

"Why, then?"

Grace sighed. "Partly because I dislike seeing any man treating any woman like dirt."

Yvonne's face flushed even as the corner of her lip curled. "Sisterly solidarity, is that it?"

"But mainly," Grace went on, ignoring her snide comment, "it's because I really *hate* knowing the effect it will have on your daughters, who will grow up thinking it's normal behaviour—behaviour that's acceptable—when you and I both know that it never has been and never should be."

70

Nick sat alone in an office whilst, in an interview suite two rooms away, his life came apart at the seams.

Modern interview rooms were different from the old days. There was no one-way glass wall posing as a mirror and fooling nobody. Instead, there was full video and audio monitoring, digital recording that caught every twitch and flicker, that could be zoomed and replayed and studied and picked apart.

Sometimes, he wished it wasn't so.

After Dylan Elliot had finally provided his alibi, Nick had come down to Kendal with Pollock and Yardley to put that alibi to the test. They'd travelled in two cars—Pollock insisted on driving Nick's Subaru. Yardley followed on in his own transport so he could take Pollock back up to Penrith afterwards.

It was clear that the DI assumed such an emotional bomb blast would leave Nick in no fit state to drive. Nick himself wasn't sure that was true. He felt shocked, yes, maybe a little numb, but distraught...? No—and that lack of devastation was a worry in itself.

Even so, the realisation of what came next was excruciating.

He wasn't allowed in the room during the interview, but that was only to be expected, all things considered. So he was shut away in here with a pair of headphones and a flatscreen. That they were letting him suffer without witnesses was little consolation.

In the interview suite, Yardley and Pollock had arranged

themselves in the usual pattern around two sides of the table. Their interviewee sat facing the camera. On the surface, she seemed poised, immaculately made up and smartly dressed. But if you looked a little deeper there were signs of nerves and she was definitely on her way to anger. Fear often manifested itself that way.

So did guilt.

The trick was being able to spot the difference.

Yardley went through the preliminaries in a completely neutral tone that impressed Nick. It gave absolutely nothing away.

He knew the usual routine would mean a reassuring friendly introduction from Pollock came next. Their subject didn't give them the chance.

"Look, what's this all about?" Lisa demanded, putting on what Nick always thought of as her telephone answering voice. "Why on earth am I here, Brian, being treated like a criminal?"

That sent Nick's eyebrows climbing. As far as he was aware, Pollock had met Nick's girlfriend maybe two or three times, briefly, at the occasional police bash he'd attended—fundraisers and the last Christmas party. They'd been introduced, of course, but were not on the kind of close terms that should have allowed her to speak to him with such familiarity. He felt a sneaking admiration for her approach.

"As I understand it, Lisa, you came here voluntarily to help us with our enquiries."

"Did I hell!" she shot back. "All I know is, I get a message from Nick asking me to meet him here—and where is *he* skulking, I'd like to know? And the next thing, I'm thrown in an interrogation cell with you pair of comedians, as if I've robbed a bank!"

Yup. She's definitely scared. He could hear it in the edge to her voice. *Now, how much of that is to do with these knock-off handbags she was telling me about, I wonder?*

"If you mean you were invited—politely, I might add—to join us in an interview suite, with a cup of tea and a plate of ginger biscuits, aye, lass, that about sums it up."

She glared at Pollock but, wisely perhaps, didn't respond.

"Do you *know* why you're here, miss?" Yardley asked.

Lisa turned her attention on the young detective, eyed him

speculatively. Yardley wasn't used to Lisa's brand of predatory confidence. Although Nick couldn't see his eyes, he caught the way his head ducked and he fidgeted with the paperwork in front of him.

Don't show weakness, Dave, or she'll eat you for breakfast.

"Surprise me," she said icily.

"Do you know a man called Dylan Elliot?"

She blinked, just once. "Y–yes. Yes, I do," she went on, with more confidence. "He's a friend of my brother's. Why?"

"Is that all he is—just a friend of your brother's?" Pollock asked. "Karl, isn't it?"

"That's right."

"Ah, that's strange, miss, because *Dylan* reckons it was *you* who introduced him to Karl, not the other way around."

"Might have been. Can you remember exactly how you met any of *your* friends? That's always supposing you have any, of course."

From the camera angle, slightly overhead, Nick saw the tips of Yardley's ears flush red. Pollock took pity on him and stepped in.

"So, how well would you say you know this particular 'friend' then?"

She shrugged. "Just socially, you know. I see him out around town every now and again."

"With Karl?"

"Sometimes. Sometimes he's with other mates, or maybe on his own."

"And you didn't happen to see him 'around town' last week, did you? Tuesday night, perhaps?"

She was starting to look shaken now, shifting in her chair as if it had suddenly become a bed of thistles. "I–I don't know. I don't remember."

Pollock watched her squirm. "Oh, dear. That doesn't speak well to young Dylan's prowess, now does it?"

"Is he saying we were…?"

Yardley said, "Dylan claims that he met up with you, by prior arrangement, at your business premises, after hours on the evening in question and the pair of you"—he took a breath —"were 'at it like rabbits' in the aromatherapy massage suite at the back of the shop."

If Lisa went any whiter, Nick considered, she'd disappear into the beige paint on the wall behind her. "It's a hair and beauty salon, not a *shop*, thank you *very* much!"

"Frankly, I don't care if it's a bloody sewage treatment works," Pollock said blandly. "And I care even less if you were discussing the metaphysical poets or shagging like two ferrets in heat. *Can you confirm he was with you or not?*"

"Aren't I allowed to say 'no comment' or something like that?"

"Well, love, you could do but, to be quite honest, if you're going to say 'no comment' instead of a straightforward 'no', that's as good as a 'yes' at this stage."

Lisa sat for a long moment in silence, biting her lip, then nodded.

"If you would speak please, miss," Yardley said. "For the benefit of the tape."

Her head shot up, eyes blazing. "Yes! All right? Yes, he was with me. We were having sex and I enjoyed every minute of it! Happy now?"

And with that she burst into tears.

Nick, peeling off the headphones with a feeling of nausea in the pit of his stomach, felt like doing much the same thing.

71

ONE OF THE takeaway food places in Appleby had local radio playing, and that's where Queenie heard the news.

Had it confirmed for her, anyway.

The bones in the river, they said, had been officially identified as those of Owen Liddell. The police investigation was described as "ongoing" with no further details given. And now the weather…

Queenie paid for her fish supper, only vaguely aware of the paper-wrapped parcels hot and damp in her hands, the smell of vinegar sharp in her nose. It was as if the outside world had taken a step back away from her, leaving her hearing muffled and sight blurry. She stumbled out into the warmth of the still-bright early evening and shivered, pulling her shawl more tightly around suddenly goose-bumped arms.

So, my sweet Owen has been dead all these years between then and now. I was right to think him cold for cutting me off without a word. Only the reason for it that was wrong…

She'd left Ocean sitting on the steps below the sundial on its pillar. He was supposed to be keeping an eye on his sister but when Queenie came along Low Wiend, it was only Sky she saw. The little girl had elbows on knees and chin on her fists, looking in bad humour to be left to her own devices. She was a bright little *racaire*, a chatterbox, who loved nothing more than an audience she could entertain.

Queenie hurried over to her. "Sky! Where's your brother?"

Sky jerked her head toward the cloisters at the front of St Lawrence's Church as she reached for a parcel. Queenie didn't like them to eat food she hadn't cooked herself at home, so this was a treat associated only with time at the Fair.

Her eyes followed the direction the girl had shown and her heart broke into a gallop.

Standing in the centre archway was Ocean, right enough. Hands in the pockets of his jeans, rocked back on his heels, still wearing his yellow waistcoat over the shirt the lady had rinsed through for him. It was a pose she'd seen her own brother take, too many times to count—Bartley, too.

And the thought that her boy was growing up, that he would soon be beyond her call or reach made her throat close up with sorrow.

But not as badly as the sight of the man he was speaking with.

The two of them stood easy, with no unease or ill-will between them. For all the world like a couple of fellows exchanging the *craic*.

Only, the last time Queenie had seen the man, she had been holding a dagger to his groin.

"Here, take these and leave them wrapped," she said to Sky, pushing the rest of the parcels toward her. The girl had a particular liking for the crispy bits of batter, and had been known to take her pick from everyone's plate as well as her own.

Queenie strode over the road, wishing she still had her dagger about her.

Even so, when the man caught sight of her, he couldn't prevent a flinch of reaction that went a little way toward reassurance.

But not far enough.

He stood his ground and let her come to him. And just before she did, his two *pals* stepped out from the shadows of the cloister and loitered, meaningfully.

"Ah, we meet again, *gudlo-pishen*," he said without expression. His eyes slid to Ocean. "Got that right, did I? A honey bee, eh?"

"Describes you, right enough, Ma." Ocean nodded and threw her a cocky grin. "Sweet as honey, but beware the sting if you rile her."

"Go get your supper, before your sister steals the bits you fancy," she said, not taking her eyes from the man's.

She knew without looking that Ocean's gaze flicked between them, picking up the vibe but not the reason why.

When he'd swaggered over to join his sister, Queenie turned her back on the two of them so they couldn't see the storm clouds gathering in her face, her eyes, and leaned in.

"What the devil d'you think you're all about, hanging around my kids?" she demanded in a savage whisper. "I've said you'll have the colt, haven't I?"

"You have," Karl agreed. "I'm just making sure you know I'm to be taken seriously, eh? You even *think* about not going through with our bargain and, well…it wouldn't take Gypsy Rose Lee and a crystal ball to tell you that pair won't have much of a future."

She felt what little colour was left in her face drop out of it. Her hands clenched into fists by her sides.

"And you'd best heed the warning *I* gave you, also," she threw back at him.

He glanced sideways and his pals closed in a little further. He smirked in response, full of bluster, let his eyes walk down her body and back up again in a way that made her want to scrub in the river.

"That's the thing about honey bees. They sting if you push 'em, like, but they can only do it once and then they're dead…"

72

NICK WAS LEANING on the railing outside Kendal police station, hands stuffed into his pockets, when the doors opened and Lisa hurried out. She had her head down and the collar of her jacket turned up, as if hoping not to encounter anyone she knew.

She didn't see Nick until he called her name. Then she froze and turned reluctantly to face him. Her eyes were swollen from crying, her face pale as mist. She braced herself, though, lifted her chin as if preparing to take whatever verbal blows he might throw.

Nick took one look at her brittle defiance and swallowed any words of reproach. He straightened, closed until they were almost toe to toe. A welter of emotions crossed her face in the time it took. They stood there for a long moment, staring at each other without speaking.

At last, Nick said, "Come on. I'll take you home."

He pulled out his keys and walked away without waiting for her to follow. He wasn't entirely sure what he would have done had she failed to do so.

In truth, his over-riding feeling was...ambivalence. Oh, he could rant and rave, call her all the names that men tended to use for women who betrayed them sexually, but he wasn't sure he could work up the energy.

He was almost at his car when he heard the clip of her heels behind him. He stopped, looked back. Her steps faltered, almost fearful, as if he was about to change his mind. Her sudden, uncharacteristic timidity wearied him for some reason. Perhaps because he was sharply reminded of Yvonne Elliot.

"What is it you think I'm going to do?" When she didn't answer, he sighed, went around to the passenger side and opened the door for her. "Just get in, Lisa."

It wasn't until they pulled up at the traffic light onto Windermere Road that she asked, in a small voice, "So, what *are* you going to do?"

He let his hands drop from the wheel into his lap, his head fall back against the seat.

"I wish I knew. I need a bit of time to get my head around it. This has been dropped on me, don't forget." He glanced across at her but she continued to stare rigidly straight ahead. "Why, what were *you* planning to do—when I found out?"

He carefully didn't say "if".

She carefully didn't correct him.

Instead, in a more detached voice, she said, "I...suppose I hoped it would have blown itself out before then."

"I see."

"Do you? Do you really, Nick?" She twisted to face him as the light dropped to green and he pulled away. "I *like* sex. I always have. Even after the baby and everything, I still *need* sex. But since I moved back in last winter, you've hardly *touched* me."

Nick clenched his jaw with the effort it took *not* to say, "Oh, so this is all *my* fault?"

But he took the ninety-degree corner onto Sandes Avenue at the bottom of the hill too fast, chirruping the tyres. Lisa threw him a glance, bracing herself on the centre console, but didn't comment.

"How do you know Dylan Elliot, if not through your brother?"

It wasn't the question he wanted to ask, by any means, but it was probably the safest option.

Even so, her eyes flashed and she tried for bravado that didn't quite overcome her embarrassment. "So, you were listening in."

"Wouldn't *you*, if you'd been interviewing a suspect in the death of his *own child*"—*OK, not technically correct, but she doesn't need to know that*—"and he gave up *my* name as his alibi?"

The next set of lights turned red against him, too. He braked late and hard. For once, he couldn't care less about mechanical sympathy.

"I've known Dylan since we were teenagers," Lisa said then. "We…went out together for a bit—nothing serious. It was before I went to train at the salon in Manchester."

Which, Nick recalled, was where he and Lisa had met, after an attempted robbery. Still in uniform back then, he'd been first on scene.

"How…long?" he asked, and didn't need to specify he was talking about the present, not the past.

"'Couple of months," she muttered, which meant at least three and probably four. Practically since she moved back from her parents' place and brought little Sophie back with her.

"You *do* know he's married, yeah? With *six* kids?"

Make that five…

"Yes, I *do* know he's married. And I *do* know how many kids he's got. Why do you think he was looking for something extra? His wife is too knackered looking after that little lot to want to—"

She broke off abruptly, which told Nick more than he wanted to know about Dylan's sexual appetites. He accelerated away from the lights and took the next corners quickly enough to keep Lisa silent. When they slowed again for Miller Bridge over the River Kent, she said, "It was just a *fling*. We were both of us just…scratching an itch, Nick. It didn't *mean* anything."

"What about Sophie?"

"W–what about her?"

"What about the effect all this might have on our daughter?"

Where was she *while you and Dylan were 'at it like rabbits' in the back of the salon?*

"Well, unless we're going to have screaming matches in front of her, why *should* it have any effect?"

The side road to their flat in the Old Organ Works was coming up. Nick stuck his indicator on but pulled over to the kerb rather than turning off the main road.

"I don't want her to get…confused about where home is."

About who her parents are.

Lisa sat for three beats with a growing look of anguish on her face.

"Nick… When I came back, I thought you wanted to make a proper go of things—between us, I mean."

"Of course I did."

"Yes, but…" She bit her lip, hesitant now. "Because of me? Or because of Sophie?"

For a second he sat immobile, unable to force an answer—the right answer—past his lips.

She nodded, as if he'd spoken anyway, and that broke him out of it.

"What about *you*, Lisa? Did you want to make a proper go of things?" he asked softly. "Only, if you found an old boyfriend so hard to resist, it doesn't exactly sound like your heart was in it, hey?"

She stared at him, eyes starting to fill again.

"And if it wasn't," he went on, "then the fact that Sophie might have been missing her daddy wasn't a good enough reason for us to get back together. She could have spent half the week with each of us. We could have worked something out."

Lisa bit her lip and said nothing. A car pulled out at the last minute to go around them, squeezed by traffic in the other lane. The driver blew his horn.

Nick sighed. "I need to get back to work. If Dylan *didn't* kill the boy, we're back to square one."

She nodded, unclipped her seatbelt and slid out of the car. But instead of closing the door she leaned down, met his gaze.

"I am truly sorry, Nick."

"Yeah," he said tiredly, "so am I."

73

By the time he'd wrapped up the examination of Dylan Elliot's vehicle and written his report for DI Pollock, Blenkinship felt lighter than he had in days. He didn't wait until he was back in Carlisle. Instead, after he'd sent Frost home, he perched in a corner of the workshop with his laptop, tapping furiously at the keys, eager to get the whole thing down and delivered.

He'd been, not *worried*, exactly, but certainly *concerned* about finding the scrap of torn fabric himself. Having Frost turn up just at the right moment, and *offer* his assistance, was the perfect solution. This way, Blenkinship was one step removed. It would not be *his* name on the dotted line.

Or, perhaps more importantly, on the witness stand when the case eventually came to trial.

What could be better than that?

In fact, when he'd suggested, oh-so casually, that Frost should be the one to test and analyse his find, the young CSI had actually looked *grateful*.

"You sure, boss?" he'd asked. "I thought, you know—case like this—you'd want to do it yourself, like?"

"No, no, credit where it's due, Ty." And, just in case the lad thought he was going soft on him, he added, "Besides, if you can't be trusted to do the job right, I've been wasting my time training you, eh?" And there were enough echoes of Blenkinship's well-regarded predecessor in that to put the lad's mind at rest.

Blenkinship finally hit Send and the email zapped along the wires to Pollock's inbox, report attached, with a copy to Frost. He was still feeling buoyed up as he sauntered out of the workshop. He checked his watch.

Not too late. Might see if I can grab a table somewhere and take Susanne out for dinner. Probably owe her a nice meal, seeing how on edge I've been this past week. Still, I can put that down to the Horse Fair…

He was even smiling as he walked toward his car. He'd parked it nose-out. Now the body shop who had the contract for all the police vehicles had finished the repairs, the front end looked good as new. No sign of any scuffs or dents. They'd turned it around in record time for him, with a bit of persuading. No point in being in a position of power if you didn't wield it every now and again.

Blenkinship felt he could, at last, begin to relax. Like he'd turned a corner, and it was all going to be all right from here on in.

"Evening, Chris. How's it going?"

He hadn't heard anyone approach and he turned fast, startled. He recognised DC Yardley right away. They played on the same Sunday league five-a-side team, although working shifts meant there was a fair sized pool of players.

Blenkinship, who'd been considered for a career in the beautiful game at one point, thought of himself as a near-professional among amateurs. But even he had to admit that Yardley had a modicum of talent.

"Ah, hi Dave. Not bad, thanks. How's about yourself?"

"Bit crap, really," Yardley admitted. "Thought we'd got our feller. Turns out he's got an alibi. Would you credit it, eh?"

Like a rock crashing through the icy surface of a lake, Blenkinship felt his composure heave and splinter. "W–what? You're not talking about Dylan Elliot are you? But… I thought you had him bang to rights! The kid wasn't his, and he lied about not going out. What *happened*, man?"

The report! Damn, I've emailed it to Pollock and there's no way I can get into his system now. Not without leaving a trail even that technological dinosaur could follow. Come on, think, man, think!

"Claims he's known the kid wasn't his for years, and says the reason he lied about his whereabouts was because he was over

in Bowness, having it away with Nick Weston's girlfriend."
Yardley's tone was a mixture of smugness that such a thing
could, of course, *never* happen to him, and shocked glee that it
had, in fact, happened to one of his colleagues.

*If Elliot's in the clear, how the hell do we excuse the 'evidence' we've
just 'found' on his car?*

"Well, bugger me," Blenkinship said faintly, his mind in
freefall. "You sure Elliot's not just trying for a wind-up?"

Yardley shook his head. "We've just had her in for interview
down at Kendal nick and she admitted it. She and Weston have a
kid together and everything—poor bugger. He must be
steaming."

"Aye, he must…" But Blenkinship couldn't help the feeling of
savage satisfaction. If, in the course of a few moments, it had all
gone horribly wrong for him then at least misery had company.

"And that's not the only thing," Yardley went on, apparently
oblivious to the grenade he'd tossed under Blenkinship's feet. "A
couple who live just down the valley from the Elliots rang in.
Reckon they saw young Jordan ride past their cottage on
Tuesday night, at a time when Dylan's lady friend claims he was
with her, thirty-odd miles away."

"Why the heck are they only coming forward *now* with this?"

Yardley threw him a sideways glance. "Been away for a few
days, apparently. Only got back today and heard the news
reports, so…"

Blenkinship tuned him out, mind working furiously.

*Wait a minute… Frost came straight from doing that damn drone
survey, didn't he? I'm sure he mentioned they'd found trace evidence of
some kind in the river. There's no reason why the lad couldn't have got
a bit…carried away with the idea, is there? He's still young, inexperienced.*

*And I gave him responsibility for gathering important evidence.
Well, he wouldn't have been human if he hadn't tried to put a belt* and
braces on it, eh?

He hardly heard Yardley's next words—something about
getting home to his missus. She was about to pup, Blenkinship
recalled. He made what he hoped were the right noises and
muttered about still having work to do.

He watched Yardley climb into his car and drive off with a
jaunty wave. When he'd gone, Blenkinship doubled back, and

hastily put together a carefully worded follow-up email to Pollock, saying, in a roundabout way, that since sending in his report on Elliot's vehicle, he'd re-examined some of CSI Frost's working methods and 'had some concerns over the integrity of the evidence gathered.' He would carry out his own inspection immediately and communicate the results as quickly as possible.

And he made sure, when he hit Send *this* time, that Ty Frost was not on the recipients list.

74

"HELLO NICK! Twice in one day. How lovely," Eleanor said when she answered her front door in response to his knock. "Do come in. Have you eaten? We're having a barbecue and there's *more* than enough food."

It was only then it occurred to Nick that he hadn't eaten all day. Lunchtime had disappeared and now his stomach felt roiling with acid, scoured and empty.

"Thank you," he said, stepping inside. "And in answer to your questions, no, I haven't, and yes, I'd like that."

"Good, my maternal instinct is satisfied. We're in the conservatory."

She beamed at him, linked her arm through his as they walked along the hallway. Just before they reached the rear of the house, though, she paused, forcing him to stop alongside her. He glanced down, caught her eyes skimming over his face. They were the same distinctive shade of polished hazel as her daughter's, flecked with copper and jade.

"Is everything all right?" she asked, voice low and serious.

He took a breath, gave himself a mental shake. "No, but I'll live."

She searched his face a moment longer, correctly divining that no, he didn't want to talk about it. Instead, she gave his arm a squeeze and led him into the conservatory.

When Nick thought of conservatories, he pictured ugly structures with white plastic frames—saunas in summer and ice houses in winter. This was old brick and young oak, beautifully proportioned, furnished with flair.

Of course…

Just outside, on a mossy flagged terrace, a man stood with his back to Nick, tending a large polished barbecue grill. Next to him, topping up the wine glass he held, was Grace. She wore her usual cargo trousers with the multiplicity of pockets she favoured, and a sleeveless shirt that seemed to showcase the long lean muscles of her arms. The man said something to her and she laughed.

Nick found himself lingering a moment, just to admire.

Then the man raised his glass, turning as he did so, and Nick recognised him. He wore a Panama hat, stylishly slanted, a dark shirt that had to be silk, and pale linen trousers. He looked confident, suave, successful—everything that Nick, right then, felt *he* was not.

"*Max.*"

He hadn't realised he'd gritted out the name of Grace's ex-husband until Eleanor said, "Yes, he's been helping me put the garden in order."

Nick flicked his eyes sideways. She was watching him again. She not only shared the colour of her eyes with her daughter, but also their ability to see far too much.

"He's been popping round quite frequently since I moved in," Eleanor went on in an entirely neutral tone. "Isn't that lovely of him?"

"Yes," Nick muttered. "Isn't it just…"

They moved into the conservatory and Eleanor waved to the pair outside. They turned and saluted with raised glasses. To Nick's discontented eye, they looked the perfectly matched couple.

"Come and join us," Eleanor said. Her voice dropped to a murmur. "And don't worry. If there's one trait Grace has had, ever since childhood, it is that she does not like to repeat her mistakes…"

Nick was suddenly aware of the tension in his shoulders. He made an effort to relax them, gave her a wry smile. "That's good to know."

As they stepped outside, Grace smiled in welcome.

"Hello, Grace," Nick said. "How was Yvonne when you left her?"

She shrugged. "It's hard to say if she'll have the courage to take it further but I suspect she won't, I'm afraid. It's not the first time this has happened, and I daresay it won't be the last."

"Hm, you may well be right."

And so Dylan gets away with it, yet again.

"But you didn't come here to talk about the Elliots' marital disputes, I'd guess. You were being very cloak-and-dagger when you rang. Have you brought those photos you want me to take a look at?"

"The originals have been logged but I took copies. No doubt your boss will be going over them tomorrow."

"Well, strictly speaking, it *is* his case."

"Maybe, but I have more faith in your eye."

"Oh, *this* sounds interesting," Eleanor said. She laid out an extra place for him at the bleached outdoor table and took a seat.

Max nudged at the cooking food with tongs, then closed the lid of the barbecue and picked up the wine bottle. He offered to pour for Nick, who shook his head. He had a bottle of Jack Daniel's he was longing to dive into—or would have been, had it not been in the flat in Kendal. The flat where Lisa was currently in situ.

Unless she's decided to seek solace elsewhere…

He slammed the door on that one, presented Max with a perfunctory smile as he took a seat. "I'm driving," he said. "And, technically, still on duty."

Max gave a tilt of his head as if conceding a point well played. That was half the trouble with the man, Nick thought savagely. He was so, damned, *pleasant.*

Now, Max joined them at the table, lounging in his chair.

"Oh, don't mind me," he said, when both Nick and Grace stared at him. "I agree—it *does* sound fascinating." He took a sip of wine. "Now, is this to do with the boy who was pulled out of the river, or the skeleton at Mallerstang?"

Grace frowned at him before Nick could do so himself. "Max, this is a serious incident—"

"Which one?"

"*Both* are suspicious deaths. You *know* we can't discuss anything in front of civilians."

"Quite right and proper," Eleanor put in.

"And that includes *you*, Mother."

Eleanor pulled a face but rose elegantly. "Ah, well, it was worth a try. Come along, Max. We'll leave these two to talk shop and you can help me put the salad together, if you wouldn't mind?"

"Of course," he said courteously, but the way he rose and strode inside gave lie to his nonchalance.

Eleanor leaned in to her daughter and whispered, "And *you* can tell me all about it later. I'm your wing-man, remember…" Then she disappeared through the conservatory after Max.

"Parents, eh?" Nick said when they'd gone. "You bring 'em up properly, you take 'em out, and look what happens."

"You don't need to tell me," Grace muttered. She fixed him with a clear eye. "Are you OK?"

He made a maybe, maybe-not gesture with his outspread hand and dug in a pocket for his phone.

She stared at him a moment longer. He could see it was on the tip of her tongue to niggle him for an answer. Then she pushed back her chair. "OK, I'll just grab my laptop."

She soon returned, firing up the machine and connecting it with Nick's phone. While the copies Nick had taken of the pictures Catherine Liddell had brought in were downloading, he gave her a brief précis of their last meeting.

"Presumably, you went through all these with the sister before she left?" Grace said as the images started to appear on screen.

"I did. I didn't bother copying the ones of him as a kid. I didn't quite think that snaps of him in his pushchair on the lake-front at Windermere, with his face covered in ice cream, would tell us much."

"So, what about these?" Grace asked. She pointed to a line of thumbnails that clearly *were* of a baby.

"That's just it. Catherine reckoned these were definitely *not* of him as a youngster. Said he had a shock of white-blond hair when he was born and it only started to turn dark when he got to three or four. And besides, in that one *there*—that's it—it's Owen himself holding the baby."

Grace clicked on the image he'd indicated, opening it up full screen. It showed a slim young man standing out on a driveway or the side of a road, with a stone wall and part of a tree in the background, and the front end of an old yellow Ford Escort just in view behind him. He was cradling a swaddled baby and, from the awkwardness of his stance, it wasn't something he did often enough to be easy with it. The infant was rather red in the face, eyes closed and mouth puckered as if he or she objected to the pose, too.

Grace zoomed in on the shot as far as the resolution would allow, studied the faces in turn. Nick helped himself to olives from the bowl on the table. There was a jug of iced water, slick with condensation, the top half chock full of ice cubes and sliced fruit. He poured himself a glass. It was cold enough to spike his forehead.

He could just see the screen, at an angle. Enough to watch Grace close out of the picture, skim through the others and come back to it again. Her fingers moved adroitly on the keys and trackpad, totally absorbed in her work.

He held his impatience in check. Crowding her, he knew, would not be to his benefit. Instead, he allowed his gaze to drift around the garden, touching on the huge oak tree with the midge cloud billowing beneath the canopy, the lichen-covered sundial, the mature borders. Whatever else she was, he considered, Grace's mother was not hurting for money.

When Nick looked toward the laptop screen once more, she had copied and divided the image so that the two faces were side-by-side, of equal size. She had overlaid them with some kind of grid which, he assumed, charted the distances between facial features. She had done something similar on a previous case, he recalled. When they had a sniper on the loose the summer before. That was the first time he'd worked with Grace —had learned to respect her abilities.

Eventually, she sat back and reached for her wine.

"Well, I'm not an expert in genetics, but I *think* the child may well be his."

Nick nodded. "And yet, as far as his sister is aware, he never had any kids."

"As far as she's aware," Grace agreed. She twisted the laptop toward him. "But if you look at the shape of the end of the nose, the inner corners of the eyes, the area around the mouth, what do you see…?"

It was no hardship for Nick to lean closer. "Hm. I'm not sure if I see similarities because they're *there*, or because I'm *trying* to see them."

"OK, how about…this?"

The picture of Owen Liddell was replaced by one of Max, looking sombre and serious, alongside the face of the baby.

"For goodness *sake*, Grace. If you're going to show me graphic images, some kind of *warning* would have been nice."

She flashed him a quick smile that managed both to censure and conspire. "All that aside, look at those same areas of the faces again and you'll see—no match. Not even close."

"OK, so where does that get us?"

"More questions than answers," she said, eyes on the screen again—back to the full shot of Owen cradling the baby. She was frowning, a deep vee formed between her eyebrows. "There's something about this picture and I can't put my finger on exactly what it is…"

"Don't chase it. It will sneak up on you when you least expect."

Eleanor reappeared through the conservatory, carrying a bowl of fresh salad. She reached between Nick and Grace to put it onto the table. But as she caught sight of the image on the computer screen, she suddenly stilled.

"Oh," she said.

"'Oh'?" Grace repeated. "Why 'oh'?"

"Well, isn't that…the little boy who was here—the one we rescued? Ocean?"

Grace blinked. "I wonder…"

Nick could hardly follow what she did next, going back to the close-up of the baby's face with the overlaid grid, then searching through folders until she came to the thumbnail she was looking for, opening that and zooming in again, overlaying the same grid lines.

"Hm," she said at last. "The angle's not quite right to get a proper comparison—he was a little too side-on to the camera—but what do you think?"

She turned the screen toward them both.

"It's hard to tell," Eleanor said after a moment or two. "When I first saw that picture—the one of the baby—there was something about the face I recognised instantly. But now, I'm not sure."

"No, no, you're right. I felt the same thing but couldn't place it..." Grace caught Nick's eye. "I wonder if the name 'Ocean' is as near as she dare get to naming him after the man who was his father?"

"Maybe."

"And how old did he say he was—ten?" She glanced at Eleanor, who nodded. "That would make him a year or eighteen months old when we think Owen Liddell went missing, wouldn't it?"

"But we don't know when that picture *was* taken," Nick pointed out.

"Don't we?" Grace smiled at him, zoomed out of the image, shifted the cursor and zoomed in again on a different point. "Back when this is *likely* to have been taken, what always *used* to be in the front passenger-side corner of a vehicle windscreen?"

"Ah, of course," Nick said, looking more closely. "A tax disc."

"Exactly—with the expiry date on it. That narrows it down to a twelve-month period at the most. If we could *really* zoom in, we could see the date-of-issue stamp but the resolution won't stand it, I'm afraid."

"The DVLA may be able to help there," Nick said, reaching for his notebook.

"Well, from the look of the foliage on that tree in the background, I'd say it's late summer, maybe early autumn—too late in the season to be Horse Fair time of year."

Nick nodded his thanks and made another scribble, then put the notebook aside. "It occurs to me, also, that if Queenie's brother and this Patrick Doherty bloke were prepared to put Owen in hospital for starting a relationship with her, just *imagine* what they might do if she got pregnant by him?"

"What, something like bludgeon him to death and bury him next to the river at Water Yat where they camp and graze their horses, you mean?" Grace asked. She sat up suddenly, eyes shooting to her mother. "Ah, the horse!"

Lost, Nick said, "What horse?"

"The *china* horse," Grace said, still focused on Eleanor. "The one Ocean took a fancy to when they were here. He tried to pinch it. It may still have enough of his epithelial cells on it to give us DNA, if—"

Eleanor's face fell. "Oh dear," she said. "I washed it. He had sticky fingers, you see, from the cake…"

She looked so disappointed that Nick felt compelled to say, "Not to worry. It gives us another line of enquiry to pursue, anyway. And my DI would probably have baulked at paying for another fast-track DNA test. He's having kittens about the budget as it is."

Eleanor beamed at him and, as her mother turned away, Grace mouthed, "Thank you."

He smiled at her. *No, thank* you.

"That picture of the chap with the baby," Eleanor said. "The background looks local. In which case, you might want to go and have a chat with old Agnes Trelawney."

"Oh?" Nick picked up his water glass and drained it. "Who is she and why is that?"

"She's retired now, I believe, but she *was* the local midwife in this area for donkey's years. And *why*, because she's delivered more babies than a whole flock of storks put together," Eleanor said. She flicked her eyes to her daughter. "She even delivered *you*, though I don't expect you to remember much about it. *I* don't remember *too* much about it, come to that, and I'm almost *certain* I was there at the time."

Nick reached for his notebook and pen again. "Any ideas where I might *find* this Agnes?"

"She had a farm on the top of Stainmore, I seem to remember. There were times in the middle of winter—if the A66 was shut because of snow—when she turned out clinging to the back of a tractor to help women in labour, but she always got through."

"Eleanor, that's great. Thank you—thank you both," Nick said. "Truly, you're amazing."

Max emerged from the conservatory just in time to hear that last remark. He gave Nick a long, level stare.

"Yes, they are rather, aren't they?" he said, with a certain proprietorial note in his voice. "Now, who's ready to eat?"

75

GRACE COULDN'T HELP NOTICING that, although Nick confessed he hadn't eaten all day, he did little more than pick at the plate put in front of him. And it was nothing to do with Max's food. The man prided himself at his skills over hot coals. Some kind of guy thing, she thought, connected to cooking in the outdoors, using real fire.

As soon as the last knife and fork had been set down, Nick stood, said his polite thanks and announced he had best be on his way. But she sensed the reluctance in him—either to leave or to stay. He was conflicted, angry. Maybe even hurting.

"I'll walk you out," she said, rising also.

Eleanor gave him a hug and offered her cheek for his kiss.

"You know you're welcome any time," she said, holding his gaze with sincerity.

"I do know, thank you."

Max held out a hand and their shake was cordial to Grace's narrowed eye. Neither man tried to crush the bones of the other —a juvenile habit which would have earned them both short shrift.

At the other end of the hallway, Grace opened the front door and pulled it almost shut behind them.

"Will you tell me what's wrong?" She put no edge into the words, kept them soft and even. No pleading, either, just calm and matter-of-fact.

"We're keeping Dylan in overnight on the assault," Nick said after a moment. "But he's in the clear as far as Jordan's death is concerned."

"I see," Grace said carefully. "That's…disappointing, yes, but what am I missing?"

He sighed. "The reason he's in the clear is that he had an alibi for that evening. He was with Lisa."

"Oh." She stared at him blankly. "*Oh*."

"Yeah, 'oh' indeed."

"I'm so sorry, Nick. That must have come as quite a shock. Or…was it?"

"Not really, if I'm honest. She's been 'working late' on days when I know full well the salon isn't open late—making excuses that don't ring true. I suppose I knew what she was doing, on some level. I just succumbed to the ostrich theory of problem solving."

"Buried your head in the sand and hoped it would all go away?"

"That's the one. And Lisa, by the sounds of it, was banking on much the same thing—that they'd be bored with each other long before I found out."

"But they weren't."

"No, they weren't."

"And…you've already talked to her about it."

He nodded.

"Talked? Or yelled?"

"Talked." He leaned on the stonework of the porch, side on to her with arms folded and jaw tense. "I mean, a part of me *was* angry, yes, as you might expect—at the sneakiness of it, more than anything. But other than that, I just felt…weary, I suppose."

Without thinking, Grace put her hand on his back, between his shoulder blades, and rubbed gently, as you'd comfort a child. Through his shirt, he was almost hot to the touch. She was acutely aware of the width of him, and the solid muscle. If he had the same kind of temper as Dylan Elliot, she thought, he could have put Lisa in hospital without breaking sweat. She let her hand drop away.

"I'm sorry, Nick. I know how much you wanted things to work out—for Sophie's sake."

"Yeah, the trouble is, I think it was more for Sophie's sake than for Lisa's, if that makes sense?"

"It does." They stood there for a moment in silence, then Grace asked, "What are you going to do?"

He drew his hands over his face, pausing there before they dropped away. She heard the rasp of stubble against his palms.

"Well, mostly that depends on Lisa," Nick said. "It's better for Sophie to have both her parents, but not if we'd end up rowing all the time. I know Soph missed me, when Lisa moved out before, even though she was too young really to understand what was going on. I don't know if it would be easier or harder for her, if it happens again. She loves all of us being together, doing stuff as a family, but…"

His voice trailed away. Grace nodded. "But, from what I've seen of her, Lisa does have a tendency to score points. And, much as I hate to say this, it won't do your little girl any good in the long run if that's how her parents' relationship ends up."

"I know." He straightened. "Look, I need to get going."

"Of course." She stepped back, cupped her elbows with her hands, suddenly feeling chilled, when a last thought occurred to her. "Is Lisa at the flat tonight?"

"Yeah."

"Well, if you need somewhere to stay"—she saw the surprise, chased away by something darker—"then there's plenty of spare room here."

"Ah, no. That's very kind but I'll manage. Thanks."

"I'm sure my mother wouldn't mind. And, to be honest, the way things are at the moment, she might be glad of having someone else in the house."

"The way things are?"

"Mm, they're starting to become somewhat uncomfortable in Appleby."

He stilled, cop instinct to the fore. "In what way 'uncomfortable'?"

"She was saying that some of the local pubs have turned away the Travellers. A couple of the shops have refused to serve them. There has been a bit of name-calling and some vandalism —windows broken, cars keyed, that kind of thing."

"I was given to understand that was only to be expected around this time of year?"

She shrugged. "Some of it, but we've now had two bodies turn up—of local people—while the Fair is in town, and the rumours are rife. I have a nasty feeling it may get worse before it gets better."

"Well, if she has any worries, she only has to call one of us," he said. He even managed a smile as he pulled out his car keys. "And if it's *you* she calls, then I hope *you'll* call *me* before you turn out to take on marauders single-handed?"

"Of course." Grace flashed him a quick smile. "Although in my defence, I'd bring Tallie as well. Her bark is definitely worse than her bite, but *they* won't know that."

She watched him walk away and climb into the Subaru, parked out on the road.

When she got back to the terrace, she found that between them, Eleanor and Max had cleared the table of debris. A pot of coffee now stood in the centre, with cups, sugar and cream. Eleanor was lighting citronella candles to deter the evening insects.

She'd left her laptop lid closed but it was now open again, and Max had taken Nick's chair. From there, he had a good view of the screen. Nick's copies of the original photographs were clearly visible.

And that in itself points to the age of the pictures—physical prints rather than digital images. She could see that Nick had laid out a series of what looked like six-by-fours, full bleed—no white border around the edge of the print—and had snapped them with his phone.

The corners were crumpled on the prints. One had a slight tear along the edge. The shot of Owen holding the baby bore the worst damage.

As though it received the most handling, had been picked up time after time…

Max lifted his cup from its saucer and gestured to the image of the baby. "She's a tiny little thing, isn't she? Is there a connection to your case?"

"*'She'*?" Grace queried.

Max shrugged. "Well, isn't it a *she*?" He leaned over and poured himself the last of the wine, gestured with his glass toward the screen. Grace wondered, briefly, if he intended driving himself home or if *he* was taking advantage of Eleanor's hospitality overnight.

Perhaps it's just as well Nick turned down the offer to stay.

"What makes you think so?"

Max said, "I rather thought the pink blanket was a bit of a giveaway."

Grace stared again. She'd thought the blanket to be white, and it still could be. Difficult to know, dealing with an old print, if the colour balance was off or if it had simply faded over the years. The light meter in the camera used to take the original shot must have been fairly rudimentary, too. And the make of film used would affect it. Kodak stock, in her experience, tended to show reds as orange. Agfa shifted them closer to crimson.

She clicked on one of the close-ups of the infant in what looked like a carry cot. The blanket was blasted out, over-exposed, dropping the background into near-darkness.

And the auto-flash had tripped, which pained Grace every time she saw it in baby pictures. The reflex responses of new-borns took a little while to develop. One of the most important was the reaction of their eyes to sudden changes in light levels. A photographic flash, fired without the short preliminary bursts modern cameras used, designed to shut down the pupil to conquer red-eye, could permanently damage the child's vision.

Grace looked again at the blanket, tilting her head on one side as if that might make the colour tone more obvious. It didn't.

"Are you *sure* it's pink?"

Eleanor moved to hover behind her other shoulder. "Well, it certainly *looks* pink to me and I've had the surgery for my cataracts, so I can see reds again. You know how bad I was before."

"Hm," Grace said. "I'm not sure I'd count the colour of the blanket as a definitive method of sexing a baby but I *will* make a note of it, nonetheless."

"Thank you," Eleanor said. She picked up the empty wine bottle. "I'll fetch another, shall I?"

"Not on my account," Grace said. "I have to get home to my dog, but you carry on, by all means."

When they were alone, Max said softly, "I always dreamed of one day seeing *you* with a baby in your arms—*my* baby."

Grace swallowed before turning to glance up at him. "It wasn't to be," she said stiffly. "I'm sorry."

"Don't be. It takes two to tango, as they say. Who knows why—"

"It was me," she said, the words coming out in a rush, as if she might lose her nerve if she didn't jettison them quickly. "I went to see a specialist, after…"

"*After* we divorced? Why on earth…?" His voice turned blank, his face followed. "You wanted a child."

This last was not a question but a flat statement. He did not add *"without me"* but they both heard it, even so.

"I…considered it, yes. But I found out the problem was mine rather than yours. They told me it was highly unlikely I would ever conceive."

She did not add that the problems of her teenage years, after the premature death of her father, her flirtations with eating disorders and her desperate attempts to control something— anything—in her life, had compromised an already borderline capacity.

Max, to his credit, had no words of recrimination or regret. He put a hand on her shoulder and when he spoke, his voice was filled with anguish. She knew a little was for himself, yes, but mostly it was for her. "Oh, *darling*…"

Grace sat staring at her computer screen without seeing it, aware of a sheen across her eyes that turned it all into a blur. She reached up and squeezed Max's hand and they stayed like that, silent in the gathering dusk.

76

Two things stood out to Blenkinship as he drove into the cul-de-sac and neared home. The first was Susanne's car on the driveway. The second was that there were apparently no lights on in the house.

He felt the familiar tightening in his belly, the hollow feeling up underneath his ribcage that he always got when he'd been out for a skinful with his football teammates, most Saturday nights in his youth. The feeling that came just before he threw his guts up.

He swallowed back the bitter taste in his mouth, fumbled in the door pocket for another antacid tablet. Last one in the pack.

Better start buying 'em in bulk if this goes on much longer…

The prospect of it stopping—of what would be the only possible cause of it stopping—made him feel sicker yet.

He hit the button for his garage door but he'd mistimed it, and had to brake sharply on the drive, waiting for the door to rise to the end of its travel. He glanced over at the silent house. No glimmer of light showed from anywhere within.

Inside, he shut down the engine and climbed out as the door lowered behind him. He stood for a moment once it was down, listening for sounds of occupation. None came. After a minute or so, the automatic light shut off, plunging him into darkness.

With a muttered curse, he blipped the car alarm on, which caused the indicators to flash enough to light his way to the internal door to the house.

As he stepped through into the darkened hallway, he opened his mouth to call Susanne's name but something stopped him. Instead, he toed off his boots and slipped quietly through the rooms on the ground floor, checking.

Initially, he thought the lounge was empty but then a shape solidified on the sofa. He felt for the switch by the door, snapping it on. Susanne sat up and winced against the sudden flood of light from the overhead bulb.

"What are you doing, pet, sitting here in the dark—?"

His words died away when he saw what was on the coffee table in front of her. His coveralls. The ones he'd worn the night he arrived back from Mallerstang—*that* night—and cleaned up the underside of his car.

He'd stripped them off and dumped them in the laundry basket, not thinking twice about it. He'd seen Susanne loading the washing machine with a text book in one hand often enough, half her mind on the job and the other half planning tomorrow's lessons. Why should this time be any different?

But, clearly, it was.

She'd laid the coveralls out as you would evidence, front-side up, with the dark smears on sleeve and leg prominently displayed. At the time, he hadn't noticed the marks were there. Hardly surprising, when he thought about it.

"What's all this?" he asked, hiding his unease behind a touch of belligerence.

"I had a call from Julie today," she said.

"Julie?"

She gave him a brief, reproving glance. "Of Julie and Steve—remember *them*? The friends you had supper with last week?" The sarcasm dripped through her tone and the acid in his gut churned in response. "The night I got landed with all that extra admin for my promotion?"

"All right, all right, I'm with you. What about it?"

"She wanted to know if you were OK. Said it had been all over the news, about that boy being killed—the one from the river. *That same night*. She said she'd been a bit concerned about you driving yourself home—that you'd all been drinking."

"*They* were drinking. Like I *told* you, I had a couple of glasses of wine with the meal, that's all."

Susanne ignored that. "She also said that you left around

eleven but you didn't come to bed 'til gone two." Her eyes were very bright, her body very tense. "So where *were* you, Chris?"

"Come on, pet, where do you think?" He pushed a note of exasperation into his voice, tried to be convincing with it. "It's fifty-odd miles and I wasn't in any mad rush. I took it steady, eh?"

"Most of it's motorway, so barely an hour door to door at that time of night—and that's if you *are* taking it steady," she shot back. "So what were you doing for the other *two hours*? And what the hell is *that* on your overalls?"

He sighed, ran a hand over the top of his head, over the bristle of the buzz-cut he favoured. "I–I hit a badger," he said at last, improvising wildly. "Decided to take a shortcut over the old Tommy Road. You know the one—cuts across the valley from Pendragon Castle over to the road down to the Fat Lamb Inn. Bloody animal ran straight under my wheels. Didn't stand a chance to avoid him…it."

He paused, eyes on Susanne's face. She was soft when it came to animals and, sure enough, he saw her face crease in sympathetic dismay. "Oh no, was it…dead?"

He nodded. "Aye, ran right over the poor beggar. So, I stopped…did what I could but"—he shrugged—"there wasn't much I *could* do. Anyway, when I got back here, I knew if you saw the car you'd be upset, like, so I cleaned it up before I came to bed."

"At *that* time of the morning?"

"Would have been harder if I'd left it to…to the next day."

"Oh." The relief in her face was plain. But it also highlighted the suspicion that preceded it, brought the two conflicting emotions into stark contrast. "Well, of course, I *never* thought for a moment you'd…"

Her words lacked conviction.

"No, no, of course you didn't," Blenkinship said.

And *his* words lacked conviction, too.

PART VI

SUNDAY

77

TURNING RIGHT off a dual carriageway was always a risky proposition, in Nick's opinion. Doing so off a main cross-country route like the A66 was even more of a hair-raising experience. It was never empty of traffic unless it was closed because of snow. Even now, early on a Sunday morning, there were plenty of vehicles heading in both directions.

When he indicated and pulled into the right-hand lane, the cars behind thought he was overtaking and accelerated after him. He waited until the very last moment before darting into the turn lane and braking hard.

No wonder there are so many fatalities along here…

The now-retired midwife Eleanor McColl had mentioned, lived out in the Pennine hills at North Stainmore. A quick records search had produced an address, which turned out to be a weather-beaten farmhouse, a stone's throw from the main road. As he approached, Nick saw an old sandstone property, hunkered down in the lee of a cavernous barn. Various outbuildings were dotted around the foot of it with dry stone walls leading off in four directions, almost like guy-ropes, holding it down.

The sandstone around here was local, he'd been told, quarried at nearby Alston and hard as iron. On the roof were stone flags, graduated from small at the peak down to huge great slabs the size of gravestones just above the guttering. They needed to be to withstand the hurricane-force winds that sometimes lashed across this desolate place, come winter.

There were times when Nick wished for more isolation than was afforded by the Kendal flat, but this was going too far the other way. There was only so much bleakness a man could stand.

Mind you, the flat had felt pretty bleak last night. He purposely stayed out late and bedded down on the sofa in the living area. He was woken early by Sophie clambering onto his legs and demanding that he read her a story. He found it hard to do so past the lump in his throat, at the thought that time with his daughter, like this, might be limited.

The door to his and Lisa's bedroom remained firmly closed throughout. He vacillated over knocking, just to check she was actually there before he left, but then he heard the shower running. So, he kissed Sophie's head as she sat crayoning a picture at the breakfast bar.

"Look, Daddy. It's you and me and Mummy!"

He went before the tears in his eyes overran.

Now, Nick parked up by the verge and climbed out of his car, suddenly aware of the thunder of trucks rolling past only a hundred metres or so away.

Maybe a place like this has more drawbacks than simply the weather.

Still, right now, with the promise of full summer on the way, it was magnificent, all far-distant hills and green fields between.

He tugged on the old-fashioned bell-pull by the front door in the porch, listened to the answering clang. Somewhere inside, a dog began to bark and a woman's voice shouted at it for silence.

Eventually, the door was opened by a woman with long greying hair, held away from her face by an Alice band. She wore a long skirt and flowered top beneath an apron, which she was drying her hands on.

"Mrs Trelawney?" Nick asked. There was a moment's hesitation before she nodded. Only fractional but he caught it, all the same. "I'm DC Nick Weston with Cumbria police, ma'am. Nothing to be alarmed about, but I wonder if I could ask you a few questions in connection with an ongoing enquiry?"

"Oh…well, yes, of course. Please—come in. Excuse the mess, won't you? I'd like to give you some important reason for it but the truth is that housework bores me silly. Kitchen's at the back, just keep going, and do watch your head on the beams. Can I offer you a cup of tea? I have herbal, if you prefer it?"

She spoke in a nervous flurry, hardly seeming to pause for breath. Nick accepted her offer just to give the woman time to settle. She bustled about the crammed kitchen, shoving a kettle onto a camping stove on the worktop and putting a match to the gas.

"Oh, I turn off the Aga during the summer, or it gets like a kiln in here," she said, following his gaze. "Do you take milk and sugar? I think there's camomile if you prefer? Or I have some peppermint—very good for the digestion."

"Just ordinary builder's tea is fine," Nick said when he could get a word in.

When the kettle had begun to whistle and she'd fussed over mugs and teapot, milk and sugar, biscuits and cake, and insisted on taking a tray out into the garden at the far end of the house, she finally sat down and said, "I've been expecting you. Well, not *you* precisely but someone *like* you—about the boy."

"Ah, it *was* a boy then?"

She looked taken aback. "You mean you didn't know?" she asked faintly. "Oh, my lord, it was worse than I thought. I mean, I hardly did more than glance at him, but still, I didn't realise…"

"You hardly did more than *glance* at him?" Nick echoed, puzzled. "But I thought you delivered him?"

"Well, it was *more* a case that *he* was delivered to *me*, as it were. I called you right away. As soon as I saw what it was they'd brought me to see—do you see?"

Nick shook his head. "Mrs Trelawney… I think we may be talking at cross-purposes here. I've come about a child we're trying to identify." He reached into his pocket and drew out copy prints of Owen Liddell with the unknown infant in his arms. "This one, here."

"Oh," she said abruptly. "*Oh.*"

Her face paled then flushed, like the swell on a beach receding before crashing further up the shoreline.

"What is it you *thought* I'd come to see you about?"

"Well…" Her hands fluttered nervously over the teapot, removing the lid and stabbing at the leaves with a spoon. "The boy who was found in the river near Kirkby Stephen yesterday. I–I was the one who called you."

"You found him?"

"Yes, well… No, no…not really." She faltered into silence. "You can't blame them, can you? I mean, most of the time the only contact they have with the police is when they're evicted, moved on. And they're often treated roughly. It's appalling, some of the things they've told me—"

"Who, Mrs Trelawney?" Nick cut in, aware of another layer peeled away from his patience.

"The Romany," she said. "Travelling people. *They* found the boy—pulled him from the weir and did their best but... Well, they could see it was already too late. So they called me, asked me to come and…wait for officialdom to arrive. And that's what I did."

With a sinking feeling in his stomach, Nick said, "You're *not* Mrs *Agnes* Trelawney, are you?"

"Oh, goodness me, no." Her relief brought laughter rather than anger, which in turn was a relief to Nick. "That's Mum."

"I'm so sorry for the misunderstanding, Mrs Trelawney—or should that be Miss?"

"Oh, no, I'm Mrs, too, but I'm Wynter. I got married, you see, but my husband's name was Bottom and I wasn't going to take that—Wynter Bottom, can you imagine it? So I kept my maiden name and then we divorced but it didn't feel right to go back to being Miss and… It's complicated. Last of the line."

Nick rubbed a hand across his eyes and rechecked his notes. "But your mother still lives here, yes? I understood she was the local midwife?"

"Oh, I see, when you said *'delivered'* you meant… Ah, yes, she does—still live here, that is." Wynter Trelawney waved a hand toward one end of the farmhouse. Nick could see another door at ground level, with its own letterbox and bell.

He put his hands on his knees, braced to stand. "In that case, thank you for your time. It's Agnes I really came to—"

"Oh, you can't see her," Wynter said, her voice entirely matter-of-fact. She poured the tea with hands that weren't quite steady. "Well, you could, but it wouldn't do you any good."

Nick subsided again, wary now. "May I ask why not?"

"Alzheimer's. It was diagnosed about six or seven years ago

and she's gone steadily downhill ever since. She barely knows *me*, most days, when I go in to get her up and clean her and feed her. Mum just sits in her chair and smiles and strokes the cat on her knee, and then asks when her daughter's coming in to see her, because she's waited *ages* and the wretched girl never comes…"

78

As GRACE PUSHED OPEN the door to the CSI office, she almost ran headlong into Ty Frost on his way out.

"'Morning, Grace!"

"Good grief, Tyson, what's the rush?"

"Summons from on high," he said cheerfully, still walking. "Mr Pollock wants me for something or other."

"Oh? Any idea why?"

"Nope. I'll tell you when I get back. See ya!"

As she slipped into the chair behind her desk and booted up her computer, she was still smiling at his puppy-like enthusiasm.

Her good humour waned a little at the amount of work awaiting her, both paper in the in-tray perched on the corner of her desktop, and in her digital inbox. She had gone straight home last night from her mother's without going back to the office first. In retrospect, perhaps that was a mistake.

Mindful of her last conversation with Dr Onatade, she looked first for an email with Jordan Elliot's post-mortem exam report attached, frowning when nothing showed up. She was about to dash off a quick request for a copy, when she leafed through the mesh tray and found a print-out with a note from Blenkinship clipped to the top.

Grace took a breath and tried to let go of her irritation. It was *her* case, even if Blenkinship had commandeered attending the PM. The fact that the report had gone to him and had to be delivered to her as an afterthought niggled at her. If nothing else, it made the timeline…untidy.

Still, she couldn't complain too much. After all, *she* had taken first look at the pictures of Owen Liddell with the mystery baby, and *that* was very definitely Blenkinship's case. When *she* had not declined to stick her nose in, how could she complain when *he* did the same?

Besides, we're a small department. We all have to muck in…

She flipped through the report. As she studied Dr Onatade's detached opinion, voiced in entirely matter-of-fact phraseology, she could not help overlaying it with the stark reality of the body as she'd photographed and detailed it at the scene.

And when she reached the conclusion, she experienced a moment's qualm at the definitive statement that the boy was dead when he went into the water. She made a mental note to ask the pathologist exactly what had tipped the balance for her, from probability into certainty.

With a sigh, Grace got up, suddenly restless. She made herself a cup of ginger and honey tea before going back to her desk, needing a moment.

When she turned her attention back to work, she did not return to the Elliot case.

Not just yet.

Instead, she clicked on the email from the forensics lab, with the results of the rush DNA test on the asthma inhaler. OK, they'd given her the gist of it when they rang the day before, but she still liked to read it for herself. Simply listening to someone else's verbal summary was not the same thing at all.

When she'd read the report on screen, Grace sent it to the printer and read it again on paper, pen in hand. Then she sat back in her chair and stared at a crack in the plaster above the doorway.

"Hm," she said out loud to the empty room.

Whatever *else* she might have been about to say was lost to the ringing of her mobile phone. She checked the incoming number as she picked up.

"Hello, Nick. How are you?"

"Hi, Grace." His voice sounded subdued. There was a low roar in the background. He was obviously driving somewhere. "Oh, I'm OK, I think."

She didn't call him a liar outright but her pause said the words for her.

"So, what can I do for you?"

"I just wanted to update you. I went to see Agnes Trelawney, as your ma suggested."

"Ah. Any use?"

"Not really. She has Alzheimer's. Totally away with the fairies, unfortunately. Her daughter looks after her. I saw the old girl but there was clearly no point in asking her anything. I didn't even try."

"Oh, what a shame. Still, presumably there must be records."

"Mm, I'll look into it as soon as I get in."

"Meanwhile, *I've* just taken a proper look at that DNA report on Jordan Elliot."

"Oh, why do I not like the sound of that? You're not going to tell me Dylan *was* his father after all, are you?"

"Quite the opposite," Grace said. "Not only was Dylan not the boy's father, Yvonne wasn't his mother, either..."

"I'm sorry... *What*?"

"Uh-huh. It took *me* a little while to get my head around it. There were two samples on the asthma inhaler—one male and one female. Jordan's sister, Ollie, tends to make free with his stuff when he's not there. When the lab rang me yesterday, they told me that there was no match between the male sample and Dylan Elliot's profile, which is on the database, but that was *all* they said."

"Sounds like they missed out a few vital bits."

"Jordan was also no match to the female sample—Ollie. In theory, she should be his half-sister at the very least. She *is* a match to Dylan, however."

"But is she a match to Yvonne as well?"

"Ah, *that* we don't know. Yvonne's profile isn't on record anywhere and I doubt we've enough to compel her for a test— that's *if* I could get the authorisation to apply in the first place."

He was silent for a moment or two. Then he muttered, "*Damn*."

"Quite."

"But we still have Dylan in custody, and we have the remainder of our forty-eight hours until we have to charge or release him... What about checking Yvonne's medical records relating to her pregnancy with Jordan? I mean, was she *really* pregnant? If not, where did the baby come from?"

"And, if she *was*, where did *her* baby go?"

"Quite," he echoed. "OK, Grace, I'll—"

But Grace wasn't listening any longer. Movement at the office doorway caught her eye. She glanced up to see Ty Frost standing there, looking pale as a ghost and utterly stunned. As she watched, he swayed, put a hand out to the door frame to steady himself and missed. He staggered, almost fell.

"Nick, I've got to go." Grace hung up without waiting for a response, jumped to her feet and hurried to guide Ty into his chair.

He looked up at her with unfocused eyes. She bent toward him, took a hand that was cold, clammy, and lifeless as a corpse.

"Ty, what's happened?" she demanded. "What's wrong?"

"I... I've been suspended," he said faintly.

"*Suspended*? Oh, Ty... Whatever for?"

He swallowed, eyes huge, flitting everywhere without seeming to settle. "Con–contaminating the evidence—from the car." He gripped her arm suddenly, voice turning fierce. "I didn't do it, Grace! I *swear* I didn't. I would *never* plant anything—"

"Wait a moment. Are they accusing you of *planting* evidence? Where on earth did they get such a stupid... Ah, *Blenkinship*, yes?"

He nodded, looking more wretched than she'd ever seen him.

Grace put her hand on his shoulder. "Tyson, listen to me. I don't believe for a second that you did anything wrong. You're an excellent CSI, careful, methodical, conscientious. No *way* would you contaminate anything, and no way in *hell* would you ever do anything dishonest. This is a mistake and we *will* get to the bottom of it, OK?"

He nodded again with all the conviction of a man on his way to the gallows.

She rose, forced a brisk note into her voice. "Right, what did you find?"

For a beat longer, he didn't move. Then, sluggishly, he swivelled back to his keyboard and brought up a folder of images. They showed part of the rear suspension of Dylan Elliot's Ford, a wide shot to give context, then a close-up of a scrap of cloth wedged into part of the coil-spring assembly. And, finally, the fabric removed from the car and laid out on a plain background. The usual graduated scale alongside showed it to be perhaps a couple of inches square, with part of a hem at one edge.

Grace leaned closer, her eyes narrowing. "This?" she queried. "*This* is what they're saying you 'planted'?"

He flinched at her tone as much as the words, but gave a single affirmative duck of his head.

"Then it's not *you* who needs to worry," she said, her voice grim, "because it's not just *unlikely* that you did any such thing, I can *prove* it's damn near impossible…"

79

"How *dare* you!" Yvonne yelled, surging out of her chair. "Accusin' me of *stealin'* a baby, are you?"

"Sit *down*, Mrs Elliot," DI Pollock said calmly.

"I—"

He cocked his head and stared at her. She subsided without another sound, folding back into herself until she was small and tightly packed away.

"For the benefit of the recording," Nick said, "I am now showing Mrs Elliot two DNA test results. These were obtained from samples taken from an asthma inhaler belonging to Jordan Elliot." He slid the two sheets across the table toward Yvonne. "One set of results has been identified as belonging to Jordan. The other is from your daughter, Olivia Elliot."

"So?" She skimmed over them, her blank expression making it clear that she did not understand their significance.

"We have your husband's DNA stored on our database from a previous offence," Nick went on. "These results prove that Jordan was not Dylan's son. *And*," he added, cutting her off when she opened her mouth for another loud denial, "they also prove that Jordan is no relation to Olivia."

"What was you takin' Ollie's DNA for, anyway?" she demanded. "You'd no right to do that!"

"It appears that your daughter had handled Jordan's inhaler," Nick said. "Her DNA was collected unintentionally. It won't be stored…once this case is over."

"So, what all this boils down to," Pollock said, "is that although we know little Olivia is Dylan's daughter, if she's *your* kiddie as well, then Jordan can't possibly be. So which is it?"

Yvonne sat there and glared between the two of them for a moment, then she folded her arms and said, "No comment."

"And what we need now, in order to clear this up, nice and easy, like, is a sample of *your* DNA for comparison."

Yvonne's eyes flew to the duty solicitor sitting alongside her, a drippy girl who kept pushing her glasses back up her nose every couple of minutes and sniffing—hay fever, she'd explained.

"Can they *make* me do that?"

"No," the girl said with more bite than Nick would have given her credit for. "They can't."

Pollock heaved a gusty sigh and eyed the solicitor with disfavour. "Might I suggest, Ms Chadwick, that you try to talk some sense into your client."

"It is not up to Mrs Elliot—or me—to do your job for you, detective inspector," she said with another sniff. "Until we know exactly what offence you're alleging has taken place here, we're not obliged to respond. My client has a right not to incriminate herself, as I'm sure you're well aware."

Pollock glowered at her for a few seconds longer, then jerked his head to Nick and got to his feet.

"Interview suspended at…" Nick logged the time, then paused the recording and followed Pollock outside, closing the interview room door behind them.

"Well, they're both right, in a way," Pollock remarked as they moved further along the corridor. "We *are* accusing Yvonne of nicking a baby, more or less—"

"We just don't know which one."

"And until we *do* know that, we can't begin to work out where the cuckoo came from, or by what means they acquired it."

"Maybe she…swapped it?" Nick suggested. "Dylan was desperate for a son, after so many girls. What if she was convinced this one was a boy and then, when it was born, it turned out to be another girl?"

"Or maybe she simply faked the pregnancy and snatched the

kid." Pollock scratched his chin. "How are we doing with her medical records?"

Medical records were subject to the Data Protection Act. Without the consent of the patient, it was hard to get hold of them, as Nick had found on numerous occasions in the past. But when the death of a child was involved—or the safety of other children—then no General Practitioner wanted to be held responsible for being obstructive.

"It took a bit of fast talking, sir, but her GP agreed to release them—under the circumstances."

"Hm, about time, too. Although, whether we can make anything from them or not is another matter."

"Ah, well, I took the liberty of calling in some expert assistance, sir," Nick said. Movement at the other end of the corridor caught his eye and he nodded over Pollock's shoulder. "And here she is now."

Pollock turned just in time to see Dr Onatade moving briskly toward them. In one hand was a folder of papers. "Brian. Nick," she greeted them.

"Ayo, thanks for coming in," Pollock said. He nodded to the folder. "What can you tell us?"

"I'm sure you will appreciate, gentlemen, that I've had very little time to study this material in depth?"

"Understood," Pollock said. "First off, can you confirm she was actually pregnant?"

"Oh yes," she said promptly. "Ante-natal clinic attendance notes, ultra-sound scans, all her appointments. She was pregnant, without a doubt."

"Did they note the sex of the baby?" Nick asked.

"Yes, a boy. She particularly wanted to know."

Nick exchanged a glance with his inspector. "What about the next pregnancy, with the little girl, Olivia?"

"That one is confirmed, also."

Nick frowned. "I suppose we could check if there were any missing babies reported at the hospital around the times they were born."

"Ah, well, there you *will* struggle," Dr Onatade said. "She opted for home births—both times." She flipped open the folder and double-checked. "Midwife in attendance. No doctor required. No complications reported." And she closed the folder again.

"So, after all that, we still don't know which one is hers," Pollock muttered.

Dr Onatade eyed him with surprise. "Oh yes, I can tell you *that*," she said. "I can say with absolute certainty that Yvonne Elliot could not *possibly* be the mother of Jordan."

"Why so sure?" Nick asked.

"Blood. According to the records, Yvonne's blood group is listed as O-positive. Nothing unusual in that—it's the most common type. Almost forty percent of the population have it. However, Jordan's blood group was *also* O-positive."

Nick frowned at the pathologist and noted Pollock doing the same. Clearly the right response. She beamed at them.

"Dylan Elliot's blood type is *AB*-positive. Not the rarest, but close. Only around three percent of us have such a type. Interestingly, it also makes him capable of receiving a donation from any *other* blood type."

Pollock cleared his throat.

Dr Onatade regarded him over her reading glasses. He refrained from whatever impatient remark had been forming. Nick held back a smile. Nice to see his boss was not the only one who'd perfected the hard stare technique.

"What this means as far as your case is concerned," she went on, "is that if the parents are types AB and O, then it is scientifically impossible for their offspring to be type O. Or type AB for that matter. They can be *only* A or B."

Pollock looked momentarily stunned. "Ayo, you're a bloody wonder."

"Yes, I know." Dr Onatade grinned as she handed over the folder. "Now, is there anywhere I can observe what happens next?"

Nick caught the doubt on Pollock's face. "Dr Onatade might be able to discount on medical grounds any arguments Yvonne tries to raise, sir," he pointed out.

"All right then. Show her the way and let's get back at it, lad, eh?"

As he led her to the office set up with the video and audio links, Dr Onatade leaned in conspiratorially. "Sod medical grounds," she murmured, "I want to catch the drama."

When Nick returned to the interview room, Pollock had restarted the recording equipment. From the sour look on the faces of both Yvonne and Ms Chadwick, he had already given them the glad tidings about Jordan's parentage as well.

"DC Weston has just entered the room," Pollock narrated. "Now, Mrs Elliot. We need some answers. So, do yourself a favour, lass."

"My client *is* now prepared to make a statement," Ms Chadwick said.

Pollock sat back in his chair. "*Is* she now?"

Yvonne's gaze was skittering around the walls as if looking for an escape. When none presented itself, she clamped her hands together in her lap.

"When I fell pregnant with me fourth, and we found out it were a boy, my Dyl' were over the moon. Only, you lot nicked him for receiving," she said, throwing them a dirty look.

That's right—blame us for catching him, Nick thought, *not him for being stupid enough to commit the crime in the first place.*

"So, when I got near me due date, he were still on remand." She stopped, stared down at her hands. "I–I knew there were summat wrong with the baby. You can't give birth to three kids and not realise…"

Ms Chadwick gave her an encouraging smile and sniffed again.

"What did the doctors say?" Pollock asked.

Yvonne shook her head. "I didn't go. Was too scared of what they was goin' to tell me, I s'pose. And Dyl' were so desperate for a boy—he would've killed me…"

That hung in the air between them.

"Go on, lass," Pollock said, almost gently.

"I was about a week or so overdue when I finally went into labour." She pushed a limp dangle of hair away from her face. "Never known anythin' like it—not even with me first. I sent for the midwife… She did her best but, when he were born, I could see he weren't breathin'…"

"Still-born," Pollock said, in a hushed tone Nick hadn't heard him use before. He glanced sharply at his DI but could read nothing from his face.

"I thought so," Yvonne agreed, face screwed up with anguish, "but…she took him away for a bit. Don't know how long. I was exhausted, like. I just…passed out. And then the midwife brought him back, all wrapped up and wailin' and it… It were like a miracle."

But her words lacked conviction.

"The midwife—that would be Agnes Trelawney, I presume?" Nick said. *Convenient to dump responsibility for the whole deception onto the one person who was in no state to answer questions.*

"Aye… Aye, that's right. Agnes."

Nick asked quietly, "Did you know, straight away, that he wasn't *your* baby?"

She shook her head fiercely—too fiercely, overdoing it perhaps.

"Not then," she denied. "But he were so *tiny*—smaller even than my eldest, and she were a week early. And then, of course, as he grew…" She looked up, met their gaze at last, her eyes brimming with tears. "Well, by that time he *were* mine, every way that mattered."

80

GRACE WAS CONCENTRATING SO COMPLETELY on the outraged email she was writing in defence of Ty Frost, that she did not immediately notice Dr Onatade hovering in the doorway.

"Good heavens, Grace. That's quite a scowl."

Grace made an effort to relax. It was only then she appreciated how tense her shoulders had become.

"What can I say?" She shrugged. "Incompetence infuriates me."

"Ah, anything I can help you with?"

Grace bit her lip. She was very tempted to vent her feelings to the pathologist about the treatment of her colleague, but something made her pause. It would be unprofessional of her. Besides, there were protocols, chains of command to be observed. And although Ayo Onatade had always seemed friendly, approachable, Grace did not know her well.

She did not, she reflected, know *any* of her colleagues particularly well outside of work.

With the exception, perhaps, of Nick Weston…

"No—thank you anyway, Ayo. I'll get to the bottom of it, I expect." She sat back in her chair. "It's lovely to see you, though. What brings you to my neck of the woods?"

"That rather dishy young detective, Nick Weston."

Grace merely raised her eyebrows and Dr Onatade laughed out loud.

"He was only after my *mind*, sadly. For the interpretation of medical records—and confirmation that the boy could not possibly be the child of his parents. I understand it was *you* who spotted the differing DNA results between the boy and his sister?"

"It's a problem with sending anything away to an outside lab for testing. If they don't know the context, they don't flag up things that could well be vital."

"Hm, I know some forces are setting up their own in-house labs, but they are not without their drawbacks—accusations of bias in favour of the prosecution, for instance."

Was that what had happened here, Grace wondered? That someone had let their enthusiasm for a conviction get the better of them?

"Ayo… When you carried out the post-mortem exam, on the boy, what happened to his clothes?"

The pathologist blinked in surprise at the apparent swerve of subject. "I photographed them in situ, removed them from the body, bagged them, labelled them, and passed them on to Chris Blenkinship to log when he got back here. Why, is something wrong?"

"I'm not sure at the moment," she said, disliking the need for evasion. "Would you be able to send me the images you took?"

"Of course," she said promptly. "I can login remotely to my system and do it from here. On *one* condition."

Grace looked up quickly at the serious note in her voice. "Which is?"

But the other woman was smiling as she nodded to the kettle and cups on top of a filing cabinet. "That you make me a cup of ginger and lemon tea. I can't *stand* vending machine stuff."

"Oh, I'm sorry, I should have offered. Please, have a seat." Grace got up, checked the water level in the kettle and flicked it on. "Actually, while you're here, would you mind taking a look at a couple of pictures for me?"

"Of course," Dr Onatade said again, taking Ty Frost's vacant chair. Grace set her laptop down on the empty desk and clicked open a folder. The pathologist unfolded her reading glasses and began scrolling through the images. "The man is Owen Liddell— I never forget a customer, as it were. But who is the child?"

"That's what we're trying to find out, although—strictly speaking—this is not really my case."

"Ah, well. Sadly, unlike the female of the species, I cannot tell from Mr Liddell's remains if he had children or not."

"Trust me, anything you can glean from the appearance of the baby in this picture might help us identify him or her."

"Hm. I would say that they *may* have been born prematurely."

"Oh?"

"Yes, the child here is not the usual chubby baby. Babies typically put on fifty percent of their body fat in the last two months of pregnancy, so these rather gaunt features are often a sign of a premature birth."

"Care to hazard a guess if *this* could be the same child?" Grace leaned across and clicked open the image she'd taken of the Gypsy boy, Ocean, at the Fair.

"To quote Sherlock Holmes: 'I never guess. It is a shocking habit—destructive to the logical faculty.'"

"I wouldn't have had you down as a Conan Doyle fan."

"Loved the stories as a child. And what is forensic science if not the ultimate in analysis of evidence, and deductive reasoning?"

"Me, too," Grace admitted. "You know he based Holmes on Dr Joseph Bell, a forensic scientist at Edinburgh, of course?"

Dr Onatade leaned forward, her face intent, and studied the two images. "Hm, it's a shame the angles aren't directly comparable but, even so, there are certainly some facial characteristics in common. Do we know anything about this boy?"

The kettle clicked off. Grace poured hot water into two mugs. "Only that he's Romany, and Owen was rumoured to be having a relationship with a Gypsy girl at the time he disappeared. And that the boy is approximately the right age to be the baby in the picture."

"Well, he does seem a likely match then." Dr Onatade accepted her lemon and ginger tea with a grateful nod. "Does this have any bearing on Mr Liddell's body being found at a location where Travellers are known to camp?"

Grace took a sip of her own tea. "It may well do. Apparently, her clan disapproved and tried repeatedly to warn Owen off— even put him in hospital with that arm fracture you identified."

Dr Onatade pursed her lips, swivelling her chair from side to side slightly as she considered. "I suppose so," she said. "He could have gone to Water Yat to see the child, perhaps been involved in an argument that turned nasty, took a whack to the head—maybe accidental—and before they know it, they've a body to dispose of."

"I thought you didn't make guesses?" Grace said mildly.

She received another laugh. "Well, at least the cause of death on *that* one was clear-cut enough not to *need* to guess," Dr Onatade said. "I'm sorry I couldn't be as definite on Jordan Elliot for you. But, by the time the river was finished with him, it was impossible to—"

"What?" Grace sat upright so abruptly that hot tea slopped out onto her fingers. "What do you mean…? Hang on a moment." She put down the tea, wiped her hand, and leafed through the paperwork on her desk. "Ah, here we go. This is the PM report on Jordan and, unless I'm mistaken… Yes, *there*."

She handed the report over with the conclusion page upper-most. Dr Onatade took it, looking puzzled. As she read through the final paragraph, her eyebrows climbed toward her hairline, then slammed downward.

"WHAT? This is *not* what I said. I *categorically* did *not* say this. It's been interfered with. I—" She let Grace peel the report out of her nerveless fingers. "I emailed the original through *only* to you and to Christopher, so who…?"

"I never received this from you electronically," Grace said quietly. "It was delivered onto my desk as hard copy—*this* copy."

"By whom?"

"Tyson said Chris Blenkinship brought it in personally."

"Oh…"

"Yeah, 'oh' indeed." She took a deep breath, thinking of Ty Frost's suspension and the reason behind it. "And that's not all…"

81

"WE'LL HAVE to let the Elliots go—for the moment," DI Pollock said. "I don't think they're going to run far and it saves all kinds of headaches with Social Services over who looks after the kiddies."

Nick nodded. "Yes, sir."

"And besides, if Jordan *wasn't* Jordan, then we need to find out who the heck he *was* before we work out what to charge 'em with."

"I'll get back on that now, sir," Nick said.

But on his way to the CID office he detoured via CSI, finding only Dr Onatade in occupation. She was studying a report and drinking pale liquid from a mug.

"Oh, hi," he said when he stuck his head round the door. "Have you seen Grace McColl by any chance?"

"I believe she's just on her way to see Mr Blenkinship," Dr Onatade said, looking unaccountably stern.

And Nick, knowing how rarely Grace actively sought out the company of her boss, frowned.

"OK. I'll perhaps catch up with her later. Oh, and thanks for your expertise earlier, doctor. It was much appreciated."

She drained the last of her tea and got to her feet. "Thank you, Nick," she said, her thunderous tone belying the words. "It's nice to know *someone* respects my work."

Nick beat a hasty retreat.

On his way up the stairs, however, he was almost knocked

flying by a figure that came galloping down them. Both men cannoned off the wall of the stairwell and, had Nick not grabbed hold of the man's arms, he would have taken a dive down the next flight.

"Steady on, Dave," Nick said, recognising DC Yardley. "Where's the fire, man?"

"It's Cheryl!" Yardley said, his eyes a little wild. "She's gone into labour, eh? I gotta get over there—"

"For God's sake, you're in no fit state to drive," Nick said. "I'll take you. Just let me grab my keys and leave a note on the board."

"OK, OK," Yardley yelped. "But hurry! Her waters have broken already."

He appeared to be making up for his absence at his wife's bedside by panting through his own phantom labour pains.

Nick took the final staircase three at a time.

82

THE LAST DAY of the Fair was upon them, and Bartley Smith could not wait for it to be over. Not the usual state of affairs at all, to be sure. He was a sociable feller, by and large, and the annual gathering of the clans was something he generally looked forward to with anticipation, and looked back on with warmth.

Not this year.

This year he'd been aware of the pressure building on the approach. A thunderhead before the storm. Looking back, he'd thought his biggest worry was the choosing of the new *Shera Rom*, but he hadn't counted on Vano and his schemes.

He even wondered if the whole thing—the way its course had run—was some devious dealing on the part of his brother-in-law. A plan to have Bartley himself seem a lesser man in the eyes of those who had the final choice to make.

And, if he was being honest, he didn't care.

No, that wasn't *quite* the case. He didn't care about the winning, or the prize. But he *did* care about the losing—of face as well as standing.

And, more than that, he cared about letting Queenie down.

Because let her down he had, and badly. Putting her in a position where she felt there was nothing else to be done but hand over her father's last colt, just to appease that *bostaris*.

O beng te poggar his men. May the devil break his neck.

If he'd asked for a child, that *gorgio* could not have chosen something she valued more. To Queenie, the colt was almost of her own blood. How could he expect her simply to give away the little horse, the *tawno gry*, when she had already lost so much?

Because what had *he* lost? Nothing he wasn't glad to see the back of, to be sure.

And look at what he'd gained—

An arm looped around his shoulders. So caught up had he been in his misery, he hadn't kept his wits about him. Unforgiveable, is what it was.

He ducked, twisted, and stepped out from under the arm with the kind of dancing lunge that had served him well in the ring.

Not this time.

Instead, he came up hard against a second man to the side of him. He started to turn, was stopped short by the bite of a blade slicing through shirt and skin, between his ribs.

He froze.

His breath hitched in his throat. The knife was barely more than tip deep, he knew, but he felt the trickle of blood slide greasily toward his hip. And he knew it would take little more than a twitch to see him gutted like a hare.

The man beyond the blade moved in close and breathed in his ear, "Well then—*Mr Smith* is it now? You're a hard man to track down. I've been waiting for a chance at you."

He recognised the harsh tones of the North in the man's voice and his belly dropped to his boots.

"McMahon," he managed past a tongue suddenly thick in his mouth. "Well, here I am. Have your say and be done with it."

The Irishman tutted slowly. "Is that any way to greet an old friend? Why, I've known you since before you were born… Back when you were still someone else. Isn't that right…*Patrick*?"

"I left that man behind me, buried him and moved on," Bartley said between his teeth.

"Did you think a change of name would ever be enough to hide behind? After what you did?"

"It was a fair fight. Your cousin was…unlucky."

"You hit him and he almost died," McMahon gritted back. "And then I find you've the nerve to use the names of not one but *two* Gypsy kings."

Bartley said nothing. He'd taken Smith to please old

Hezekiah, to make him worry less about losing a daughter, and think more about gaining another son.

And as for the Bartley, well, what fighter would not be proud to carry the name of Bartley Gorman V? A fellow Irish Traveller, he was undefeated bare-knuckle boxing champion of the United Kingdom and Ireland for twenty years or more.

Now, it seemed a poor disguise.

Bartley flicked his eyes at the man who still had an arm clamped tight across his shoulders, for all the world like an old *pal* saying a long hello. But the man was half a head taller and, though thickset, his bulk was muscle not fat. Still, for the moment it was McMahon and the blade that had his attention and concern.

Bartley knew that Appleby was crawling with *gavvers*, as it always was come the Fair. He could see them now, strolling along The Sands on the opposite bank of the river, with their hands tucked into the arm-holes of their stab vests. A peculiar habit, he'd always thought, that didn't leave your fists where you might need them in a hurry.

Mostly, he walked wide of them. This must be the only time he could remember willing a pair to turn his way. To take a long hard look, and work out what lay beneath the false appearance of friendly bonhomie.

But, of course, they did not.

Bartley turned his head away from McMahon toward his *pal*. He may be a big man and a fighter but he was no champion. Too lumbering to have the agility the ring demanded. And not careful enough to have a nose that wasn't oft-times broken. Bartley tilted his head back, as if to get a better look at the man's slack features.

"Sure and don't I know you?" he asked.

The man frowned, distracted. Bartley uncoiled his neck and flicked his forehead forward viciously. The blow landed hard, sending the man's already beleaguered nose halfway across his face in a welter of blood.

He let loose a roar, like a lion Bartley had once seen in a circus in County Mayo. The bellow of it echoed across the surface of the river. Heads whipped away from the horses and the ponies tied to the orange plastic barriers that lined The Sands. Instead, they turned to stare across the river.

Bartley shimmied out of the big man's grasp and tried to jerk away from the knife between his ribs. He unstuck himself, yes, but not without the sting of it biting harder. The rip of flesh, the tear of skin, the welter of his own blood.

I could be a dead man walking, and not know it 'til I drop.

McMahon let his temper get the better of him then. Instead of palming the knife and backing away, as if Bartley was the one who'd started the scuffle for no reason at all, he leapt in with fists flying. Bartley avoided him, mostly. Not easy with your insides making for the emergency exit like there'd been a fire.

But McMahon's actions brought the knife into plain view.

On the other side of the Eden, the *gavvers* set up a hue and cry. One ran for the edge of the river and looked like he might jump in and try to wade across, more fool him. Others ran for the bridge, heads cocked, shouting into their radios.

Beside him, McMahon swore under his breath. "We're not *done*," he said fiercely. Then he and his *pal* ran onto the cricket field behind them and were gone.

Bartley tried to straighten. He quickly found himself bent around the pain that was coming, ever greater, in waves with every breath. His shirt was barely enough to hold it in. He tried to move, also, to flee. His legs had other ideas. They folded.

And as the first burly copper came thundering along the river path, red-faced and breathless, Bartley gave up his battle with gravity and slid to his knees in the grass.

83

DC DAVE YARDLEY lived in Alston, a small market town at the top of Hartside Pass, high in the Pennines. Driving up the steep, switchback road, Nick had trouble keeping the big grin off his face, glad of the excuse to put his foot down

In the passenger seat, Yardley braced himself between door and dashboard. Nick caught the occasional sharp intake of breath at some of the hairpin corners, but otherwise Yardley said nothing until they were approaching the first signs of habitation.

"This is us—opposite the garage," he said. "And thanks, mate. You got us here in half the time it would've taken me. This thing's a right rocket-ship, eh?"

"It has its moments," Nick agreed. "D'you mind if I just use your facilities before I head back? I'm assuming you don't need me to wait. I mean, *you're* not likely to be back in the office yourself for a bit, are you?"

"I think I'm allowed the time off—in the circumstances," Yardley agreed. He glanced across at the row of parked cars outside the pair of stone cottages. "And the midwife's here. I can always get a lift down with her to pick up my car."

The cottages were three storeys high and built tucked into the hillside that rose behind them. The ground floor housed an integral garage, leading almost straight out onto the road. A set of worn stone steps led up to the main entrance at the side of the property. Yardley galloped up them and charged through the front door, shouting, "Cheryl!"

"We're up here!" called a voice.

Yardley shot along the hallway and up the next flight.

"Loo's up here, mate," he said over his shoulder as he went. "Excuse me if I…" And he was gone.

Nick followed him upstairs at a more moderate pace. The bathroom was the door facing him at the top. When he emerged onto the landing again, he paused a moment, wondering whether to simply let himself out quietly or wait to wish his colleague goodbye and good luck.

The decision was taken out of his hands.

"Nick?" Yardley's voice came from the front bedroom, if he was any judge. And there was enough off-kilter about it to have Nick pushing the door open and walking in without a second thought.

A woman lay propped up in the double bed, holding a very pink and wrinkled baby in her arms, wrapped in a yellow blanket.

Nick came to an abrupt halt. "Oh. Wow."

The woman gave him a tired smile, although she was looking remarkably composed considering what she'd just gone through. "'Wow' is about right," she said.

"Nick, meet Cheryl, my wife—and…our daughter."

Nick nodded to the woman. "Congratulations," he said warmly. "I'm sorry I didn't get him here sooner."

"If you drove any faster, mate, we would have been airborne, eh?"

"And once she decided she was coming, there was no stopping this little lady," said the midwife from over by the window.

Nick turned. They recognised each other at the same moment. A cocktail of emotions flitted across the woman's face, from embarrassment, through dismay, to a hint of defiance.

"Hello Mrs Trelawney," Nick said. "How is your mother? You didn't mention that you'd followed in her footsteps…"

———

"So, *was* it your mother who delivered Jordan Elliot?" Nick asked. "Or was it you?"

They were downstairs in the small sitting room. Old-fashioned furniture at odds with the latest flat-screen TV stuffed into one of the alcoves. Yardley had made tea for the three of them, letting his wife and their new offspring grab a nap uninterrupted.

Wynter Trelawney perched uncomfortably on the edge of the sofa, as if she might need to jump up at any moment and flee. Nick made sure to stand between her and the door, just in case.

It was hard to reconcile the neat and businesslike midwife with the flamboyant scatterbrain he'd met at the farm. Her wild grey hair now hung in a tight plait over her shoulder, any stray ends pinned away from her face. She was gripping her mug so her knuckles gleamed whitely through the skin.

She took a deep breath, blew it out unsteadily, looked up and met Nick's eyes without flinching.

"In the end, it was both of us—in a way."

Nick said nothing, just waited for her to continue. After a moment or two, she did.

"I'd split up with my husband, come back north to live with Mum. And for want of another career, I suppose, I'd started training to be a midwife, too."

"Agnes was still working then?"

She nodded. "It was Fair time. We'd bow-tops and vardos camped all along the lane by us, and in the field at the back, when Mum got word a Romany girl had gone into labour."

"Who was the girl?"

"All I know is, she was young—very young. Hadn't even known she was carrying. Mum didn't ask questions and I didn't either. She just packed up her bag and went, same as she always did. And then, a little while later, Yvonne Elliot rang. She'd been in labour for hours, she said, and the baby wasn't coming. She'd had three by then, knew probably better than *I* did how it all *should* go. But she couldn't feel the baby moving and she was scared, sobbing at me down the phone. So…I went to her."

"What about her GP? Or an ambulance?"

"She said she'd tried but couldn't get through. And anyway, what with the Fair and everything, it would have taken them too long to get out to Mallerstang."

"So you went to her," Nick echoed, trying to keep any judgement out of his voice.

Even so, she flushed. "What else could I do? Leave her to struggle on alone? The baby was breech. I'd just learned about it —about how you can turn them using ECV."

"Which is?" Nick asked.

"External Cephalic Version," Yardley supplied. Both of them stared at him. His neck stained pink above his collar. "Cheryl was breech at thirty-six weeks. The doc had to manipulate her abdomen to turn the baby into the right position for delivery, eh? Explained all about it."

"So, what happened with Yvonne?"

"It was too late to try that method when she'd already gone into labour. She needed a caesarean section—and quickly. Even so, I'm not sure, by then, if it would have made much difference. She'd been trying too long—she was exhausted, panicking about what her husband would do to her if anything happened to his son…"

"So Yvonne's baby was still-born," Nick said quietly. The realisation settled over him like snow, softly chilling.

"Yes." It was almost a whisper.

"And the Gypsy girl?"

Wynter swallowed. "When I got back to the farm, Mum was in the kitchen. She'd put the girl's baby in the bottom oven of the Aga."

He started. "She'd done *what*?"

"He was early—a tiny little mite. It was the only way to keep him warm enough. We used to do it with lambs all the time, back when Dad was still farming."

"What of the girl herself?"

"She was hysterical, Mum said. Hadn't known she was pregnant and was convinced her family would kill her if they found out."

"So you did a swap."

She nodded. "Mum said the girl begged her to take him, not to tell anyone. So it seemed the perfect solution all round. She drove him down to Mallerstang and…gave him to Yvonne. I don't know if Yvonne suspected—I mean, surely she *must* have done. But she never said…"

"And the other child—Yvonne's still-born baby?"

Wynter met his gaze again. "I'd brought him away with me.

Not quite sure why. But Mum took him and…" Her eyes shimmered bright with unshed tears. "She never said what she'd done with him and I, God help me, never asked."

84

OUTSIDE THE DOOR, Grace lifted a hand and hesitated, just for a second.

Then she reached for the handle, opened the door and stepped through before rapping her knuckles on the wood panel.

Chris Blenkinship looked up sharply at the intrusion. He was sitting behind his desk near the window. There were two desks in the CSI office at Carlisle but, since the reshuffle of staff, only one was occupied. The other was utterly empty. Almost like a symbol, she thought, that he neither wanted nor needed any assistance.

"McColl," Blenkinship greeted her coolly, only his raised eyebrows betraying his surprise. "I'd say 'come in' but it *seems* you already are."

"I need to speak to you."

His eyes dropped back to the screen of his laptop and he resumed pecking at the keys.

"Well, pet, I'm a bit busy at the moment. If you'd called to make an appointment before you drove up, like, I could have saved you a wasted journey."

Grace ignored the dismissal and waited, her expression bland, to see whose nerve broke first. After only a few moments, something ticced in his face and he sat back with an exasperated sigh.

"All right, sit yourself down, seeing as you're here anyway." He checked his watch pointedly. "I can spare you *five* minutes."

"That's fine, Christopher. I won't need long."

She disregarded the visitor's chair and chose instead to lean on the edge of the spare desk. She put down her bag on the desktop, close to hand, and withdrew a plain folder. From it, she picked out the top sheet of printed paper, which she offered. He folded his arms, almost childishly, forcing her to place it on the desk in front of him.

Blenkinship leaned forward with obvious reluctance, just enough to peer at the page. "What's this?"

"It's the summary from the post-mortem examination report on Jordan Elliot," Grace said with calm precision. "The PM *you* attended."

"Yes, I *do* know where I've been, thank you all the same, McColl." And the flash of something in his eyes *could* simply have been irritation, but somehow she thought not.

"If I might draw your attention to the text I've highlighted…? You see, that is a copy of the report which *you* delivered to me yesterday. Whereas *this*"—she removed a second sheet from the folder, also highlighted, and placed it alongside the first—"is the same page of the *original* report, which Dr Onatade emailed through to both of us."

"So?"

"Three little letters," Grace said. "That was all it took. The erasure of N-O-T to turn 'cannot' into 'can' at the end of that line, and suddenly the whole tone of the conclusion changes, wouldn't you agree?"

"Making a bit of a meal out of this, aren't you, McColl? It's clearly a mistake. No doubt Dr Onatade sent me an earlier version of the report, realised she'd cocked up, and is now trying to cover her arse. And like I said, I'm busy and—"

"Then I'll be brief," she cut across his further attempt at dismissal. She took out a number of print-out images and lined them up in front of him, then pointed to the first. "These two are my crime-scene photographs when Jordan Elliot was taken from the river. No, *look* at them, Christopher!" she snapped, when he would have pushed his chair away. "Look at his shirt. It's torn and ragged, yes, but the hems are intact."

"So?" He glared at her with defiance rather than do as he was bid, but couldn't hold it long. "What of it?"

She ignored his question, stabbed a finger at the next image.

"*This* is the photograph Dr Onatade took of the shirt when she'd removed it from Jordan's body. See—hem *still* intact."

"All right, McColl. No need for theatrics. Just say what you have to say, will you?"

"This last shot is the one Ty Frost took of the 'evidence' he recovered from the underside of Dylan Elliot's vehicle. A vehicle *you* were working on, alone, immediately prior to that discovery."

He did look then, slowly, from the first pictures to the last. His face reddened as the blood rushed to it, to the tips of his ears. As his fight-or-flight response fired.

"You altered the PM report and you planted the evidence for Ty to find," Grace said quietly. And, almost to herself, "You know, if I thought it was because you were trying to protect someone else, I might *almost* admire you. But this is all about *you*, isn't it?"

She saw it then, the kaleidoscope of emotions that flickered through his face. Anger, dismay, fear and—finally—guilt. *Confirmation.* He swallowed, didn't speak right away. And when he did so, he chose his words with care.

"What…proof do you have? Of any of this?"

"What more proof do I need, Christopher?" she asked. "What more is there to find?"

He shook his head, putting up a hand as if to ward off further questions. Then let it drop back into his lap helplessly.

"Who else have you told…about this?"

She eyed him for a split-second, somehow knowing this moment was pivotal.

And, quite possibly, dangerous.

"Dr Onatade knows there's a discrepancy in the reports but, other than that, nobody. I rather thought it was *your* job to… bring it to light."

"Thank you."

"*Don't,*" she said, her voice clipped with revulsion—at herself for giving him this chance as much as at the man who had been her colleague, and was supposed to be her superior. "Don't *thank* me. I'm not the keeper of your secrets. I simply don't want all the evidence we've gathered to be discredited by your actions. Nor will I stand by and let you ruin Ty's career. He's a good CSI."

Unlike you. The words hung unspoken between them. "He doesn't deserve this."

"I know. It wasn't—"

"Don't," Grace said again, but with more tiredness than heat. She slid the empty folder back into her bag and rose. "You need to turn yourself in, Christopher. *You* need to do it, not have me do it for you. I'll give you that, at least. You have until tomorrow. Then…"

And with that she walked out of the office, leaving him slumped in his chair, staring with eyes that saw nothing but his own downfall.

85

THE BATTER of a fist on the outside of the vardo made them both jump. Bartley, leaning against a bunch of pillows on the bunk at the far end, clutched the bandaged wound in his side and gave a muttered curse. Queenie had her hands in a bowl of cold water, scrubbing the blood from his shirt. Looking down, she saw the ripples spread outward from the sudden tremble of her fingers.

"Stay there," she told him, shaking off the excess water.

She opened the top doors only and stood in the gap, wiping her hands on a towel.

Below her, on the grass, was the *gorgio* she knew only as Karl. The man she'd threatened with a blade, and been threatened by in her turn. She felt her spine stiffen, her chin lift.

"And what is it *you're* wanting?"

He looked up at her, squinting against the bright sun. He didn't like having the lower ground, but short of dragging her out there wasn't much he could do about it.

"You know *that* well enough," he said. "Come for my horse, haven't I?"

"Oh, and it's *your* horse, is it now?" she tossed back at him.

"We had a deal."

"So we did." She nodded. "And if you'd kept up *your* end of it, then so would I do the same."

His brows drew down, making his forehead seem bulbous and heavy. From this angle, she could see the depth of his shoulders as well as the width. Like those of a dray animal who leaned into the collar, and built up layer upon layer of muscle for the task.

"What're you *on* about, girl? You promised me the horse so that miserable bugger you call a husband could hide behind your skirts, instead of standing up for himself like a man."

"Oh, I promised you the horse all right," she agreed, "but only *if* there were no comebacks. Your man sticking a *churi* between Bartley's ribs is not what *I'd* call 'no comebacks', is it now?"

Just for a second, she caught the surprise in the big *gorgio's* eyes, then the glower was back.

"A what?"

"A knife. A blade. Call it what you will. And your man McMahon behind it."

He shook his head. "*If* he did anything, it wasn't on *my* time."

"So? You can't set loose your dog and then say it's not your problem when he bites."

"Not *my* dog. Got a mind of his own, that one, eh?"

"*You* brought him here," Queenie insisted, a set to her jaw. "*You* turned him loose."

Karl gave a grunt, his patience with her argument clearly exhausted. "*I* didn't bring him nowhere or tell him to do 'owt," he said. "Now, I'm taking *my* horse and I'm going."

He nodded to someone standing off to the side of the wagon, out of Queenie's sight. She leaned out, craning, as two more of them appeared, moving toward where the mare was tethered, the colt alongside her. One of the men carried a leather foal slip headcollar, the other a long whip.

Queenie threw open the lower door and leapt down, ignoring Bartley's shout from behind her. She ran for the man with the whip first, bowling him off his feet with sheer momentum and weight and rage. She snatched the whip from his hand and turned on the other man with a snarl.

Karl wrapped both arms around her from behind, pinning hers to her sides. He lifted her clear off the ground, her feet still striding in the air. She gave a shriek of fury and struggled against his grasp, but to no avail. He had her fast.

Bartley jumped down from the vardo, wincing as he landed. He'd refused to go to the hospital, insisting that the ambulance people on The Sands simply patch him up. They had stitched or glued him back together, but it hadn't held. Blood now seeped through the top layer of the dressing.

Still, as he stood there without his shirt, there was no mistaking the wiry strength of his build, the numerous old scars of his chosen craft, the tattoos and the battered knuckles.

"Leave her *be*," he growled.

Karl ignored him, continuing to hold Queenie off the ground without apparent effort. She took as deep a breath as she was able to with her ribs being crushed, then bent her knees and kicked back her heels as hard as she could.

One foot missed but the other boot thudded into Karl's knee. She heard the graunch, the groan, felt him sag and his grip slacken.

"You little—"

That was as far as he got before Bartley was upon him, putting his all into the blows even though it made him nearly cry out with the effort of doing so. The blood escaped the bandage and overran his belt.

Karl let go of Queenie so abruptly that she dropped on all fours, scrambling away from the pair of them and jumping back to her feet. She whirled just in time to see the other *gorgio* wrap the leather foal slip over Bartley's head and yank him backwards.

She threw herself back into the fray. Her father had taught her how to punch—wrist straight, fingers tight, thumb tucked outside. She used that knowledge now. Taking a run at the man with the headcollar, her fist connected with the side of his jaw hard enough to spin him off his feet. He went down like a cut tree in the forest.

In her blinkered frenzy she barely saw the blur of a figure coming in from her right. She jerked, expecting another attack. It was no *gorgio*, she saw, but one of Jackson's *pals*. The man who'd been with him that day he threatened Bartley, and she'd threatened him right back.

Only, now he was grappling with Karl on her behalf.

More men arrived, of her own clan and the others. Anyone nearby, until the three *gorgios* were surrounded a dozen deep.

"*Dosta*," Queenie shouted. "Enough."

It took a moment—and a few blows—before they fell

back into a wide circle with the three left swaying in the centre. She pushed through them and stepped out to face Karl.

He stared at her over a split lip as he spat blood into the grass between them.

Queenie flicked her eyes around the group. She noted *familiya*, extended family, other members of her *vitsa*, her clan, and even *kampaniyi*, those from alliances of other families. All standing beside and behind her.

She straightened, her father's daughter. "We agreed terms, you and I," she said. "*You* broke those terms."

"You cheated me."

"You cheated yourself." She sensed someone move up by her shoulder—Bartley, holding his side, pale, but still on his feet. She gave him a grateful nod, turned back to the *gorgio*. "Now, I suggest you leave while you still have your legs under you."

As if by command, the circle parted, created an opening, a line of retreat. Two of the men shuffled toward it, one of them limping. It took Karl longer to move. And before he did so, he stabbed an accusing finger toward Queenie's chest.

"This," he said, "is *not* over."

86

THE KNOCK on the door came suddenly. Sharp enough that Dylan jumped, the tea slopping out of his mug and straight down the front of his T-shirt. Damn those bloody coppers, setting him right on edge!

He stomped into the hall and yanked the door open with a rising temper, that ebbed as he took in the startled figure standing outside.

"What *you* doin' here?"

Lisa had been looking around, as if afraid someone was going to see her. At the edge in his tone she stiffened, bristling. "Aren't you going to invite me in?"

He stepped back. "Yeah, 'course. Go on through."

He followed her into the kitchen, his eyes on the way the floaty little sundress she wore alternately outlined and fluttered around her trim backside.

Inside the room, she hesitated, turned to face him with hands twisted together.

"Now then, to what do I owe the pleasure?" he asked, calmer now. He put down the mug of tea, took a bite of the toast slathered with peanut butter that he'd been making when she arrived.

"You told him!" Lisa blurted out. Her voice rose. "How could you? You told Nick—about us!"

He tried a cajoling smile. "Didn't have no choice, did I? They had me down the cells, grillin' me about the boy. No alibi, otherwise. What else could I do?"

"I don't know—anything but that!"

The knuckles of her linked hands gripped white, shoulders pinching upward. "We've got a kid, Nick and me. You might have…"

"Look, if I could've done it any other way, I would've. You gotta realise that. But you don't know what it's like, havin' the cops after you! Always had it in for my dad and got it in for me, too. They've *never* given me a break, and this time it's worse than ever."

She bit her lip, blinked a bit.

Oh, don't you try the tears routine. Not with me, Lisa…

He sighed as he put down the toast, wiped his mouth with the back of his hand and stepped in, reaching for her waist. She felt tiny as he pulled her in toward him, her flesh firm without the squashy excess roll his 'Vonne had acquired over the years, between ribcage and hip.

"Look, sweetheart, it wasn't so long ago you and him wasn't together anyway, was it?' he said, more gently. "You said yourself that he was sniffin' around that redheaded CSI woman. And what's sauce for the goose, eh?"

"Yeah, but…"

Tired of convincing her with words, he slipped a hand beneath her chin and tipped her mouth to his. After only a moment, she kissed him back, like she couldn't help herself. The want zipped down his spine. In heels, she was almost his height so they were hip to hip.

He hauled her closer, needing the full contact, wanting to grind his pelvis hard into hers, but she wedged a hand against his chest.

"Dylan, no, you're all covered in tea. My dress—"

He ignored her, more demanding now with hands and teeth and tongue. In the past, she'd liked him to go a bit rough, so it took him maybe longer than it should have done to realise she was still trying to push him away.

Abruptly, he released her. She tottered back, leaned against the sink with her knees clamped together like some blushing virgin. When she wiped her mouth with one hand, he saw it was shaking. She looked close to tears again.

"I'm s–sorry. I didn't come here for… I just got carried away, that's all."

"So, what *did* you come here for, then?"

"I don't know. A mistake, clearly, wasn't it? It's just…DI Pollock dragged me into Kendal nick for questioning, like I was some kind of *criminal*. I didn't know what to *do* with myself." She let out a long, shaky breath and shook her head, voice bitter now. "And when they were done, there was Nick waiting for me, all deadly calm, like he used to get when he was on Firearms. And I knew he'd been listening to the whole thing. You even told them how I had my bikini-line waxed, for God's sake, just to prove it. Honest, I nearly *died* of embarrassment."

Dylan stilled, picked up what was left of his tepid tea just for something to do with his hands. "So, what did you say to him?"

"What d'you mean, *what did I say to him*? What *could* I say to him?"

Dylan hesitated, warring between the need for his alibi to hold, and not wanting to have some psycho copper after him— especially not one who might come tooled up and after his balls on a skewer.

Then she sighed. "I told him it wasn't serious, just a bit of fun." Her voice was miserable.

"And how did he take that, like?"

"Honestly?" She shook her head. "I don't know."

He eyed her with a certain amount of cynicism. "What else did you come here for, Leese? Not just to tell me nothin', was it?"

She took a deep breath. "Those bags," she said, looking furtive now. "The knock-off ones Karl got from you."

He moved further into the kitchen, plonked himself down at the table and sprawled in the chair. She wasn't wearing a wire— not unless it was hidden somewhere *very* personal—but he knew better than to confirm it out loud. Instead, he just raised an eyebrow.

"I brought them with me," she said. "In the car. I–I need you to take them back."

He smiled. "If you wanted rid of 'em, sweetheart, you should've just dumped 'em in the first skip you came to."

"Nick *knows* about them," she gritted out.

He stilled. "What—where they came from, you mean?"

"No, no, not that. I told him Karl had got hold of a few from some bloke he met in a pub. I think he can make it all go away, but you've *got* to take the rest back."

"Oh, I do, do I?"

The lazy insolence in his voice made her redden, like she knew she was asking the impossible and was asking it anyway.

Should have got on your knees rather than shovin' me away, sweetheart, he thought acidly. *A quick blow job might've made me feel a bit more generous, like.*

Unaware, she stumbled on. "I mean, you don't have to give me the money right now, if you haven't—"

He did laugh then, a raucous burst that stopped her in her tracks. "Oh, that's priceless! So, you not only want me to take the gear off your hands but you want a *refund* as well. What am I, Marks & Spencer? Kept the receipt, did you?"

He surged out of his chair, gratified by the way she flinched at the grate of its wooden feet along the tiles. He crowded her against the sink and, when she would have ducked out past him, closed his fingers around her exposed throat. Just hard enough to make the fear jump in her eyes.

"Let me tell you how this is goin' to work, *sweetheart*. See, *I* won't be takin' nothin' back. And *you* won't be saying *nothin'* to nobody. You got me?"

87

A UNIFORMED SERGEANT stopped Nick on his way into the station at Hunter Lane.

"I don't know what kind of aftershave you wear, DC Weston, but it certainly seems to be working," she said grimly.

"Excuse me?"

"You've *another* young lady waiting in Reception to talk to you." she said with a sniff. "I wouldn't be skipping your vitamin pills, if I were you."

Still mystified, Nick detoured to the front desk. Standing with her back to him, studying the Crime Prevention posters, was a slim girl with a mass of wild black curls. She wore a short leather jacket that enabled her to stick both hands in the back pockets of her skinny jeans.

"Hi," Nick said. "I was told you wanted to see me..."

The girl turned, revealing a stunning North African face. He couldn't help giving her a quick appraisal, realised she was doing the same right back.

"So, you must be DC Weston," she said. "I'm Alex."

"Alex...?"

She flashed him a quick grin. "The *bloke* in Tech Support, remember?"

Nick felt his face heat. "Ah, yeah. Look, I'm sorry about that —" he began but she waved away his apology.

"No worries," she said. "You wanted the text messages from Owen Liddell's mobile. Got the last six months the phone was active, right here." She patted the canvas messenger bag slung over her shoulder. "Thought I'd deliver them personally, take a look at *you* while I was at it."

"And?"

"Not shy, are you? Glad I did, though, if you want to know."

Nick raised an eyebrow. "I meant, was there anything interesting in the texts?"

"Oh yeah," she said. "That, too…"

88

GRACE HAD no sooner sat down behind her desk at Hunter Lane, than Nick stuck his head round the office door.

"Ah, you're back," he said, then stilled. "Everything OK?"

She forced a smile. "Er, yes, I think so. What's up?"

He regarded her a moment longer, took a breath. "I've just got back from speaking to the midwife who delivered Yvonne Elliot's baby."

"But I thought you said Agnes Trelawney wasn't capable of being questioned—"

"Not *Agnes*—her daughter, Wynter. She's the local midwife now, but back then she was in training and she delivered Yvonne's real child, which was still-born, apparently. Wynter said her mother was dealing with a young Gypsy girl giving birth at the same time, and *that* was the baby given to Yvonne to pass off as her own."

"So who was the mother?"

Nick shook his head. Leaning in the aperture, hands in the pockets of his suit trousers, he owned the doorway. "Wynter claims Agnes never told her, and we've no means of proving that either way."

"Rather convenient," Grace observed.

"Yes, it is, isn't it?" He frowned. "Did you say that Owen Liddell's DNA didn't come up a match to the boy, because the story about a young Gypsy girl is very familiar. And we know from the photographs that Liddell had a kid."

"Let's not jump to conclusions," Grace said. "We know he was *photographed* with a baby, but that doesn't signify ownership. *I've* been photographed in front of the Taj Mahal, but I won't be taking up residence anytime soon."

"Well, considering I understood it was built as some kind of tomb, I'm glad to hear it."

She smiled. "Can you leave this with me, Nick? Let me get the lab to run Jordan's DNA through the database again."

"What will that do?"

"I'll ask them to widen out the search. Before, we were looking for close relatives only. But if we've any aunts, uncles or cousins on file, that might get us closer to either of his birth parents."

"Great," Nick said. "Will you let me know the results as soon as you can? I'm just waiting for the DI and then we're off to have another word with the Elliots."

She looked up. "About Jordan?"

"Not this time," he said. "I've just had Owen Liddell's last text messages delivered. And the last one he received and replied to, it was from Yvonne Elliot."

"Really? That's…interesting. What did it say?"

But the clatter of boots on the stairs had him glancing over his shoulder, as DI Pollock joined him in the doorway.

"We may well need CSI down there, Grace. Have you seen Blenkinship anywhere?"

Grace schooled her face into a bland expression. "Last I knew, he was in Carlisle."

"Hm, well he's not there now and nobody seems to know where he's disappeared to," Pollock said. "So, unless you're up to your neck in something urgent, grab your kit. You're with us."

89

BLENKINSHIP DROVE into a street of squat terraced houses in Workington and slowed to a crawl.

The houses were identical cramped boxes, two up, two down, with kitchen and bathroom extensions bumped out into the yard at the back. An attempt had been made to relieve the uniformity of their pebble-dashed fronts, by painting the door and window reveals a variety of bright colours. It only served, in his opinion, to make them look like a slightly mismatched set of old plates.

The house he was looking for was next to the end of the row. A sludgy shade of mud brown had been chosen as its accent colour. Blenkinship parked and climbed out, hearing the harsh cackle of seagulls wheeling overhead. He could smell the sea, too, less than half a mile away to the west. He straightened his shoulders and rang the doorbell.

It was only as he did so that he noticed the tiny camera lens drilled into the plastic surround of the door frame, at the top corner. He stared straight up into it and mouthed, "Let me in."

After a long pause, the door opened and Ty Frost stood in the gap. He wore what might have been tartan pyjama bottoms, with a stained T-shirt and socks but no shoes.

"Hi boss," he said, without enthusiasm. "What're you doing here?"

"I've just come to see how you are, like," Blenkinship said, ignoring Frost's sceptical expression. "Aren't you going to ask us in?"

Frost moved back with obvious reluctance and jerked his head. Blenkinship stepped through straight into the living room. The space was almost entirely taken up with a leather corner sofa. A large flat-screen TV hung on the wall opposite. There appeared to be no other furniture in the room. The walls were hung with classic movie posters—mainly sci-fi epics.

"Make yourself at home," Frost mumbled, clearing his laptop and a games controller off to one side.

They sat in awkward silence for a moment while Blenkinship searched for the best way into his story.

"Look, Ty, I just wanted you to know that I don't believe for a *second* you planted that evidence, all right?"

Ty looked up at him blankly. "But… I thought it was *you* who reported me?"

"Well, obviously, yeah. As soon as I realised there was something amiss, I didn't have a choice," he said hastily. "But that doesn't mean *you* were the one who put it there, eh?"

"I suppose that would've been a bit dumb—me planting it *and* then finding it myself an' all," he agreed.

"Aye." Blenkinship hid a wince. "But I think I've an idea who *might* have done it."

That got his attention. "*Who*?"

Blenkinship eyed him for a moment. He'd worked out all the angles on the drive over to the coast, but now he was actually here…

"Weston," he said.

"No way," Frost said faintly but there was no weight behind it. "You sure?"

Blenkinship let his breath out slowly, only then aware he'd been holding it. "Well…let's just say I have my suspicions, eh?"

"Can you prove it, like?"

He made a face of regret. "That's the thing. I *thought* there might just be something on my dash-cam. It records if anybody interferes with the car, not just when you're driving, doesn't it?"

"Well, yeah, but…"

"The clothing from the post-mortem exam on the boy was in the boot when Weston ran into me in the car park. He could have accessed it then—while I was distracted, like." Blenkinship had practised talking about this, saying the words out loud during the drive until they sounded natural to his own ears, almost convincing. And the best lies, he knew, were those which stuck closest to the truth. "I can't prove it but...I could've sworn there was already some damage on the front corner of his vehicle."

"Oh," Frost said. And, as the import struck home. "*Oh.*"

"Yeah. So, are you *sure* you threw away that SD card—the one from my dash-cam? Because, if not, I wondered if I could have it back—see if I can get anything off it."

"If it is corrupted, you'll struggle," Frost said.

Blenkinship tried not to let his relief show. *So, he hasn't looked at it.* The use of present-tense did not escape him, though. His eyes narrowed.

"Does that mean you *didn't* chuck it?"

Frost lifted a shoulder. "Well..."

"It's OK, Ty. Just let me have it back and I can check it out, yeah?"

"I might be better taking a look at it myself. No offence, boss, but I'm probably better on the tech side of things and—"

"No!" Blenkinship said. He swallowed, lowered his voice. "No, if you do it, it looks like you're trying to push the blame onto someone else, eh? But if *I* do it, as your boss, I'm simply carrying out a thorough internal investigation. All above board and proper. See what I mean?"

There was another agonising pause, then Frost nodded. "Yeah."

"So...can I have it then, mate?"

"Ah, well, that's the problem," Frost said awkwardly. "I don't have it anymore..."

90

"OH NO, NOT *YOU* LOT AGAIN." Yvonne Elliot answered the front door jiggling the baby, bawling, on her hip. "What d'you want *this* time?"

DI Pollock sighed. "Just give it a rest, Yvonne, and let us in, eh?"

"I don't s'pose you've got a warrant *this* time, neither?"

"Funny you should say that, lass…"

She seemed about to say more, Nick thought. But then she looked at the paperwork the detective inspector was holding out to her, past him to where Nick and the uniforms stood behind him, and to Grace, climbing out of her pick-up in the yard, with her crime-scene kit in hand. Yvonne stepped back without a further word, holding the door wide. Even the baby momentarily stopped crying.

"Thanks," Pollock murmured. "Dylan about, is he?"

"In his workshop."

Pollock turned and nodded to the uniforms, who moved off toward one of the barns where the crackle of a welding rig could be heard.

She led them through to the sitting room at the back of the house again. Two of the older girls were watching TV in there, lounging on one of the sofas. Yvonne picked up the remote and muted the sound.

"Upstairs," she said. "Now."

The girls scowled but took one look at the obvious police

presence and hurried out. Yvonne blinked, as if she hadn't quite expected to be obeyed. She plonked herself down in one of the vacated spaces and stared mutinously at Pollock. He picked up the discarded remote and shut the TV off completely. For a moment, the only sound in the room was the air fizzing out of the compressed seat cushion where she sat.

"Tell me about Owen Liddell," Pollock said quietly.

Yvonne opened her mouth, then closed it again, eyes skating. "Who?"

"Don't, lass. We found his phone with the body and we've recovered his text messages—his *final* text messages."

Her hands tightened around the infant, who let out a protesting wail. Yvonne turned the baby's face into her chest to lessen her cries, and busied herself rocking her until she quietened.

"All right, I knew Owen, what of it?"

"Friend of the family, was he?"

"Sort of, yeah."

"Sort of," Pollock echoed flatly. "You must have known him better than that, Yvonne. Why else would it be Owen you contacted in an emergency?"

"I–I don't know. Can't remember."

"Must have been something memorable, like. Something important. What was that message again, DC Weston?"

Nick made a show of consulting his notes, knowing it carried more weight if people saw something was in writing. "'Emergency! Come quick!'"

She effected a nonchalant shrug. "When am I s'posed to 'ave sent *that*?"

"Why? Send out a lot of SOS messages, do you, lass?"

Nick read out the date. Late September, eight years ago. "You must have known Owen quite well, Mrs Elliot," he said. "Because he doesn't query it at all. A couple of minutes later he sends back, 'On my way!' and, as far as we know, that's the last communication anybody had from him. Ever."

The statement, delivered without inflection, hung in the air like dust, swirling in the sunlight that streamed through the windows.

Pollock lowered himself gingerly onto the opposite end of the sofa. "Come on, Yvonne. He must have meant…*something* to you, if he were the first person you turned to in a crisis. So, what was it, lass?"

"Our eldest—Jess," Yvonne said dully. "She was still at primary school then. She fell, in the playground, cut her forehead and knocked hersel' out. Dylan were…away somewhere when they rang me—the school. They'd sent for an ambulance. I needed to go with her but…the other kids…the baby. There weren't nobody else I could call at that notice."

Nick frowned. "But Owen lived up near Penrith. Surely it would have taken him too long to—"

She shook her head. "He rented part of the workshop from our Dyl' to do some stuff on that old Escort of his, and he'd been here already that day. Only been gone about ten minutes. Said he was goin' to stop off in Kirkby on his way home. Knew he wouldn't have got far."

"So, you texted him, and he texted back," Pollock said, encouraging her on. "What then?"

"I saw him comin' up the drive and went out. I'd got me coat on, and the baby in me arms. I handed him over and got straight in me car."

"That was it? He didn't say anything to you?"

She was crying now, tears bubbling over her lower lids and sliding down her cheeks. "He smiled at me and said how I wasn't to worry. He'd take good care of him… But, when I got back, Owen was gone…"

She bent forward, curled over the baby, sobbing.

Along the hallway came the sound of the front door opening. Nick heard Dylan's whiny voice protesting, as one of the uniforms hustled him in. The man had a tight grip on Dylan's arm.

"Sir," he said to Pollock, his eyes flicking uncertainly over the woman weeping on the sofa.

"Well, lad, spit it out."

"The barn, sir. There's something out there you might like to see."

91

GRACE STARTED her methodical search in the hallway, drawing a blank. Once everyone had cleared the sitting room, she moved on to there, then finally into the kitchen.

Yvonne Elliot, she decided quickly, was not the most house-proud of women. But, to be fair, if *she* had half-a-dozen kids to look after, Grace supposed she wouldn't be too bothered about keeping the corners free of cobwebs or the work surfaces tidy, either.

Grace's brief from DI Pollock before they left Hunter Lane was a broad one.

"*If* Liddell did meet his end inside the Elliot house, it could have been eight years ago, which means there won't be a lot left for you to find," he'd told her.

"You'd be surprised what people leave behind," was her reply.

"Aye, lass. Well, just do your best."

"I always do."

Even in a room with as much gathered grease and dust as this kitchen, she didn't expect to find Owen's hair or skin cells, or any other cast-off DNA. Not after all this time. Even if she did, there were any number of reasons why it might legitimately be there—none of them sinister.

But she was bearing in mind that Owen had died from blunt-force trauma to the back of his skull. It was likely to have bled—

and bled heavily. That kind of bleed, Grace knew, was hard to clean up and harder still to eradicate entirely.

So, her search was more in the way of a sweep. If *that* came up empty, she would start again at the beginning.

"Anything I can do to help, Ms McColl?"

She glanced up. One of the uniformed PCs stood in the doorway. A youngster, not long out of probation, a slim figure bulked up by her stab vest and equipment.

"It's Grace," she said. "And yes, if you'd stay by the door and get ready to hit the lights. It's Rhona, isn't it?"

"That's it." The young PC grinned. They were always so pleased when anyone remembered their name. "Are you doing a Luminol test?"

"Ah, you've been studying your forensics," Grace said.

The girl laughed. "Well, I've been watching *CSI*, if that's what you mean."

Grace knelt on the draining board to tape a blackout cloth over the single window, disturbing the cobwebs as she did so. The window was deep set and relatively small, not letting in much light, but for her purposes she needed even less.

Noting the way the girl leaned closer as Grace opened her kit, she said, "Actually, I use a fluorescein spray rather than Luminol."

"What's the difference? Er, that's if you don't mind me asking questions?"

"Oh, I don't mind. Fluorescein doesn't react with household bleach the way Luminol does, and it's thicker so it tends to stick better on vertical surfaces."

Standing in the centre of the room, Grace sprayed the chemical outward around her, aiming for the lower cabinet doors under the sink. She worked her way along the doors, walls, the legs of the table and chairs, and finally round onto the face of the Aga. Then she nodded for the overhead strip light to go off, and passed over the areas she'd sprayed with a UV hand lamp.

When she reached the Aga, the rail and part of the front doors lit up.

"Wow," the PC said. "*That's* impressive."

Grace sprayed the Aga again, up onto the hotplate covers and down onto the floor in front of it as well, then scanned with the UV lamp. The result was the same, but more so.

"*You're* impressed," Grace murmured. "*I'm* horrified…"

With the light back on, she carefully inspected the grubby chequerboard of black and terracotta quarry tiles on the floor. They were probably original to the house, and several were no longer stuck down to the sub-surface. Grace managed to lever up one of the loose ones, sprayed the back of the tile and the area beneath it.

"More blood," the PC said quietly.

In the leg pocket of her trousers, Grace's mobile began to buzz. She had to delve awkwardly under her protective Tyvek suit to get to it. She answered with her mind still on the task in front of her.

"CSI McColl."

It was only when the woman from the forensics lab introduced herself that Grace's attention focused on the call. And the fact that the woman seemed to be apologising to her.

"I'm sorry, *what* was that?"

"It's a cock-up," the woman said. "Or a mis-communication, if you will. Normally, it's something I would double-check at the time I passed on the results but, to be honest, your Mr Blenkinship was so abrupt that—"

"So, what exactly has happened?"

"The Owen Liddell results." The woman sounded mortified. "Well, it appears we thought *you* were running them through the database."

"We managed to find a match via his dental records," Grace recalled. She had assumed that Blenkinship would have run the dead man's DNA anyway. But perhaps he had been too preoccupied by other concerns…

"And also, the two results were uploaded more or less at the same time, so that might also explain it."

Grace took a breath. "Just so I'm clear, spell it out for me, would you?"

"OK… The DNA from Owen Liddell is a familial match to your other victim—the boy, Jordan Elliot. They're father and son."

Grace stilled, absorbing it. In a strange way, it made perfect sense. And, she realised, Yvonne knew. She *must* have known. Or why else would Owen be the one she called to look after the child in an emergency? Who else could she trust but the boy's real father?

Even the reason for the pink blanket wrapping the baby in the photograph suddenly became clear. Up to that point, Yvonne had given birth only to girls. They were not a well-off family. No surprise that the same baby blanket had been brought out and used again.

"But still no indication of his mother?" she asked.

"We widened out the search, as requested, and found a partial match to one Vano Smith. Uncle, possibly?" The woman paused. "Look, we're embarrassed about the misunderstanding here. I've spoken to the lab manager at home and she's prepared to take the cost of the fast-track off what's owing—"

"*It's owing…*"

"Of *course*!" Grace said out loud. "Not *owing* but *Owen*… *That's* what she said…"

"I'm sorry?"

"No, no, don't be. That's wonderful. Send those through to me, would you? And thank you. Thank you very much."

"Er…you're welcome?" the woman said.

As Grace ended the call, the PC said, "You look like you've just had a eureka moment."

"Yes, I rather think I have." Grace speed-dialled the Kendal CSI office and, when the phone was answered, said, "Ah, Steve. I could do with a hand processing a scene up near Kirkby Stephen. Are either you or Tony free?"

"You've just caught me on my way out the door to a stabbing. But Tony's up at a farm robbery just past Grayrigg, so he's halfway there already. I'll let him know. Where are you and what's up?"

She gave him the address of the Elliots' farmhouse. "Tell him the PC on the door, Rhona, will give him all the details when he arrives," she said, receiving a big smile from the officer in question. "I've got to get over to Appleby before the Fair packs up and we miss our chance."

92

Dylan was fuming.

Being handcuffed, stuffed in the back of a cop car, and dragged into the cells at Penrith *once* was bad enough. But to haul him in *again*—and for *this*? He reckoned he had the right to show a bit of temper. *It's what anyone would do, if they* was *innocent*...

He didn't know what 'Vonne had told 'em this time, but she'd find out what he thought about *that* as soon as they came to their senses and let him go. Something they were in no hurry to do. They'd processed him and stuck him in a cell, kicking his heels until the drippy bird, Ms Chadwick, arrived again. Then it was back to the same interview room as last time, facing Pollock and Weston across the same scarred table.

Whatever the reason for it, he was getting heartily sick of this. He was being victimised, that's what it was. No way would they try this on if he was some ethnic minority—they wouldn't dare.

As Pollock ran through the preliminaries, Weston was eyeing Dylan across the table. Something about him made Dylan uncomfortable. He was a bit too focused, a bit too predatory. Pollock was old-school and Dylan knew where he stood. Pollock would nick him if he could, but he wasn't going to make a life's work out of it. Somehow, Dylan knew that if DC Weston ever really got his teeth into him, he'd have a job ever shaking the man off.

Just for a second, he wondered if maybe it was *Lisa* who'd given him up—tit for tat, for not taking those hooky bags back. He took a quick sideways glance at Weston again. Either the man had ice running through his veins, or she hadn't said anything. No way could anyone look so…detached if he'd found out the bloke his girlfriend was shagging had also supplied her with knock-off gear.

"So, my officers found in your barn an old Ford Escort that's registered in the name of Owen Liddell," Pollock said. "Care to explain why you were hiding the car?"

"*Hidin'*? Hang on, I was just *storin'* it for him, like. How was I s'posed to know he were dead?"

Weston raised an eyebrow, like he didn't believe for a moment that Dylan *hadn't* known. A trickle of sweat itched between his shoulder blades. He fought the urge to squirm it away.

"He lived up near Penrith. Why would he store his car all the way down at Mallerstang?"

"He was rent—er, borrowin' the workshop, like. And I'd lend him a hand with it, if I were about. Did a bit of rallyin' when I was younger, you know?"

"So, you were *mates*, then, you and him?"

Dylan hesitated, his mind skittering ahead, trying to ease his way past the traps without stepping into one. He snuck in a glance at Ms Chadwick, but got nothing. "Er, yeah, I s'pose…"

Weston's phone, which he'd put down on the table-top with his notes, buzzed once with an incoming text. Pollock scowled, not so much at the message but at the fact Weston picked the phone up and checked it. Dylan saw the DC's eyebrows quirk, just once—his only reaction.

"So, what ended it?" Pollock asked, dragging Dylan's attention back into the room. "Had a falling out, did you?"

"Well, no, not really. He just…stopped comin' round. Did a bit of a runner, by all accounts."

"And why would that be?"

He shrugged. "Dunno. Rumour was, he'd taken a bit of a fancy to some Gypsy girl and her people had it in for him…"

"Who was she, this lass?"

He shrugged. "Can't recall a name—if I ever knew it in the first place—not after all this time. I do know she had a brother, though, and *he* were a nasty piece of work, that one. Came lookin' for Owen a time or two."

"Can you remember *his* name?"

"Smith? Jones? Summat like that. I only remember because it was so *un*-memorable, if you get me?"

"What about you, yourself? You got on all right with Owen, did you?"

"Me? Fine."

Weston put the next question like Pollock had just tagged him in a wrestling bout.

"What about *Mrs* Elliot?"

"What about her?"

"How well did *she* know Owen? On equally *friendly* terms, were they?"

Dylan fixed him with a sullen stare. He knew where this was going, all right.

"Friendly enough, I s'pose."

Weston rode the pause. "Friendly enough that young Jordan, the boy you were raising as your own son, was actually Owen Liddell's child?"

Pollock's head snapped round, like he'd rick his neck.

"Message from CSI, sir," Weston murmured, nodding to his phone. "The lab results came back."

"So what?" Dylan said, making an effort not to fidget. "Already told you I knew he wasn't mine, like, didn't I? What difference did it make *whose* he was, after that?"

"You already knew he was Owen's," Weston said. A statement rather than a question.

Dylan cursed inside his head. Still Ms Chadwick had not lifted her nose out of the file in front of her. *Come on, darlin', give me a clue!* Would it have been better to fake surprise? Pretend that he hadn't known *who* was Jordan's real father? Surely, that wouldn't make any difference after all this time…

"Yeah," he admitted, cautiously. "Yeah, I knew."

"How?"

"Saw 'em together, didn't I? It was kinda obvious, when you saw him and Jordan, side by side. Had his look about him."

"When did you realise this?"

"Does it matter?"

"Oh, it matters, lad," Pollock growled. "Was it eight years

ago, for instance, on the day your wife texted him to come and baby-sit, in a hurry? The day your eldest gave herself a nasty bump on the head at school and had to be carted off to hospital? Ring any bells, does it? *The very same day,*" he went on, "that Owen Liddell was last heard from *alive*?"

"I—"

"Is that what happened, Mr Elliot?" Weston chimed in, both in the ring now, scoring dirty punches when the ref's back was turned. "Did Owen want his son back? After all, he had a better claim to him than either you *or* your wife, didn't he?"

"What does *that* mean?" Dylan was aware his voice was rising, couldn't stop it. "He were 'Vonne's kiddie, too. She had just as much right to him!"

"Your wife didn't tell you?" Weston's voice sounded cruelly casual to Dylan's ears. "Jordan wasn't *her* child, either. *Her* baby was still-born, apparently. Agnes Trelawney somehow arranged a replacement."

Dylan hunched down in his chair, his thoughts fractured, spinning off in all directions. He hardly heard Ms Chadwick arguing for a suspension so she could consult with her client. Hardly heard Weston continuing to rain down his verbal blows.

"Are you also aware, Mr Elliot, that Owen Liddell was killed by a single blow to the back of his skull? And that our CSI has also just confirmed the presence of a significant amount of blood in your kitchen?"

That, finally, penetrated.

"*What?*" Dylan yelped. He would have jumped to his feet but Ms Chadwick's hand was suddenly on his arm in warning. "Never! Where? You show me where!"

"Oh, attempts have been made to clean it up, but that's the thing about blood. Just because you can't see it anymore, doesn't mean we can't still prove it's there."

93

Ms Chadwick lost her cool then, ordered they suspend the interview and practically kicked them out of the room. Nick logged the time and paused the recording. He gathered his stuff and followed Pollock out into the corridor. The door slammed shut behind them.

"Why the heck are we only *just* finding out about Liddell's connection to Jordan *now*?" Pollock demanded as soon as they were alone.

"I don't know sir," Nick said. Grace's message had been detailed in some places but vague in others—deliberately vague, he felt. Which, he somehow knew meant it wasn't her fault. If it *had* been, she would have said so, straight out. He could make an educated guess who'd slipped up, but it wasn't his place to start apportioning blame.

"Hm," was all Pollock said, giving him a narrow-eyed glare that said he knew *exactly* what Nick was doing.

"So, what do you reckon—did he know the whole story about Jordan, or is he just a better liar than we give him credit for?" Nick asked.

"He's good, but not *that* good," Pollock said after a moment's reflection. "I've known Dylan Elliot a long time, for one reason or another, and I've never seen him look quite so shattered as he did when you told him the little lad didn't belong to him *or* his missus."

Nick raised an eyebrow. "I'd got the impression that the fact he knew Jordan wasn't his made him...almost *resent* the boy."

"When he thought the lad was proof Yvonne had a bit on the side, aye," Pollock said. "But now? Now he knows she's been telling him the truth all along. And if he's been taking it out on her—and the lad—all these years, well"—he shrugged—"if he's got half an ounce of human decency left in him, he's going to feel pretty badly about that, isn't he?"

Nick nodded slowly. There were times when he thought of Pollock as an unreconstructed old-generation copper. A bit of a chauvinist perhaps, certainly not very politically correct. But at his core, Pollock had an understanding of what made people tick that was sharp and savvy.

Nick was still searching for the words to express this, when the door to the interview room opened and Ms Chadwick stuck her head out into the corridor.

"We're ready for you," she said with another of her sniffs. "My client wishes to make a statement—against my advice, I might add."

"Right you are," Pollock said and, when the head withdrew, he murmured, "*This* ought to be good..."

When they were seated again with the recorder running, Dylan launched into his story, about driving home from Kirkby Stephen along the Mallerstang valley that day in autumn, about three or four months after Jordan was born.

"I was just goin' into that narrow stretch before Outhgill, where there isn't room for two cars to pass side-by-side, when who comes t'other way but my 'Vonne, headin' down toward Kirkby. She nearly runs head-on into me—goin' like a right idiot, she was. I had to back up or neither of us would've got through."

"Are you quite sure this is relevant, Ms Chadwick?" Pollock asked.

"If you'd let him *finish*, detective inspector, then we'll see, won't we?"

Pollock sat back and waved Dylan on. Nick studied the man's face as he spoke, looking for the tells of a liar. Dylan, he'd noticed, tended to get shirty when he thought he wasn't going to be believed, but spoke with far more apparent confidence when he was telling an outright lie, almost over-egging it. He was picking up neither of those traits.

"Well, I stopped to give her what for, drivin' like that, only I saw she was on her own in the car. She was bletherin' on about the school callin' to say our Jess had fallen off the slide in the playground. Knocked herself out good and proper, so they reckoned, and they'd sent for an ambulance. About how she had to get to the school before the ambulance got there, or 'Vonne wouldn't know for certain where they was takin' her."

"What was *your* reaction?" Nick asked, knowing that, if it was Sophie who was hurt, nothing would have kept him away.

"What *d'you* think?" Dylan's tone was scornful. "I wanted to know what she'd done with my...with the baby. Who was lookin' after him? She's so ditzy half the time, I could believe she might'a just run out the house and left him."

"But she hadn't."

"No, she hadn't," he agreed. "She gabbled somethin' about how Owen had got him and she was off like a rocket."

"You knew he'd been at the house earlier in the day?"

"Yeah, he'd been puttin' a new gearbox in that old Escort. And he was good with the kids," he added, almost grudgingly. "They seemed to like him."

"So you weren't...surprised or alarmed to hear your wife had left the children in his care?"

"Well, no, I s'pose not. Not really. Still got there as fast as I could, like."

Dylan paused long enough for Pollock to prompt him with a careful, "And?"

He looked up then, but Nick could see his gaze wasn't in the room any longer.

"Don't remember the rest of the drive back, if I'm honest. I *do* remember rushin' into the house, though, findin' Owen in the kitchen, holdin' *my* kid in his arms, rockin' him. It was the look on his face that did it, stopped me in my tracks, it did. Don't know how to describe it, even—a kind of wonder and pride and...love."

He shifted in his chair, restless with embarrassment at the memory. Not a bloke who found it easy to talk about his feelings, Nick would bet. He kept his face impassive, knew without looking that Pollock would be doing the same. Sure enough,

Dylan flicked them both an aggressive little glance, just to check they weren't mocking him, before he continued.

"I–I don't mind admitting, it proper shook me, did that. Not just the way he was holdin' him, but…I s'pose it was the first time I'd seen 'em together—real close, like. And that was when it really hit me."

"What did?"

"The likeness," Dylan said. "I always thought it was a load of rubbish, when people say, 'oh, he looks just like his dad,' or whatever. Family resemblance and all that. But when I saw Owen with Jordan that day… Well, there weren't no use denyin' it any longer, even to myself."

"And what did you do then?" Pollock's voice was almost gentle.

"I asked him, straight out, didn't I? Should've stopped to think about it, but"—he shrugged—"by the time I realised that, it was too late. I said to him, 'Is he yours?' and he never even took his eyes off the baby's face. He just said, 'Aye, he is,' real quiet, like. And that were it."

"What was, Mr Elliot?"

Dylan glanced at his solicitor, as if needing the reassurance. She sniffed and gave him a slight nod. He swallowed.

"I lost my temper, didn't I? Same as any red-blooded man would've done. Started yellin' at him, and the kid were screamin' at the top of his lungs and I just…hit him."

"Jordan?" Pollock asked, sharper now.

"No—Owen," Dylan said, his voice hollow. "With what he'd just admitted—what I *thought* he was admittin', about shaggin' my wife, passin' his kid off as mine—what did you expect? I belted him."

"With what?"

"My fist, what else? Proper left to the chin he never saw comin'. One punch. Knocked his lights out for him."

"You hit him, when he was holding your child?" Nick couldn't stop himself from asking the question, despite Pollock's twitch of irritation alongside him.

"He'd just admitted the kid wasn't *my child* at all, hadn't he?" Dylan shot back, as if that made it all OK. "'Sides, he stayed on his feet for a moment, even if his eyes had rolled back. Time enough for me to grab the boy from him, before he went down, like. Dropped like a stone, he did, right there on the kitchen floor."

There it was, Nick thought, a confession if ever there was one. So why did Dylan look like he'd just played his best Get Out of Jail Free card?

Pollock must have been thinking the same. He cleared his throat and said, "Mr Elliot, just to be clear—you admit to hitting Owen Liddell, hard enough that he fell, unconscious, onto your kitchen floor?"

Dylan shrugged. "Yeah."

Nick glanced at his file again. "Did Mr Liddell fall forward or backwards?"

Dylan frowned, his face pulled into a scowl by the force of his concentration. "I dunno. He just sort'a dropped. I wasn't paying him no attention, what with the boy screechin' in my ear. I just got outta there."

"Where did you go?"

"Stuck him in the car and just drove, didn't I? Wasn't givin' much notice to direction."

"For how long?"

"Couple of hours, maybe three or four? Ended up down at Morecambe. Sat on the seafront and looked out across the bay."

"Why Morecambe?"

Dylan shifted again in his seat, then slouched a little further. "Remembered that story what was all over the news, from a few years back, about them Chinese cockle pickers who got caught by the tide. How fast it turns there, with it being so flat. They used to say the incomin' tide across the bay at Morecambe could outrun a gallopin' horse. And I watched it start to come in, and I looked at Jordan, all wrapped up, asleep in his blanket on the back seat, and I thought about... That is, I considered..." His voice petered out into a harsh whisper. He took a long unsteady breath. "But in the end, I couldn't do it. Couldn't even do it *then*, right after I found out—when I *thought* I'd found out... So, how you could think I'd lay a finger on him *now*, all these years later..."

Don't mind laying more than a finger on your wife, though, do you?

Beneath the level of the table, Nick's hands tightened convulsively. Not trusting his voice, he left it to Pollock to ask the next question.

"What about Owen Liddell? When did you get rid of the body?"

Dylan gaped. His eyes flew briefly to the solicitor. Nick recognised both alarm and accusation in the glare.

"What you *talkin'* about? I never *buried* him! He were *fine* when I left, and he'd gone by the time I got back! He must've come round and taken himself off, mustn't he? And there weren't no *blood*, neither." He gulped down a breath, like he'd just been running. "If you want to point the finger at anyone, mate, you should be lookin' at them gyppos! They was there, with their horses and their caravans, on Water Yat that day, when they'd no good reason to be. And the next day, they was gone!"

94

"GRACE? YOU IN HERE?" Blenkinship called as he stepped through the open front door of the farmhouse.

He'd driven from Workington to Penrith as fast as he dared, then wasted precious time searching Grace McColl's desk for the SD card Ty Frost admitted giving to her. Now, he'd tracked her to this crime scene and his time and temper were wearing thin.

Instead of Grace, it was a small female PC who hustled out of one of the doorways off the hall in response to his shout.

"Excuse me, sir, but I'm afraid you can't—"

"Lead CSI Blenkinship, pet. Where's CSI McColl?" His ID was in his hand and he was already looking past her, already *moving* past her. He stuck his head into what proved to be a kitchen. A white-suited figure was kneeling on the floor, its back to the doorway, bending low to inspect the tiles in front of the Aga. "Grace?"

The figure straightened and twisted to face him.

"Oh, hiya Chris," Tony Marsh said. "Though, if you can mistake me for Grace McColl, you might want to think about an eye-test, mate, eh?"

Tony was close to retirement age, a rotund figure whose belly strained against the restriction of his Tyvek oversuit. What little hair remained on his head had long-since turned grey, as had his beard. He and Blenkinship worked together for several years in Carlisle before the reshuffle of personnel last summer.

"Where is she?" Blenkinship demanded, fighting to keep his tone even.

As it was, Marsh regarded him impassively for a moment before he said, "Don't know, mate. She rang Steve. Steve rang me. Next thing *I* know, I'm sent up here to carry on processing the scene. By the time I arrived, she'd already legged it."

"Dammit. She should have checked in with me before she went haring off somewhere else. She's no grasp of protocol, that woman." His eyes flicked briefly around the room. "I don't suppose Mr Pollock's still about, is he?"

Marsh shook his head. "'Fraid not. He carted Elliot back to Penrith for questioning. If that lad spends any *more* time in the cells up there, they'll be charging him rent."

"Dylan Elliot?" Blenkinship asked. "I thought he'd been cleared...?"

"That was for young Jordan. This is in connection with Owen Liddell's death, apparently. 'Round up the usual suspects', eh?"

"But...Liddell is *my* case," Blenkinship grumbled.

"Well, you're welcome to take over if you feel that way about it." Marsh heaved himself to his feet with a grunt. "Besides anything else, tiled floors are murder on my knees these days."

"Oh, you may as well carry on now you've started," Blenkinship said quickly. He shook his head. "What the *hell* does she think she's playing at...?"

"As I understood it, *sir*," the PC said tartly, "Mr Pollock tried to get hold of *you*, but nobody knew where you were and your phone was switched off."

He turned to find her hovering in the hallway behind him and eyed her with disfavour. It was mutual. "I don't suppose *you* know where CSI McColl has disappeared off to?"

"Well, believe it or not, it just so happens I *do*..."

95

NICK AND DI POLLOCK were back in the CID office, staring at the murder boards for Jordan Elliot and Owen Liddell. Dylan Elliot was back in a holding cell, and the indomitable Ms Chadwick was back coiled in the centre of her web somewhere, Nick presumed—probably still sniffing.

"So, Dylan is pointing the finger at the Gypsies," Pollock said to the assembled detectives. In fact, with Yardley taking paternity leave there were only two others—DS Rebecca Hodgson and DC Asif Khan. "The question is, do we believe him?"

"It is a bit...convenient, is it not, sir?" Khan said.

And Nick recalled Grace's comment that the Horse Fair was considered a good time to settle old scores. For locals to get their own back on their neighbours and to blame the Gypsies.

"Maybe, lad," Pollock agreed. "But, as far as we know, Dylan is unaware that there's a strong possibility Jordan's real mum is a member of the Travelling community."

"He could have worked it out, sir," Nick said. "After all, it was common knowledge that Owen was seeing a Gypsy girl. As soon as we told Dylan that Yvonne wasn't Jordan's mother, he could easily have realised what that meant."

"And do we have only Dylan's word for it that there *were* any Gypsies camped at Water Yat, around the time we believe Liddell was killed?" Hodgson asked.

Nick frowned. "I'm sure Dave said something about Vano Smith..." He moved over to Yardley's vacant desk and leafed through his notes. "Ah, yes, here we go. Smith was done for a minor traffic offence in Kirkby Stephen, the day *before* the last text message was sent."

"Not conclusive, but enough to bring the lad in for questioning, that's for sure," Pollock said. He looked to Khan. "What news on the blood found at the Elliots' place?"

"Well, sir, CSI can confirm it is definitely blood. But what they cannot tell without lab work is if it is *human* blood or not."

Pollock's eyebrows shot up. "What else might they be doing —sacrificing goats in there?"

"Actually, sir, you'd be amazed what gets done in these old farmhouse kitchens," Hodgson put in, and Nick remembered hearing that her family were hill-farming people somewhere in the Scottish borders. "My gran used to butcher whole sheep in hers."

"All right, all right. Let's get samples sent to the lab. See if we can get a match to Liddell, while we're at it."

"They might not be able to, sir," Hodgson warned. "Depends how degraded it is by time and the chemicals used to clean it up in the first place."

"Yes, I *am* aware of that fact, detective sergeant," Pollock said. "They can but do their best, eh?" His eyes roved over the boards as if looking for something that might have been missed. "Mr Blenkinship may be able to give us a better idea of timescale on this. Has anybody seen him yet?"

"Er, he arrived here while you and DC Weston were interviewing Mr Elliot," Khan said. "He was looking for CSI McColl. I told him she was processing the Elliot scene, and I believe that is where he was heading."

Perhaps I should call Grace and give her a heads up… Nick checked his watch. He calculated how much time might have passed and decided it would probably be too late to do so.

"Well, until the forensics come back on the farmhouse," Pollock continued, "we're just going to have to sit on Dylan for the time being and—"

"I don't *think* so, detective inspector," said a sharp voice from the doorway.

They all turned as Superintendent Waingrove strode in. She didn't seem able to enter a room any other way. Nick instinctively straightened away from the desk he was leaning against, and Hodgson got to her feet.

"Oh, ma'am?" Pollock queried. His voice was mild but Nick did not miss the way he tensed, like a mastiff in the presence of another big dog. "Why's that, then?"

Waingrove's eyes narrowed. A muscle twitched at the side of her jaw.

"When were you going to tell me about the planted evidence in the Elliot case?" she demanded, clearly annoyed enough by Pollock's stance not to do this in private.

"You mean the *allegation* of planted evidence, ma'am? The CSI in question has been suspended, pending further investigations. No doubt there will be a report on your desk in due course."

"Not good enough," Waingrove snapped. "I've just had my *arse* handed to me by Dylan Elliot's solicitor. She's accusing us of some kind of witch-hunt involving her client. First we bring him in for his *son's* death—"

"Er, actually, ma'am," Hodgson interjected, "It appears that Jordan was *not* Dylan's son."

Waingrove pinned her with a look so toxic Nick could almost *see* it melting Hodgson's chances of ever making detective inspector.

"*As I was saying,*" Waingrove continued, not shifting her gaze from the squirming Hodgson, "first we bring him in for Jordan Elliot's death, and then we bring him in *again* for Owen Liddell. Don't you have any *other* suspects?"

"Oh aye," Pollock said. "But none who had the means, the motive and the opportunity, *and* who've *admitted* assaulting the dead man on their property, where a large quantity of cleaned-up blood has just been found." He paused deliberately. "Ma'am."

Nick wondered idly if the filing cabinet to his left would be enough to shield him from the blast radius, if Waingrove *actually* exploded, as she looked liable to do at any moment.

He saw her take a breath and will herself calm. "Can you confirm it's Liddell's blood?"

"Not at present, ma'am. That's why we need to sit on Dylan for a day or so—just until we get the lab results back."

"The only way to do *that* would be to fast-track them," Waingrove said. "Do you have *any* idea how much of the budget you're blowing on having all these tests rushed through the lab?"

It was clearly a rhetorical question and, wisely, nobody tried to answer it.

After a moment, Waingrove nodded, as if silence signified capitulation. "Let him loose," she said. And when Pollock would have argued she held up a hand, palm outward. "You can always pick him up again, *if* the evidence comes back with a solid link."

"Yes, ma'am."

"Good. Now, who else *might* be in the frame for Liddell?"

Pollock straightened again. "A Traveller called Vano Smith, ma'am. He had a long-standing grudge against the victim and was known to be in the vicinity around the time Liddell was last heard of."

"Vano Smith? Not *him* again." She swung in Nick's direction. "I understand *you* found a way to speak to him about Jordan's death without causing a riot, detective constable."

"In a way, ma'am," Nick murmured.

"Well, whatever method you employed before, go and do it again."

"We need to bring Smith in and question him under caution, ma'am," Pollock said. "Whatever Nick gets from him otherwise will be hearsay."

"All right. Weston, go and *invite* Smith to come and help us with our enquiries."

"And if he *declines* that invitation?" Pollock asked, saving Nick from trying to find a way to voice the same question. His relief was short lived.

"Oh, I'm sure Weston will use his initiative to ensure a satisfactory outcome, detective inspector," Waingrove said, baring her teeth. "Despite the lack of *Shera Rom*, this year's Fair is almost over and has so far passed off without major incident. It *will* stay that way. Is that understood?"

Pollock huffed out a sigh. "With all due respect, ma'am, you're tying my hands here."

"With all due respect, detective inspector," she shot back. "Tough."

QUEENIE PACKED up the wagon ready to travel without the usual feeling of regret that the Fair was almost done. The truth of it was, she couldn't wait to be on the road home. The vardo was as much home as anywhere else, this was true. As long as she was with Bartley and Ocean and Sky.

All together.

Safe.

And this year she would not feel safe until Fair Hill, Appleby-in-Westmorland and all it contained, was a distant speck on the road behind them.

She'd brought out the little carpet and was beating the dust from it, perhaps more fiercely than was needed. But Bartley and Ocean had taken the mare and the colt down to The Sands for the last time. And she didn't need to be told that they would return richer in *luvvo* but poorer in *gry*.

Right now, Queenie knew she'd rather keep the horses and may the devil take the money they would fetch. But as her husband and her son had led them away, with even the old piebald bellowing his despair, she couldn't find her own voice to call them back again.

Sky had begged away from her chores to have a final hour or so with the other *tawnie yecks*, the little ones. It was only then it struck Queenie that Ocean hadn't wished to do the same. She thought of the hiding he'd taken from the boys of Jackson's clan.

Maybe Queenie wouldn't be the only one glad to see the back of this Fair.

She gave the carpet a final whack, carried it back up the steps to the porch and unfurled it onto the polished wooden floor, straightening it just so.

When she alighted again and turned, there was a woman waiting for her.

Queenie hid the jolt of surprise it gave her behind a haughty stare.

"What would you be wanting *this* time?" she asked.

"Want? Nothing," the woman, Grace, said. "Actually, I'm here to give something to *you*—the ending to a story."

Queenie continued to stare, although she'd be the first to admit that something of her haughtiness softened. "And in return?"

"I was hoping you might be able to tell me the parts of the story that are missing."

She was dressed much the same as she had been when Queenie last met her, at the old lady's house up the hill, her mother's. And she still looked tall and cool and elegant. Not like a woman who'd just been sweating over a dusty carpet in the sun.

Queenie eyed her for a moment longer, then jerked her head toward the wagon.

"Come," she said, nerves making her brusque. "We'll sit."

She climbed the steps herself first and Grace followed her up. Queenie was interested to note the woman toed off her boots on the front porch, left them there.

When she caught the glance, Grace said, "I wouldn't walk dirt into my own home, why should I do so into yours?"

Queenie gave a nod of thanks and gestured her onto the locker seat next to the bed. She took the other, opposite the stove and nearer the door.

As she settled herself, Grace looked about her with an appreciative eye. "The work in here is quite beautiful," she said, in a detached tone that gave no hint of talking down.

Queenie found herself fiddling with the folds of her skirts. "You said you had a story."

"I did," Grace agreed. She reached into the canvas bag that was over her shoulder and brought out a photograph, handed it across. "It starts with this man—Owen Liddell. And, I believe, with you."

Queenie took the picture. *There* was the face she remembered from so long ago. Her first love—her first lover, come to that. Behind him was the old car he'd so treasured and, in his arms, a child. She smoothed a thumb over both the faces as if hoping to sense something more than the shiny surface of the paper. Nothing came.

"Yes." She swallowed. Her eyes lingered on the baby. "So, he…took a wife, did he? Had a family?"

But Grace shook her head. "No," she said, voice gentle. "He did not."

Queenie looked up sharply. "But who—?"

Grace held her gaze. "How about I tell you what I know, and you can stop me if I'm going wrong, yes?"

Just for a second, Queenie hesitated. Sometimes the *not* knowing was better—safer. But then she remembered her words to Bartley, when he'd kept the news of Owen's death from her. She nodded.

Somewhere in Grace's clothing, a phone began a muffled buzz. She reached into the leg pocket of her cargo trousers and silenced it, without looking to see who might be calling.

And then she began to speak. She wasn't entirely accurate in the story of Owen's presence at the Fair, his fondness for the horses, his first meeting with Queenie, their becoming lovers. But she was close enough for Queenie to sit with breath caught in her throat, not wanting to break the spell.

It became harder to listen to the calm voice recounting Queenie falling with child, her fear—both of the consequences of her condition and the wrath of her father.

"No," she said then. "Not wrath. Not my father. Had he known, he would have been disappointed, yes, but never angry."

"So who *were* you afraid of?" Grace asked.

"My brother," Queenie whispered. "It would be Vano who would have killed me, if he'd known. Him and—" She stopped abruptly, aware she'd almost said too much.

"And Patrick Doherty?" Grace supplied.

"Yes. Patrick, too."

"And because you didn't have a mother, or an older sister or aunt you could turn to, when your waters broke, early, while you were up here for the Fair, you were understandably frightened."

"I was terrified," she recalled. "Thought I was dying."

"So you went to Agnes Trelawney, who was known and trusted by the Travellers, as is her daughter, Wynter, now. And she delivered your son."

"Mine and Owen's."

"Did he know?"

Queenie shook her head. "Appleby the year before, that was when Vano and…and *Patrick* laid about Owen, broke his arm, warned him off. We met up a few times between—the Traveller Fair at Kenilworth in the September, and again just before Christmas. And then I saw nothing of him until Appleby in June."

"By which time you were how far along? Twenty-nine weeks or so?"

She nodded. "Thereabouts."

"So he was premature," Grace murmured, almost to herself. "No wonder he was tiny."

The hair began to prickle at the nape of Queenie's neck. "What do you mean? How do you know that about him, if… if…" But she couldn't finish.

Grace looked at her and something passed through her face, her eyes, like the shadow from clouds across the sun. And when she spoke her voice was careful.

"Queenie, what do you *think* happened to your baby?"

"He died," she said, the burn in her throat rasping in her voice. "My fault… All my fault. I didn't even know I was carrying him, not for months. Just thought I was getting *fat*. Cut back on my food when I should have been eating more… Eating for the both of us."

Giving her a look Queenie couldn't fathom, Grace asked, "How did he die?"

"How? I don't know. Can a soul truly die if they have never even lived?" She sat very straight and very still, refusing to let the sorrow in her voice reach her eyes. "All I *do* know is that I struggled too long and too hard to bring him into this world. I know that now. I was so scared—of everything. Of having him, of not having him, of him living or him dying. *Hours*. It felt like days. And by the time he was out of me, I craved him gone with all my heart." She tried to smile but her mouth would not curve. "They tell you to beware of what you wish for…"

She took a last look at the photograph and offered it back to Grace, who shook her head. "Keep it, if you want to," she said. "I admit, when I first saw that picture, I thought the baby might be Ocean. That *he* might be Owen's child."

"He has something of the look of my *yeckoro chavo*, as a baby —my only son. But Ocean was born a year after I married…"

Grace frowned. "I thought he said he was ten."

"Ah, how fast they wish to grow into men. He's barely nine."

They both fell into silence until Queenie said, "Now, have you decided?"

"Decided what?"

"If you're going to tell me the ending to this story that you promised. It will bring no happiness, will it?"

"I thought Gypsies fortune-telling was a myth," Grace said.

"Ah, I've no need of *dukkering* to know evasion when I see it," Queenie said. "So tell me, straight and tell me quick, before I lose all my nerve."

Grace seemed to take a breath and gather herself. Then she came forward off the locker seat and went to her knees in front of Queenie, grasping both hands in hers.

"Hold onto me," Grace said when she would have pulled away. "With what I'm about to tell you, trust me—you'll need someone to cling to…"

97

"*Stop*! *Please*. Don't you hurt my mummy!"

Dylan already had his fist cocked and loaded for another blow, when the little voice finally penetrated his rage. He became aware that fists much smaller than his own were beating a furious tattoo against his thigh. Looking down, he found Ollie, face flushed with effort and anger, attacking him.

Irritated, he hoisted his daughter up by both wrists and swung her away.

"Will you give it a *rest*," he growled, throwing her onto the sofa.

She landed in a flurry of arms and legs, thumping against the cushions, letting out a shriek.

That, finally, got a reaction from Yvonne. She levered her head from the carpet and glared at him through the eye she could still open.

"Leave. Her. *Alone*." The words came out slurred past the split lip.

"*Don't*." Dylan stabbed a finger at her. "Don't you tell me what to do, 'Vonne. How many times do I have to tell *you*, eh? How many times do I have to say it—you don't tell the cops *nothin'*! And *still* you just *have* to go shootin' your mouth off, don't you?" He shook his head. "You brought this on *yourself*. Don't try and make out otherwise."

"Leave both of 'em alone."

The echoed order came from a different voice, a different

direction. Dylan turned to find his eldest, Jess, hovering in the doorway. She was seventeen now, tall for her age. And she'd been learning tae kwon-do, after hours at the Grammar School in Kirkby Stephen. Not that Dylan would ever allow himself to be wary of *any* woman, let alone one little more than a child. But even so…

"Or what?" he sneered. "Goin' to take me down with that Japanese nonsense you been learnin', are you?"

"It's Korean," Jess said.

"What?"

"Tae kwon-do—it's Korean, not Japanese."

"Who cares? What gives *you* the right to think you can question *anythin'* I do in *my* house, eh?"

"Not *your* house, is it?" Jess said, her voice scornful. "It's Mum's. Came from *her* nana and granddad, didn't it?"

"Why you cheeky little—"

"Jess, please," Yvonne croaked. She'd managed to get a hand under her enough to sit up, the other pressed to her ribs. Ollie slid off the sofa and latched her arms around her mother's neck. Yvonne winced but didn't make her let go. "Please, love…don't wind him up even more."

Jess's chin came out, even if her bottom lip gave a betraying wobble. "He *can't* keep doin' this to you, Mum…"

"I can do as I please and don't you forget it!"

Jess glanced over her shoulder and, just for a second, Dylan worried who else might be out there in the hallway, listening, unseen. He never hit 'Vonne *that* much—not where it would show—but she'd really provoked him this time. He'd have to make sure she stayed in the house, just until the black eye and the bruises faded.

Another figure sidled into view, then another, and he realised all his daughters, barring the baby, were here now. Watching him, judging him. He saw the condemnation in their eyes and it infuriated him beyond measure. *What right do any of them have?* He wanted to lash out and keep doing so. To stamp and punch and kick and throw until everything was broken. The depth of his own anger surprised him.

It maybe even scared him, just a little.

He would have gone to his grave rather than admit it.

But now, the girls slipped past him, giving him as wide a

berth as the confines of the room allowed, and went to their mother. They clustered around her, like a human shield, and stared him down.

"You really want to do this, do you?" he asked, aiming his question at Jess, the apparent ringleader. "Really want to take me on?"

"Why not? 'Bout time *somebody* did," Jess threw back. Her voice turned soft and vicious. "Besides, you gotta sleep sometime…"

In that moment, Dylan had no doubts about Jess's parentage.

She was every inch of her *his* daughter.

"Ach, to hell with the lot of you! You're none of you worth the effort." He threw up his arms in apparent disgust. "I'm goin' out."

And he whirled away before they saw the thin layer of his bravado for what it was.

98

"GRACE! At *last*. Don't you *ever* check your messages?"

Ty Frost's voice on the phone was a squawk in Grace's ear.

"I've been at the Elliot house in Mallerstang. You know how hit-and-miss it is down there for mobile coverage," she said. "And then I was…tied up for a while."

She thought of Queenie's reaction to her story, and wondered again at the kind of woman Agnes Trelawney must have been— to tell one mother of a new-born baby her child was dead, and then to tell another her dead child lived.

Surely, she must have known it couldn't remain a secret forever?

And it hadn't, she realised. Somehow, Owen Liddell had found out. The question was, how?

"Grace, are you listening to me?"

She shook herself out of her thoughts. "I'm so sorry, Tyson. Say that again."

"Chris Blenkinship. He came to see me—at *home*. I didn't think he knew where I lived."

"What did he want?"

"Well, he sort-of took me by surprise. I wasn't really prepared…"

"Ty, just tell me what he wanted."

"To let me know he didn't believe I planted that evidence—"

"Because *you* didn't."

"And how he suspected Nick Weston might have had something to do with it."

"What?"

How could *he?* Grace was suddenly aware of feeling a terrible misgiving. That she might have trusted a dishonourable man to do the honourable thing. Instead, was he taking the opportunity *she* had given him, to lay the blame at yet another's door?

"Oh, Ty. You…don't *really* think that, do you?"

"Grace, Mr Blenkinship is my *boss.*" She heard the anguish in his voice. "When he wants to, he can turn on the charm. He and I will never be mates, like, but…he's a CSI. We're here to, I don't know, make sure cases can be proven in court by scientific *fact*—to see justice done. Not to…set each other up."

"I know," she said, more quietly. "I know."

"He was after that SD card. The one out of his dash-cam. You remember—the one I gave you."

"Yes." As she spoke, she tried to recall what she'd done with it. They'd been just about to launch the drone to find Jordan Elliot's entry point into the Eden…

Her hand went to the pocket of her cargos, reached right down into the bottom corner and found a small flat piece of plastic. *Ah!*

"I–I'm afraid I *might* have mentioned to him that *you'd* got it."

"When you say 'might have' you mean…?"

"Yeah, I told him. I'm sorry. Like I said, he caught me on the hop. It didn't occur to me that I'd need to lie to him."

She could almost see him hanging his head and scuffing his toes into the carpet.

"Ty, it's fine. Don't worry about it." She paused. "Thank you for letting me know now."

"It wasn't until after he'd gone that I started to think about it, and I realised there was just something off about the whole thing. Did you try running the card? I mean, *is* there anything on it or not?"

"I don't know," Grace said. "We've been rushed off our feet. But I've got my laptop in the car, and a card reader. I'll take a look now." *Just to find out what's so important he went chasing off to find you, just to make sure…*

"I'm really sorry, Grace," Ty said. She heard him take a deep breath. "I hope I haven't put you in an awkward position. You know that's the *last* thing I'd want."

"Don't worry about it," Grace said, keeping her voice light.

"I'm sure it will be fine. And," she added, making a joke of it, "it's not as if Christopher knows where to find me..."

99

BLENKINSHIP DROVE ONTO THE FIELD, feeling the tyres of his car sink through the grass and into the mud lurking beneath. Even when it was sunny for a few days, the memory of the recent storm was always near to the surface.

He'd just handed over an extortionate amount of money, in his opinion, for the convenience of parking close to the centre of Appleby, rather than allowing himself to be shunted off into one of the outlying car parks. Some of the local landowners took advantage of visitors to the Fair something rotten. It was practically gouging.

He locked his car and joined the crowds. The last day—a last chance to see the Gypsy horses being paraded and haggled over —always drew a crowd.

In some ways, Blenkinship was thankful for them. It gave an illusion of safety, of cover from which to stalk his prey.

The very fact he was thinking of Grace McColl in those terms brought him up short, put a hitch in his stride so the family behind him almost ran their pushchair into his heels. They swerved around him, giving him a scowl as they went by. The little boy in the pushchair gazed at him with sticky fingers outstretched.

There was something almost accusing in the child's eyes.

Blenkinship looked away, scanned the people lining each side of Battlebarrow, leading down toward The Sands. His chances of spotting one woman among all those gathered here were slim, he recognised.

And, even if he *did* find Grace, what then? Did he intend to plead with her? Reason? Threaten, even?

The familiar acid burned in his chest. A timely reminder that guilt, like mud, was also never far from the surface.

100

Dylan met with Karl on St Lawrence's Bridge over the River Eden in Appleby.

Karl was on the down-river side, smack bang in the centre of the bridge, where a rounded pedestrian refuge butted out over the water. It overlooked The Sands and the slipway down to the river. One or two horses were still being washed and swum, making the refuge a good spectator spot, but Karl had it all to himself.

One glance was enough to tell Dylan why.

There was something about the set of those massive shoulders, emerging hairily out of a T-shirt with the sleeves torn off. It made people unwilling to get too close, just in case. Even Dylan found himself edging in alongside the big man.

"Heard you been spending a lot of time as a guest of our local constabulary," Karl said without so much as a hello. "Should I be worried, like?"

Dylan masked his unease by taking a sip from the can of cola he was holding. Yvonne always bought own-brand stuff from one of the cheap supermarkets. It was only made drinkable by the generous slug of vodka he'd added. There were laws about drinking alcohol in public and, at Fair time, the cops would be all over him if he didn't do it on the sly. He felt the spirit burn down the inside of his chest. Maybe it was that put the jut into his tone.

"Worried about what?"

Karl nudged his wrap-around sunglasses just far enough down his nose to give him a pointed look over the top of them. A look that said, *"Don't play dumb with me…"*

"I didn't say anything about that little business deal we got goin', if *that's* what you mean?" Dylan said, checking other onlookers were too far away for eavesdropping.

"I'm not interested in what you *didn't* say, mate, but what you *did*, eh?"

"Well, they got bigger fish to fry than a few fake handbags, that's for sure," Dylan said bitterly. "Tryin' to fit me up for *murder*, aren't they?"

"Oh aye," Karl said. "And did you do it, like?"

"Which one?" Dylan muttered. "Seems any crime that's got 'em stumped at the moment, they're tryin' to throw it my way. Even accused me of killin' my *own kid*, for God's sake…"

He stared sullenly across the river toward a large group of Travellers, who were lounging on the grassy bank. Their dress and manner set them apart. They were rowdy and boisterous, raucous enough to be attracting a few irked glances. Their laughter mocked him to the point of fury,

"High time they put a stop to all this," Dylan said darkly. "If I had *my* way…"

"Aye, well, it's tradition, eh?" Karl said. "No matter how much trouble they cause, you can't interfere with their 'human rights', or some such nonsense."

"Huh, it figures." Dylan took another swig from his can, still scowling at the Travellers. "Amazin', isn't it? My mate Owen goes missin' and his body turns up buried in the middle of where *that lot* was campin' at the time, and do the coppers bring 'em in for it? 'Course not."

He took another long swallow. The anger he'd felt when he left home still writhed just under his skin, glad of an outlet now. "Then *my* kid gets killed and there *they* are again—large as life, twice as ugly. And do the coppers haul 'em in and give 'em the third degree? Do they heck as like!"

"So, what're you gonna do about it, eh mate?" Karl asked, his eyes hidden behind his sunglasses again, his pose apparently relaxed.

Dylan shifted his feet, restless with the same urge to destroy something—*anything*—that he'd felt in the sitting room at home. He rubbed a hand over his jaw.

"Dunno," he said, hunched forward now, leaning on the low parapet. "What *can* I do?"

"Depends how far you're prepared to go, like," Karl said.

Something in his voice had Dylan's head coming round, his eyes narrowing. "What you up to then?"

"Well, you're not the only one who's been shafted by the gyppos, mate," Karl said. "I was s'posed to be getting my hands on a nice bit of horse-flesh today. Already had a buyer lined up an' all. But they cheated their way out of the deal, and I don't have to tell *you* I don't take kindly to that."

Dylan kept a grip on his impatience. When Karl got like this there was no hurrying him. Trying was likely to flip his switch, and that was the *last* thing Dylan wanted to do. So he gulped down the dregs of his can and waited.

Karl lit a cigarette, taking his time.

"I got a few handy kind of lads from up north on their way down here, right now," he said at last. He checked the chunky stainless steel watch embedded in the fur of his wrist. "Gonna teach these thievin' beggars a bit of a lesson, eh?" He turned his head. All Dylan could see was his own reflection in the mirrored lenses, the bitter twist of his own features. "You want in, like?"

"*Hell*, yeah."

101

Blenkinship quickened his pace toward the far side of the bridge, trying to keep it all casual. He reckoned he'd just heard all that he needed to.

So, there's going to be a bit of a ruckus, eh?

His first thought was to call it in. To let DI Pollock—or, better still—Superintendent Waingrove know. *She* was the one who had most to lose if the Fair did not run smoothly. She'd be suitably grateful for the heads-up.

And he was going to need all the friends in high places he could get, once Grace McColl dropped her bombshell. Far better if he could get *his* side of the story—or some permutation of it—in first. As he moved onto The Sands and weaved around a couple of RSPCA inspectors standing by one of the temporary barriers, he was already reaching for his phone.

But something stayed his hand.

A bit of a ruckus…

He'd recognised Karl from old mug shots. Blenkinship had talked with Steve Scott, one of the CSIs based in Kendal, only a week or so ago about a batch of ladies' designer bags that had appeared in local markets. Rumours were, Karl was the man behind them—or the middle-man, anyway. Blenkinship tried to keep track of all the open cases in the force area. When you were in overall command of the team, it came with the territory.

He hadn't known Dylan Elliot by sight, but he worked out who he was fairly quick.

So, they've got it in for the Gypsies, have they?

He'd no idea what *kind* of trouble the men had planned but any kind would do, providing it was sudden enough, and violent enough, for a little bit of collateral damage not to go amiss.

And Grace McColl wouldn't be able to *resist* sticking her nose in, getting involved and trying to play the heroine role…*again*.

Even if she didn't, it wouldn't matter. Even if she tried to stay well clear, something *unfortunate* might still happen to her. After all, he knew how to make any scene look authentic. And if it seemed that she'd got too close to the action this time, and come to a sticky end, would anyone *really* be surprised…?

102

Driving east from Penrith, Nick saw the tailbacks on the opposite carriageway of the A66. Some of the Travellers were already leaving the Fair, scattering to all points of the compass.

His hands tightened around the rim of the Subaru's steering wheel. If they didn't manage to track down Smith and Doherty before the end of today, then the truth about Owen Liddell's death was never likely to emerge.

If I don't manage it.

Oh, he had a good idea who was going to carry the can for this one. He hadn't dealt much with Superintendent Waingrove since her arrival, but he got the distinct impression she was not the forgiving type.

On impulse, he called up Grace's number on his mobile. It took maybe half-a-dozen rings before she answered.

"Grace, hi." And when she didn't immediately respond. "It's Nick. Is everything OK?"

"Er, yes," she said, the doubt in her voice almost turning it into a question. She must have heard it herself because she cleared her throat. "Yes, I'm fine. What can I do for you?"

In the background he heard a burst of loud voices.

"Are you still at the Elliots'?"

"No. There was something I needed to do over at the Fair. I'm in Appleby, why?"

"Perfect. I was going to ask if you knew where I might be able to find the Gypsy woman who was at your mother's—

Queenie? I really need to talk to her brother. Thought getting her on-side might be my best chance. What do you think?"

"Hm, you may be right. And I've just been speaking with her, as a matter of fact."

"Great. Look, I'm just coming up to the turn-off. Can I meet you somewhere?"

"If you can get close to Fair Hill, I'll be there."

"That would be fine...*if* I knew where Fair Hill was." He glanced across at the packed sea of caravans off to the left of the road, which seemed to go on for field after field.

He expected her to laugh but there was no hint of a smile in her voice when she said, "Turn right when you get to the T-junction. It's the first big field gateway on your left."

"OK. Grace...are you *sure* you're all right?"

"Not really," she said, "but I *will* be."

And she disconnected the call before he had a chance to ask which of them she was trying to convince.

103

Queenie stood with her arms crossed, defensive. She had refused to go down to the gateway itself. Too many people would see her there and she wasn't convinced she wanted this meeting in the first place, never mind for all to gossip over. Instead, she stood partway up the sloping field, between a couple of horse trailers, and kept a watch on the entrance from there.

"I'm still not so sure about this," she said, nerves lending an edge to her tone.

"Don't worry," Grace told her. "You can trust Nick to do what's right."

"Aye, but there's often some distance travelled between what's *right* and what's right by the *law*."

"And he knows the difference. I'd stake my life on it."

She snorted out a breath, like the old piebald after a steep grade. "Easy words."

"Not when they come from experience."

Queenie shot her a quick glance but the other woman's face was unreadable.

"I'll hear him out," she said finally. "Can't promise more than that."

"I can't *ask* more than that. Ah, there's his car. Shall I bring him to your caravan?"

Queenie nodded and watched the tall redhead walk away.

The fair-haired copper had stopped to talk to one of the

marshals through his open window. Whatever he said to the man was enough to get him permission to leave his car inside the gate. He climbed out and met Grace on the way up. Queenie eyed the two of them together, looking for signs of tension. Signs that he might not be quite as open-minded with regard to the law as Grace had promised.

Instead, she saw tension of a different kind.

Ah, it's like that *between them, is it? No wonder that he risked his life for her…*

The pair started up the hill and Queenie hurried for the vardo, wanting to be there well ahead of them.

As she climbed the steps to the front porch, she looked through the open doors and saw her husband and her brother already inside. Bartley was laid on the bed, shirt open to reveal his bandaged ribs. Vano had taken the locker seat nearby. He rose at the sight of her, bullish.

"What *is* this?" Vano demanded.

"A reckoning," Queenie said. "And not before time." She glanced at Bartley. "Did you sell the colt?"

"I did, but—"

She flashed up a palm. "Then let that be the end of it. I don't need to know any more."

His face twisted. "Queenie, listen—"

But a firm knock on the wooden side panel cut off whatever he'd been about to say. She moved to the doorway. Grace and the *gavver*, Nick, waited below. She jerked her head without speaking and they climbed up.

As before, Grace left her boots on the porch. Nick, Queenie noticed, kept his on but he did at least tap any loose dirt off them against the top step before he came inside. She accepted the compromise for what it was.

"What *is* this?" Vano repeated, harsher now. "What are *they* doing here?"

He was still on his feet, making the floor space overcrowded.

"Sit *down*," Queenie told him. "We *will* have a reckoning. One we should have had a long time ago." And when still he made no move, she said, more quietly, "Don't make me have you called before a *kris Romani*."

She saw him pale at the words, as well he might. It was the highest court, with the power of *marimé*—of banishment. It was capable of ordering permanent separation from his family, of declaring the very blood in his veins changed to *gorgio*.

It was not a threat ever to be used lightly and Queenie did not do so. She *meant* it.

Vano sank back onto the locker seat with his mouth agape. Even Bartley held his tongue.

She waved Grace onto the locker seat opposite the stove, hopped up onto the edge of the bed alongside Bartley, letting her feet dangle, and nodded to the copper.

"Shut the door and ask your questions," she said.

He nodded back, closing them in before he let his eyes skim across the three, coming to rest upon Vano.

"I'm not going to spin you any tales or try to trip you up," he said. "I'll level with you, and I hope you'll do the same, OK?"

"Go on," Vano said cautiously, which was no reply and he knew it. Queenie scowled at him fiercely. He ducked his head as if she'd swung for him. "All right, yes."

"We *know* you were in Kirby Stephen the day before Owen Liddell disappeared. And we *think* it was you who camped at Water Yat that night." He paused, expectant.

"I hear no question there," Vano said with the same stubborn tilt to his head he'd had since they were *tawnie yecks*.

She did swing for him then, letting the toe of her boot thud into his knee—something *she* had done since they were children. He clutched at it and cursed her more than the injury warranted.

"Yes, I was there."

"I also think," the copper said, speaking more carefully now, "that you went to the Elliots' farmhouse, looking for Owen. What I hope you'll tell me is what happened when you got there."

Queenie was suddenly aware how important this answer was to her, by the fact she was holding her breath.

Vano looked down at his hands, braced on his thighs. She saw his fingers clench briefly. Then he looked up.

"We found him dead on the floor," he said. "In the kitchen there, and not another soul in the place." He cleared his throat. "So we cleaned away the blood...so much blood...and took him back with us and buried him near the river. And the next day, we moved on."

Queenie scanned Nick's face. He seemed thoughtful rather

than disbelieving, for which she was thankful. She'd listened to her brother lie many times over the years. This had truth woven into it, she could tell.

"Why take him?" Nick asked. "Why not call for us or simply leave him to be found by someone else?"

"Because we'd been there and we knew, if you had reason to look closely, you would prove it—what with DNA and tyre prints and all of that scientific stuff." At Nick's raised eyebrow he shrugged and said, "We do have a television set at home, you know. And if a man dies by violence and there are Gypsies nearby, we *know* we'll always be your first port of call. Besides, we'd…history with him, you might say."

Grace had remained silent. But now, once again, the phone in her pocket began to buzz. She pulled it out and checked the display.

"I'm sorry but I think I'd better answer this," she murmured, and took herself off outside, closing the doors behind her. Queenie heard her slip on her boots and descend the ladder.

"The man you had with you when you were pulled over in Kirkby Stephen," Nick said when Grace had gone. "He gave his name as Patrick Doherty." His eyes flicked to Queenie. "That name keeps coming up. You told me he was 'no longer with us', which is not *quite* the same thing as saying he's actually dead, is it?"

Queenie felt the denial on her lips but there it stayed. He'd been true to his word, this *gavver*. He'd kept his mind open, questioned them, yes, but not questioned their word. She couldn't bring herself to repeat the evasion.

"Because, as I recall, it's a Romany tradition that you don't ever speak the names of the dead," the copper went on. "But you spoke Patrick Doherty's name to me without a flicker."

"He's gone," Bartley said. "But not dead, no. I changed me name, is all. Got tired of being the man I was. And when Queenie said she'd have me, I wanted to honour that—and Queenie's father—by leaving Patrick Doherty behind me."

Nick frowned. "We didn't find any outstanding warrants for Doherty."

"Ah, there are more kinds of trouble than just the sort that's of interest to the likes of *you*, my friend."

Nick nodded at that, as if he understood. And maybe he did,

Queenie thought. From the looks of his face, his hands, he was no stranger to the rougher side of life.

"I just have one *last* question," he said. "Why were you there in the first place—at the Elliots', I mean? Were you *looking* for Owen?"

Bartley tensed so suddenly it sent an obvious barb through the wound—which, she noticed, the *gavver* had carefully avoided mentioning.

"Old Agnes," he said when he could speak again, which had Queenie's gaze jerking to meet his. "She told me…what she'd done. I think she knew she was losing her grip, even back then. She wanted to…confess, while she still had her wits about her. Sent you a letter, she did."

"I never got any letter…" Her voice was a whisper.

Vano cleared his throat. "You didn't," he said, and the colour in the tips of his ears and the sides of his neck gave her the reason.

"*You* took it. You *read* it!" Her voice rose, outraged.

"He did," Bartley said gently, reaching for her hand. "We went to see if we could find him—your son. And what we *did* find meant we daren't risk fighting for him…"

Queenie gave a reluctant nod. When she looked at Nick again, her eyes were bright and fierce with the effort it took her to be strong.

"Does that answer all you had to ask?" she demanded.

"I think it does."

Bartley gave her hand a squeeze. "And…will there be charges laid against us?"

"Well, that's not up to me but, seriously? I very much doubt it. The worst we could bring is possibly prevention of a proper burial—maybe perverting the course of justice?" His lips twitched, perilously close to a smile. "I have a feeling my superintendent would not like the adverse publicity it would bring."

He nodded to them, opened the doors and climbed down from the wagon. Queenie moved to the doorway.

"You know the worst thing?" she said. He paused, looked up at her. "He and Ocean played together, whenever we camped on Mallerstang. They were friends, the pair of them. And never knew they were half-brothers."

"GRACE! HEY, WAIT UP A MINUTE!"

Blenkinship broke into a jog the moment he recognised the unmistakable figure. For all her faults, being hard to look at was not one of them, he decided.

Almost makes it a shame…

She paused and let him come to her, like it was some kind of *right*. He forced a relieved and friendly look onto his face.

They were on one of the fields that had been opened up for the Travellers to camp, to the west of the town. After a fruitless search he'd finally resorted to calling her, told her it was urgent to meet face-to-face. The fact she'd agreed, and given him her location without apparent hesitation, gave him hope.

"What was so important, Christopher?" she asked.

"Look, I know we don't always see eye-to-eye," he said, "but I've just received some major intel and we need to act on it fast or there's going to be proper bloodshed."

"Oh?"

He gritted his teeth. Never had one word sounded so condescending as when she uttered it, like that, so cool and distant.

"Aye. A couple of the locals have got a gang of lads together and they're on their way down here, tooled up—*right now*—and out to start a pitched battle with the Gypsies."

Grace frowned and he resisted the urge to hold his breath while he waited for her to bite. From her past actions, it seemed to him that she liked the limelight, and wasn't averse to taking a few risks if it put her centre stage.

Still she hadn't reacted. A couple of young kids ran past, one chasing the other. Both were whooping with laughter.

"Come on, Grace!" he urged. "Can you imagine what will happen if they get loose in here with this lot—women and kiddies? It'll be mayhem."

She looked at him more closely then. "Christopher…we're crime scene, not armed response. What is it, exactly, that you think we're going to be able to *do*?"

As if to confirm what he was telling her, a police van appeared on the nearby road, heading up from the direction of the town. It was travelling at speed on blue lights. As it reached the slip road for the dual carriageway, they heard the wail of its siren, too.

Frustrated by her lack of willingness, Blenkinship tried to take her arm, to hustle her toward the field exit. Grace dug her heels in and twisted easily out of his grasp.

"Well, we're not going to be able to do *anything* if we don't give it a try, pet, are we?" He was aiming for persuasive. Instead, all he heard was desperation.

She stepped back away from him, wary now. He was losing her…

"Oh, for—" He lunged for her, grabbed her at elbow and wrist, his grip hard this time, his voice harsh. "For *once* in your life will you just do as you're damn well *told*, woman!"

The next moment, he was lifted and spun, like he weighed nothing. Just for a split-second, he thought Grace had done this to him. He had no idea how.

Then he hit the ground with a thud that knocked most of the breath from his lungs. A heavy knee between his shoulder blades did the rest. Both arms were wrenched behind his back and he heard the ratchet of handcuffs bracelet his wrists. He tried to protest but could only produce a wheeze.

He heard Nick Weston's voice ask, "Are you OK, Grace?"

"Yes, I'm fine." She leaned down into Blenkinship's field of view. "But if you honestly believed I would go *anywhere* with you, Christopher, after watching what was on that memory card, you've got another think coming…"

NICK HAULED Blenkinship to his feet, reciting his rights more out of habit than anything else. As he did so, he became aware that a couple of people around them had become half-a-dozen, with more approaching all the time.

"Nick, it was him—*he* killed Jordan," Grace murmured, jerking her head in Blenkinship's direction. "You have to get him out of here before they lynch him."

Nick almost argued. There were so many questions he hardly knew where to begin. Then he looked about him, saw the focus of the gathering crowd was fixed only on the handcuffed man, and felt ice pool at the base of his skull.

"You're coming, too."

But she shook her head. "I need to explain to Queenie...what happens next—I owe her that," she said. "I'll be fine. Go—*now*."

He hesitated a second longer. It felt like running away.

She mouthed, "*Please!*" and he did as he was ordered, dragging Blenkinship along by one arm. In much the same way, it occurred to him, that the man had *tried* to drag Grace. Nick had no doubts that she would have fended him off successfully on her own. But he had tackled Blenkinship on the basis of why have a big dog on hand and go to the trouble of biting somebody yourself?

Blenkinship, slower to read the situation, began to drag his feet, to protest about his treatment, his rights.

Nick whirled, got right in his face. "Do you *really* have a death-wish? Or are you just *stupid*?"

Then he caught on a little *too* well, putting on a burst of speed. Nick had to yank him back, muttering, "For God's sake, man. *Walk*, don't run."

In fact, he reckoned that appearing to handle Blenkinship on the rough side probably worked in their favour. It made the arrest seem less like a rescue. As it was, he marched the disgraced CSI down the hill and shoved him into the passenger-side rear seat of the Subaru, without intervention.

There, Nick quickly unlatched the handcuffs from Blenkinship's right wrist, threaded his left arm through the seatbelt, and snapped the loose cuff around the grab handle above the door.

He'd already made the driver's seat before the swell of people began to move, firing the engine and hustling the car out of the gateway.

Getting down Long Marton Road and under the long railway bridge was slow going. The road itself was filled with wandering pedestrians, strung-out family groups too busy gawping to hear the motor revving behind them. And too many horses to count, going to and from the flashing lane further up the hill.

As Nick reached the turning for the A66, two more police vehicles were heading up Battlebarrow toward him. The first shot past and disappeared. But the second slowed and curtly waved him on ahead. Nick did as he was bid, frowning. When you were on blue lights, in his experience, road manners went by the board.

He put his foot down as they left the town behind them, feeling the Subaru squat as the aerodynamic spoilers came into effect and sucked it to the tarmac. By the time he reached the dual carriageway, he was doing close to eighty. He glanced in the rear-view mirror. The squad car following him slowed abruptly and slewed across the slip-road, blocking it to further traffic.

Ah, so that's why you let me go first...

They were closing the road.

He shifted his head slightly and checked his mirror again, this time making eye contact with Blenkinship in the back seat.

"What's going on, Chris?"

"You should be asking your brother-in-law *that*, mate," Blenkinship said, lip curling.

Nick did not bother to point out that he and Lisa were not married. "Karl? What's *he* been up to?"

"He's got a beef with the Gypsies, hasn't he? Arranged some mob from up north to come down and sort them out. What do you think I was *trying* to get through to McColl? But, would she listen—?"

He stopped speaking abruptly as Nick saw the stationary vehicles just up ahead and, beyond them, more flashing blues, and began to brake. On the other side of the road was a large single-decker coach—the kind his gran would have taken on trips to the Continent. It had not been pulled over so much as forced to stop, at an angle across its lane. There were two squad cars, one stopped in front and the other alongside.

Some of the coach passengers were already spilling out of the vehicle onto the verge. They were nothing like Nick's gran—consistently big blokes, clearly not at all awed by the two officers who were doing their best to control the situation.

If Nick's swift appraisal was accurate, the uniforms were hanging on by their fingernails. And if what Blenkinship had just told him was true, the coach-load were here on the promise of a fight. They did not look concerned who that might be with.

The traffic on his carriageway was mostly at a standstill now anyway. Nick glanced in his mirrors, then twisted the wheel and swerved over to the left and onto the verge himself. He switched off the engine and punched the hazard lights.

"What the hell are you doing?" Blenkinship demanded.

Nick opened the door and threw him a hard stare over his shoulder. "My job."

Can you remember a time when you did yours?

As an afterthought, he added, "Stay here."

Blenkinship rattled the cuff still firmly attached to the grab rail. "Oh yeah, *very* funny."

Nick jogged between the idling cars. Just as he reached the centre of the road, he saw two men get out of a van that had stopped a little way ahead. He recognised the pair immediately —Lisa's brother, Karl, and Dylan Elliot. He was aware of a tightening in his gut, a buzzing in his ears. His hand ached, as if to remind him of the last time he'd walked *toward* something when he should have walked away from it.

Just for a second, the physical reaction shook him.

I thought I was over this.

And that's when Karl turned his head and looked straight into Nick's eyes. There was no fear there, he saw, just a condescending sneer. An overwhelming confidence that, whatever he had planned, Nick had neither the balls nor the ability to stop him.

Before he could shout, Karl swaggered over to join the men from the coach in haranguing the two uniforms.

"Dylan, what the hell are you trying to do?" Nick called to the other man. "Because, trust me, *this* is not going to achieve anything."

"You reckon?" Dylan threw back. "Those Gypsy scum killed my kid—he was mine as much as anyone's. And they killed my mate. And you spineless lot have done *nothin'* but try to frame *me* for it. So why in hell should I trust anythin' *you* say?"

Nick edged nearer, hoping he could grab Dylan's arm if he needed—stop him doing something he'd regret when the truth had come out.

The uniformed copper from the second car caught sight of them. He moved forward, gesturing furiously.

"Hey, you two. Get back in your vehicles!"

Dylan saw his chance and dashed across to join Karl. The uniform glared at Nick, then a light bulb seemed to come on, bringing relief with it. "Weston! What are *you* doing here?"

"Whatever you need me to," Nick said, eyes on the milling crowd. They were still getting off the coach. *Hell, how many of them* are *there?*

"Back-up's on its way," the uniform said, jaw tight. "Sliproads are blocked. Traffic's being kept back. We just need to hold 'em here for another ten or fifteen—"

But as he spoke they both became aware of a thundering noise, fast approaching. As he listened, Nick realised it was the thudding of many hooves, moving at a gallop, until the air itself seemed to thicken and vibrate.

Everyone quietened as the sound grew louder. Their heads turned almost as one, toward the field on the other side of the wire fence that separated the low embankment from the carriageway.

And then, over the grassy crest came the first wave of horses. Piebalds and skewbalds, mostly ridden bareback, some still with driving harness attached. All of them carried one Gypsy rider and many were two-up. Some of the Gypsies had whips, or clubs, or any other makeshift weapons they'd found close to hand. Nick saw several machetes, even a scythe. They rode right up to the fence line and slithered to a stop, looking down furiously on the enemy.

"When you said back-up was on its way," he murmured to the uniform, "I didn't think you meant the cavalry…"

No sooner had Nick driven away than the Gypsies started to gather in earnest. Grace reached for her phone and called Hunter Lane. Blenkinship may have been spinning her a line to get her alone but not about the root cause. There was indeed a coachload of trouble on its way, she was told. Appropriate steps were being taken. Every available officer was being rounded up and sent to help deal with the incident.

As Grace ended the call, she began to silently query if the word 'incident' was anywhere near enough to cover the activity around her.

It looked like an army, under attack and prepping for war.

Queenie reappeared at that moment. Grace had not even been aware that she'd gone. But she was now riding the thickset piebald Grace had last seen grazing peacefully alongside their caravan. He'd looked staid and steady, maybe a few years past his best.

Not anymore. He was lifting his knees high, jittery with transmitted tension, and throwing his head about to reveal the whites of his eyes behind the blinkers of his bridle. Grass-coloured froth flew from his open mouth. Behind Queenie, her brother arrived on his own mount. She looked about her, took in the numbers, and nodded.

"We heard what your man said," she told Grace. "It's nothing we haven't been expecting."

"The A66 will be blocked off," Grace said. "They won't let you get anywhere near."

Queenie flashed her a quick smile. "There's other roads," she said, and wheeled away.

An old man arrived with a skinny chestnut mare pulling a two-wheel lightweight cart, similar to a racing sulky. He jumped down and offered the reins and whip to Bartley with a toothless grin.

"Go on, *chavo*," the man urged. "You're more a *cooroboshno* than I'll ever be."

Bartley clapped him on the shoulder and hopped up onto the bench seat. In doing so he forgot about the bandages covering his ribs, Grace saw, and whatever injury lay beneath them. The pain brought him up short, almost bent him double. He paused to catch his breath.

She used the opportunity to climb up alongside him.

The old man gave her a dubious glance and said something to Bartley. Grace heard the words, "*Rawniskie dicking gueri*," but nothing more.

Bartley flicked his eyes toward her, said, "Oh, I'll not forget," and slapped the reins against the chestnut's rump. The horse bounded forward, and then Grace was more concerned with hanging on for grim death—or was it dear life? She could never quite remember.

They shot out of the field gateway and instantly turned back on themselves, up a dusty track that ran parallel to the camping field in a dead straight line.

"What is this—a footpath?"

"It's the old Roman road," Bartley said, loud enough to be heard over the thumping hoof beats. There were more horse-drawn vehicles in front and behind them, and a young lad on a pony shot past in the narrow gap between sulky and hedge.

The track jinked over a bridge crossing the railway line, which Grace was pretty sure was not something the Romans had to take into account. Then Bartley was tugging the chestnut's head away from the track. The wheels bounced clear of the ruts and they struck out across the field. She could see the flattened trails through the grass where the other Gypsy horses had come this way before them.

"What did the old man say to you, back there?"

Bartley glanced at her, face tight from the jolting of the rough ride. "He said I was more of a *cooroboshno*—a fighting cock—than he'd ever be."

"Not that part—after?"

"Ah, he told me you were a 'lady-like looking woman' and I should bear that in mind."

"What's that got to do with anything?"

"I think he meant that I should try to keep you out of the fight."

"Really?" Grace said. "I thought you'd only let me come along as some kind of human shield, in case the police got heavy-handed."

He let his surprise show. "Well, me darlin'—that, too…"

The hedge between that field and the next was straggling, reinforced with stretches of post and wire. The wire had been cut and peeled back, and Bartley drove through without slowing. As they reached the high ground, midway across, the A66 sprang into view. Horses lined the fence before the low embankment. The Gypsies themselves had vaulted over to surround a coach standing on the road below.

There were half-a-dozen police vehicles, with more just arriving, Grace saw. Even so, none of the outcomes she could envisage would be good.

The men on the coach had come expecting a brawl and would take some talking out of it. She knew it was inherent in Gypsy culture never to back down from a challenge. And if the police tried to keep the two sides apart, they were liable to find themselves pitched against both.

Bartley brought the chestnut to a ragged halt just before the fence down to the road. He jumped from the sulky, stumbling as he again forgot to take the wound in his side into account. The chestnut stayed where they'd left her, flanks heaving, her head low and nostrils flared.

Grace got to the fence first. Bartley offered his hand, but she grabbed the nearest post, got a toe-hold in the sheep netting halfway up and jumped from there, landing neatly on the other side. She looked back at him, raised an eyebrow and offered *her* hand. He grinned and wouldn't take it.

One of the police cars below disgorged Superintendent Waingrove, very upright in her uniform, cap firmly in place.

She was handed a megaphone, which she switched on without a fumble and barked at the crowd to disperse. They were contravening Section 14 of the Public Order Act 1986 and would be liable to *immediate* arrest.

None of the outnumbered uniforms present looked pleased at this pronouncement.

From the crowd milling around the coach, one man stepped forward.

Dylan Elliot.

"Arrest, eh?" he bellowed, waving an arm toward the Gypsies. "So, you'll arrest this lot just for *standin' around*, but you won't do it for killin' *my* kid? How is that *justice*?"

From the ranks of the Gypsies, a smaller figure elbowed her way through. Grace heard Bartley let out a low groan alongside her. She hardly needed to see the woman to know it was Queenie.

"That was *my* child, stolen from *me*!" she shouted, jabbing a thumb toward her own heart. "You *gorgios* with your stories of Gypsies as child-stealers and thieves. Hah! You should look to *yourselves*."

A murmur of agreement, of anger, rumbled among the Gypsies. Their stance hardened, fists were waved. The men from the coach closed up together like a Roman legion. Grace saw bike chains appear in their hands, knuckle dusters and baseball bats. Probably knives, too, being kept out of sight for now.

"Well, you *would* say that, wouldn't you?" Dylan shouted. He turned to the men from the coach. "Never *their* fault, is it lads?"

Then, from the far side of the road came Nick, and it was Grace's turn to suck in a dismayed breath. He was propelling Chris Blenkinship just ahead of him. Both the big CSI's arms were behind him, clearly cuffed. He struggled but was unable to do anything other than comply.

"Weston! What the *hell* do you think you're doing?" Superintendent Waingrove had momentarily laid aside her megaphone. She hardly needed it.

"You want the man who killed Jordan Elliot? Well, here he is."

"Weston, STAND DOWN!" Waingrove sounded incandescent. "That's a *direct* order."

Nick ignored her. Instead, he shoved his foot into the back of

Blenkinship's leg, dropping him to his knees in the centre of the road. "Tell them," he said roughly. "You tell them or *I* will, and I won't make it sound pretty."

Blenkinship threw him a look of utter hatred. But he said, "I… It was an accident."

"*Louder.*"

"It was late. It was dark. He had no lights on his bike, all right? What was a kid that age doing out at that time without—" He broke off abruptly as Nick must have twisted the solid bar connecting the two steel cuffs. They dug into the delicate bones of his wrists, alive with nerve-endings, and stopped him in his tracks. "I–I killed him. I didn't mean to. It was an accident. I'm so…*so*…sorry."

Complete silence followed his cracked confession. A few of the men from the coach shuffled their feet, glanced at each other as if not sure of their next move. Even Waingrove seemed lost for words.

Then Dylan shook himself out of it, he looked around, aware he was losing ground, losing support. That his chance for vengeance, the outlet for his anger, was fading fast.

"What about Owen?" he yelled. "What about my mate? Killed him and buried him right in the middle of their own camp, didn't they, eh? What're you goin' to do about *that*?"

Grace glanced at Bartley. "If we do right by you, will you do right by us?"

"Meaning?"

"No bloodshed," she said. "No reason for the naysayers to try to put an end to the Fair."

He hesitated a second, then nodded.

Grace stepped forward. The Gypsies nudged each other and opened a path to let her through. She came down the embankment, stopped when she reached the edge of the road.

"The Gypsies buried Owen, yes," she agreed, loud enough to be heard.

Dylan spun, crowing. "You see—"

"*But* you've already admitted that *you* were the one who punched him, in your kitchen, and that he fell. What you didn't tell us—maybe you didn't even realise it—was that *as* he fell, he hit his head on the front rail of your Aga. It crushed the back of his skull. And because you ran out and left him, he bled to death, right there on your kitchen floor." She paused, saw the sickly realisation on his face. "So, Dylan, the Gypsies didn't kill your 'mate'. That was all down to you…"

One of the uniforms came forward then and took control of Blenkinship, hauling him back to his feet. Nick walked toward Dylan. Grace could see the wariness in him but Dylan just stood there, shocked and unresisting, as Nick took him by the arm.

"Dylan Elliot, you are under arrest in connection with the death of Owen Liddell. You do not have to say anything. But it may harm your defence…"

By the time he'd finished reciting the man's rights, most of the Gypsies had already climbed back over the fence into the field. Grace noticed Queenie among them. Their eyes met and she received a cool nod by way of acknowledgment.

They gathered their horses and walked away.

PART VII

MONDAY

EPILOGUE

NICK WAS ALREADY WAITING at Water Yat when Grace and her mother arrived. He'd got there early, not having much else to occupy him. Now, he leaned against his car as he watched Max Carri's Mercedes pull off the road onto the grass.

It did not surprise him that Grace's ex-husband was driving them. Just another example of the man trying to re-insert himself into her life. With a rueful twist of his lips, Nick supposed he couldn't blame him for that. He'd always thought Max a fool for letting her get away in the first place.

The car came to a halt. Max hopped out and trotted round to the passenger side to open both doors, handing Eleanor out of the front with exaggerated courtesy. The action shielded Grace emerging from the rear seat. It wasn't until she stepped away from the car that Nick got a good look at her.

"Wow," he murmured.

Grace wore a knee-length dress in pale cream with a short jacket over the top, and a broad-brimmed hat to match. On her feet were, he presumed, the reason she had not driven herself—a pair of sky-high red heels that made her legs go on forever.

Nick pushed away from his car and buttoned the jacket of his own suit. It was standard black, although he'd been forewarned about the colours associated with Romany funerals, enough that he'd put on a red tie.

Not that this was a funeral—more of a memorial service for

Jordan Elliot and Owen Liddell. He had no idea what the Romany etiquette was for that.

He headed across the rough ground on an intercept course, joining them halfway to the river. Grace saw him coming and held back from the others, allowing him to come to her. It reminded him of the first time they'd met. He kept his stride easy, refusing to hurry.

"Grace," he said, smiling as he reached her. "You look…charming."

She laughed. "I look wildly overdressed, but apparently it's expected." She looped her arm through his. "You can stop me breaking an ankle in these ridiculous shoes."

With them, she was eye-to-eye, a rare experience for Nick. As she searched his face, she frowned. "I haven't seen you this week," she said, a little too casually.

"I expect you've been busy." Then he took a breath, keeping his own eyes on the ground ahead. "And Waingrove suspended me."

She stopped, pulling him to face her. "Oh, Nick, I *am* sorry. For what you did with Christopher?"

He nodded and she allowed herself a brief mutter of frustration.

"For how long? I mean, doesn't she realise you stopped a *riot*?"

"Who knows." Nick shrugged and started walking again, if only to escape that penetrating gaze. "Anyway, *you* stopped things escalating just as much as I did."

After a few strides, she asked, "How has Lisa taken her brother's arrest?"

Nick gave a half-snort. "Well, she went in voluntarily and made a statement about Dylan supplying those bags," he said. "So she must have known Karl would be implicated, too."

"Perhaps she was finally showing you where her loyalties lay?"

Perhaps.

"So, how are things with you, Grace? Has there been a lot of upheaval over Blenkinship?"

"Quite a bit, as I'm sure you can imagine. We'll be lucky not to lose convictions over this."

They reached the cluster of people gathered by the side of the

Eden. Queenie in her finest, with heels even higher than those Grace wore, Bartley and Vano, both in suits and dark glasses, despite the overcast day.

Nick noted that Yvonne Elliot wore dark glasses, also. But he knew *that* was to cover up what he sincerely hoped was the last beating she'd ever suffer at the hands of her husband. Four of her daughters stood round her like personal bodyguards—only the baby was not present.

He recognised Owen's sister, Catherine and her partner, Shanaya. They stood very close together but without touching, as if they weren't certain how their relationship would be viewed or accepted.

Last to arrive was not someone Nick had expected to see—Wynter Trelawney. She arrived alone and stood apart from the others, as if she wasn't sure of her welcome, either.

Queenie stepped forward without a word. She turned to face them and the chatter died away.

"It's not our way to speak of the dead," she said, her voice cool and clear. "But that doesn't mean we won't think of them often, and carry them in our hearts."

Vano and Bartley moved alongside her. Each man held a tall vase—one of white carnations, the other red gladioli. They put them down at the edge of the river and stepped back. Bartley also carried a tumbler of amber liquid, which he handed to Queenie.

"When someone passes on, it's our custom to toast them only in spirits," Queenie said, raising the glass. "Not knowing he'd passed, this toast is a long time coming. But I hope he'll understand, and forgive me."

Owen, Nick thought.

She took a sip, raised the glass and, with a flick of her wrist, sent the remainder of the contents out over the river. It hung in a rainbow shimmer for a second, then pattered into the water and swirled away.

Queenie put down the glass. She picked a single stem from each of the vases and held them up to be seen.

"The white carnation is for innocence and pure love. The red gladiolus is for strength of character, faithfulness, and honour." She tossed the two flowers into the water. "And now, I hope you'll all cast your own, to help send them both on their journey."

Vano passed her two more single blooms in pink and purple. Nick, not an expert on flowers, didn't recognise them. Queenie paused a moment without speaking, then let the remaining blooms drop into the river.

"That's so sad," Eleanor murmured alongside him.

"What were those last two?"

She looked at him as if surprised he didn't know. "A pink carnation, to signify the love of a mother, and a purple lilac for first love."

When he looked back to Queenie, Wynter had thrown her carnation and gladiolus into the river and was hovering nearby.

"I swear to you, Queenie, I never knew," she said. "Mum never told me. But I think she might have told—"

"It's all right," Queenie said. She took a deep breath, as if needing to tear herself away from her own thoughts. "Bartley said…it was *you* who bought the colt."

"I did. I've space at the farm and…it seemed the least I could do." She offered a tremulous smile. "I'll always think of him as still yours, though."

Yvonne Elliot was close enough behind Wynter to hear her last words and she paled. Her eyes were still hidden behind the dark glasses, but her lip wobbled as she approached.

"You were given a precious gift," Queenie said, her voice expressionless. "A child to cherish and raise as your own. And you…lost him."

"I know," Yvonne said helplessly. "I know, I've made so many mistakes, over the years. Let my Dyl' get away with so much. But…all this has made me realise I gotta make some big changes. An' if ever I'm weakenin', all I gotta do is think of my —*your*—son."

Queenie hesitated a moment, then she sighed and drew the other woman into her arms. "*Our* son," she said. "We can both of us mourn him equally."

Yvonne held on tight for a moment, then twisted free and hurried away, surrounded by her children.

Grace moved forward and picked out one red and one white flower. "Thank you," she said to Queenie, "for allowing us to come today. It means a lot."

"Thank *you*," Queenie said, her composure intact. "Without you, there would have been no reckoning, no justice."

Grace simply smiled. "I hear congratulations are in order—that *you* have succeeded your father as the new *Shera Rom*. Or should that be *Shera Rawnie*?"

But Queenie merely smiled and said, "I'm not the only one to be congratulated, am I not?"

Nick picked out two flowers, and glanced at Grace with eyebrow raised. She was staring blankly at Queenie.

"How on *earth* did you know that?"

"What?" Nick asked.

"That they've…they've offered *me* Chris Blenkinship's job."

"Congratulations," he said, meaning it, despite his own misfortunes. "That really is great news, Grace. You deserve it."

She pulled a face. "Hm, the jury's still out on that one. It's certainly not quite the route to promotion I would have envisaged—or wanted, come to that."

He stepped up alongside her. The two of them tossed the blooms into the water and the river carried them rapidly out of sight.

———

HIGH OVER MALLERSTANG, out of the peat bogs on Black Fell Moss, the River Eden rises. Once she was in Westmorland. Now she has one foot in the Yorkshire Dales, another in Cumbria, holding the front line and shaping the border.

Born as Red Gill Beck, she toboggans the steep valley side, rips and stumbles, blossoms into Hell Gill Beck. With a bellow, she launches over Hell Gill Force to tumble into Ais Gill Beck. Their twinned spirits trip and twine, combine, to become the Eden.

AFTERWORD

Liked it?
If you've enjoyed this book, there is no greater compliment you can give an author than to leave a review on the retailer site where you made your purchase, or on social media. Doesn't have to be long or in great detail, but it means a huge amount if you'd write a few words to say what you liked about it, and encourage others to give my books a try. Thank you so much for taking the time.

I'm only human…
We all make mistakes from time to time. This book has gone through numerous editing, copyediting, and proofreading stages before making it out into the world. Still, occasionally errors do creep past us. If by any chance you do spot a blooper, please let me, the author, know about it. That way I can get the error corrected as soon as possible. Plus I'll send you a free digital edition of one of my short stories as a thank you for your eagle-eyed observational skills! Email me at **Zoe@ZoeSharp.com**.

Please Note
This book was written in British English and UK spellings and punctuation have been used throughout.

ABOUT ZOË SHARP

Zoë Sharp opted out of mainstream education at the age of twelve and wrote her first novel at fifteen. She created her award-winning crime thriller series featuring ex-Special Forces trainee turned bodyguard, Charlotte 'Charlie' Fox, after receiving death threats in the course of her work as a photojournalist. She has been making a living from her writing since 1988, and since 2001 has written various novels: the highly acclaimed Charlie Fox series, including a prequel novella; standalone crime thrillers; and collaborations with espionage thriller author John Lawton, as well as numerous short stories. Her work has been used in Danish school textbooks, inspired an original song and music video, and been optioned for TV and film. Find out more at **www.ZoeSharp.com**

For Behind the Scenes, Bonus Features, Freebies, Sneak Peeks and advance notice of new stories, sign up for Zoë's **VIP list** at **www.ZoeSharp.com/newsletters**.

Zoë is always happy to hear from readers, reader groups, libraries or bookstores. You can contact her at **Zoe@ZoeSharp.com**

Visit Zoë's Amazon Author Page

facebook.com/ZoeSharpAuthor

twitter.com/authorzoesharp

goodreads.com/authorzoesharp

amazon.com/author/zoesharp

instagram.com/authorzoesharp

ACKNOWLEDGEMENTS

Ayo Onatade
Brian Price
Daniel Macintosh
David Penny
Derek Harrison
Doug Lyle MD
Emma Yates
John Lawton
Jill Harrison
Judith O'Reilly
Jules Farrer
Kate Hollamby
Katrinna Bristow
Lewis Hancock
Michelle Wilbye
Rachel Amphlett
Tim Winfield

THE STORIES SO FAR...

Charlie to improvise as never before. And this time she can't rely on Sean to watch her back.

ABSENCE OF LIGHT #11: In the aftermath of an earthquake, Charlie's working alongside a team who dig out the living and ID the dead, and hoping they won't find out why she's *really* there.

FOX HUNTER #12: Charlie can never forget the men who put a brutal end to her army career, but she swore a long time ago she would never go looking for them. Now she doesn't have a choice.

BAD TURN #13: Charlie is out of work, out of her apartment and out of options. Why else would she be working for a shady arms dealer?

TRIAL UNDER FIRE #0: The untold story. Before she was a bodyguard, she was a soldier... (Coming soon)

FOX FIVE RELOADED: short story collection. Charlie Fox. In small bites. With sharp teeth. (Coming soon)

the Lakes Thriller trilogy

DANCING ON THE GRAVE: #1 A sniper with a mission, a CSI with something to prove, a young cop with nothing to lose, and a teenage girl with a terrifying obsession. The calm of the English Lake District is about to be shattered.

BONES IN THE RIVER: #2 Driving on a country road, late at night, you hit a child. There are no witnesses. You have *everything* to lose. What do you do?

standalone crime thrillers

THE BLOOD WHISPERER Six years ago CSI Kelly Jacks woke next to a butchered body with the knife in her hands and no memory of what happened. She trusted the evidence would prove her innocence. It didn't. Is history now repeating itself?

AN ITALIAN JOB (with **John Lawton**) Former soldiers Gina and Jack are about to discover that love is far deadlier the second time around.